UNCANNY BANQUET

Books by Ramsey Campbell

Anthologies

Novels

Novella

Short Stories

UNCANNY BANQUET

Edited by

RAMSEY CAMPBELL

LITTLE, BROWN AND COMPANY

A *Little, Brown* Book

First published in Great Britain in 1992
by Little, Brown and Company

A CIP catalogue record for this book
is available from the British Library.

ISBN 0 316 90311 6

Photoset in North Wales by
Derek Doyle & Associates, Mold, Clwyd.
Printed and bound in Great Britain by
BPCC Hazells,
Aylesbury, Bucks, England.

Little, Brown and Company (UK) Limited
165 Great Dover Street
London SE1 4YA

ACKNOWLEDGEMENTS

'Behind the Stumps', copyright © 1979 by Russell Kirk, from *The Princess of All Lands*. By permission of the author and his agent, the Pimlico Agency Inc.

'A Horizon of Obelisks', copyright © 1981 by Dorothy K. Haynes, from *Peacocks and Pagodas*. By permission of John S. Gray.

'The Loony', copyright © 1984 by Alison Prince, from *Nightmares 2*. By permission of the author and her agent, Marilyn Malin.

'The Hill and the Hole', copyright © 1947 by Fritz Leiber, from *Night's Black Agents*. By permission of the author.

'Ravissante', copyright © 1968 by Robert Aickman, from *Sub Rosa*. By permission of the Estate of Robert Aickman and its agent, Artellus Limited.

'The Lady in Gray', copyright © 1988 by the Estate of Donald Wandrei, from *The Eye and the Finger*. By permission of the Estate of Donald Wandrei and its Executor, Harold Hughesdon.

'A Mote' by Walter de la Mare, copyright © 1971 by Arkham House, from *Eight Tales* by 'Walter Ramal'. By permission of Arkham House.

'McGonagall in the Head' by Ramsey Campbell, copyright © 1992 by Ramsey Campbell. By permission of the author.

For Kirby and Kay McCauley, with love –
something older than all of us

CONTENTS

UNCANNY BANQUET

INTRODUCTION

THE tale of supernatural terror is in danger of losing touch with its own traditions. No single author, and perhaps no author at all, is to blame for this. If hordes of living writers have been imitating the bestsellers in their field, this need not be altogether a bad thing in itself. After all, they must learn somehow, just as their predecessors learned from such models as H.P. Lovecraft and M.R. James, both of whom acknowledged earlier models themselves. Nor is it new that most of the imitators read like no more than that, and in some cases even less: too many followers of James and Lovecraft merely imitate the style or the set-pieces of their favourites, rather than setting themselves the more difficult tasks of examining how the stories work and trying to achieve freshly what they achieved. Now we have the Stephen King school and more recently the school of Clive Barker, and the problem is even clearer and, I venture to suggest, more acute. At least, it's my impression that many of the writers who have modelled their work on the stories of Barker and King were previously unaware of the field, and may still have read nothing that led up to them – quite possibly no fiction older than themselves.

I repeat that this is no fault of (for example) King and Barker. King has written at length in *Danse Macabre* about his influences, the most important of which I take to be the tales of Richard Matheson, and Barker hasn't been shy in the past of citing writers he admires, Machen and Aickman among them. Why then are so many of the

1

classics so neglected? Presumably not because of any lack of taste for the subtler kind of material, given the continuing popularity of books as restrained as (to list a few personal favourites) Kingsley Amis's *Green Man*, Peter Ackroyd's *Hawksmoor* and *First Light*, and Shirley Jackson's *Haunting of Hill House*. Perhaps it is rather that the material is difficult to come by, and that is a situation I've tried in this book, if not to rectify, at least to address.

I remember a time when anthologies of horror and the supernatural seemed to consist quite largely of their predecessors, which is taking the duty to acknowledge one's roots too far. Ironically, because many of the key stories were so often reprinted anthologists now avoid them, with the result that they are often hard to find. It would be tempting and, leaving aside the unreason-ableness of some of the agents for the authors' estates, relatively easy to put together a fat anthology of them – the kind of volume which it is worth haunting second-hand bookshops for – but *Uncanny Banquet* isn't such a book. I rather hope it collects a range of stories as remarkable as the accredited classics of the field but less well known. I think it demonstrates that if indeed there was a Golden Age of supernatural fiction, that age isn't over – not that I'm claiming my own story as evidence of this, but perhaps it may add an extra bit of variety. This is a book for people who love tales of the supernatural rather than of gross gruesomeness, or who would like to find out if they do.

Ramsey Campbell
Merseyside, England
23 April 1992

BEHIND THE STUMPS

by Russell Kirk

RUSSELL AMOS KIRK (1918–) is the most unjustly neglected – at least by British readers – living master of the ghost story. His tales were initially collected as *The Surly Sullen Bell*, a book which later appeared as a Paperback Library Gothic, retitled *Lost Lake*, with one of a thousand covers showing a lady in a long dress fleeing a castle. These tales, and more, were given more permanency in two Arkham House books, *The Princess of All Lands* and *Watchers at the Strait Gate*. In 1977 he received the World Fantasy Award. Some of the later stories tend to foreground his philosophy as an American right-wing thinker, as do his two novels, *Old House of Fear* and *A Creature of the Twilight*. However, in 'Behind the Stumps', taken from his first collection, his main and entirely praiseworthy aim seems to be to make us shiver.

And Satan stood up against Israel,
and provoked David to number Israel.

1 CHRONICLES 21:1

POTTAWATTOMIE County, shorn of its protecting forest seventy years ago, ever since has sprawled like Samson undone by Delilah, naked, impotent, grudgingly servile. Amid the fields of rotted stumps, potatoes and beans grow, and half the inhabited houses still are log cabins thrown up by the lumbermen who followed the trappers into this land. In Pottawattomie there has been no money worth mentioning since the timber was cut; but here and there people cling to the straggling farms, or make shift in the crumbling villages.

An elusive beauty drifts over this country sprinkled with little lakes, stretches of second-growth woods and cedar swamps, gravelly upland ridges that are gnawed by every rain, now that their cover is gone. As if a curse had been pronounced upon these folk and their houses and their crops in reprisal for their violation of nature, everything in Pottawattomie is melting away.

Of the people who stick obstinately to this stump-country, some are grandchildren and great-grandchildren of the men who swept off the forest; others are flotsam cast upon these sandy miles from the torrent of modern life, thrown out of the eddy upon the soggy bank to lie inert and ignored. Worn farmers of a conservative cast of mind, pinched, tenacious, inured to monotony, fond of the bottle on Saturday nights, eccentrics of several sorts; a silent half-breed crew of Negro-and-Indian, dispersed in cabins and sun-stricken tar-paper shanties along the back roads, remote from the county seat and the lesser hamlets that conduct the languid commerce of Pottawattomie – these are the Pottawattomie people. Decent roads have come

7

only lately; even television is too costly for many of these folk; the very hand of government is nerveless in this poverty of soil and spirit.

Yet not wholly palsied, the grip of the State, for all that. Tax assessments necessarily are modest in Pottawattomie, but there are roads to be maintained, poaching of deer and trout to be repressed, public relief to be doled out. There exists a sheriff, intimate with the local tone, at the county seat; also a judge of probate; and the county supervisors are farmers and tradesmen without inclination to alter the nature of things in Pottawattomie. So far, government is a shadow of a shade. But now and again the State administration and the Federal administration gingerly poke about in the mud and brush of the stump-land.

A special rural census had to be compiled. Down in the capital, a plan had been drawn up concerning commodity price-levels and potential crop yields and tabulated prices. Acres of corn were to be counted, and pigs and people. Enumerators went out to every spreading wheat farm, to every five-acre tomato patch; and Pottawattomie County was not forgotten.

Always against the government, Pottawattomie; against the administration that ordained this special census, most vehemently. This new survey, Pottawattomie declared, meant more blank forms, more trips to the county seat, higher taxation, and intolerable prying into every man's household – which last none resent more than do the rural poor.

So the Regional Office of the Special Census began to encounter difficulties in Pottawattomie. Doors were shut in the faces of certified enumerators, despite threats of warrants and writs; the evasive response was common, violent reaction not inconceivable. Reports particularly unsettling were received from the district of Bear City, a decayed village of two hundred inhabitants. Despite his pressing need for the stipend attached to the office, the temporary agent there resigned in distress at a growing unpopularity. A woman who took his place was ignored by half the farmers she endeavored to interview.

Put out, the Regional Office dispatched to Bear City a

Special Interviewer: Cribben. They let him have a car and a stack of forms and rather a stiff letter of introduction to the postmaster in that town, and off he drove northward.

Being that sort of man, Cribben took his revolver with him. Once he had been a bank messenger, and he often told his associates, 'The other messengers carried their guns at the bottom of their briefcases, so there'd be no chance of having to pull them if there was a stickup. But I kept my .38 handy. I was willing to have it out with the boys.'

Tall, forty, stiff as a stick, this Cribben – walking with chin up, chest out, joints rigid, in a sort of nervous defiance of humanity. He looked insufferable. He was insufferable. Next to a jocular man, an insufferable man is best suited for the responsibilities that are a Special Interviewer's. Close-clipped black hair set off a strong head, well proportioned; but the mouth was petulant, and the eyes were ignorantly challenging, and the chin was set in lines of pomposity. In conversation, Cribben had a way of sucking in his cheeks with an affectation of whimsical deliberation, for Cribben had long told himself that he was admirably funny when he chose to be, especially with women. Years before, his wife had divorced him – in Reno, since (somewhat to her bewilderment) she had been able to think of no precise ground which would admit of obtaining a divorce in their own state. He lived chastely, honestly, soberly, quite solitary. He laughed dutifully at other men's jokes; he would go out of his way to write a friendly letter of recommendation; but somehow no one ever asked him out or looked him up. A failure in everything was Cribben – ex-engineer, ex-chief clerk, ex-artillery captain, ex-foundry partner. He told himself he had been completely reliable in every little particular, which was true; and he told himself he had failed because of his immaculate honesty in a mob of rogues, which was false. He had failed because he was precise.

'Corporal, about the morning report: I see you used eraser to clean up this ink blot, instead of correction fluid. Watch that, Corporal. We'll use correction fluid. Understand?' This is the sort of thing the precise Cribben would say – if with a smile, then the wrong kind of smile; and he would compliment himself on his urbanity.

Cribben did not spare himself; no man ever was more methodical, more painstaking. Reliable in every little particular, yes; but so devoted to these particulars that generalities went to pot. Subordinates resigned and read the 'help wanted' columns rather than submit to another week of such accuracy; superiors found him hopelessly behind in his work, austerely plodding through tidy inconsequentialities. Truly, Cribben was intolerable. He knew the mass of men to be consistently inaccurate and often dishonest. Quite right, of course. Sensible men nod and shrug; Cribben nagged. His foundry went to pieces because he fretted about missing wrenches and screwdrivers. He thought his workmen stole them. They did; but Cribben never would confess that moderate pilferage was an item of fixed overhead. In Cribben's pertinacity there would have been something noble, had he loved precision for the sake of truth. But he regarded truth only as an attribute of precision.

So down to that sink of broken men, petty governmental service, spun Cribben in the vortex of failure. Having arrived at the abyss, which in this instance was a temporary junior clerkship, Cribben commenced to rise in a small way. In this humorless precisian the assistant chief of the Regional Office discerned the very incarnation of the second-best type of public functionary, and so set him to compelling the reluctant to complete interminable forms. Cribben became a Special Investigator, with every increase of salary authorized by statute. To entrust him with supervisory duties proved inadvisable; yet within his sphere, Cribben was incomparable. It was Cribben's apotheosis. Never had he liked work so well, and only a passion to reorganize the Regional Office upon a more precise model clouded his contentment. With the majesty of Government at his back, the hauteur of a censor in his mien as he queried the subject of a survey or interrogated the petitioner for a grant – a man like Cribben never dreamed of more than this. For Cribben was quite devoid of imagination.

And Cribben drove north to Bear City.

False-fronted, dry-goods shops and grocery stores and saloons, built lavishly of second-grade white pine when pine was cheap and seemingly inexhaustible, are strung along a broad gravelled road: this is Bear City. They are like discolored teeth in an old man's mouth, these buildings, for they stand between grass-grown gaps where casual flames have had their way with abandoned structures. One of these shops, with the usual high, old-fashioned windows and siding a watery white, is also the post office. On Saturday afternoons in little places like this, post offices generally close. But on this Saturday afternoon, in Bear City – so Cribben noted as he parked his automobile – not only the dry-goods half of the shop, but the post office too was open for business. This was tidy and efficient, Cribben reflected, striding through the door. It predisposed him to amiability.

'Afternoon,' said Cribben to the postmaster. 'I'm J.K. Cribben, from the Regional Office. Read this, please.' He presented his letter of introduction.

Mr Matt Heddle, Postmaster, Bear City, was behind the wrought-iron grille of the old post-office counter, a relic of earlier days and more southerly towns; and his shy wife Jessie was opposite, at the shop counter. They were not lacking in a dignity that comes from honorable posts long held in small places. Mr Heddle, with his crown of thick white hair and his august slouch, his good black suit, and his deep slow voice, made a rural postmaster for one to be proud of.

'Why, I wish you luck, Mr Cribben,' Matt Heddle said with concern, reading the letter of introduction. Mr Heddle desired to be postmaster for the rest of his life. 'I'll do anything I can. I'm sorry about the fuss the other census man had.'

'His own damned fault,' Cribben said, largely. 'Don't give a grouch a chance to make a fuss – that's my way. Take none of their lip. I've handled people quite awhile. Shoot out your questions, stare 'em down. I won't have much trouble here.'

He didn't. Whatever Cribben's shortcomings, he was

neither coward nor laggard. Only six or seven hours a day he spent in the tourist room he had rented; and by the time six days had passed, he had seen and conquered almost all the obdurate farmers around Bear City. Their sheds and their silos, their sheep and their steers, their hired men and their bashful daughters, the rooms in their houses and the privies behind them – all were properly observed and recorded in forms and check-sheets. What Cribben could not see with his own eyes he bullied out adequately enough from the uneasy men he cornered and glowered upon. He was big, he was gruff, he was pedantically insistent. He was worth what salary the Regional Office paid. He never took 'no' for an answer – or 'don't know', either. He made himself detested in Bear City more quickly than ever had man before; and he paid back his contemners in a condescending scorn.

His success was the product, in part, of his comparative restraint: for he seemed to those he confronted to be holding himself precariously in check, on the verge of tumbling into some tremendous passion, like a dizzy man teetering on a log across a stream in spate. He was cruelly cold, always – never fierce, and yet hanging by a worn rope. What brute would have had the callousness, or the temerity, to thrust this man over the brink? It was safer to answer his questions and endure his prying.

Over the rutted trails of Pottawattomie County in muddy spring he drove his official automobile, finding out every shack and hut, every Indian squatter, every forlorn old couple back in the cedar thickets, every widow who boasted a cow and a chicken run. They were numbered, all numbered. This spring the birds were thick in Pottawattomie and some of the lilacs bloomed early, but Cribben never looked at them, for they were not to be enumerated. He had not an ounce of fancy in him. Six days of this and he had done the job except for the Barrens. Of all Pottawattomie, Bear City district was the toughest nut for the Special Census, and the Barrens were the hard kernel of Bear City's hinterland.

Who lives in the Barrens, that sterile and gullied and scrub-veiled upland? Why, it's hard to say. A half-dozen scrawny families, perhaps more – folk seldom seen, more seldom heard, even in Bear City. They have no money for the dissipations of a town, the Barrens people – none of them, at least, except the Gholsons; and no one ever knew a Gholson to take a dollar out of his greasy old purse for anything but a sack of sugar or a bottle of rot-gut whiskey. The Gholsons must have money, as money goes in Pottawattomie, but it sticks to them.

On Saturday afternoon, a week after his arrival in town, Cribben entered the post office, self-satisfied and muddy. Matt Heddle was there, and Love the garage-man – Love already lively from morning libations. 'Started on the Barrens this morning, Heddle,' Cribben said ponderously. 'Easy as falling off a log. Covered the Robinson place, and Hendry's. Eight kids at the Robinsons', dirty as worms.' He looked at his map. 'Tomorrow, now, I begin with this place called Barrens Mill. Not much of a road into it. It's right on Owens Creek. What d'you know about Barrens Mill, Heddle?' He pointed, his heavy forefinger stiff, at a spot on his map.

Mr Matt Heddle was a good-natured old man, but he did not like Cribben. Pottawattomie people said that Mr Heddle was well read, which in Pottawattomie County means that a man has three reprints of Marie Corelli's novels and two of Hall Caine's, but they were not far wrong in Heddle's case. The appetite for knowledge clutched at him as it sometimes does at pathetic men past their prime, and his devotion to the better nineteenth-century novelists, combining with some natural penetration, had made him shrewd enough. His good nature being unquenchable, he looked at grim Cribben and thought he read in that intolerant face a waste of loneliness and doubt that Cribben never could confess to himself, for terror of the desolation.

He looked at Cribben, and told him: 'Let it go, Mr Cribben. They're an ignorant bunch, the Gholsons; they own Barrens Mill. Let it go. It'll be knee-deep in mud up there. Look up the acreage in the county office, and the assessment, and let it go at that. You've done all the work anybody could ask.'

'We don't let things go in the Regional Office,' Cribben said, with austerity. 'I've already looked in the county book: five hundred and twenty acres the Gholsons own. But I want to know *what* Gholson.'

Matt Heddle started to speak, hesitated, looked speculatively at Cribben, and then said, 'It's Will Gholson that pays the taxes.'

Love, who had been leaning against the counter, a wise grin on his face, gave a whiskey chuckle and remarked, abruptly: 'She was a witch and a bitch, a bitch and a witch. Ha! Goin' to put *her* in the census?'

'Dave Love, this isn't the Elite; it's the post office,' Mr Heddle said, civilly. 'Let's keep it decent in here.'

'Yes, Will Gholson pays the taxes,' Cribben nodded, 'but the land's not in his name. The tax-roll reads "Mrs Gholson" – just that. No Christian name. How do you people choose your county clerk?'

'Mrs Gholson, old Bitch Gholson, old Witch Gholson,' chanted Love. 'You goin' to put *her* in the census? She's dead as a dodo.'

'Will Gholson's mother, maybe, or his grandmother – that's who's meant,' Heddle murmured. 'Nobody really knows the Gholsons. They aren't folks you get to know. They're an ignorant bunch, good to keep clear of. She was old, old. I saw her laid out. Some of us went up there for the funeral – only time we ever went inside the house. It was only decent to go up.'

'Decent, hell!' said Love. 'We was scared not to go, that's the truth of it. Nobody with any brains rubs the Gholsons the wrong way.'

'Scared?' Cribben sneered down at Love.

'God, yes, man. She was a damned witch, and the whole family's bats in the belfry. Old Mrs Gholson have a Christian name? Hell, whoever heard of a witch with a Christian name?'

'You start your drinking too early in the day,' Cribben said. Love snorted, grinned, and fiddled with a post-office pen. 'What kind of a county clerk do you have, Heddle, that doesn't take a dead woman's name off the books?'

'Why, I suppose maybe the Gholsons wanted it left on,'

Heddle sighed, placatingly. 'And there was talk. Nobody wants to fuss with the Gholsons. Sleeping dogs, Mr Cribben.'

'If you really want to know,' Love growled, 'she cursed the cows, for one thing. The cows of people she didn't care for, and the neighbors that were too close. The Gholsons don't like close neighbors.'

'What are you giving me?' Cribben went menacingly red at the idea of being made the butt of a joke: this was the one thing his humorless valor feared.

'You don't have to believe it, man, but the cows went dry, all the same. And sometimes they died. And if that wasn't enough, the Gholsons moved the fences, and the boundary-markers. They took over. They got land now that used to be four or five farms.'

Mrs Heddle, having been listening, now came across the shop to say in her shy voice, 'They did move the posts, Mr Cribben – the Gholsons. And the neighbors didn't move them back. They were frightened silly.'

'It'll take more than a sick cow to scare me, Mrs Heddle,' Cribben told her, the flush fading from his cheeks. 'You people don't have any system up here. What's wrong with your schools, that people swallow this stuff? How do you hire your teachers?'

'Barrens Mill is a place to put a chill into a preacher, Mr Cribben,' said Matt Heddle, meditatively. 'There's a look to it . . . the mill itself is gone, but the big old house is there, seedy now, and the rest of the buildings. John Wendover, the lumberman, built it when this country was opened up, but the Gholsons bought it after the timber went. Some people say the Gholsons came from Missouri. I don't know. There's stories . . . Nobody knows the Gholsons. They've another farm down the creek. There's five Gholson men, nowadays, but I don't know how many women. Will Gholson does the talking for them, and he talks as much as a clam.'

'He'll talk to me,' Cribben declared.

Over Matt Heddle came a sensation of pity. Leaning across the counter, he put his hand on Cribben's. Few ever had done this, and Cribben, startled, stepped back. 'Now, listen, Mr Cribben, friend. You're a man with spunk, and you know your business; but I'm old, and I've been hereabouts a while. There are people that don't fit in anywhere, Mr Cribben. Did you ever think about that? I mean, they won't live by your ways and mine. Some of them are too good, and some are too bad. Everybody's growing pretty much alike – nearly everybody – in this age, and the ones that don't fit in are scarce; but they're still around. Some are queer, very queer. We can't just count them like so many fifteen-cent stamps. We can't change them, not soon. But they're shy, most of them; let them alone, and they're likely to crawl into holes, out of the sun. Let them be; they don't signify, if you don't stir them up. The Gholsons are like that.'

'They come under the law, same as anybody else,' Cribben put in.

'Oh, the law was made for you and me and the folks we know – not for them, any more than it was made for snakes. So long as they let the law alone, don't meddle, Mr Cribben, don't meddle. They don't signify any more than a wasps' nest at the back of the orchard, if you don't poke them.' Old Heddle was very earnest.

'A witch of a bitch and a bitch of a witch,' sang Love, mordantly. 'O Lord, how she hexed 'em!'

'Why, there's Will Gholson now, coming out of the Elite,' Mrs Heddle whispered from the window. A greasy, burly man with tremendous eyebrows that had tufted points was walking from the bar with a bottle in either hip-pocket. He was neither bearded nor shaven, and he was filthy. He turned toward a wagon hitched close by the post office.

'Handsome specimen,' observed Cribben, chafing under all this admonition, the defiance in his lonely nature coming to a boil. 'We'll have a talk.' He strode into the street, Matt Heddle anxiously behind him and Love sauntering in the rear. Gholson, sensing them, swung round from tightening his horse's harness. Unquestionably he was a rough customer; but that roused Cribben's spirit.

'Will Gholson,' called out Cribben in his artillery-captain voice, 'I've got a few questions to ask you.'

A stare; and then Gholson spat into the road. His words

were labored, a heavy blur of speech, like a man wrestling with a tongue uncongenial to him. 'You the counter?'

'That's right,' Cribben told him. 'Who owns your farm, Gholson?'

Another stare, longer, and a kind of slow, dismal grimace. 'Go to hell,' said Gholson. 'Leave us be.'

Something about this earth-stained, sweat-reeking figure, skulking on the frontier of humanity, sent a stir of revulsion through Cribben; and the consciousness of his inward shrinking set fire to his conceit, and he shot out one powerful arm to catch Gholson by the front of his tattered overalls. 'By God, Gholson, I'm coming out to your place tomorrow; and I'm going through it; I'll have a warrant; and I'll do my duty; so watch yourself. I hear you've got a queer place at Barrens Mill, Gholson. Look out I don't get it condemned for you.' Cribben was white, from fury, and shouting like a sailor, and shaking in his emotion. Even the dull lump of Gholson's face lost its apathy before this rage, and Gholson stood quiescent in the tall man's grip.

'Mr Cribben, friend,' Heddle was saying. Cribben remembered where he was, and what; he let go of Gholson's clothes; but he put his drawn face into Gholson's and repeated, 'Tomorrow. I'll be out tomorrow.'

'Tomorrow's Sunday,' was all Gholson answered.

'I'll be there tomorrow.'

'Sunday's no day for it,' said Gholson, almost plaintively. It was as if Cribben had stabbed through this hulk of flesh and rasped upon a moral sensibility.

'I'll be there,' Cribben told him, in grim triumph.

Deliberately Gholson got into his wagon, took up the reins, and paused as if collecting his wits for a weighty effort. 'Don't, Mister.' It was a grunt. 'A man that – a man that fusses on Sunday – well, he deserves what he gets.' And Gholson drove off.

'What's wrong, Mr Cribben?' asked Heddle, startled: for Cribben had slipped down upon the bench outside the post office and was sucking in his breath convulsively. 'Here, a nip,' said Love, in concern, thrusting a bottle at him. Cribben took a swallow of whiskey, sighed, and relaxed. He drew an envelope out of a pocket and swallowed a capsule, with another mouthful of whiskey.

'Heart?' asked Heddle.

'Yes,' Cribben answered, as humbly as was in him. 'It never was dandy. I'm not supposed to get riled.'

'With that heart, you don't want to go up to Barrens Mill – no, you don't,' said the postmaster, gravely.

'She's a witch, Cribben.' Love was leaning over him. 'Hear me, eh? I say, she *is* a witch.'

'Quiet, Love,' the postmaster told him. 'Or if you do go to the Barrens, Mr Cribben, you'll take a couple of the sheriff's boys with you.'

Cribben had quite intended to ask for a deputy, but he'd be damned now if he wouldn't go alone. 'I'm driving to the judge for a search warrant,' he answered, his chin up. 'That's all I'll take.'

Heddle walked with him to the boardinghouse where Cribben kept his automobile. He said nothing all the way, but when Cribben had got behind the wheel, he leaned in the window, his big, smooth, friendly old face intent: 'There's a lot of old-fashioned prejudice in Pottawattomie, Mr Cribben. But, you know, most men run their lives on prejudice. We've got to; we're not smart enough to do anything else. There's sure to be something behind a prejudice. I don't know all about the Gholsons, but there's fact behind prejudice. Some things are best left alone.'

Here Cribben rolled up his window and shook his head and started the motor and rolled off.

After all, there was no more he could have said, Matt Heddle reflected. Cribben would go to Barrens Mill, probably count everything in sight, and bullyrag Will Gholson, and come back puffed up like a turkey. Misty notions. . . . He almost wished someone would put the fear of hell-fire into the Special Interviewer. But this was only an oldfangled backwater, and Cribben was a newfangled man.

On Sunday morning, Cribben drove alone up the road towards the Barrens. In his pockets were a set of forms, and a warrant in case of need; Cribben left his gun at home, thinking the devil of a temper within him a greater hazard than any he was liable to encounter from the Gholsons. Past abandoned cabins and frame houses with their roofs fallen in, past a sluggish stream clogged with ancient logs, past mile on mile of straggling second-growth woodland, Cribben rode. It was empty country, not one-third so populous as it had been fifty years before, and he passed no one at this hour.

Here in the region of the Barrens, fence wire was unknown; enormous stumps, uprooted from the fields and dragged to the roadside, are crowded one against another to keep the cows out, their truncated roots pointing toward the empty sky. Most symbolic of the stump-country, jagged and dead, these fences; but Cribben had no time for myth. By ten o'clock he was nursing his car over the remnant of a corduroy road which twists through Long Swamp; the stagnant water was a foot deep upon it, this spring. But he went through without mishap, only to find himself a little later snared in the wet ground between two treacherous sand hills. There was no traction for his rear wheels; maddened, he made them spin until he had sunk his car to the axle; and then, cooling, he went forward on foot. Love's Garage could pull out the automobile later; he would have to walk back to town, or find a telephone somewhere, when he was through with this business. He had promised to be at Barrens Mill that morning, and he would be there. Already he was within a mile of the farm.

The damp track that once had been a lumber road could have led him, albeit circuitously, to the Gholsons. But, consulting his map, Cribben saw that by walking through a stretch of hardwoods he could – with luck – save fifteen minutes' tramping. So up a gradual ascent he went, passing on his right the wreck of a little farmhouse with high gables, not many years derelict. 'The Gholsons don't like close neighbors.' Oaks and maples and beeches, this wood, with soggy leaves of many autumns underfoot and sponge-mushrooms springing up from them, clammily white. Water from the trees dripped upon Cribben, streaking his short coat. It was a quiet wood, most quiet; the dying vestige of a path led through it.

Terminating upon the crest of a ridge, the path took him to a stump fence of grand proportions. Beyond was pasture, cleared with a thoroughness exceptional in this country; and beyond the pasture, the ground fell away to a swift creek, and then rose again to a sharp knoll, of which the shoulder faced him; and upon the knoll was the house of Barrens Mill, a quarter of a mile distant.

All round the house stretched the Gholsons' fields, the work of years of fantastic labor. What power had driven these dull men to such feats of agricultural vainglory? For it was a beautiful farm: every dangerous slope affectionately buttressed and contoured to guard it from the rains, every boulder hauled away to a pile at the bend of the stream, every potential weed-jungle rooted out. The great square house – always severely simple, now gaunt in its blackened boards from which paint had scaled away long since – surveyed the whole rolling farm. A low wing, doubtless containing kitchen and woodshed, was joined to the northern face of the old building, which seemed indefinably mutilated. Then Cribben realized how the house had been injured: it was nearly blind. Every window above the ground floor had been neatly boarded up – not covered over merely, but the frames taken out and planks fitted to fill the apertures. It was as if the house had fallen prisoner to the Gholsons, and sat Samson-like in bound and blindfolded shame.

All this was apprehended at a single glance; a second look disclosed nothing living in all the prospect – not even a dog, not even a cow. But one of the pallid stumps stirred.

Cribben started. No, not a stump: someone crouching by the stump fence, leaning upon a broken root, and watching, not him, but the house. It was a girl, barefoot, a few yards away, dressed in printed meal-sacks, fifteen or sixteen years old, and thoroughly ugly, her hair a rat's-nest; this was no country where a wild rose might bloom. She had not heard him. For all his ungainly ways, Cribben had spent a good deal of time in the open, and could be meticulously quiet. He stole close up to the girl and said, in a tone he meant to be affable, 'Well, now?'

Ah, what a scream out of her! She had been watching

the blind façade of Barrens Mill house with such a degree of intensity, a kind of cringing smirk on her lips, that Cribben's words must have come like the voice from the burning bush; and she whirled, and shrieked, all sense gone out of her face, until she began to understand that it was only a stranger by her. Though Cribben was not a feeling man, this extremity of fright touched him almost with compassion, and he took the girl gently by the shoulder, saying, 'It's all right. Will you take me to the house?' He made as if to lead her down the slope.

At that, the tide of fright poured back into her heavy Gholson face, and she fought in his grasp and swore at him. Cribben – a vein of prudery ran through his nature – was badly shocked: it was hysterically vile cursing, nearly inarticulate, but compounded of every ancient rural obscenity. And she was very young. She pulled away and dodged into the dense wood.

Nothing moved in these broad fields. No smoke rose from the kitchen, no chicken cackled in the yard. Overhead a crow flapped, as much an alien as Cribben himself; nothing more seemed to live about Barrens Mill. Were Will Gholson crazy enough to be peering from one of the windows with a shotgun beside him, Cribben would make a target impossible to miss, and Cribben knew this. But no movement came from behind the blinds, and Cribben went round unscathed to the kitchen door.

A pause and a glance told Cribben that the animals were gone, every one of them, to the last hen and the last cat. Driven down to the lower farm to vex and delay him? And it looked as if every Gholson had gone with them. He knocked at the scarred back door: only echoes. It was not locked; and, having his warrant in his pocket, he entered. If Will Gholson were keeping mum inside, he'd rout him out.

Four low rooms – kitchen, rough parlor, a couple of topsy-turvy bedrooms – this was the wing of the house, showing every sign of a hasty flight. A massive panelled door shut off the parlor from the square bulk of the older house, and its big key was in the lock. Well, it was worth a try. Cribben, unlocking the door, looked in: black, frayed blinds drawn down over the windows – and the windows upstairs boarded, of course. Returning to the kitchen, he got a kerosene lamp, lit it, and went back to the darkened rooms.

Fourteen-foot ceilings in these cold chambers; and the remnants of Victorian prosperity in mildewed love seats and peeling gilt mirrors; and dust, dust. A damp place, wholly still. Cribben, telling his nerves to behave, plodded up the fine sweep of the solid stairs, the white plaster of the wall gleaming from his lamp. Dust, dust.

A broad corridor, and three rooms of moderate size, their doors ajar, a naked bedstead in each; and at the head of the corridor, a door that stuck. The stillness infecting him, Cribben pressed his weight cautiously upon the knob, so that the squeak of the hinges was faint when the door yielded. Holding the lamp above his head, he was in.

Marble-topped commode, washbowl holding a powder of grime, fantastic oaken wardrobe – and a tremendous Victorian rosewood bed, carven and scrolled, its towering head casting a shadow upon the sheets that covered the mattress. There *were* sheets; and they were humped with the shape of someone snuggled under them.

'Come on out,' said Cribben, his throat dry. No one answered, and he ripped the covers back. He had a half-second to stare before he dropped the lamp to its ruin.

Old, old – how old? She had been immensely fat, he could tell in that frozen moment, but now the malign wrinkles hung in horrid empty folds. How evil! And even yet, that drooping lip of command, that projecting jaw – he knew at last from what source had come the power that terraced and tended Barrens Mill. The eyelids were drawn down. For this only was there time before the lamp smashed. Ah, why hadn't they buried her? For she was dead, long dead, many a season dead.

All light gone, Cribben stood rigid, his fingers pressed distractedly against his thighs. To his brain, absurdly, came a forgotten picture out of his childhood, a colored print in his *King Arthur*: 'Launcelot in the Chapel of the

Dead Wizard', with the knight lifting the corner of a shroud. This picture dropping away, Cribben told his unmoving self, silently but again and again, 'Old Mrs Gholson, old witch, old bitch,' as if it were an incantation. Then he groped for the vanished door, but stumbled upon the wire guard of the broken lamp.

In blackness one's equilibrium trickles away, and Cribben felt his balance going, and knew to his horror that he was falling straight across that bed. He struck the sheets heavily and paused there in a paralysis of revulsion. Then it came to him that no one lay beneath him.

Revulsion was swallowed in a compelling urgency, and Cribben slid his hands sweepingly along the covers, in desperate hope of a mistake. But no. There was no form in the bed but his own. Crouching like a great clumsy dog, he hunched against the headboard, while he blinked for any filtered drop of light, show him what it would.

He had left the door ajar, and through the doorway wavered the very dimmest of dim glows, the forlorn hope of the bright sun without. Now that Cribben's eyes had been a little time in the room, he could discern whatever was silhouetted against the doorway – the back of a chair, the edge of the door itself, the knob. And something *moved* into silhouette: imperious nose, pendulous lip, great jaw. So much, before Cribben's heart made its last leaping protest.

A HORIZON OF OBELISKS

by Dorothy K. Haynes

DOROTHY KATE HAYNES (1918–1989) was born and lived in Lanark all her life, apart from four years in an orphanage, an experience which she described in her autobiography, *Haste Ye Back*. Her short stories were collected in two books, *Thou Shalt Not Suffer a Witch* (illustrated by Mervyn Peake) and *Peacocks and Pagodas*, with some overlapping of material. Whether witty or macabre, her tales have an authentically Celtic tang.

⟩

THEY opened the grave in the evening, digging deep, beyond the grass roots, and the roots of small things tangled in the mould like hairs.

The man in the grave felt the chill just before dawn. Soil pattered, rotten wood cracked, and he shrank as the air pressed on him. 'Cold,' he thought, 'right through to my bones,' and he moved the bones, disconnected now, under the flesh he thought was there. 'Cold,' he thought. His arms folded, hugging himself, and there was a wetness of dew, and a weakness over him. He remembered the weakness, and the light going down low, and a queer pinpoint of it lingering on after they had washed and bound him and knelt by his side. Now the light was growing again, and he scrabbled up and lay on the ground like a newly hatched bird, waiting for the day to dry him out.

The sun came up like polished copper, and the angel on the mortuary dome preened its wings and curved them like pincers. Weakly, the man went down the paths, left and right, looking for the way out. It seemed to take a long time. What he remembered about the graveyard went back to his childhood, hot days among the tombstones and daisies, and his mother watching him, smiling on the grass beside a cypress tree. He had always enjoyed going to the graveyard. Heaven, he had thought, would be just like this, smooth grass, bright beds of flowers, and a horizon of obelisks and angels. Perhaps this *was* Heaven . . .?

He accepted the fact that he had died, remembering how life had narrowed to a needlepoint and gone. But what, then, of the Resurrection? He had always pictured it as a great flapping of wings and an uprush of souls, all crying together and vanishing into the sun, but there had been no trumpets splitting the air, nothing ascending from the green mounds. The angel on the mortuary was rigid

29

against the sailing sky, and he himself had nothing about
him that was celestial. In his mind he was as he had once
been, a raw, red man in working clothes with a fuzz of
ginger over his baldness. He passed his hand over his
eyes, and looked about him distractedly. All through the
chill of his waking he had heard a bleating and lowing and
the flustered clucking of hens, and he remembered how it
had once been a comfort to him to know that, when he
died, he would lie within sound of the cattle market. That
was where he had worked; but how long ago, he could not
remember.

Here now was the way out, a little arch let into the grey
wall. He looked over his shoulder, as if to ask permission,
but no-one stopped him as he laid his hand on the latch,
and there was no fiery sword to bleed and burn through
him. He stepped out on to the pink grush, and weakly,
meekly, made his way past the grave-digger's lodge to the
blue tar of the roadway.

It was early yet, the sun level along the streets, and he
went with the determined plod of a child making for
home. The school playground was a wash of sunlight, and
all the pointed windows stood open. By ten o'clock the
place would echo like a church with the plainsong of the
multiplication tables, but now there was only the janitor,
whistling in his peaked cap and boiler suit.

Downhill, where the road narrowed, the butcher was
dressing his floor. He walked backwards, blue and white,
like a sailor on the golden sawdust, and the man paused,
idle and interested; but there was an uneasiness, too, in
the death around him, the great bull swinging in chains,
the sheep's heads, the bones pink on their ashets – he did
not know whether it was kinship or pity. Quickly, he
backed out of the shadowed street to where the sunlight
sliced the pavement.

What was the time? The clock blazed gold, and the
weather vane was as small as a golden bee. It was so high
that he had to lean back, his eyes screwing up and up the
weathered stone, past the frets of the belfry and the white
scuds of bird lime. Half past seven. The clouds raced and
dizzied him, and his eyes darkened and dropped to the

ground. The street was bare, the whole proud sweep of it smiling and empty, but the birds were busy, brown sparrows and slate-coloured doves feeding and fluttering together.

The man went down among the shabby houses behind the church. He was holding himself in as a hurt child holds itself till it reaches home. Down here the pavements were scrabbled with yesterday's games, and the doorsteps dipped in the middle. He paused in a close, and listened in brown shadow. Away up the stairs he heard his own door slam, and he knew that a white flake had fallen from the gas mantle. Every crack in the plaster was familiar, the dusty windows on the landings, the gas pipes branching from the wall. When his mother came to the door he would cling to her and let himself go, put his head on her lap and clutch her skirt and sob and sob and stay with her for ever. . .

The knocker was a grinning brass cat with a bow on its neck, but he poked, two-fingered, at the letterbox. Nobody answered. He knocked harder, listening for a footstep inside, and then he turned away. He did not want to disturb the neighbours, to have them coming out in their dustcaps and aprons, rubbing at the doorknobs as they spied. Down the stairs again, he searched in the yard, in the wash house, among the house-proud scorings of pipe-clay. She might be filling the coal bucket, or emptying the ashes, or shaking the rugs. She was so clear in his mind that he could almost touch her; but she was not there, and he went away with the love in him taut and swollen.

He hung about, hoping to meet her in the streets. The shops put their shades out, and he wandered up and down, remembering this kind of day, the bright joy of it, long ago. No-one spoke to him, and he did not look at faces. The things he added to the turmoil of his mind were little pleasures his mother had shown him, secret things, the amber glass of a door handle, a fluted light in a fruit shop, an alley where the cobbles were sea-rounded and smooth; but he was at a loose end, like a child playing truant . . .

Playing truant . . . from what? He would not think about it. The school emptied, the streets filled with yells and running feet. Every cafe in the town was bursting full, steaming with beef and broth and custard; and then it was afternoon. The clock on the station kept at its eternal semaphore, the signals shifted, the trains fussed and sighed; and past the station wall and the horse trough went the orphan children, four deep, with a Sister of Mercy behind them. Her boots kicked up the hem of her long blue skirt, and her white flyaway hat was like an arum lily. The man wanted to speak to her, because nuns were good women who would help anyone who asked, but he could not explain what troubled him. Time eluded him, like the memory of what had come after this repeated present. He could not think beyond this day, with the dust blowing, and the farmers jostling in the streets, and the brown droves of cattle going by with lowered horns and a yapping at their heels. He did not know what was going to happen next, but when it did happen, it was as if someone had jogged his memory. On a day like this, his mother had taken him into an icecream shop, and in the cool dark they had supped from little glass dishes. Outside, a beggar had squeezed his accordion, with a dirty capful of pennies in the gutter – and there was the beggar, his grey head frowsy, his hands grained with dirt. 'No,' his mother had said, as he tugged at her sleeve, 'No, he'll just drink it,' and she had dragged him away from the sighing music and the man's turned up eyes.

The orphan children had gone now, through the chapel gates, and the man stood, lost for a moment, by the dusty horse trough. The roadway filled with a carpet of fawn fleeces, and a car crawled behind them, another and another car, all black. Rigidly, the man stood, watching the funeral. This had happened too, a long time ago. He and his mother would stand on the edge of the pavement, not staring, but taking it all in, the long coffin in the glass hearse, the rainbow wreaths, and the stuffed-looking mourners, not looking out of the window in case they should enjoy the ride. He had had to take off his cap . . . stiffly, he put his hand up, but the cars had passed, round the corner by the market.

He could not follow them. His mother had never intruded when a funeral was on, but later, when it was all over, they would tiptoe in, and look at the wreaths, and read the black-edged cards among the petals. Vaguely, with a sense of filling in time, he made his way to the market. Soon the selling would be over, the rings silent, the pens empty, and children would run round in the empty space gathering feathers and handfuls of white down.

The afternoon was ebbing away in lessening enchantment. A lone cow filled the barns with its bellowing, and men with stiff brooms were sweeping the cobbles. These were none of the men he knew, and they did not pass the time of day. The day was nearly over for them, and all they wanted was to finish and go home for tea.

Timidly, he rubbed a hand over his face. The day, this peculiar day, was ending for him as well. The workers would go to their separate homes, wash at the running tap, and sit down at the table with a woman to wait on them; but he could not go back to that. He was still living out his childhood, the past condensed into a few bright hours, and the hours' slow saddening towards evening. The house would grow dark, the teaplates sour with beetroot and vinegar, the kettle whining as the fire died. And after he had washed, and climbed into the recess bed, listening to his father clearing his throat and knocking out his pipe, the curfew bell would ring, knell, knell, knell, and he would want to sob, thinking of all the evening hymns.

'Change and decay in all around I see. . . .' But he would hold back his weeping because his mother would be tired by that time, and she might not have patience with him. . . .

Weary, a little bewildered, he turned away from the dunged cobbles and the mournful lowing. Opposite were the main gates of the cemetery, wrought-iron gold-embossed, with a humble little door at the side for those who entered on foot; and through this door went the man, shutting it after him as his mother had taught him when he was a child.

This, he had thought, must be like entering Heaven; but surely Heaven was never meant to be so lonely? There had been no joy in his day, nothing but a yearning and an ache in the heart. If this was Heaven, his mother would come now, surely, in the cool of the evening, walking reverently past the grave, poking among the flowers with stiff gloved fingers . . .

He knelt to look at the cards, but his eyes were blurred, and it was a long time before he realized that she was buried there, and that hers was the funeral he had seen in the wake of the jogging sheep. There was no sorrow in knowing that she was dead. She would sleep as he had done, under the roots and the small pebbles, but if God was willing she would not wake till the Resurrection. He prayed that she would not waken. He himself had been meant to sleep on, but the early cold had roused him.

He sat on an iron bench marked FOR THE USE OF THE PUBLIC, and his arms folded, hugging himself. The ache inside him had eased a little with understanding. At least there would be no more searching; and maybe tomorrow, or one of the grey or golden tomorrows in store, the trumpet would sound, the graves would open, and eternity would begin – or end.

He sat for a long time, telling himself that there was nothing to be afraid of. The lone cow mourned in the market, and far away, a train trailed its own scream after it. The angel on the mortuary dome flapped its wings against the green sky, and then huddled down to sleep, but the man on the bench could not sleep for the chill. 'Cold,' he thought. 'Right through to my bones . . .'

THE LOONY

by Alison Prince

ALISON PRINCE (1931–) originally trained as an artist, and still illustrates most of her many books for children. Her collections of supernatural stories include *Haunted Children*, *The Ghost Within*, and *A Haunting Refrain*. For adults, her most recent book is a study of creativity, *The Necessary Goat*. In recent years the classical British ghost story has flourished in children's fiction penned by such writers as John Gordon, Robert Westall, Laurence Starg and Alison Prince (not to mention the streak of the macabre and disturbing in the tales of Alan Garner and Diana Wynne Jones, among others). I offer 'The Loony', originally published in an anthology of fiction for teenagers, as evidence.

'MAMA,' said Cathy, 'Lucy Claythorpe at school says the house Papa has bought used to have a lunatic woman shut up in it. The other girls say so, as well. The woman used to scream, they said, but nobody took any notice because they were used to it. The windows of her room were barred so that she couldn't get out, and at last she died in there but nobody knew.'

It was a relief to blurt it all out. Cathy had been wondering whether the dreadful story was true and, if so, whether her parents had heard it.

'My darling child,' said Mrs Palfrey, 'you must not listen to gossip.' She was always so beautiful, Cathy thought. Pearl buttons fastened the high neck of her blouse tightly round her throat, but she never looked hot or flustered. Cathy, who was often both of these things, envied her. 'Your father,' Mrs Palfrey continued, 'feels that we should have a house more in keeping with his status as a successful umbrella manufacturer. Blackstone Villa has a certain – distinction.'

Cathy thought of the house, standing in its yew-shrouded grounds on the edge of the town, backing on to the moor. It had tall windows, steep gables, and a stone path leading to its front door. A wall surrounded it, with a spiky pattern of wrought-iron along the top. It was on its own, not tucked between its neighbours like their present house. Perhaps that was what her mother meant by distinction. Cathy sighed.

'In any case,' Mrs Palfrey went on, 'people are absurdly superstitious about simple-mindedness. The very word, lunatic, shows a depth of ignorance. It comes from the Latin, *luna*, meaning moon. So lunatic is thought to mean moon-struck. As if the moon could have anything to do with it!' She laughed, then her face was again composed in its faint smile of unchallengeable good sense. 'Nobody in *this* family is likely to go mad,' she said.

Impulsively, Cathy flung her arms round her mother's neck and kissed her. She was so sensible and lovely – so utterly to be relied on.

'There, my pet,' said Mrs Palfrey, disentangling herself calmly after returning Cathy's kiss. 'Now, tea is ready in the dining-room.' She stood up gracefully. 'Your father says we should have a cook-housekeeper when we move into the new house,' she added. 'But I hardly feel that it is necessary.'

Cathy smiled as she followed her mother from the room. Of course it wasn't necessary. As well as being beautiful and wise, her mother was a wonderfully efficient housekeeper.

A week later, they moved into the new house. School had ended for the summer holidays, to Cathy's relief. She was tired of Lucy Claythorpe's taunts of 'Loo-ny! Loo-ny! Living in the mad-house!' People like Lucy, she tried to remind herself, could not be expected to understand about the Latin, *luna*. It was not Lucy's fault that she was absurdly superstitious. But the teasing hurt, and Cathy hoped that by next term the novelty of the Palfreys living in Blackstone Villa would have worn off.

It was very late by the time she got to bed. Her furniture looked strange, rearranged in the new room, and the curtains had not yet been hung at the tall window whose sills, Cathy had noticed, bore the scars of deep screw holes at approximately four-inch intervals. Her mother had fingered them lightly as she gazed round at the faded wallpaper. 'We will redecorate this room,' she had said. 'Ecru and ivory, I think. Very light. Very restrained.' Now, she bent to kiss Cathy. 'Good night, darling,' she said. 'Sleep tight.' She stood up and reached to turn off the gently-hissing gas lamp above Cathy's bed. 'No need to get up too early tomorrow,' she added. Her figure was still clearly visible in the moonlight which flooded in through the uncurtained window. 'I will bring you a cup of tea.'

'Thank you,' said Cathy, smiling. Then her mother went out.

I was silly to worry, Cathy thought as she gazed at the

waxy face of the moon, whose roundness was still slightly flattened on one side. There is nothing malign about this house. The bars have been taken down from the window and all traces of the last people who lived here will soon have gone. The only reality is what is happening here and now. And everything is all right.

Filled with trust, she closed her eyes in the cool radiance of the moon, and fell asleep.

'Here is your tea.'

'Oh!' said Cathy sleepily. 'Thank you.'

It was broad daylight. The woman who stood by Cathy's bed with a cup and saucer in her hand was not Cathy's mother. She wore a long white apron over a black dress with the sleeves unbuttoned and pushed up over her mottled arms. Her wiry, reddish hair escaped from the white cap she wore, and her face was crumpled into angry grooves. A huge purple birthmark spread from her left eye down to her chin. Cathy stared at it in horrified fascination.

'Come along,' said the woman impatiently. 'Sit up and drink your tea.'

'Who are you?' asked Cathy. 'Where is Mama?'

'Don't start any of your nonsense,' said the woman. She put the cup of tea down on a chest of drawers that stood against the wall, then turned back to the bed. Without further words, she gripped Cathy by the arms and hauled her into a sitting position, punching the pillows into place behind her. Cathy uttered a cry of fright, and the woman said, 'Scream as much as you like. Everyone is used to it. If you were sane, poor creature, you would understand that it's useless. As it is—' She shrugged, then retrieved the cup of tea and thrust it into Cathy's hands. 'Now, drink it,' she commanded. 'And don't you dare make a mess.'

Cathy sipped the tea. 'It's cold,' she said.

The woman laughed with contempt. 'Can't give hot tea to a loony,' she said. 'We don't want you scalding yourself, do we? Though I don't know why not,' she added bitterly.

Cathy drank the cold tea with a shudder, then pushed

the bedclothes aside. She would go and find her mother and ask her to get rid of this person.

'And where are you going, Miss?' enquired the woman. Cathy tried to dodge past her but the woman caught her and flung her back on to the bed. This time Cathy did scream, again and again, loudly, kicking and wriggling as the woman held her down on the bed, her arms pinioned above her head. The door opened and a man came in. Cathy, struggling, caught a glimpse of dark trousers, waistcoat and watch chain as he strode quickly to the head of the bed. She felt the woman shift her grasp to let the man pull some sort of garment over Cathy's head. It had endlessly long sleeves, as Cathy found when she was hauled again into a sitting position, the sleeves crossed and tied so that her arms were pulled tightly across her chest. Then they left her, trussed like a helpless parcel.

'Here is your tea,' said Cathy's mother.

'Oh!' said Cathy sleepily. 'Thank you.'

It was broad daylight.

'Are you feeling better now?' asked Mrs Palfrey. She did not smile.

'Better?' asked Cathy. She sipped her tea. It was lovely and hot. Why was she glad it was hot, she wondered? Tea was always hot.

'You had a bad dream,' said Mrs Palfrey. 'You were making such a noise in the night that I had to come and see what was the matter. You got out of bed, but I don't think you were awake. When I tried to persuade you to go back to bed you struggled and screamed like a mad thing. I had to call your father.'

Cathy frowned, vaguely disquieted. 'I don't remember,' she said. 'I think I dreamed about a cup of tea.'

'I hope it will not become a habit,' said Mrs Palfrey with some disapproval. 'Your father was not at all pleased to be so rudely awoken.'

Cathy's father was an impressive figure. The heavy formality of his clothes, the smell of the pomade he wore on his dark hair and the resounding boom of his voice combined to make Cathy feel a respect for him which bordered on fear. 'I'm very sorry,' she said, appalled to think what she must have done.

'We will say no more about it,' conceded her mother. She smiled kindly and added, 'It was probably the effect of the move. Tonight, things will not be so strange.'

In bed that night, Cathy stared at the bland face of the moon, almost a full circle tonight, and wondered what lay on the other side of sleep. What had happened last night to cause her parents to regard her so gravely today? And what lay in store in the unknown darkness of a dream? She tried hard to stay awake.

'Here is your tea,' said the woman.

Cathy opened her eyes and stared up at the purple-blotched face. This had happened before. They said it was a dream. 'No,' she said. 'It's not true.'

'Don't start any of your nonsense,' said the woman. 'Sit up.'

Cathy knew she must be careful. Obediently, she sat up.

'That's better,' said the woman. She put the cup of cold tea into Cathy's hands and said, 'Drink it.'

Cathy did so. It was very unpleasant. Opposition was useless, she knew. She had to be good and do as she was told until she hit on some way to break this nightmare and get back to real life. 'What must I do?' she asked meekly.

The woman laughed. '*Do*, you poor loony?' she said contemptuously. 'What do you think you can do? Put your clothes on, to start with, then sit on your chair by the window. That's what you *do*, isn't it?'

'Oh,' said Cathy. 'I see. Thank you.' She handed the woman her empty cup.

'We're having one of our good days, are we?' said the woman sarcastically. 'All right, clever Miss, see if you can dress yourself while I take this cup to the kitchen. I'll be back in a minute to see what sort of muddle you've made of it. Then I'll take you for a walk to the bathroom.'

She went out, and Cathy heard the key being turned in the lock. There were clothes folded in a pile on the chair by the window. She got up and inspected them. A clumsy grey dress, thick black stockings and flannel underwear, and a knitted cardigan which had once been blue but was dirty and tea-stained. Holes in it had been roughly darned with ill-matched wool. A pair of heavy black lace-up shoes stood on the floor under the chair.

In a kind of desperate haste, Cathy struggled into the clothes, hating the idea that the woman would come and help her. It was bad enough without that. She stared out into the dew-wet garden as she buttoned the dress, and realized that the window was protected by vertical iron bars about four inches apart. This is a dream, she told herself fiercely, fighting down her panic. I must not worry about the bars. Or about these clothes I am wearing. It is all a dream. Soon it will stop.

Turning away from the window, Cathy ran her fingers through her hair. Her comb should be on the dressing-table with the silver-backed brushes and mirror, but the furniture in this room was different. She saw that there was a rather blotched unframed mirror standing on top of the chest of drawers, and crossed the room to look into it.

The face that looked back was not hers.

Cathy felt her mouth open in a scream of silent horror, and, as if mockingly, the mouth of the reflection opened also, dry lips parting in a gaunt face whose red-rimmed eyes stared out senselessly at a world which meant nothing. The hair which straggled through the fingers of the still-upraised hand was streaked with grey.

Sick horror flooded through Cathy and made her feel as if every joint had turned to water. Desperately, she assured herself again that this was merely a dream. She picked up the mirror in both hands and carried it to the barred window where, in the stronger early morning light, she stared again at the alien reflection. And again, the face that stared anxiously back was that of a middle-aged, demented woman.

To her own surprise, Cathy found within herself a cold ability to reason. Waking or sleeping, she argued, somewhere in this house was the real world where her parents slept in their real bed. All she had to do was to break through this nightmare, then she would re-establish contact with normality. She thought carefully. The woman with the purple-marked face was a kind of gaoler. She would have to be destroyed.

A part of Cathy's mind recoiled from the plan she was formulating, but she reminded herself that this was only a dream. The face in the mirror proved it. And anything one did in a dream was unreal. One could not be held responsible, because these events were not really happening.

Very carefully, Cathy placed the mirror at an angle between the wall and the floor. Then she stood upright and kicked it with her heavily-shod foot. It was surprisingly difficult to break. She turned sideways to it and re-attacked it with a stamping action – and the mirror smashed into shards of splintered glass. Forgetting that she could not hurt herself in a dream, Cathy wrapped her hand in the blue cardigan before picking up a long sliver. She could hear footsteps coming up the stairs. She ran back to the bed and lay huddled on her side with the glass stiletto shrouded in its cardigan as she hugged it to her chest like a slender, lethal doll.

The door was unlocked. 'If she's turned violent,' the woman was saying to someone, 'it'll take both of us to restrain her. I certainly heard a crash.'

Cathy hoped that her nightgown, thrown over the back of the chair, would hide the evidence of the broken glass. It was odd how cool she felt. Mama would be proud of her, she thought.

'Now, what have you been up to?' demanded the woman, leaning over Cathy and shaking her roughly by the shoulder. Blindly, Cathy struck out with the splinter of glass. It met the resistance of a thick sleeve and she struck again and again. In the confusion of blows and shouting voices, she realized with angry satisfaction that blood was trickling over her hand. In a minute, she would be free.

There were voices downstairs. Cathy opened her eyes and saw that it was dawn. Grey light crept into the room, and birds were singing.

She sat up in bed. Why were people talking in the drawing-room below her at such an early hour? She noticed a dark stain on the patchwork quilt which covered her bed. She touched it and found that it was blood.

Dread and terror flooded through Cathy like some fatal weakness, and she lay back against her pillows feeling faint. What had happened? She tried to throw her mind back into the darkness of the sleep which had just ended, but was met by a baffling wall which defied her memory. Slowly, she got out of bed and put on her dressing-gown. Then she saw that her hand-mirror lay smashed on the floor by the window, its silver frame twisted and broken. She almost put her foot on a long, pointed sliver of glass which lay by her bed. She gathered her dressing-gown round her in fresh horror, and pushed her feet into their slippers. Then she made her way across the room to her door. For some obscure reason, she was glad to find that it was not locked, and wondered why this should be so. Her bedroom door had never been locked.

Cathy crept down the carpeted stairs and crossed the hall to where the drawing-room door stood slightly ajar. She crouched down and peered through the crack.

Dr McClintock was bandaging Cathy's father's arm. Mrs Palfrey watched intently, sitting very upright in an arm chair. She had evidently dressed hastily, and the unbraided mass of her dark hair hung almost to her waist. Even at this moment, Cathy thought it looked wonderful.

'I would not expect blood-poisoning from such clean slashes as these,' Dr McClintock remarked in his pleasant Scottish voice. 'Not in the ordinary way, that is. But after what happened in this house on a previous occasion, you understand, I feel it is necessary to be doubly vigilant. You must inform me at once if there is any sign of infection setting in.'

Cathy saw her parents look at each other. 'What *did* happen in this house?' enquired Mr Palfrey as he sat with his arm extended to the doctor's ministrations. A bowl of red-coloured water stood on the floor beside his chair.

Dr McClintock's hands were suddenly still. 'Had you not heard?' he asked, looking up from his bandaging. 'Oh, dear. I had stupidly assumed that you knew all about it, local gossip being what it is.'

'We do not gossip,' said Mrs Palfrey icily. 'But now that you have raised the subject, doctor, I think you had better tell us what you mean.'

The doctor's round face creased with distress. He tied the bandage neatly and clipped off its ends, then returned his scissors to the open bag which stood beside him. He sat back in his chair and sighed.

'It was a few years ago now,' he said. 'As you'll know, the house has stood empty a while. Mrs Knarr, who was housekeeper here, came banging on my door one night, saying that old Mr Grayson had cut his arm badly and she feared he would bleed to death. I was not Mr Grayson's regular doctor, you understand, but I was the nearest, and it was an emergency. So I came with her to this house where I found— ' The doctor laughed in some embarrassment— 'injuries very similar to your own, Mr Palfrey. Now, I know you and your wife have told me the truth concerning this brainstorm or whatever it was that afflicted your lassie – and we must decide what to do about that in a moment.'

Cathy, crouched at the door, took a deep, shuddering breath. But the doctor was going on. 'In Mr Grayson's case, however, I was told a doubtful story about the breaking of a wine glass. And then the housekeeper came in from the kitchen and, to Mr Grayson's very evident embarrassment, gave me an elaborate explanation concerning a slip on a polished floor which caused him to put his hand through a window. I had a strong feeling that both of them were lying, and wondered why. Anyway, dawn was breaking as I left the house. I was half way to the gate when I heard a howling which made the hair stand up on the back of my neck.'

'Howling?' enquired Mr Palfrey. He sat with his dressing-gown sleeve rolled back over his bandaged arm, nursing his wrist in the other hand as if he was in considerable pain. 'A dog, you mean?'

'This was no dog,' said Dr McClintock. 'I looked back at the house and there, in the grey light of dawn, I saw a woman standing at the window of the room upstairs, directly above where we sit now. She was shaking the bars which guarded it and howling like an imprisoned animal. There was no doubt in my mind that it was she who had caused the injuries to old Mr Grayson, and I could understand that he and his housekeeper were anxious to conceal the fact that they had temporarily lost control of her. Had I been at all indiscreet, the public outcry would have been considerable.'

Mr and Mrs Palfrey nodded in understanding, and Cathy, huddled miserably outside the door, shivered in dread.

'Anyway,' the doctor continued more rapidly, as if anxious to get the dreadful story finished, 'the arm turned gangrenous, and of course a man of Mr Grayson's age has little resistance. He was dead in a few weeks. His own doctor had taken over the case – to my relief, I can tell you. But the worst thing of all was yet to come. Now, Mrs Knarr had never been a sociable woman, you must understand. Possibly she was acutely conscious of a disfiguring birthmark which covered the left side of her face, but at any rate, she was reclusive. As a result, nobody thought it strange that she was not seen about following Mr Grayson's death. But one day the postman knocked at the door with a letter too broad to go through the slot, and nobody answered. He looked through the letter-box and saw that a pile of letters lay uncollected on the mat, and raised the alarm. The police broke the door down eventually, and found the house empty. Then they discovered the poor, demented creature in the upstairs room, lying dead. It seemed that she had starved to death. The housekeeper had simply packed her bags and gone, leaving the unfortunate prisoner to her fate.'

Mrs Palfrey shuddered and said, 'How appalling!'

Her husband asked, 'Was the housekeeper ever brought to justice?'

'Fate provided its own justice,' said the doctor. 'The woman bought an isolated house on the moors with the money she had acquired from Mr Grayson – not entirely legally, I may add – and lived there under an assumed name. But the place was struck by lightning one stormy night and she was burnt to death. The subsequent investigations revealed her identity.'

'And who was the unfortunate creature upstairs?' enquired Mr Palfrey. 'A member of the family, I take it?'

'She was Mr Grayson's daughter,' said the doctor. 'I think he cared for her, in his way. But as he grew old, he became completely dependent on the housekeeper. His wife, I gather, had died in childbirth – and it is not easy to find domestic staff who are willing to take on the care of a lunatic.'

Cathy burst into the room, all caution abandoned. 'You mustn't say lunatic!' she cried incoherently. Tears were streaming down her face. Lucy Claythorpe's teasing had come back to make the nightmare finally intolerable. 'It's *luna*, for the moon. Mama said so.' Sobbing overwhelmed her and she dived to her mother's knees and buried her face in her lap. A small residue of sense in the centre of her tormented mind assured her that this was the only security. Mama was utterly to be relied on.

The room was terribly silent, and Cathy knew that her parents and the doctor were looking at each other in unspoken discussion. She could feel her hair being stroked in an absent sort of way.

Dr McClintock gently raised Cathy to her feet and led her to a chair. 'Sit down, Cathy,' he said kindly, 'and don't distress yourself, my dear. Tell me, did you have a dream tonight? Can you remember anything about it?'

Cathy struggled. Fragmented visions came back to mind.

'There was a woman,' she said. 'With a big purple mark on her face.'

The doctor smiled. 'Now, if you were listening at the door, lassie, you heard me say that,' he said. 'Try again. Just cast your mind back to what really happened.'

'Bars,' said Cathy wildly. She did not know if it was memory or imagination. 'Bars across the window. Someone brought me a cup of tea.' It was all very confusing.

Dr McClintock looked at Cathy's parents. Eyebrows

were raised, heads shaken. Then he turned back to Cathy and said, 'I think what you need is a long sleep, Cathy. A proper sleep with no bad dreams. From what I hear, you've had some pretty disturbed nights lately.' Cathy nodded. Tears were still trickling down her face, and her mother handed her a hanky. Cathy mopped and blew, but the tears kept coming. The doctor was pouring something from a bottle into a small glass. 'We'll have a proper talk about it tonight, when you're feeling better,' he said, 'but just now I want you to drink this.' He handed Cathy the glass and she drank obediently.

Cathy's mother carried the bowl out to the kitchen, and her father talked to Dr McClintock about things to do with money and trade which Cathy did not understand. Tears continued to well up, and it seemed too much effort to try and stop them. Her arms and legs began to feel very heavy. She hardly remembered being led back to her room.

When Cathy woke, it was late at night. Her limbs felt heavy and inert, as if they were still sleeping. How strange it was, she thought, to wake up in the dark, yet feel as if it should be morning.

The moon shone fitfully through scudding clouds. It was totally circular tonight, as perfect as a great pearl, but a wind had sprung up, and the yew trees in the garden moved their branches, casting erratic shapes across the wall of Cathy's room. There was darkness for a moment as clouds covered the moon, then it sailed clear of them, and the shadows danced again.

Cathy stared at the great white circle which hung so serenely in the dark sky. '*Luna*,' she murmured aloud, dwelling on the word. It sounded smooth and calm, like the moonlight itself. And, quite suddenly, she understood it all. For the first time, the dream experiences were clear in her mind. Horrified, she lay and thought about it. The people of her nightmare must be the ghosts of dead Mr Grayson and the terrible housekeeper, Mrs Knarr. The two of them seemed to be treating her, Cathy Palfrey, as the imprisoned madwoman. But why? Cathy stared round her room with the moving shadows of the yew trees flickering across the walls, and began to feel afraid. What if it should happen again? She tried to quell the thought, assuring herself that the fact of understanding it all made her safe. She was here, in the real world. The dream could not overwhelm her again. Or could it? She felt desperately alone and vulnerable. 'Mama!' she called loudly. 'Mama!'

She was immensely glad to hear a door opening down-stairs in response. She heard her mother go to the kitchen, then, after a pause, come up stairs, stopping at the door of Cathy's room to unlock it. Hearing the key turn, Cathy was in terror that it would be the woman with the blotched face who came in, for, in real life, her door was never locked. But when the door opened it was her mother who stood there, beautiful and real, with a cup of tea in her hand. She said, as if everything was quite ordinary, 'Here is your tea.' Cathy gave a small sigh of relief. Her mother stood the cup and saucer on the dressing-table and added, 'I'll light the gas.'

Warm and comfortable, Cathy smiled up at her mother as she reached up in a graceful movement to light the gas lamp above the bed.

'There!' said Mrs Palfrey as the light flared up. 'That's better.' She waved the match out and placed it carefully in an ash tray beside the cup and saucer on the dressing-table. Then, with her hands clasped before her, she gazed down at Cathy and said, 'Darling, for your own safety, your father and I feel that it may be wise to replace the bars across your window for a while.'

Bars. Imprisonment. Lunacy. Suddenly, the intentions of dead Mr Grayson and dead Mrs Knarr were clear. They wanted it all to happen again. They had condemned Cathy Palfrey to be imprisoned in this room. Cathy gave a gasp of terror as the taunting words rose in her mind: 'Loony, loony, living in the mad-house.' Living in the mad-house for ever.

'No,' said Cathy unsteadily. 'Mama, you mustn't. Please.'

'You might hurt yourself, darling,' her mother explained. 'Walking in your sleep, you see, you might fall out of the window.'

Cathy turned among her pillows to follow her mother's gaze as she looked with concern at the long window. The full moon was obscured by silver-edged clouds which parted as she watched, letting the cool light beam out. Then Cathy gave a scream of terror. The face reflected in the window's glass was blotched with dark shadows. It was the housekeeper. The round moon hung in the centre of the ghostly purple-marked face like a pearl, grotesquely beautiful amid such ugliness.

'No!' Cathy screamed. 'No! Go away! Leave me alone!' The figure she had thought to be her mother leaned anxiously over the bed, and the face was blotched with dark shadows as the yew trees moved in the moonlight. 'Mama!' Cathy screamed to the closed door, convinced that her mother had somehow left the room when the terrible stranger had come in. She leapt up, still screaming, and pushed the terrifying person away with all her might. The figure staggered back, caught off balance, and clutched at the embroidered runner on the dressing-table. It slipped off and brought brushes and combs, the ash tray and the still-hot cup of tea crashing to the floor – and the figure plunged through the window and fell outwards in a shower of sparkling shards, each one reflecting a tiny, shattered fragment of the full moon.

Cathy covered her face with her hands. She could hardly breathe. Where, oh, *where* was her mother? And how had the awful Mrs Knarr come into the room? A grain of common sense told her that ghosts had no need of doors. Downstairs, the French window had opened. Cathy's father and the doctor had run out on to the lawn. Peeping through her fingers, she moved to the window and forced herself to look down.

The woman who lay on the moonlit grass moved once, in a kind of slow convulsion, then was still. The white, upturned face of Cathy's mother was still beautiful, even in death. The doctor was bending over her. He looked up at Mr Palfrey and shook his head.

Cathy's father brought his clenched fists to his chest and stood with hunched shoulders in silent agony. Then, slowly, he raised his head and stared up to where his daughter stood at the shattered window. 'Dr McClintock,' he ground out, and his voice was terrible in Cathy's ears, 'kindly go to the carpenter's house. Get the man out of bed if necessary, and bring him here. That window must be barred. At once, and for ever.'

Upstairs, standing in the moonlight, framed by the jagged remains of the glass, Cathy thought that she was crying. But, even to her own ears, it sounded like the howl of an imprisoned animal.

THE FIRST-NIGHTER

by Henry Normanby

HENRY NORMANBY wrote stories for the *Grand* and the *Westminster Gazette*, and they were collected in his sole book *Destinies* (Sisley's, 1908). Neither I nor Richard Dalby, a better scholar of the field than I, can unearth anything further about him, but he deserves to be remembered for tales as dark as this.

I

WITHOUT, the night was warm and reminiscent of summer, but in my room it was already chill and dank, although the man had but that moment come. He brought his loathsome cold breath into my house as into the theatre, and now, as then, I shuddered at the touch of it – for it veritably touched me as with a finger of ice. Against my will I made him welcome, but the sight of his cadaverous face and luminous eyes struck such fear into me that I talked with averted head, looking aimlessly about my room, glancing down at my plate, blinding myself by staring at the lights, gazing anywhere rather than into his eyes again. Could I have closed my ears as easily to his voice I would have done so – nay, more, I would have deprived myself of my five senses in his presence, so entirely and appallingly did he dominate me.

He spoke in a rough but quiet tone which sank often to a raucous whisper, and never rose above a hoarse ejaculation. It was not so much that his voice grated on my hearing as that it seemed to chant a harsh accompaniment to everything he said, some strange and cryptic undersong whereof the key was hidden.

To his desultory conversation I, in truth, paid little heed. The burden of unwilling hospitality had fallen upon me, and I found myself wondering, at times, as our strained talk languished, why I had asked him to come; why I had insisted on his coming, but in my heart there lay the knowledge that come he would have, whether I had asked him or not.

For so many dreadful 'first-nights' had I sat by this man, not knowing who he was nor whence he came, so often had we conversed between the scenes, that his mordant wit and facile chatter had become almost a part of my life. It seemed that I must always be with him, sit next to him, listen unwillingly to his words. I pushed my plate aside petulantly and my hand touched the clammy skin of his wrist. He had moved his chair nearer to mine, bringing the damp, noxious odour that clung about him nearer to my nostrils. Imperceptibly I drew my chair and glass a minute space away; unseen by me, he lessened that space.

Three times I crept away from him; three times he drew closer. I could have laughed at our folly, and the grim humour of it, as we followed each other persistently round the table, gave me new courage such as a man may feel who is freshly fed and warmed with wine. My vagrant eyes sought his face, again his cold breath chilled my cheek, once more I was listening to his voice. It was retelling the story of that playwright, who, after long years of toil, produced one play, magnificent, immortal; but the Fates bent their brows over it, and it died to live hereafter. The dramatist thereupon laid down his quill and presently died also.

'It only ran one night,' the voice said. My bitterness against this intruder on my peace grew intense.

'You, I take it, were there on that first and last night?'

'Yes, what of it?'

The luminous eyes burnt into mine. I would not answer him. I knew, and he knew, that every play, good, indifferent, or bad, that he, sitting by me unwillingly, had ever seen on its first night, had been damned beyond redemption.

'I knew that man,' he said, after a short silence.

'You knew him?' I asked, and my mind flashed back to the half century since his death.

—'was his friend, knew him better than anyone, read his play – judged it for him. Do you know he had it buried with him, in his coffin? It is so indeed. . . . *I wrote that play.*'

II

WHAT in the name of all that is past and forgotten should I be doing by that open grave? What had I done that my hands should bleed and be soiled with the stain of that black earth? In the darkness an indefinable, penetrating, dank odour rose from the pit beneath. A clod of wet earth fell with a splashing thud and I knew, from the squelching sound of its impact, how shapeless it had become – as shapeless as the thing beneath the coffin-lid. My clammy flesh shrank from the colder, clammier earth of the grave; my eyes, fearing to look into the sinister darkness of that fearsome hole, yet dared not turn away to the relief of the blackness of the open sky. My wet feet were frozen to the ground, I tried to fly from the accursed place, but could not stir. A moment later, with the utmost fear and horror, I was clinging to the slippery, broken edge of the oblong pit and lowering myself into its appalling gloom.

Clay from above splashed upon me, upon my hair, into my eyes, and I dropped the lever with a horrible crash as I raised my hands to wipe it away. The screws had rusted out of their sockets and the sharp edges of the coffin were worn round and uneven. It was easy to raise the lid, but I had to stand off it, at the side, and lean against the wet and slimy earth of the grave. Let it be recorded, as evidence of my obsession, that I groped with my hands in that ghastly casket. The occupant had ceased to be definite and had become amorphous. It was no longer a cold, silent shape, but a soft, yielding, horrible mass. As I searched, the clay kept falling – but the thud of the clods on that box which sounded empty but was so hideously full, was not so loud or so irregular as the unsteady beating of my fearful heart. The dripping of night-dews from outstretched, silent branches was not so clear as the splash of blood from my tortured hands. The sound of living bells mourning the dead hour drowned the insidious creeping of my feet. The black trees stole away, the white grave-stones wandered by, the great iron gates closed upon the past, the road slid strangely behind, the houses walked with laggard step, the stream sobbed in the darkness, the lights rose and fell, the pale stars gleamed in the clear spaces, and the moon loomed large through the drapery of mist.

III

HE was there when I entered my room, and the thought came to me that never more would he leave it, or me. His luminous eyes met mine and though he spoke no word I knew he wished me to write. The pen was in my fingers without my taking it, and my torn hand was resting on the paper and smearing it with earth and blood at each turn of the wrist. The pen flew across the paper, impelled by my uncertain touch. The lights flared and danced and showed red in the fog which had penetrated into my room. The guest, who was remaining, although I had not asked him to remain, and whose departure God alone knows how eager I was to see, watched me with his strangely bright eyes. The bright wood fire crackled and smoked, filling the air with aromatic fumes, but in my nostrils was still the smell of the damp night, of things earthly and unearthly, on my eyes the pall of darkness, in my ears the tearing of decayed wood.

Who was this man that I should obey him? Why should I write and write and write, with palsied hand, at his bidding? If only to lessen the time that he should sit with me I forewent the asking, and wrote and wrote.

At length the task was done; between us lay the pile of copied sheets. He gathered up the damp and mouldered papers from before him and put them on the fire. The flames went out in a rush of dirty smoke, the fire died down and went out also as he beat the charred remains into dust. Together, for no longer could I show the repulsion I had felt, we turned over the leaves of the play, arranged them, bound them together. The first pages were soiled with dried blood and clay; he damped his handkerchief in the carafe and tried in vain to wash off the signs of my unholy toil.

It was finished. The great work accomplished. Months

of labour, that had passed in a few infernal hours, bringing with them night and sick dread, pain and the open grave. Years of purgatory that shall be counted for my hell, centuries of doubt and waiting and despair.

I bowed my head for a brief space, then raised it and looked at him. The fire of his eyes had burnt out; his hands that had lain before him, continually moving and twisting about, rested with upturned palms upon the disordered table, inert and lifeless. He had an air of profound lassitude, his lower lip hung, his eyelids drooped, his lank, wiry neck was bent. Even as I watched him in the greyness of dawn, his eyes became dull and fixed, his nose grew sharp, his jaw fell . . . and I knew that the ghostly terror of my life was a thing of the past.

I dared gaze no longer on his cadaverous face. I rose and drew aside the blind.

The white day showed me only the mouldered chair where he had sat, and the impress of thin fingers on the blood-stained leaves.

THE HILL
AND THE HOLE

by Fritz Leiber

FRITZ REUTER LEIBER, JR (1910–) has won many awards for science fiction and fantasy, but I venture to suggest that his achievements in the field of supernatural fiction are even more considerable. In his first collection, *Night's Black Agents*, he united the British and American traditions of the field, and perfected the tale in which the uncanny element is as much an expression of modern life as an invasion of it. Later books – the novels *Conjure Wife* and *Our Lady of Darkness*, and the collection *Shadows with Eyes* – develop this theme further, but 'The Hill and the Hole', showing what a master of the macabre can do with a sunlit country landscape, comes from his first book.

TOM Digby swabbed his face against the rolled-up sleeve of his drill shirt, and good-naturedly damned the whole practice of measuring altitudes with barometric instruments. Now that he was back at the bench mark, which was five hundred eleven feet above sea level, he could see that his reading for the height of the hill was ridiculously off. It figured out to about four hundred forty-seven feet, whereas the hill, in plain view hardly a quarter of a mile away, was obviously somewhere around five hundred seventy or even five hundred eighty. The discrepancy made it a pit instead of a hill. Evidently either he or the altimeter had been cock-eyed when he had taken the reading at the hilltop. And since the altimeter was working well enough now, it looked as if he had been the one.

He would have liked to get away early for lunch with Ben Shelley at Beltonville, but he needed this reading to finish off the oil survey. He had not been able to spot the sandstone-limestone contact he was looking for anywhere but near the top of this particular hill. So he picked up the altimeter, stepped out of the cool shadow of the barn behind which the bench mark was located, and trudged off. He figured he would be able to finish this little job properly and still be in time for Ben. A grin came to his big, square, youthful face as he thought of how they would chew the fat and josh each other. Ben, like himself, was on the State Geologic Survey.

Fields of shoulder-high corn, dazzlingly green under the broiling Midwestern sun, stretched away from the hill to the flat horizon. The noonday hush was beginning. Blue-bottle flies droned around him as he skirted a manure heap and slid between the weather-gray rails of an old fence. There was no movement, except a vague breeze rippling the corn a couple of fields away and a

69

farmer's car raising a lazy trail of dust far off in the opposite direction. The chunky, competent-looking figure of Tom Digby was the only thing with purpose in the whole landscape.

When he had pushed through the fringe of tall, dry-stalked weeds at the base of the hill, he glanced back at the shabby one-horse farm where the bench mark was located. It looked deserted. Then he made out a little tow-headed girl watching him around the corner of the barn, and he remembered having noticed her earlier. He waved, and chuckled when she dodged back out of sight. Sometimes these farmers' kids were mighty shy. Then he started up the hill at a brisker pace, toward where the bit of strata was so invitingly exposed.

When he reached the top, he did not get the breeze he expected. It seemed, if anything, more stiflingly hot than it had been down below, and there was a feeling of dustiness. He swabbed at his face again, set down the altimeter on a level spot, carefully twisted the dial until the needle stood directly over the middle line of the scale, and started to take the reading from the pointer below.

Then his face clouded. He felt compelled to joggle the instrument, although he knew it was no use. Forcing himself to work very slowly and methodically, he took a second reading. The result was the same as the first. Then he stood up and relieved his feelings with a fancy bit of swearing, more vigorous, but just as good-natured as the blast he had let off at the bench mark.

Allowing for any possible change in barometric pressure during the short period of his climb up from the bench mark, the altimeter still gave the height of the hill as under four hundred fifty. Even a tornado of fantastic severity could not account for such a difference in pressure.

It would not have been so bad, he told himself disgustedly, if he had been using an old-fashioned aneroid. But a five-hundred-dollar altimeter of the latest design is not supposed to be temperamental. However, there was nothing to do about it now. The altimeter had evidently given its last accurate gasp at the bench mark and gone blooey for good. It would have to be shipped back east to be

fixed. And he would have to get along without this particular reading.

He flopped down for a breather before starting back. As
he looked out over the checkerboard of fields and the larger
checkerboard of sections bounded by dirt roads, it occurred
to him how little most people knew about the actual dimensions and boundaries of the world they lived in. They
looked at straight lines on a map, and innocently supposed
they were straight in reality. They might live all their lives
believing their homes were in one county, when accurate
surveying would show them to be in another. They were
genuinely startled if you explained that the Mason-Dixon
line had more jags in it than a rail fence, or if you told them
that it was next to impossible to find an accurate and
up-to-date detail map of any given district. They did not
know how rivers jumped back and forth, putting bits of
land first in one state then in another. They had never
followed fine-looking, reassuring roads that disappeared
into a weedy nowhere. They went along believing that they
lived in a world as neat as a geometry-book diagram, while
chaps like himself and Ben went around patching the edges
together and seeing to it that one mile plus one mile
equaled at least something like two miles. Or proving that
hills were really hills and not pits in disguise.

It suddenly seemed devilishly hot and close and the bare
ground unpleasantly gritty. He tugged at his collar, unbuttoned it further. Time to be getting on to Beltonville. Couple
glasses of iced coffee would go good. He hitched himself
up, and noticed that the little girl had come out from behind
the barn again. She seemed to be waving at him now, with a
queer, jerky, beckoning movement; but that was probably
just the effect of the heat-shimmer rising from the fields. He
waved too, and the movement brought on an abrupt spell
of dizziness. A shadow seemed to surge across the landscape, and he had difficulty in breathing. Then he started
down the hill, and pretty soon he was feeling all right again.

'I was a fool to come this far without a hat,' he told
himself. 'This sun will get you, even if you're as healthy as a
horse.'

Something was nagging at his mind, however, as he

realized when he got down in the corn again. It was that he did not like the idea of letting the hill lick him. It occurred to him that he might persuade Ben to come over this afternoon, if he had nothing else to do, and get a precise measurement with alidade and plane table.

When he neared the farm, he saw that the little girl had retreated again to the corner of the barn. He gave her a friendly, 'Hello.' She did not answer but she did not run away, either. He became aware that she was staring at him in an intent, appraising way.

'You live here?' he asked.

She did not answer. After awhile, she said, 'What did you want to go down there for?'

'The State hires me to measure land,' he replied. He had reached the bench mark and was automatically starting to take a reading, before he remembered that the altimeter was useless. 'This your father's farm?' he asked.

Again she did not answer. She was barefooted, and wore a cotton dress of washed out blue. The sun had bleached her hair and eyebrows several degrees lighter than her skin, giving something of the effect of a photographic negative. Her mouth hung open. Her whole face had a vacuous, yet not exactly stupid expression.

Finally she shook her head solemnly, and said, 'You shouldn't of gone down there. You might not have been able to get out again.'

'Say, just what are you talking about?' he inquired, humorously, but keeping his voice gentle so she would not run away.

'The hole,' she answered.

Tom Digby felt a shiver run over him. 'Sun must have hit me harder than I thought,' he told himself.

'You mean there's some sort of pit down that way?' he asked quickly. 'Maybe an old well or cesspool hidden in the weeds? Well, I didn't fall in. Is it on this side of the hill?' He was still on his knees beside the bench mark.

A look of understanding, mixed with a slight disappointment, came over her face. She nodded wisely and observed, 'You're just like Papa. He's always telling me there's a hill there, so I won't be scared of the hole. But he doesn't need to. I know all about it, and I wouldn't go near it again for anything.'

'Say, what the dickens are you talking about?' His voice got out of control, and he rather boomed the question at her. But she did not dart away, only continued to stare at him thoughtfully.

'Maybe I've been wrong,' she observed finally. 'Maybe Papa and you and other people really do see a hill there. Maybe *They* make you see a hill there, so you won't know about them being there. *They* don't like to be bothered. I know. There was a man come up here about two years ago, trying to find out about *Them*. He had a kind of spyglass on sticks. *They* made him dead. That was why I didn't want you to go down there. I was afraid *They* would do the same thing to you.'

He disregarded the shiver that was creeping persistently along his spine, just as he had disregarded from the very beginning with automatic scientific distaste for eeriness, the coincidence between the girl's fancy and the inaccurate altimeter readings.

'Who are *They*?' he asked cheerfully.

The little girl's blank, watery blue eyes stared past him, as if she were looking at nothing – or everything.

'*They* are dead. Bones. Just bones. But *They* move around. *They* live at the bottom of the hole, and *They* do things there.'

'Yes?' he prompted, feeling a trifle guilty at encouraging her. From the corner of his eye he could see an old Model-T chugging up the rutted drive, raising clouds of dust.

'When I was little,' she continued in a low voice, so he had to listen hard to catch the words, 'I used to go right up to the edge and look down at *Them*. There's a way to climb down in, but I never did. Then one day *They* looked up and caught me spying. Just white bone faces; everything else black. I knew *They* were thinking of making me dead. So I ran away and never went back.'

The Model-T rattled to a stop beside the barn, and a tall man in old blue overalls swung out and strode swiftly toward them.

'School Board sent you over?' he shot accusingly at Tom. 'You from the County Hospital?'

He clamped his big paw around the girl's hand. He had the same bleached hair and eyebrows, but his face was burnt to a brick red. There was a strong facial resemblance.

'I want to tell you something,' he went on, his voice heavy with anger but under control. 'My little girl's all right in the head. It's up to me to judge, isn't it? What if she don't always give the answers the teachers expect. She's got a mind of her own, hasn't she? And I'm perfectly fit to take care of her. I don't like the idea of your sneaking around to put a lot of questions to her while I'm gone.'

Then his eye fell on the altimeter. He glanced at Tom sharply, especially at the riding breeches and high, laced boots.

'I guess I went and made a damn fool of myself,' he said swiftly. 'You an oil man?'

Tom got to his feet. 'I'm on the State Geologic Survey,' he said.

The farmer's manner changed completely. He stepped forward, his voice was confidential. 'But you saw signs of oil here, didn't you?'

Tom shrugged his shoulders and grinned pleasantly. He had heard a hundred farmers ask that same question in the same way. 'I couldn't say anything about that. I'd have to finish my mapping before I could make any guesses.'

The farmer smiled back, knowingly but not unfriendlily. 'I know what you mean,' he said. 'I know you fellows got orders not to talk. So long, mister.'

Tom said, 'So long,' nodded good-bye to the little girl, who was still gazing at him steadily, and walked around the barn to his own car. As he plumped the altimeter down on the front seat beside him, he yielded to the impulse to take another reading. Once more he swore, this time under his breath.

The altimeter seemed to be working properly again.

'Well,' he told himself, 'that settles it. I'll come back and get a reliable alidade reading, if not with Ben, then with somebody else. I'll nail that hill down before I do anything.'

*

Ben Shelley slupped down the last drops of coffee, pushed back from the table, and thumbed tobacco into his battered brier. Tom explained his proposition.

A wooden-bladed fan was wheezing ponderously overhead, causing pendant stripes of fly paper to sway and tremble.

'Hold on a minute,' Ben interrupted near the end. 'That reminds me of something I was bringing over for you. May save us the trouble.' And he fished in his brief case.

'You don't mean to tell me there's some map for this region I didn't know about?' The tragic disgust in Tom's voice was only half jocular. 'They swore up and down to me at the office there wasn't.'

'Yeah, I'm afraid I mean just that,' Ben confirmed. 'Here she is. A special topographic job. Only issued yesterday.'

Tom snatched the folded sheet.

'You're right,' he proclaimed, a few moments later. 'This might have been some help to me.' His voice became sarcastic. 'I wonder what they wanted to keep it a mystery for?'

'Oh, you know how it is,' said Ben easily. 'They take a long time getting maps out. The work for this was done two years ago, before you were on the Survey. It's rather an unusual map, and the person you talked to at the office probably didn't connect it up with your structural job. And there's a yarn about it, which might explain why there was some confusion.'

Tom had pushed the dishes away and was studying the map intently. Now he gave a muffled exclamation which made Ben look up. Then he hurriedly reinspected the whole map and the printed material in the corner. Then he stared at one spot for so long that Ben chuckled and said, 'What have you found? A gold mine?'

Tom turned a serious face on him. 'Look, Ben,' he said slowly. 'This map is no good. There's a terrible mistake in it.' Then he added, 'It looks as if they did some of the readings by sighting through a rolled-up newspaper at a yardstick.'

'I knew you wouldn't be happy until you found something wrong with it,' said Ben. 'Can't say I blame you. What is it?'

Tom slid the map across to him, indicating one spot with his thumb-nail. 'Just read that off to me,' he directed. 'What do you see there?'

Ben paused while he lit his pipe, eyeing the map. Then he answered promptly, 'An elevation of four hundred forty-one feet. And it's got a name lettered in – "The Hole". Poetic, aren't we? Well, what is it? A stone quarry?'

'Ben, I was out at that very spot this morning,' said Tom, 'and there isn't any depression there at all, but a hill. This reading is merely off some trifle of a hundred and forty feet!'

'Go on,' countered Ben. 'You were somewhere else this morning. Got mixed up. I've done it myself.'

Tom shook his head. 'There's a five-hundred-eleven-foot bench mark right next door to it.'

'Then you got an old bench mark.' Ben was amusedly skeptical. 'You know, one of the pre-Columbus ones.'

'Oh, rot. Look, Ben, how about coming out with me this afternoon and we'll shoot it with your alidade? I've got to do it some time or other, anyway, now that my altimeter's out of whack. And I'll prove to you this map is chuck-full of errors. How about it?'

Ben applied another match to his pipe. He nodded. 'All right, I'm game. But don't be angry when you find you turned in at the wrong farm.'

It was not until they were rolling along the highway, with Ben's equipment in the back seat, that Tom remembered something. 'Say, Ben, didn't you start to tell me about a yarn connected with this map?'

'It doesn't amount to much really. Just that the surveyor – an old chap named Wolcraftson – died of heart failure while he was still in the field. At first they thought someone would have to re-do the job, but later, when they went over his papers, they found he had completed it. Maybe that explains why some of the people at the office were in doubt as to whether there was such a map.'

Tom was concentrating on the road ahead. They were

getting near the turn-off. 'That would have been about two years ago?' he asked. 'I mean, when he died?'

'Uh-huh. Or two and a half. It happened somewhere around here and there was some kind of stupid mess about it. I seem to remember that a fool county coroner – a local Sherlock Holmes – said there were signs of strangulation, or suffocation, or some other awful nonsense, and wanted to hold Wolcraftson's rodman. Of course, we put a stop to that.'

Tom did not answer. Certain words he had heard a couple of hours earlier were coming back to him, just as if a phonograph had been turned on: 'Two years ago there was a man come up here, trying to find out about *Them*. He had a kind of spyglass on sticks. *They* made him dead. That's why I didn't want you to go down there. I was afraid *They* would do the same thing to you.'

He angrily shut his mind to those words. If there was anything he detested, it was admitting the possibility of supernatural agencies, even in jest. Anyway, what difference did her words make? After all, a man had really died, and it was only natural that her defective imagination should cook up some wild fancy.

Of course, as he had to admit, the screwy entry on the map made one more coincidence, counting the girl's story and the cockeyed altimeter readings as the first. But was it so much of a coincidence? Perhaps Wolcraftson had listened to the girl's prattling and noted down 'The Hole' and the reading for it as a kind of private joke, intending to erase it later. Besides, what difference did it make if there had been two genuine coincidences? The universe was full of them. Every molecular collision was a coincidence. You could pile a thousand coincidences on top of another, he averred, and not get Tom Digby one step nearer to believing in the supernatural. Oh, he knew intelligent people enough, all right, who coddled such beliefs. Some of his best friends liked to relate 'yarns' and toy with eerie possibilities for the sake of a thrill. But the only emotion Tom ever got out of such stuff was a nauseating disgust. It cut too deep for joking. It was a reversion to that primitive, fear-bound ignorance from which science had slowly lifted man, inch by inch, against the most bitter opposition. Take this silly matter about the hill. Once admit that the dimensions of a thing might not be real, down to the last fraction of an inch, and you cut the foundations from under the world.

He'd be damned, he told himself, if he ever told anyone the whole story of the altimeter readings. It was just the silly sort of 'yarn' that Ben, for instance, would like to play around with. Well, he'd have to do without it.

With a feeling of relief he turned off for the farm. He had worked himself up into quite an angry state of mind, and part of the anger was at himself, for even bothering to think about such matters. Now they would finish it off neatly, as scientists should, without leaving any loose ends around for morbid imaginations to knit together.

He led Ben back to the barn, and indicated the bench mark and the hill. Ben got his bearings, studied the map, inspected the bench mark closely, then studied the map again.

Finally he turned with an apologetic grin. 'You're absolutely right. This map is as screwy as a surrealist painting, at least as far as that hill is concerned. I'll go around to the car and get my stuff. We can shoot its altitude from right off the bench mark.' He paused, frowning. 'Gosh, though, I can't understand how Wolcraftson ever got it so screwed up.'

'Probably they misinterpreted something on his original manuscript map.'

'I suppose that must have been it.'

After they had set up the plane table and telescopelike alidade directly over the bench mark, Tom shouldered the rod, with its inset level and conspicuous markings.

'I'll go up there and be rodman for you,' he said. 'I'd like you to shoot this yourself. Then they won't have any comeback when you walk into the office and blow them up for issuing such a map.'

'Okay,' Ben answered, laughing. 'I'll look forward to doing that.'

Tom noticed the farmer coming toward them from the field ahead. He was relieved to see that the little girl was not with him. As they passed one another, the farmer winked triumphantly at him. 'Found something worth coming back for, eh?' Tom did not answer. But the farmer's manner tickled his sense of humor, and he found himself feeling pretty good, irritation gone, as he stepped along toward the hill.

The farmer introduced himself to Ben by saying, 'Found signs of a pretty big gusher, eh?' His pretense at being matter-of-fact was not convincing.

'I don't know anything about it,' Ben answered cheerfully. 'He just roped me in to help him take a reading.'

The farmer cocked his big head and looked sideways at Ben. 'My, you State fellows are pretty close-mouthed, aren't you? Well, you needn't worry, because I *know* there's oil under here. Five years ago a fellow took a drilling lease on all my land at a dollar a year. But then he never showed up again. Course, I know what happened. The big companies bought him out. They know there's oil under here, but they won't drill. Want to keep the price of gasoline up.'

Ben made a noncommittal sound, and busied himself loading his pipe. Then he sighted through the alidade at Tom's back, for no particular reason. The farmer's gaze swung out in the same direction.

'Well, that's a funny thing now, come to think of it,' he said. 'Right out where he's going, is where that other chap keeled over a couple of years ago.'

Ben's interest quickened. 'A surveyor named Wolcraftson?'

'Something like that. It happened right on top of that hill. They'd been fooling around here all day – something gone wrong with the instruments, the other chap said. Course I knew they'd found signs of oil and didn't want to let on. Along toward evening the old chap – Wolcraftson, like you said – took the pole out there himself – the other chap had done it twice before – and stood atop the hill. It was right then he keeled over. We run out there, but it was too late. Heart got him. He must of thrashed around a lot before he died, though, because he was all covered with dust.'

Ben grunted appreciatively. 'Wasn't there some question about it afterward?'

'Oh, our coroner made a fool of himself, as he generally does. But I stepped in and told exactly what happened, and that settled it. Say, mister, why don't you break down and tell me what you know about the oil under here?'

Ben's protestations of total ignorance on the subject were cut short by the sudden appearance of a little tow-headed girl from the direction of the road. She had been running. She gasped 'Papa!' and grabbed the farmer's hand. Ben walked over toward the alidade. He could see the figure of Tom emerging from the tall weeds and starting up the hill. Then his attention was caught by what the girl was saying.

'You've got to stop him, Papa!' She was dragging at her father's wrist. 'You can't let him go down in the hole. *They* got it fixed to make him dead this time.'

'Shut your mouth, Sue!' the farmer shouted down at her, his voice more anxious than angry. 'You'll get me into trouble with the School Board, the queer things you say. That man's just going out there to find out how high the hill is.'

'But, Papa, can't you see?' She twisted away and pointed at Tom's steadily mounting figure. 'He's already started down in. *They're* set to trap him. Squattin' down there in the dark, all quiet so he won't hear their bones scrapin' together – stop him, Papa!'

With an apprehensive look at Ben, the farmer got down on his knees beside the little girl and put his arms around her. 'Look, Sue, you're a big girl now,' he argued. 'It don't do for you to talk that way. I know you're just playing, but other people don't know you so well. They might get to thinking things. You wouldn't want them to take you away from me, would you?'

She was twisting from side to side in his arms trying to catch a glimpse of Tom over his shoulder. Suddenly, with an unexpected backward lunge, she jerked loose and ran off toward the hill. The farmer got to his feet and lumbered after her, calling, 'Stop, Sue! Stop!'

Crazy as a couple of hoot owls, Ben decided, watching them go. Both of them think there's something under the ground. One says oil, the other says ghosts. You pay your money and you take your choice.

Then he noticed that during the excitement Tom had gotten to the top of the hill and had the rod up. He hurriedly sighted through the alidade, which was in the direction of the hilltop. For some reason he could not see anything through it – just blackness. He felt forward to make sure the lens cover was off. He swung it around a little, hoping something had not dropped out of place inside the tube. Then abruptly, through it, he caught sight of Tom, and involuntarily he uttered a short, frightened cry and jumped away.

On the hilltop, Tom was no longer in sight. Ben stood still for a moment. Then he raced for the hill at top speed.

He found the farmer looking around perplexedly near the far fence. 'Come on,' Ben gasped out, 'there's trouble,' and vaulted over.

When they reached the hilltop, Ben stooped to the sprawling body, then recoiled with a convulsive movement and for a second time uttered a smothered cry. For every square inch of skin and clothes was smeared with a fine, dark-gray dust. And close beside one gray hand was a tiny white bone.

Because a certain hideous vision still dominated his memory, Ben needed no one to tell him that it was a bone from a human finger. He buried his face in his hands, fighting that vision.

For what he had seen, or thought he had seen, through the alidade, had been a tiny struggling figure of Tom, buried in darkness, with dim, skeletal figures clutching him all around and dragging him down into a thicker blackness.

The farmer kneeled by the body. 'Dead as dead,' he muttered in a hushed voice. 'Just like the other. He's got the stuff fairly rubbed into him. It's even in his mouth and nose. Like he'd been buried in ashes and then dug up.'

From between the rails of the fence, the little girl stared up at them, terrified, but avid.

RAVISSANTE

by Robert Aickman

ROBERT FORDYCE AICKMAN (1914–1981) was among the most important, least imitated and most individual masters of supernatural fiction. Perhaps it is a tribute to the abiding sense of mystery in his work that so little has been written about it, though there is an excellent essay in John Clute's book *Strokes*. His strange tales, as Aickman preferred to call them, were collected in several volumes, of which at present the least difficult to obtain are probably *Cold Hand in Mine* and *The Wine-Dark Sea*. Among his other published books were a novel, *The Late Breakfasters*; a novella, *The Model*; and two volumes of, alas, an uncompleted autobiography, *The Attempted Rescue* and *The River Runs Uphill*.

In an essay prefacing his story 'Pages from a Young Girl's Journal' in *The First World Fantasy Awards* (1977), Aickman wrote: 'One reason why we do not wish to survive is that there is no longer anything to survive for. Man does not live by bread alone, if only because ordinary day-to-day living is mainly horrible; so that to think otherwise is a major neurosis – or to think that one thinks otherwise. If life can be justified at all, it is, and always has been, by the belief in, and hope for, "a world elsewhere", as Coriolanus put it; and however the expression is interpreted. We ignore this truth at our utter peril.' I think 'Ravissante' needs no further introduction.

I HAD an acquaintance who had begun, before I knew him, as a painter but who took to 'compiling and editing' those costly, glossy books about art which are said to sell in surprising numbers but which no person one knows ever buys and no person one sees ever opens.

I first met this man at a party. The very modern room was illuminated only in patches by dazzling standard lamps beneath metal frames. The man stood in one of the dark corners, looking shy and out of it. He wore a light blue suit, a darker blue shirt, and a tie that was pretty well blue-black. He looked very malleable and slender. I walked towards him. I saw that he had a high, narrow head and smooth dark hair, cut off in a sharp, horizontal line at the back. I saw also that with him was a woman, previously invisible, though, as a matter of fact, and when she had come into focus, rather oddly dressed. None the less, I spoke.

It seemed that I was welcome after all. The man said something customary about knowing almost none of the guests, and introduced the nearly invisible woman to me as his wife. He proceeded to chat away eagerly but a little anxiously, as if to extenuate his presence among so many dark strangers. He told me then and there about his abandonment of painting for editorship: 'I soon realized I could not expect my pictures to sell,' he said, or words to that effect. 'Too far-fetched.' About that particular epithet of his I am certain. It stuck in my mind immediately. He offered no particulars, but talked about the terms he got for his gaudy pictorial caravanserais. I have, of course, written a little myself from time to time, and the sums he named, struck me as pretty good. I avoided all comment to the effect that it is the unread book which brings in the royalty (after all, modern translations of the 'Iliad' and the 'Odyssey' are said to sell by the hundred thousand, and the Bible to be more decisively the best seller of all with every year that passes); and observed instead that his life must be an interesting one, with much travel, and, after all, much beauty to behold. He agreed warmly and, taking another Martini from a passing tray, described in some detail his latest business excursion, which had been to somewhere in Central America where there were strange things painted on walls, perfect for colour photography. He said he hoped he hadn't been boring me. 'Oh, no,' I said. All the time, the man's wife had said nothing. I remark on this simply as a fact. I do not imply that she *was* bored. She might indeed have been enthralled. Silence can, after all, mean either thing. In her case, I never found out which it meant. She was even slenderer than he was, with hair the colour (as far as I could see) of old wheat, collected into a bun low on the neck, a pale face, long like her husband's, and these slightly odd, dark garments I've mentioned. I noticed now that the man had a rather weak, undeveloped nose. In the end, the man said Would I visit their flat in Battersea and have dinner? and I gave my promise.

It will be noticed that I am being discreet with names. I think it is best because the man himself was so discreet in that way, as will be apparent later. Moreover, at no time did I become a close friend of the pair. One thing, however, must have had importance.

The Battersea flat (not quite overlooking the Park) did exhibit some of the man's paintings. I might compare them, though a little distantly, with the once controversial last works of the late Charles Sims: apparently confused on the surface, even demented, they made one doubt while one continued to gaze, as upon Sims's pictures, whether the painter had not in truth broken through to a deep and terrible order. Titles of the Sims species, 'Behold I Am Graven on the Palm of Thy Hand' or 'Am I Not The Light in the Abyss?', would have served with this man's pictures also. In fact, with him there was no question of titles, not, I thought, only out of compliance with the contemporary attitude, but more because the man did not appear to see his works as separate and possibly saleable objets d'art. 'I found that I couldn't paint what people might want to buy,' he said, smiling beneath his weak nose. His wife, seated on a hard chair and again oddly dressed, said nothing. As a matter of fact, I could imagine quite well these strange pictures being ingathered for a time by fashion's flapping feelers, though, obviously for entirely wrong reasons. I remarked to the two of them that the pictures were among the most powerful and exciting I had ever seen, and what I said was sincere, despite a certain non-professionalism in the execution. I am not sure that I should have cared to live surrounded by such pictures, as they did, but that is another matter. Perhaps I exaggerate the number: there were, I think, three of these mystical works in the living room, all quite large; four in the matrimonial bedroom, into which I was conducted to look at them; and one each in the small bedroom for visitors and in the bathroom. They were framed very casually, because the painter did not take them seriously enough; and mingled them on his walls with framed proofs from the art books, all perpetrated at the fullest stretch of modern reproductive processes.

I went there several times to dinner, perhaps six or seven times in all; and I reciprocated by entertaining the two of them at the Royal Automobile Club, which at that time I found convenient for such purposes, as I was living alone in Richmond. The Battersea dinners were very much of a pattern: my host did most of the talking; his wife, in her odd clothes, seemed to say less and less; the food, cooked by her, was perfectly good though a trifle earnest; I was treated very consciously as a guest. From this last, and from other things, I deduced that guests were infrequent. Perhaps the trouble was that the establishment lacked magic. The painter of those pictures should, one felt, have had something to say, but everything he brought out, much though there was of it, was faintly disappointing. He seemed eager to welcome me and reluctant to let me go, but entirely unable to make a hole in the wall that presumably enclosed him, however long he punched. Nor, as will be gathered, can his wife be said to have been much help. Or, at least, as far as one could see. Human relationships are so fantastically oblique that one can never be sure.

Anyway I fear that the acquaintanceship slowly died, or almost died. The near-death was slow because I made it so. I felt, almost at the beginning, that anything quicker would have meant a painfulness, conceivably even a dispute. Knowing what I was doing (within the inevitable – exceedingly narrow – limits), I fear that I very slowly strangled the connection. I was sad about it in a general sort of way, but neither the man nor his wife had truly touched anything about me or within me, and associations that are not alive are best amputated as skilfully as possible before the rot infects too much of one's total tissue and unnecessarily lowers the tone of life. If one goes to parties or meets many new people in any other way, one has to take protective action quite frequently, however much one hates oneself in the process; just as human beings are compelled to massacre animals unceasingly, because human beings are simply unable to survive, for the most part, on apples and nuts.

Total death of the connection, however, it never was. The next thing that happened, was a letter from a firm of solicitors. It arrived more than four years after I had last seen the Battersea couple, as I discovered from looking through my old engagement books after I had read it; and two years, I believed, after the last Christmas Card had passed between us. I had moved during that latter period from Richmond to Highgate. The letter told me that my Battersea acquaintance had died ('after a long illness,' the solicitors added) and that he had appointed me joint executor of his will. The other executor was his wife. Needless to say, it was the first I had heard of it. There was a legacy which the testator 'hoped I would accept': the amount was £100, which, I regret to say, struck me at once as having been arrived at during an earlier period of Britain's financial history. Finally, the letter requested me to communicate as soon as possible with the writers or directly with their client's wife.

I groaned a little, but when I had reached the office where I worked before my marriage, I composed a letter of sympathy and in a postscript suggested, as tactfully as I could, that an evening be named for a first meeting of the

executors. The reply came instantly. In the smallest
number of words possible, it thanked me for my sympathy
and proposed the evening of the next day. I put off an
engagement to meet my fiancée and drove once more to
Battersea.

I noticed that my co-executor had abandoned the
unusual style of costume she had previously favoured,
and wore an unremarkable, even commonplace, dress
from a multiple store. Perhaps it was her response to the
inner drive that until recently swept the bereaved into
black. In no other respect could I observe a change in her.

She did not seem broken, or even ruffled, with grief,
and she had little more to say than before. I did try to
discover the cause of death, but could get no clear answer,
and took for granted that it had been one of the usual
bitter maladies. I was told that there was no need for me to
put myself to trouble. She would do all there was to be
done, and I could just come in at the end.

I did remark that as an executor I should have to see a
copy of the will. She at once handed the original to me in
silence: it had been lying about the room. It was simple
enough. The body was to be cremated, and the entire
estate was left to the testator's wife, except for my £100,
and except for the fact that all the testator's pictures were
to be offered to the National Gallery of British Art; if
refused, to a long list of other public galleries, ten or
twelve of them; and if still refused, to be burnt. I saw at
once why I had been brought into the settlement of the
estate. I had been apprehensive ever since I had heard
from the solicitors. Now I was terrified.

'Don't worry,' said my co-executor, smiling faintly. 'I
dealt with that part myself while he was still alive. None of
the places would touch the pictures with a bargepole.'

'But,' I said, 'as an executor I can't just leave it at that.'

'See their letters.' She produced a heap of paper and
passed it over to me. 'Sit down and read them.'

She herself drew back her normal hard chair, and sat
half watching me, half not; but without taking up any
other occupation.

I thought that I might as well settle the matter, if it really were possible, there and then. I checked the letters against the list in the will. Every named gallery was accounted for. All the letters were negative: some courteously and apologetically negative; some not. The correspondence covered rather more than the previous twelve months. Many public servants are slow to make up their minds and slower to commit themselves.

'Did he know?' I asked.

That was another question to which I failed to get a clear answer, because she merely smiled, and even that only slightly. It seemed difficult to persist.

'Don't worry,' she said again. 'I'll look after the bonfire.'

'But don't *you* want to keep the pictures?' I cried. 'Perhaps you've lived with them so long that they've become overfamiliar, but they really are rather remarkable.'

'Surely as executors we have to obey the will?'

'I am certain you can keep the pictures, as far as the law is concerned.'

'Would *you* like to take them? Bearing in mind,' she added, 'that there's about a hundred more of them stored in Kingston.'

'I simply haven't room, much though I regret it.'

'Nor, in the future, shall I.'

'I'd like to take *one* of them, if I may.'

'As many as you wish. Would you like the manuscripts also? They're all in that suitcase.' It was a battered green object, standing against the wall. I think it was largely her rather unpleasant indifference that made me accept. It was quite apparent what would happen to the manuscripts if I did not take them, and one did not like to think of a man's life disappearing in a few flames, as his body.

'When's the funeral?' I asked.

'Tomorrow, but it will be quite private.'

I wondered where the body *was*. In the matrimonial bedroom? In the small room for guests? In some mortuary?

'We neither of us believed in God.' In my experience of her, it was the first time she had taken the initiative in making such a general pronouncement, negative though it had proved to be.

I looked at the pictures, including the one I had mentally

selected for myself. She said nothing more. Of course, the pictures had been painted a number of years earlier: perhaps before the painter had first met her.

She offered me neither a cup of coffee nor a helping hand with the picture and the heavy suitcase down the many flights of stairs in a Battersea block of flats. Driving home, it occurred to me that for the amount of work involved, my executor's legacy was not so inadequate after all.

The picture has travelled round with me ever since. It is now in the room next to the one which used to be the nursery. I often go in and look at it for perhaps five or six minutes when the light is good.

The suitcase contained the tumbled typescript for the art books, apparently composed straight on to the machine. They were heavily gashed with corrections in different coloured inks, but this did not matter to me, because it had never been in my mind to read them. All the same, I have never thrown them away. They are in the attic now, still in the green suitcase, with labels stuck on it from Mussolini's Italy. To that small extent, my poor acquaintance lives still. He must presumably have felt that I, more than most, had something in common with him, or he would not have made me his executor.

But the suitcase contained something else: a shorter, more personal narrative, typed out on large sheets of undulating foreign paper, and rolled up within a thick rubber band, now rotten. It is to introduce this narrative, so strange and so intimate, to explain how it came my way and how it comes to be published, that I have written the foregoing. The sheer oddity of life seems to me of more and more importance, because more and more the pretence is that life is charted, predictable, and controllable. And for oddity, of course, one could well write mystery.

Under the will, a publication fee belongs to the widow, who plainly holds the copyright. I give notice that she has but to apply. Remembering that last evening, on the day before the funeral, I am not sure that she will. But we shall see. The rest I leave to the words of my poor acquaintance.

Yesterday I returned from three weeks in Belgium. While

there, I had an experience which made a great impression on me. I think it may even have changed my entire way of looking at things; troubled my soul, as people say. Anyway, I feel that I am unlikely ever to forget it. On the other hand, I have learned that what one remembers is always far from what took place. So I am taking this first opportunity of writing down as many of the details as I can remember and as seem important. Only six days have passed since it happened, but I am aware that already there are certain to be gaps bridged by imagination, and unconscious distortions in the interests of consistency and effect. It is possibly unfortunate that I could not make this record while I was still in Brussels, but I found it impossible. I lacked the time, or, more probably, the application, as people always say of me. I also felt that I was under a spell. I felt that something terrible and alarming might happen as I sat by myself in my bedroom writing it all down. The English Channel proves to have loosened this spell considerably, though I can still feel all those textures on my hands and face, still see those queer creatures, and still hear Madame A.'s croaking voice. I find that, when I think about it, I am frightened still, but attracted overwhelmingly also, as at the time. This, I believe, is what is properly meant by the word fascination.

As others may read this, even if only in the distant future, I set forth a few basic facts. I am a painter, and 26 years old: the age when Bonnington died. I have about £300 a year of my own, so can paint what interests me; at least I can while I remain on my own. Until now I have been quite happy on my own, though this fact seems to upset almost everyone I know. So far I have had very little to do with women, mainly because I cannot see that I have anything to offer that is likely to appeal to them, and because I detest the competitive aspect of the relations between the sexes. I should hate it for a woman to pity me, and, on the other hand, I should hate to be involved with a woman whom I had to pity; a woman, in fact, who was not attractive enough to be in the full sex war, and who might therefore, be available for such as me. I should not care to be involved with a woman who was anything less than very beautiful. Perhaps that is the artist in me. I do not really know. I feel that I should want only the kind of woman who could not conceivably want me. I cannot say that the whole problem does not trouble me, but, by the standard of what I have read and heard, I am surprised that it does not trouble me more.

I find also that I have no difficulty in writing these things down. On the contrary, I find that I like it. I fancy that I could produce a quite long narrative about my own inner feelings, though this is obviously not the occasion, for I think I have already said all that is necessary. I have to strike a balance between clearing my own mind and imparting facts to strangers. I conceive of this narrative, if I finish it, as being read only by myself and by strangers. I should not care for someone intimately in my life to read it – if there ever is such a person. I doubt whether there ever will be. Sometimes this frightens me, but sometimes it reassures me.

At this point, I remember to mention, for the strangers who may read, that both my parents died seven years ago in an aeroplane accident. It was my Mother who insisted on their going to Paris by air. I was present when my Father argued with her. It was the usual situation between them. All the same, I loved my Mother very much, even though she was as bossy towards me as she was towards my Father. No doubt this has affected me too. I fear that a woman would steal my independence – perhaps even kill me. Nor, from what I have seen, do I think these particularly unreal fears.

On the whole, I do not like people. I seem incapable of approaching them, but I find that when they approach me, I am often quite successful with them – more so, indeed, than many of those who have no trouble with bustling in and making the first gesture. When once I am started, I can talk on fluently and even amusingly (though I believe inwardly that I have no sense of humour at all), and frequently, usually indeed, seem to make a strong impression. I suppose I must get some pleasure out of this, but I do not think I ever exert any real influence. It is almost as if someone else were talking through me –

wound up by an outsider, my interlocutor. It is not I who talk, and certainly not I who please. I seriously suspect that I myself never speak, and I am certain that if I did, I should never please. This is, of course, another reason why I could not sensibly think of living with anyone.

Similarly with my art. My pictures are visionary and symbolical, and, from first to last, have seemed to be painted by someone other than myself. Indeed, I have the greatest difficulty in painting anything to command. I am useless at portraits, incapable of painting at all in the open air, and quite indifferent to the various kinds of abstract painting that have followed the invention of the camera. Also I am weak on drawing, which, of course, should be a hopeless handicap. I have to be alone in a room in order to paint, though then I can sometimes paint day and night, twenty hours at a stretch. My father, who was quite sympathetic to my talent, arranged for me to attend a London school of art. It was quite pointless. I could achieve nothing, and was unhappier than at any other period of my life. It was the only time when I felt really lonely – though worse may, of course, lie ahead. I am thus almost entirely self-taught, or taught by that other within me. I am aware that my pictures lack serious technique (if there is a technique that can be distinguished from inspiration and invention). I should have given up painting them some time ago, were it not that a certain number of people have seemed to find something remarkable in them, and have thus identified me with them and made me feel mildly important. If I were to give up, I should have to give up altogether. I could not possibly paint, as so many do, just as a hobby or on Sundays only. I am sure that soon I *shall* give up – or be given up. When I read about the mediumship of Willi and Rudi Schneider, and of how the gift departed first from one brother and then from the other, and when both were quite young, I felt at once that something of the same kind will happen to me, and that I shall settle down, like Willi Schneider, as a hairdresser or other tradesman. Not that I wish to suggest any kind of mediumistic element in my works. It is simply that they contain a glory which is assuredly not in the painter, as the few who know him will confirm. It is a commonplace that there is often more than one soul in a single body.

I must admit also to certain 'influences'. This sounds pretentious, but it has to be said because it explains what I have been doing in Belgium and how I came to visit Madame A. I find that certain works, or the works of certain painters, affect me strongly, almost agonizingly on occasion, but only *certain* pictures and *certain* painters, really very few. Art in general leaves me rather cold, I regret to say, especially when put on public display to crowds, most of them, inevitably, insensitive. I am sure that pictures should always belong to single individuals. I even believe that pictures suffer death when shared among too many. I also dislike books about art, with their dreadful 'reproductions', repellent when in colour, boring when not. On the other hand, in the painters who *do* affect me, I become almost completely absorbed; in their lives and thoughts, to the extent that I can find out about these things or divine them, as well as in their works. The look of a painter and the look of the places where he painted, can, I think, be very important. I have no use for the theory that it is the picture only that matters and the way the paint has been stuck on it. That idea seems to me both lazy and soulless. Perhaps 'my' painters are my true intimates, and them only. I cannot believe I shall ever be so close to any living person as I was to Magnasco when first I sought him out. But there again, I should emphasize that these 'influences' seem to me far from direct. I can see little sign of other people's mannerisms in my own pictures. The influence is far deeper than that. The 'only-the-picture' people would not understand at all.

It has been possible for me to travel a little in search of my particular pictures because at all times I live simply and spend hardly anything. It was to look at pictures that I have been to Belgium: not, needless to say, the Memlings and Rubenses, fine though I daresay they once were, but the works of the symbolists and their kind, painters such as William Degouve de Nuncques, Fernand Khnopff, Xavier Mellery, who said (and who else has ever said it?)

that he painted 'silence' and the 'soul of things', above all,
of course, James Ensor, the charming Baron. I had worked
for months before I left, to equip myself with a list of
addresses, many of the finest paintings of the school being
happily still in private hands. Almost everyone was kind
to me, though I can speak very little French, and for the
first fortnight I was totally lost and absolutely happy. Not
all the owners gave signs of appreciating their various
properties, but, naturally, I did not expect that. At least
they were prepared, most of them, to leave me alone and
in peace, which was something I had seldom found
among the private owners who survive in Italy. Of them
many seemed to think they might sell me something; most
made a great noise; and all refused me privacy.

One of the Belgian authorities with whom I exchanged
letters, told me that the widow of a certain painter of the
symbolist school still survived in Brussels. Not even to
myself, in the light of what has happened, do I wish to
write the name of this painter. I shall simply call him A.,
the late A. The informed may succeed in identifying him.
Even if they do, it will not matter so much by the time they
are likely to read this report. If strangers read sooner than I
expect, it will only be because I am dead, so that the
burden of discretion will be upon them and not upon me.

The Belgian authority, without comment, gave me an
address in Brussels to which I wrote from England in my
basic French, not seriously expecting any kind of reply.
My habitual concern with the lives and personalities of
'my' painters may, however, have made me write more
urgently and persuasively than I supposed. It seemed a
considerable opportunity for me. Despite my great
interest, I had never met one of my particular painters nor
even a widow or relative. Many of the painters, in any
case, had lived too long ago for such a thing. If now I
received no reply, I was quite prepared to stand about
outside the house, and consider in the light of what I
observed, how best to get in. That proved unnecessary.
Within three days, I heard from Madame A.

She wrote in a loose, curving hand, and confined herself
to the centre of a large sheet of dark blue paper. Her letter

looked like the springs bursting out of a watch in a nineteenth-century comic drawing. It would have been difficult to read even if it had been in English, but in the end I deciphered most of it. Madame A. said she was extremely old, had not left the house for years or received any visitors, but was enchanted that anyone should go out of his way to see her, and would receive me at six o'clock on an evening she named with exactitude. I had given her the dates of my proposed stay in Belgium, but none the less was surprised by her decisiveness, because it was without precedent. People with pictures had always left to me the time of a visit, and an embarrassing responsibility I had often found it. Madame A. ended by asking how old *I* was.

When the time came, I spent the afternoon at the Musée Wiertz, because it seemed to be in much the same part of the city as the abode of Madame A. 'Wiertz's work is noted rather for the sensational character of his subjects than for artistic merit', states, in true Beckmesser fashion, the English guide book I had borrowed from my public library. Possibly it is true in a way. It was not true for me. I was enthralled by Wiertz's living burials and imminent decapitations; by his livid, gory vision of that 'real' world which surely is livid and gory, though boring and monotonous also, which Wiertz omits. Wiertz's way of painting reality seems to me most apt to the character of reality. I was delighted also by the silence and emptiness of Wiertz's enormous, exciting studio. His official lack of merit keeps out the conducted art-lover.

All the same, anxiety was rising in me about my commitment with Madame A. I had remained fairly confident through most of my visits to picture owners, even in Italy, but these had been accepted as business transactions, and I had had no difficulty in concealing that for me they were stations on a spiritual ascent. With Madame A. I might have to disclose much more of myself and find words, even French words, for comments that were not purely conventional. She might be very infirm and intractable. It was probable that she was. It is September, and I sat on a bench before 'The Fight for the

Body of Patroclus', all alone in the high studio, except for the attendant, who was mumbling to himself round the corner, while evening fell and the many clocks chimed and boomed me forward to my ambiguous assignation.

The power of solitude, not least in the Musée Wiertz, delayed me, in fact, too long. I found that I had underestimated the distance from the Rue Wiertz to the street in the direction of the Boulevard de Waterloo where Madame A. lived. They are beautiful streets through which I walked, though unostentatious; quiet, well-proportioned, and warmly alive with the feel of history. I have seen no other part of Brussels that I like so much. I loved the big opening windows, filling so much of every façade, and so unlike England. I even thought that this would be a perfect district in which to spend my life. One never really doubts that one will feel always what one feels at any given moment, good or bad; or, when the moment is good, at least that one *could* always feel it if one might only preserve the attendant framework and circumstances. The activity of walking through these unobtrusively beautiful streets quietened me. Also I commonly notice that for the *very* last stretch, I cease to be anxious.

Madame A. lived in just another such house: only two storeys high, white and elegant, with rococo twirls in the fanlight above the handsome front door, a properly sized front door for a house, wide enough for a crinoline, tall enough for an admiral, not a mere vertical slit for little men to steal through on the way to work. The houses to left and right repeated the pattern with subtle minor variations. I am glad to have been born soon enough to see such houses before either demolition or preservation: so far all was well.

There was a light in an upper window. It was of the colour known as old gold.

There was a bell and I heard it ring. I expected some kind of retainer or relative, since I visualized Madame A. as almost bed-ridden. But the door opened, and it was obvious that this was Madame A. herself. She looked very short and very square, almost gnomelike in shape; but the

outline of her was all I could see because it was now
almost dark, the street lighting was dim (thank goodness),
and there was no light at all in the hall.

'Entrez,' said Madame A. in her distinctive croak.
'Entrez, monsieur. Fermez la porte, s'il vous plait.' Though
she croaked, she croaked as one accustomed, if she spoke
at all, to speak only in terms of command. Nothing less, I
felt at once, interested her in the context of human
discourse.

Up from the hall led a straight, uncarpeted staircase,
much wider than in an English house of that size, and
with a heavy wooden baluster, just visible by a light from
the landing above.

'Suivez, monsieur.'

Madame A. went clambering upwards. It is the only
word. She was perfectly agile, but curiously uncouth in
her movements. In the dim light, she went up those stairs
almost like an old man of the woods, but I believe that age
not infrequently has this effect on the gait of all but the
tallest. I should say that Madame A.'s height was rather
under than over five feet.

The light on the landing proved to hang by a thick
golden chain in an art nouveau lantern of lumpy old gold
glass speckled with irregular dabs of crimson. I followed
Madame A. into a room which traversed the whole depth
of the house, with one window on to the street and,
opposite it, another at the back of the building. The door
of the room was already open. Standing ahead of me in
the big doorway, Madame A. looked squatter than ever.

The room was lighted by lanterns similar to that on the
landing. They were larger than the lantern outside but the
old gold effulgence of the room remained distinctly dim,
and the crimson dabs cast irregular red splashes on the
shiny, golden wallpaper. The furnishings were art
nouveau also. Everything, even the common objects of
use, tended to stop and start at unexpected places; to
spring upwards in ecstasy, to sag in melancholia, or
simply to overhang and break away. One felt that every
object was in tension. The colours of the room coalesced
into strikingly individual harmony. Almost as soon as I

entered, it struck me that the general colouration had something in common with that of my own works. It was most curious. The golden walls bore many pictures, mostly in golden frames: mainly, I could see, the work of the late A., as was to be expected, and about which I must not further particularize; but also some esoteric drawings manifestly by Felicien Rops, and stranger than his strangest, I thought as I sat amongst them. In the substantial, art nouveau fireplace blazed a fire, making the room considerably too hot, as so often on the Continent. None the less, I again shut the door. As I did so, I saw that behind it was a life-size marble figure of a woman in the moment of maternity. I identified it at once as the work of a symbolist sculptor well known for figures of this type, but, again, I had better not name him because about this particular figure was something very odd – odd even to me who knows about childbirth only from works of art, not least the works of this particular man.

'Mais oui,' said Madame A., as I could not withdraw my gaze from the figure. 'C'est la naissance d'un succube.'

But at this point I think I had better stop trying to remember what was said in French by Madame A. In the first place, I cannot succeed in doing so, though her very first words, those that I have set down, remain clearly with me. In the second place, Madame A. soon disclosed that she could speak English perfectly well – or rather, perhaps, and as I oddly felt, as well as she could speak French. There was something about her which suggested, even to an unsophisticate like me, that she was no more a native of Belgium or France than she was of Britain. I am trying to set down events and my feelings exactly as they were, or as nearly as possible, and I am not going to pretend that I did not sense something queer about Madame A. from the very start, because there is nothing in the whole story of which I am more certain than of that.

And now there she was standing dumpily before the big, bright fire with her long bare arms extended, almost as if to embrace me.

Yes, despite the impending autumn, despite the blazing fire, her arms were bare; and not only her arms. Her hairy legs were bare also, and her dull red dress was cut startlingly low for a woman of her years, making her creased bosom all too visible. My absurd impression was that this plain red scrap of a garment was all she was wearing, apart from the golden slippers on her small, square feet.

And yet old she certainly was; very old, as she had said in her letter. Her face was deeply grooved and grained. Her neck had lost all shape. Her stance was hunched and bowed under the weight of time. Her voice, though masterful, was senile. I imagined that her black hair, somewhat scant, but wiry and upstanding, could only be dyed. Her head was like an old, brown egg.

She made me sit and sweat before the fire, constantly urging me nearer to it, and plied me with cognac and water. She herself remained on her feet, though, even so, her corrugated brown cheekbones and oddly vague black eyes were almost on a level with mine. The chair in which she had put me, had wings at the level of the sitter's head, thus making me even hotter, and, every now and then, as she spoke, she leant forward, put a hand on each of these wings, and, for emphasis or to indicate a confidence, spoke right at my face, coming almost near enough to kiss me. She appeared to drink very little herself, but she made me drink far more than I wanted, praising the quality of the brandy and also (little did she know, I thought) the power and strength of my youth. Her very first question when we had settled ourselves was: How old had I said I was? And, she continued, born in Scorpio? Yes, I replied, impressed but not astonished, because many people have this particular divination, even though the materialists say otherwise. And how do you interpret that? I went on; because different people emphasize different aspects. Secrecy and sensuality, she croaked back. Only the first, I smiled. Then I must direct myself to awakening the second, she replied rather horribly.

And yet, I thought, how hard I am, how unsympathetic, after all; and, at the same time, how weak.

She did soon begin to talk about art, and the painters she had known long, long before. Perhaps she thought that this was the topic which would awaken me. She tended to lose the way in her long, ancient chronicles, and to fill or overfill my glass while she recovered direction.

It was noticeable that she seemed neither to admire nor to have liked any of the men she spoke of, many of whom were and are objects of my particular regard. At least I hope they still are: an object of admiration is impaired by hostile criticism of any kind, however ill judged, and there is nothing the admirer can do to mend the wound, even though his full reason may tell him that the critic has no case. Madame A.'s comments were hardly reasoned at all and thus all the more upsetting. They were jeers and insinuations and flat rejections.

'X.,' she would say, 'was an absurd man, always very dapper and with a voice like a goat.' 'Y.!' she exclaimed. 'I had a very close friendship with Y. – as long as I could stand him.' 'Z.'s pictures are supposed to be philosophical but really they're not even successfully pornographic.' All the time she implied that my own enthusiastic assessments were grotesquely immature, and, when I argued back, sometimes with success, because she was not much of a hand with logic and not too accurate with her facts either, she flattened me with personal reminiscences of the comic or shady circumstances in which particular works had come to be painted, or with anecdotes which, as she claimed, showed the painter in his true colours.

'J.,' she asserted, 'was madly in love with me for years, but I wouldn't have used him as a pocket handkerchief when I had the grippe, and nor would any other woman.' Madame A. had a fine turn of phrase, but as I knew (though we did not mention) that J., painter of the most exquisite oriental fantasies, had hanged himself in poverty and despair, her line of talk depressed and disconcerted me very much. I felt that in too many cases, even though, I was sure, not in all, her harsh comments were true, even though doubtless not the whole truth. I felt that, true or not by my standards, so many people (among the few interested at all) would agree with these comments as thereby to give them a kind of truth by majority vote. I felt, most sadly of all, that what I have called harshness in

Madame A. was simply a blast of life's essential quality as it drags us all over the stones; artists – these selected divinities of mine among them – included.

As so often, it would have been better not to know.

'K.!' croaked Madame A. 'K. worked for three years as a police spy and it was the happiest period of his life. He told me so himself. He was drunk at the time – or perhaps drugged – but it was the truth. And you can see it in his pictures if you only look. They are the pictures of a self-abuser. Do you know why K.'s wife left him? It was because he was impotent with a real woman, and always had been. He knew it perfectly well when he married her. He did it because she had inherited a little money and he was on cocaine already and the good God knows what else. When I read about K.'s pictures being bought for the Musée Royal des Beaux-Arts, I laugh. I laugh and I spit.' And Madame A. did both. She had a habit of snatching at the neckline of her red dress as she spoke, and dragging it yet further down. It seemed by now to have become an unconscious reflex with her, or tic.

'L.,' she said, 'started as a painter of enormous landscapes. That was what he really liked to paint. He liked to spend days and weeks entirely by himself in Norway or Scotland just painting exactly what lay before him, bigger all the time. The trouble was that no one would buy such pictures. They were competent enough but dull, dull. When you saw them lined up against the walls of his studio, you could do nothing but yawn. And that's the way people saw them when he hoped they might buy them. You couldn't imagine anyone ever buying one. You wanted only to get out of the studio and forget about such dull pictures. All those pictures of L. that you talk about, the 'Salomés' and 'Whores of Babylon', weren't what he liked at all. He turned to them because two things happened at once: L.'s money ran out and at about the same time he met Maeterlinck. He met Maeterlinck only once, but it did something to him. Maeterlinck seemed fashionable and successful, and L. couldn't see why he shouldn't be too. But it really wasn't in the little man, and before long he gave it all up and became a fonctionnaire, as you know, though it was a bit late in the day for that.'

'No, madame, I didn't know.'

'Why, he's alive still! He's got the jumps, some kind of disease that gives you the jumps. The 'Whore of Babylon' might have given it to him, but he never got near enough to her to make it possible. L.'s alive all right – just. I used to go and see him when I still went out. He liked to borrow my old art papers. I've got hundreds of them, all from before the war. Ah, les sales Boches,' added Madame A. irrelevantly, but as many people do in Belgium and France from force of habit.

Despite everything, I suppose my eyes must have lighted up at the mention of the pre-war art journals. In such publications is often information not to be found anywhere else and information of just the sort that I find most valuable and absorbing.

'Ah,' croaked Madame A. almost jubilantly. 'That's better. You are getting accustomed to me, hein?' She grasped my hands.

By now, she was flowing on in English. It was a relief. At one moment, she had spoken several sentences in a language I could not even identify. She had doubtless forgotten about me, or was confusing me with someone else.

'But you look hot,' cried Madame A., releasing me. 'Why do you not remove your jacket?'

'Perhaps,' I replied, 'I could walk round the room and look at the pictures.'

'But certainly. If you wish.' She spoke as if it were a remarkably ridiculous wish, and perhaps discourteous also.

I struggled away from her, and proceeded from picture to picture. She said nothing while I promenaded, but remained standing with her back to the fire, and her short legs well apart; gnomic in more than one sense. I cannot say that her eyes followed me with ironical glances, because her eyes were too vague for such a thing. The light in the room, though picturesque was quite unsuited to the inspection of pictures. I could see hardly anything.

At the end of the room away from the street and away from the fire, it was almost dark. It was absurd for me to persist, though I was exceedingly disappointed.

'It is a pity my adopted daughter is not here,' said Madame A. from the brightness. 'She could entertain you better than I can. You would prefer her to me.'

She spoke in a tone of dreadful coyness. I could think of no convincing reply. 'Where *is* your adopted daughter?' I asked lamely and tamely.

'Away. Abroad. With some creature, of course. Who knows where?' She cackled. 'Who knows with whom?'

'I am sorry to have missed her,' I said, not very convincingly, I am sure. I was indignant that I had not been invited for some hour when I could see the pictures by daylight.

'Come back over here, monsieur,' cried Madame A., pointing with her right forefinger to my hot armchair and then slapping her knee with the palm of her hand, all as if she were summoning a small, unruly dog. It was *exactly* like that, I thought. I have often seen it, though I have never owned a dog myself. I forebore from comment and returned reluctantly to the hot fire. Madame A., as I have said, was commanding as well as coy.

And then an extraordinary thing happened. A real dog was there in the room. At least, I suppose I am now not sure how real it was. Let me just say a dog. It was like a small black poodle, clipped, glossy, and spry. It appeared from the shadowy corner to the right of the door as one entered. It pattered perkily up to the fire, then round several times in a circle in front of Madame A. and to my right as I sat, then off into the shadow to my left and where I had just been standing. It seemed to me, as I looked at it, to have very big eyes and very long legs, perhaps more like a spider than a poodle, but no doubt this was merely an effect of the firelight.

At that moment, there was much to take in fairly quickly, but one thing was that Madame A., as I clearly realized, seemed not to see the dog. She was staring ahead, her black eyes expressionless as ever. Even while I was watching the dog, I divined that she was still thinking of her adopted daughter, and was entranced by her thoughts. It did not seem particularly remarkable that she had missed the dog, because the dog had been quite silent, and she might well have been so accustomed to seeing it around the house that often she no longer noticed it. What puzzled me at that stage was where the dog had hidden itself all the time I had been in the room with the door shut.

'Nice poodle,' I said to Madame A., because I had to break the silence, and because Englishmen are supposed to be fond of dogs (though I am, comparatively, an exception).

'Comment, monsieur?' I can see and hear her still, exactly as she looked and spoke.

'Nicely kept poodle,' I said, firmly sticking to English.

She turned and stared at me, but came no nearer, as at such moments she usually did.

'So you have seen a poodle?'

'Yes,' I said, and still not thinking there was anything *really* wrong, 'this moment. If it's not yours, it must have got in from the darkness outside.' The darkness was still on my mind, because of the pictures, but immediately I spoke, I felt a chill, despite the blazing fire. I wanted to get up and look for the dog, which, after all, must still have been in the room; but at the same time I feared to do any such thing. I feared to move at all.

'Animals often appear in here,' said Madame A. huskily. 'Dogs, cats, toads, monkeys. And occasionally less commonplace species. I expect it will have gone by now.'

I think I only stared back at her.

'Sometimes my husband painted them.' It was the only reference she had made to her husband, and it was one which I found difficult to follow up. She dragged down the front of her dress in her compulsive way.

'I will talk to you,' said Madame A., 'about Chrysothème, my adopted daughter. Do you know that Chrysothème is the most beautiful girl in Europe? Not like me. Oh, not at all.'

'What a pity I cannot have the pleasure of meeting her!' I said, again trying to enter into the spirit of it, but wondering how I could escape, especially in view of what had just happened. On the instant, and for the second time, I regretted what I had said.

But Madame A. merely croaked dreamily, staring straight ahead. 'She appears here. She stays quite often. For a quite long time, you understand. She cannot be expected to remain longer. After all, I am far from being her mother.'

I nodded, though it was obscure to what I was assenting.

'Chrysothème!' cried Madame A. rapturously clasping her hands. 'My Chrysothème!' She paused, her face illumined, though not her eyes. Then she turned back to me. 'If you could see her naked, monsieur, you would understand everything.'

I giggled uneasily, as one does.

'I repeat, monsieur, that you would understand everything.'

It dawned on me that in some way she meant more than one would at first have thought.

One trouble was that I most certainly did not *want* to understand everything. I had once even told a fortune teller as much; a big-nosed but beautiful woman in a tent when I was a schoolboy.

'Would you like to see her clothes?' said Madame A., quite softly. 'She keeps some of them here, to wear when she comes to stay.'

'Yes,' I said. 'I should.' I cannot fully analyse why I said it, but I said it. Madame A. being what she was, I could claim that I was given very little voice in the matter. Perhaps I wasn't. But that time it didn't arise. I undoubtedly chose.

Madame A. took me lightly by the wrist and drew me out of the chair. I opened the big door for her, and then another big door which she indicated. There were two on the opposite side of the landing, and she pointed to the one on the right.

'I myself sleep in the next room,' said Madame A. on the threshold, making the very wall sound like an invitation. 'When I can sleep at all.'

The room within was darkly panelled, almost to the ceiling. The corner on the left behind the door was filled by a panelled bed, with a coverlet of dark red brocade. It seemed to fill more space than a single bed, but not as much space as a double bed. From the foot of it, the plain, dark panelling of the wall continued undecorated to the end of the room. In the centre of the far wall stood a red brocaded dressing table, looking very much like an altar, especially as no chair stood before it. On the right was a window, now covered by dark red curtains, of the heavy kind which my Mother used to say collected the dust. Against the wall on each side of this window, stood a big dark chest. There were several of the usual art nouveau lanterns hanging high on the walls, but the glass in them was so heavily obscured that the room seemed scarcely brighter than the dim landing outside. The only picture hung over the head of the bed in the corner behind the door.

'What a beautiful room!' I exclaimed politely.

But I was looking over my shoulder to see if the black dog had emerged through the open door on the other side of the landing.

'That is because many people have died in it,' said Madame A. 'The two beautiful things are love and death.'

I went right into the room.

'Shut the door,' said Madame A.

I shut it. There was still no sign of the dog. I tried to postpone further thought on the subject.

'Most of her clothes are in here,' said Madame A. She pulled at the panelling by the foot of the bed, and two doors opened; then another pair; then a third. All that part of the bedroom panelling fronted deep cupboards.

'Come and look,' said Madame A.

Feeling foolish, I went over to her. All three cupboards were filled with dresses, hanging from a central rail, as in a shop. If they had been antiquarian rags or expectant shrouds, I should hardly have been surprised, but they were quite normal women's clothes of today; as far as I could tell, of very high quality. There were garments for all purposes: winter dresses, summer dresses, and a great

number of those long evening dresses which one sees less
and less frequently. All the dresses appeared to be
carefully looked after, as if they were waiting to be sold. It
struck me that in that direction might lie the truth: that the
dresses might never have been worn. Certainly the room
looked extremely unoccupied. Apart from the dresses, it
looked more like a chapel than a bedroom. More like a
mortuary chapel, it suddenly struck me; with a sequence
of corpses at rest and beflowered on the bier-like bed
behind the door, as Madame A. had so depressingly
hinted.

'Touch the clothes,' said Madame A., reading my mind.
'Take them out and see the marks of Chrysothème's
body.'

I hesitated. Unless one is a tailor, one instinctively
dislikes the touch of other people's clothes, whoever they
may be; and of unknown strangers' clothes not least.

'Take them out,' repeated Madame A. in her commanding way.

I gingerly detached a random dress on its hanger. It was
a workaday, woollen garment. Even in the poor light, the
signs of wear were evident.

That point made silently between us, Madame A.
showed impatience with my timid choice. She herself
drew out an evening gown in pale satin.

'Marvellous, exquisite, incomparable,' she exclaimed
stridently. I think that if she had been tall enough, she
would have held the dress against her own body, as the
saleswomen so curiously do in shops; but, as it was, she
could only hold it out at the end of her long arms, so that
most of it flowed across the dark red carpet like a train.
'Kneel down and examine it.' I hesitated. 'Kneel,' cried
Madame A. more peremptorily.

I knelt and picked up the bottom hem of the dress. Now
I was down on the floor, I noticed a big dark patch which
the dark carpet was not dark enough to hide.

'Lift the dress to your face,' ordered Madame A. I did so.
It was a wonderful sensation. I felt myself enveloped
in a complex silky nebula. The owner, the wearer of
that elegant garment, began, even though entirely

without definition, to be much more present to me than Madame A.

Madame A. dropped the dress and on the instant was holding out another in the same way. It also was a long dress. It was made of what I believe is called georgette, and was in some kind of mottled orange and red.

The pale satin dress lay on the floor between us.

'Kneel on it. Tread on it,' directed Madame A., seeing me about to circumvent it. 'Chrysothème would approve.'

I was unable to do such a thing, and crawled round the edges of the satin dress to the georgette dress. Immediately I reached the georgette dress, Madame A. threw it adroitly over my head, so that I had a ridiculous minute or two extricating myself. I could not but notice, and more than just notice, that the georgette retained a most enchanting scent. Her scent made the wearer of the dress more real to me than ever.

Away to my left, Madame A. now extended a third long dress; this time in dark blue taffeta, very slender and skimpy.

'You could almost wear it yourself,' cackled Madame A. 'You like wearing blue and you are thin enough.' I had, of course, not told her that I liked wearing blue, but I suppose it was obvious.

Madame A. twisted round a chair with her foot and laid the dress on it, with the low top hanging abandonedly over the back of it.

'Why don't you kiss it?' asked Madame A., jeering slightly.

Kneeling at the foot of the chair, I realized that my lips were only slightly above the edge of the seat. To refuse would be more foolish than to comply. I lowered my face and pressed my lips against the dress. Madame A. might be ridiculing me, but I felt now that my true concern was with that other who wore the dresses.

When I looked up, Madame A. was actually standing on another chair (there were only two in the room, both originally in the corners, both heavy, dark, and elaborate). She was holding up a short dress in black velvet. She said nothing, and I admit that, without bidding, I darted towards her and pressed the wonderful fabric against my face.

'The moon,' gurgled Madame A., pointing to the pale satin dress on the floor. 'And the night.' She flapped the black velvet up and down and from side to side. It too smelt adorably. I clutched at it to keep it still and found that it was quite limp, inert in my grasp.

Madame A. had leapt off the chair with one flop, like a leprechaun.

'Do you like my adopted daughter's clothes?'

'They are beautiful.'

'Chrysothème has perfect taste.' Madame A.'s tone was entirely conventional. I was still sniffing the velvet dress. 'You must see the lingerie,' Madame A. added, merely as if to confirm the claim she had just made.

She crossed to the chest at the left of the curtained window and lifted the unlocked lid. 'Come,' said Madame A.

The big chest was full of soft underclothes in various colours; not ordered like the dresses, but tangled and clinging apparently at random.

I suppose I just stood and stared. And the same scent was rising hypnotically from the chest.

'Take off your blue jacket,' said Madame A., almost with solemnity. 'Roll up your blue sleeves, and plunge in your white arms.'

Without question, I did what she said.

'Sink your face in them.'

I hardly needed to be instructed. The scent was intoxicating in itself.

'Love them, tear them, possess them,' admonished Madame A.

All of which I daresay I did to the best of my ability. Certainly time passed.

I began to shiver. After all, I had left a very over-heated room.

I found that all my muscles were stiff with kneeling; and I suppose with concentration too. I could hardly rise to my feet in order to rescue my jacket. As I rolled down my shirt-sleeves, I became aware that the hairs on my forearms really were standing on end. They seemed quite barbed and sharp.

'Blue boy!' exclaimed Madame A., waiting for me to make the next move.

I made it. I shut the lid of the chest.

'The other chest contains souvenirs,' said Madame A., dragging at the neckline of her dress.

I shook my head. I was still shaking all over, and could no longer smell that wonderful scent. When one is very cold, the sense of smell departs.

And at that moment, for the first time, I really apprehended the one picture, which hung above the wide bed in the corner. Despite the bad light, it seemed familiar. I went over to it, and putting one knee on the bed, leant towards it. Now I was certain. The picture was by me.

But there were two especially strange things. Though I was quite certain that the picture could only be mine (my talent may be circumscribed, but it is distinctive), I could not remember ever having painted it, and there were things about it which could at no time have been put there by me. Artists, in their later years, do sometimes forget their own works, but I was, and am, sure that this could never happen in my case. My pictures are not of a kind to be forgotten by the painter. Much worse was the fact that, for example, the central figure which I might have painted as an angel, had somehow become more like a clown. It was hard to say why this was, but, as I looked at it, I felt it irresistibly.

My attack of shivering was turning to nausea, as one often finds. I felt that I was in danger of making a final fool of myself by being actually sick on the floor.

'Quite right,' said Madame A., regarding the picture with her vague eyes, and speaking as she had spoken in the other room. 'Not a painter at all. Would have done better as a sweeper out of cabinets, wouldn't you agree, or as fetcher and carrier in a horse-meat market? It is kept in here because Chrysothème has no time for pictures, no time at all.'

It would have been absurd and undignified to argue. Nor could I be sure that she was clear in her mind as to who I was.

'Thank you, madame,' I said, 'for receiving me. I must detain you no longer.'

'A souvenir,' she cried. 'At least leave me a souvenir.'

I saw that she held a quite large pair of silvery scissors.

I did not feel at all like leaving even a lock of my hair in Madame A.'s keeping.

I opened the bedroom door, and began to retreat. I was trying to think of a phrase or two that would cover my precipitancy with a glaze of convention, but then I saw that, squatted on the single golden light that hung by a golden chain from the golden ceiling of the landing, was a tiny fluffy animal; so very small, that it might almost have been a dark furry insect with unusually distinct pale eyes. Moreover, the door into the big, hot room on my left was, of course, still open. I was overcome. I merely took to my heels; clattering idiotically down the bare, slippery staircase. I was lucky not to slide headlong.

'Mais, monsieur!'

I was struggling in the dark with the many handles, chains, and catches of the front door. It seemed likely that I should be unable to open it.

'Mais, monsieur!' Madame A. was lumbering down after me. But suddenly the door was open. Now that I could be sure I was not trapped, a small concession to good manners was possible.

'Good-night, madame,' I said in English. 'And thank you again.'

She made a vague snatch in my direction with the big, silvery scissors. They positively flashed in the light from the street lamp outside. She was like a squat granny seeing off a child with a gesture of mock aggression. 'Begone,' she might have said; or, alternatively, 'Come back at once': but I did not wait to hear Madame A. say anything more. Soon I found that I was walking down the populous Chausée d'Ixelles, still vibrating, and every now and then looking over one shoulder or the other.

Within twenty-four hours I perceived clearly enough that there could have been no dog, no little animal squatted on the lantern, no picture over the bed, and probably no adopted daughter. That hardly needed saying. The trouble was, and is, that this obvious truth only makes things worse. Indeed, it is precisely where the real trouble begins. What is to become of me? What will happen to me next? What can I do? What am I?

THE LADY IN GRAY

by Donald Wandrei

DONALD WANDREI (1908–1987) is overdue for rediscovery as a writer of weird fiction. His early work was championed by H.P. Lovecraft, some of whose fiction Wandrei in turn managed to sell to magazines other than *Weird Tales*, where the horror fiction of both writers appeared. After Lovecraft's death Wandrei and August Derleth founded Arkham House, the first and most important publisher devoted to the macabre and fantastic. Sadly, when *Weird Tales* folded in 1954, Wandrei apparently stopped writing fiction. He leaves a novel, *The Web of Easter Island*, a book of poetry, *Poems for Midnight*, and three collections of short stories – *The Eye and the Finger, Strange Harvest*, and the posthumous *Colossus*. His poems *Sonnets of the Midnight Hours* were based on his frequent nightmares, and it feels to me as if 'The Lady in Gray' may have been. Certainly it has all the qualities of one.

DURING the whole of my life, the hours from sunset to sunrise, when other people sleep, have been oppressive with fear. Since early childhood, I have been subject to terrifying dreams, from which neither physicians nor psychologists have been able to offer me the slightest relief. Doctors could find no organic derangement save for a few minor troubles such as are common to all men. My life has been singularly free of accidents, shocks, tragedies, and misfortunes. Financial worries have never beset me. I have pursued my career, at which success came steadily. Psychiatrists have devoted months to analyzing me, probing my life, my emotional development, my conscious and subconscious minds, hypnotizing me, making innumerable tests, and searching for secret fears or obsessions that might account for my nightmares, but in vain. Sedatives, opiates, dieting, travel, rest: these have been urged upon me at one time or another, and I have tried them without success. To doctors, I am a healthy man of thirty-four. To psychiatrists, I am a mentally sound, normal, and balanced person whose extraordinary dreams they either discount or discredit.

This is no comfort for me. I have come to dread the hours when night approaches. I would gladly expend my fortune if I could be relieved of the visions that possess my nocturnal mind, but the great diagnosticians of America and the foremost psychiatrists of Europe have alike labored in vain.

As I sit here now, writing these last words, a calm and a despair burden me, though my head seems clear as seldom before, despite the horror, the loathing, the terror, the revulsion, and the fear that combined in the first, and I believe final, profound shock which annihilated only a few minutes ago, and in full daylight, what hopes I had of fulfilling my life. That dreadful thing is at my elbow while

I write; and when I have written, I shall destroy.

Let me go back for many years. I have been, I repeat, subject since early childhood to hideous dreams. Disembodied heads that rolled after me; cities of colossal and alien statuary; fire that burned and beasts that leaped; falls downward from titanic precipices; falls skyward up from pits of ancient evil; the old ones, waiting and waiting; flights through eternal blackness from nothing or something I only sensed; the grind of infernal torture machines against my flesh; monsters all of flowers and animals, fish and birds and stones, wood and metal and gas united incredibly; the pale avengers; descent into necrophilic regions; the leering of a bodiless eye in the midst of vast and forlorn plains; a corpse that rose and turned upon me the visage of a friend, with tentacles and ribbons of tattered black flesh writhing outward as though blown by gusts of wind; the little ones who pattered toward me with strange supplications; sunlight upon an oak-covered hill, sunlight whose malignance, nameless color, pulse, and odor instilled in me the unreasoning hate that is allied with madness; orchids lifting blooms like children's faces, and sipping blood; the dead ones who came, and came again; that awful moment when I drowned, and a fat thing swam out of the sea-depths to nibble; mewing blades of grass which purred avidly as my feet trod upon them; these and countless other such nightmares, inflicted through slumber as far back as I can remember, bred in me a deep and rooted aversion to sleep. Yet sleep I must, like all mortal men. And what shall I say of those darker dreams, those fantasmal processions that did not and do not correspond with any knowledge I possess? What of the city beneath the sea, all of vermilion marble and corroded bronze, in whose queerly curved geometry rest the glowing configurations of things that earth never bore? What of the whisperer in darkness, and the call of Cthulhu? I saw the seven deaths of Commoriom, and the twenty-three sleepers where Hali raises its black spires in Carcosa. Who else has witnessed the dead titans waken, or the color out of space, or the ichor of stone gods?

These, these tormented me and wakened me to fever and to sweat in the hours past midnight, and the silence before the gray of dawn. But they were small things, old dreams, compared with those of late.

I can not now narrate the events leading up to my acquaintance with Miriam, nor the brief but boundless love that we enjoyed, the eternal marriage we planned, and her tragic death when the airplane in which she was nearing the city from a visit to her parents fell upon the eve of our wedding. Perhaps the shock of that waking nightmare completed the slow devastation to which sleeping nightmares had almost brought my mind. I am not the one to say. Miriam was dead, all her strange beauty, the gray of her eyes, the gray and subdued mood of her personality, the pallor of her cheeks, the haunted and roving spirit prisoned within her, gone. I thought of her as the lady in gray, as she lay in her bier, like a woman from Poe, or an eery creature out of *The Turn of the Screw*. So lovely, so unreal, so alien, and yet so eerily sweet. Dead, and not for me. Even the day was gray, that wild, autumnal afternoon, and the leaves that the wind blew rustled with a dry, sad sound, until the rain began falling later, and the world turned to a duller gray where the noise of slashing drops rivalled the sodden howl of gusts, and I was alone with my loneliness.

In the sanctuary of my chamber that night, I dreamed a dream. I dreamed that Miriam came to me, and took my hand, and led me forth. Now we came to a great and slimy sea, whose frightful color appalled me more than its stench. The blackness of the sea, its viscidity, and the universal atmosphere of decay, made me sick before ever she led me into it, so that the touch of that fluid brought a double horror. Far out in the sea, as I struggled with choking lungs, the lady in gray, who floated luminous above its surface, turned without reason or warning, and guided me back.

I could not account, in the morning, for the awful stuff that coated me, or the mephitic smell in my chamber. Only after arduous labors was I able to remove it from my person, and I was compelled to burn every article that the slimy, sticky, nauseating stuff had stained.

That night, I dreamed merely of skies of flame, and lands

whose sinister red masses of rock soared from sere valleys where nothing lived and no plant flourished toward a cyclopean metropolis suspended in the heavens; and thus, for many nights, my old dreams recurred, until there came a time when I visioned again the lady in gray; and in my sleep, she took me by the hand, and raised me from my bed. We walked across plains of dusty gray, and she led me to a pillar. Now there dwelt in this pillar a great white worm, yet not a worm; a fat thing, like a slug, all gray, and with the face, if I may call the hideous thing such, of a rational creature; a horned visage whose red, white and gray pulp sickened me; but Miriam commanded, and I obeyed. I strode to the pillar, and lo, it fell apart. Out of those shards rose the loathly worm, and I gathered it in my arms. It curled. Then my lady in gray led me across that tremendous and desolate plain to my chamber, where she left me, committing to my care the dweller of the pillar. Over me she bent, and the gray thing kissed the gray woman with its beaked mouth; and then she leaned above me and caressed my lips, and she drifted upon her way, like a fog, soundless, and without visible steps.

I was frightened in the morning when I discovered that huge and horrible slug beside me. As I remember, I leaped from bed and with the tongs from my fireplace I beat and crushed it to a froth. Then I wrapped the pulp in the stained sheets, and burned it in the furnace. Then I bathed. Then I found the gray dust on my shoes, as I was dressing, and fear came to me anew.

There is, indeed, in Afterglow Cemetery, where they had buried Miriam, a kind of ashy soil; and though the grass grows green, and tall grow the wild flowers, they have never conquered the soil; so that in spring the gray shows through, and in autumn the dust lies lightly upon dead leaf and dying blade.

But I would not go there to find my tracks; for if I found my prints, I would have the horror of somnambulism added to my delirium; and if I did not find my footsteps, I would have a more poignant fear. *Where had I been? Whence came the gigantic worm?*

Thereafter, for many nights, so many nights that the loss of Miriam became a dull ache partly obliterated in time and memory, I dreamed the old dreams, of falling and fleeing and cities beneath the sea; of torture, of unknown beasts, and of unsocketed eyes.

Then the lady in gray came again one night in early winter, when I was beginning to forget, as much as I could. That night was yesternight. All the day, the snow had been falling, and the northwest wind, with a prolonged wail, had driven it onward, and whipped it into drifts, while the branches of naked trees ground and soughed mournfully together, so that, as the bleakness of evening drew near, I became a prey to melancholy, and depressed by thoughts of Miriam, who was dead. The frozen scream of the wind shrilled higher, and to that far-away cry I fell asleep. And when I slept, she came to me, to lead me forth.

Through the desolate plains she led me, and into the shadows of a forest, whither we penetrated deeper and deeper with the boles of tremendous trees rising ever taller around us; and thus we reached the cavern that she entered; and I followed after, striving to approach her, yet unable to close by one inch the distance between us. Now a strange thing happened, for the cavern swept sharply downward, until it became vertical, plunging toward the bowels of earth; and now a stranger thing happened, for we sank, as though falling gently, and yet we must make an effort, as though we were walking normally, but the horizontal had become the vertical. And slowly I drew closer at last to Miriam, until after age-long falling, we came to rest far, far, incredibly far beneath the surface of earth. And now I found us in the midst of a vault whose ceiling swept onward in arches of ever vaster scope and huger curves, while the walls receded like the naves of a cosmic and buried cathedral; and so I followed her down the aisle of that spacious edifice; and ghostly tapers, rising like giant torches beside our way, cast, in the little damp gusts of wind which fretfully stirred them, grotesque and wavering shadows upon the floor; and the gray robes of Miriam, the gray death-garments, fluttered behind her, streaming almost to my face as the distance between us lessened. Thus we came to the blackwood door, which swung wide and silent upon its great hinges as we approached; and the lady in gray drifted within, and I followed. Now I found myself within a crypt, whose three red tapers, guttering to their end, cast a somber and sinister glow; one at her head, and one at her feet, and one dripping scarlet drops upon her breast. For there lay Miriam, my lady in gray, in repose upon everlasting marble. At her head, a bowl of the slime of the black sea; at her feet, the white worm resurrected; and in her hands, folded across her breast, one the taper, and one a gardenia, whose fragrance, spicy and virginal, overpowered the odor of the chamber of death.

Now in my dream, with the queer logic of dreams, I thought this natural and had no fear; so I went to my lady in gray, and lo, at my coming, the bowl spilled over, but I brushed it aside, and the great worm rose, but I trampled it under, while the candles guttered out, and the gardenia glowed weirdly phosphorescent. By that luminescence, faint as it was, I saw that Miriam stirred, and a sigh passed across her, and I lifted her in my arms. Now the gardenia palely lighted my way, and through the rustling darkness I carried her, and the gray of her robes swept downward and around my ankles as I walked; until I came to the gusty corridor, and the tapers that flared, and the stately march of arches in cathedralesque tiers. So, with the curious illogic of dreams, the vertical corridor disappeared, and I walked onward through the vast chamber, until I emerged upon the plain. The gray dust rose, but the gray robes of Miriam fell about me, and the dust passed away. The heavens were empty of stars. In blackness I walked, save for the single flower whose scent sweetened the air, and whose glow lighted a path. Thus I clung to Miriam, and carried my lady in gray to my chamber.

Only a little ago, I wakened from my dream.

I stared and stared for all eternity, with cycles of oppressive and wildly swirling circles of frozen blackness alternating with red holocausts of flame to shatter the tranquility of my mind, and for ever. Not again for me the ways of man, or the mortal habitations of earth, or the transitory and ephemeral uncertainties of life. I have written, and now I shall die, of my own hand, and by my own choice.

For, when I wakened, I wakened to see the lady in gray seated beside my bed. In her face were the rotting vestiges of the grave, and her robes hung tattered and moldy; but these three things corrupted me from being: the fresh gardenia in her hands; her finger-nails, long and yellow, as only the finger-nails of those dead and buried six months or more have ever grown; *and the dreadful way in which her hands were twirling the flower, while her black, liquescent eyes centered upon me!*

A MOTE

by Walter de la Mare

WALTER JOHN DE LA MARE (1873–1956) was one of two writers who most consistently demonstrated Robert Aickman's notion that the ghost story is akin to poetry. (The other, of course, was Aickman himself.) Apart from his novel *The Return*, a remarkably subtle story of possession, his ghostly tales are scattered through his various collections, most of which are out of print. It would be a great boon to the field if some publisher were to bring them out as a single volume. His earliest tales, including 'A Mote', were written under the pseudonym Walter Ramal, and eventually collected by Arkham House as *Eight Tales*. In his introduction to his brother Colin's anthology *They Walk Again* de la Mare said of ghost stories 'To those who delight in them any defence of them is superfluous, and none perhaps is of much use.' Need I say more?

I AWOKE from a dream of a gruesome fight with a giant geranium. I surveyed, with drowsy satisfaction and complacency, the eccentric jogs and jerks of my aunt's head. Dozing in her basket chair, she reminded me of an Oriental doll decked in a bunch of gaudy fabrics. Her cap squatted unsafely and awry upon her pendulous curls; her yellow, glossy-skinned, emerald-ringed hands lay loosely upon her silken lap. I sat in my chair like some gorged spider surveying his grey expanse of web, more placid than malevolent concerning this meagre fly. The sleepy sun leered upon the garden with blowzy face. I turned from my aunt to the black cat. The luminous green of his eye glowered with lazy spitefulness upon the manoeuvres of a regiment of gnats. Him too, with sleepy amusement, I wove into the tapestry of my dreams. Presently, beyond measure vexed, the beast sprang into the air and buffeted right and left with his fore paws. I turned towards my uncle to enjoy with him a smile at his behaviour, and thus on a sudden perceived his odd posture. His bald mauve head was propped upon his right hand, and his elbow was supported by his chequered knee. He seemed to be watching with minute attention a sun-beetle diligently labouring between the stubborn grass-blades. His attitude was conventional, but his gaze was extraordinary; for he was looking at the beetle with the whites of his eyes.

So that there might be no doubt in the matter, I dropped cautiously upon my knees and peered up at his face from underneath. His mouth was open, just wide enough to betray the glint of gold between his teeth; a faint, infantile flush reddened his cheeks; his lids were uncommon wide apart, disclosing, not two grey pupils, but simply two unrelieved ovals of yellowish white. I was amazed. In my amazement I forgot discretion; I stayed upon my knees in the soft turf – thus becoming an insurmountable obstacle to the beetle – and thought hard. Perhaps my fixed attention troubled my uncle; perhaps he heard me breathing. For, on an alarming sudden, his orbs revolved as it were on greased hinges, and his two pale grey pupils, with an unwonted glitter in them, gazed full into mine. The pink flush upon his cheek deepened into an unwholesome ruddiness. His teeth clicked together. He fastened an icy finger and thumb upon my wrist, and, stealthily craning his neck, looked back upon my aunt. Audibly satisfied with her serene helplessness, and still bent almost double, he beckoned me over the lawn towards the apple trees. This obscure conduct in a man of transparent respectability – the admiration of every comfortable widow of the neighbourhood, a man of ponderous jollity and bellicose good-humour – gave me not a little satisfaction. I congratulated myself on his lapse from sobriety. It had always seemed to me a misfortune that so potential a Falstaff should be a saint. Under cover of the apple trees, with red cheeks made ruddier by the belated beams of the sun through the twinkling leaves, he looked as bibulous a sinner as one might wish. I was to be disappointed.

'What were they like?' said he anxiously.

'All white,' said I laughing.

'Ah! don't giggle, my boy!' said he. 'I see, I see, you are yet in your veal. Drunkenness and women are the whole duty of the twenties. I am not drunk.' (His manner defied incredulity.) 'One minute's silence, my boy. I must see the end of this. The place is black under the pines, and soon the moon will be swallowed up by the drift. Two minutes!' Whereupon he rolled back his pupils, and with white blind eyes stood gently swaying to and fro in a yellow ribbon of sunlight. Through the green of the trees I could see the unrhythmic flutter of my aunt's lavender ribbons. Patiently, and with some alarm, I awaited the return of uncle's pupils. Presently they again revolved, and returned to their normal position. 'Trouble is brewing,' said he, blinking at the sun, 'but yet he stalks on inscrutable.' He heaved a prodigious sigh, and clutched at my wrist. 'My heart will knuckle under some day,' said he.

'Feel that!' He placed my hand upon a piston-rod just above his watch fob. Blue had mingled with the red in his face. I deemed it better to be dumb. 'You see, my boy,' he continued in an asthmatic voice, 'if your aunt knew of these things, it would be farewell to quiet. She would never cease to worry. Besides, your aunt is not fanciful. Why should she be?' he asked himself strenuously.

'Can I be of any help?' said I. 'I have skimmed a few medical books. I know a chap in Guy's. I might, you know – '

'Medical books be damned!' said my uncle. This I took to be a reassuring symptom. 'I am not a monstrosity,' he added irritably; 'my carcase is my own. Hang it! I'll tell you, Edmond. Let me tell you all from the beginning; the burden grows irksome upon my back. Only the night shares it with me. He is on his trackless travels even now, and I am not there to see. Scoff if you please, but do not preach. Sit down, my boy; your aunt is good for ten minutes.'

His gravity astonished me even more than his eccentricity. I sat down at the foot of an apple tree and leaned my back against its whitewashed trunk. My uncle did likewise.

'I remember,' said he, wrinkling his lids, 'I remember a dream frequently dreamed when I was about six or seven years old, I used to wake wet and shaking. It was a simple dream of an interminable path between walls of white smooth stone. By that way one might walk to eternity, or space, or infinity. You understand?'

I nodded my head.

'Remember, my boy, I find it hard work to prose – I would sooner be watching. The dream never came back to me after I was twelve years old, but since then I have had other dreams, as false to the Ten Commandments. I have seen things which Nature would spit out of her mouth. Yet each one has been threaded, each has been one of an interminable sequence. There's a theory written under the letter D in a little book I used to keep when I first entered the bank, "A Theory concerning Dreams expressed algebraically" – the result of mental flatulency. So far you are clear?'

'Yes,' said I.

'Well, last autumn, towards the end of October, a time of

strong winds, I was troubled with many sleepless nights. Being retired from the bank I could not occupy my mind with mental arithmetic, so, having no dry goods to carry in my head, I simply gave unlimited rope to my thoughts. Now *I* wear the halter. On the fifth November, Guy Fawkes' Day (I remember that your aunt complained of a strong smell of gunpowder in the bedroom), at a quarter to two, by St. Simon's clock, I was lying flat upon my back and wide awake. My eyes were naturally attracted by the white circle of light thrown by the gas globe upon the ceiling. Your aunt will not sleep without a glimmer of light in the room. Without danger of lying I may say that I was thinking absolutely of nothing. It is a vulgar but discredited practice. However, let it be agreed that whatever thoughts I had, lay between my retina and the end of my optic nerve. Theory is easier than science. Suddenly, as I watched idly, a little figure – a tiny insect-like figure crawled in at the left of my eye, and slowly traversing a small segment of the luminous disc upon the ceiling crawled out at the right. In my astonishment my lids blinked rapidly, my eyes moved of their own volition in an odd, perplexing manner. Please to mark that it was precisely at that moment when I discovered that my eyes had tricked me. Perhaps they had revolted from the uncommon and disagreeable fixity of sleeplessness and had revolved upon their axes inward. Perhaps I do not know the reason. Whatever it may have been, I know now that I had been looking under the bows of my eyebones into my skull. In all likelihood the grey circle of light which I had seen was the natural stored light of my eyes glowing in the darkness. If this was so, I had mistaken the personal, perhaps imaginary, light of my eye for the actual light of the gas-globe. It's not science, but it's common sense. Such, I say, were my conclusions some time subsequently, after many nights' experience. Try as I pleased in my wakefulness, the creature would not walk again upon the ceiling, for the very excellent reason that in my excitement and ignorance *I was looking in exactly the opposite direction*. But invisible, unfelt, undreamed, there it was, there it had always been, and there it will be until – Heaven knows.'

My uncle patted his brow, eyes, and cheeks with his bandana handkerchief, and (in a manner not unlike that of the black cat) gazed up at the patches of blue between the green boughs. 'The boom of that bee seemed to make the scent of the blossoms stronger, didn't it?' said he, with his handkerchief poised on the top of his head.

'What happened then?' said I.

'Upon the next night,' continued my uncle, 'as I purposely lay in the same position, I fancy that I almost fell asleep. So it seemed, although all the time I could hear your aunt snoring – 'twas time reckoned by a dream-clock. There was the circle of light; there was the gas-globe, the venetian blind, the embroidered watch-holder. But almost imperceptibly the light circle was becoming blurred at the circumference; it still possessed the same shiver, but now there were faint marks upon it, permanent stains in its whitest places; it was not without shadows. I gripped the bed-clothes and strangled my thoughts. And again, again, Edmond, the tiny figure walked out of the east into the west. I watched. The dim shapes in the centre moved and trembled, but took no nameable form. Again I saw the transit of the figure, but now it toiled more slowly. Soon the circumference seemed to widen. The figure took bulk and distinction. At the base of the disc a flatness became discernible encompassed by a huge bow of grey (my skull, perhaps) lightening and deepening into white and pink. A white thread suddenly crept out of the obscurity at the base, crept and wriggled between masses of black (masses like flour seen through a microscope). Presently the black masses caught colour and motion. Sudden glaring spots pricked my eye, and slow-moving blotches writhed into being with a dull pain as though my eyeballs were bringing them forth. Then I perceived slender lines and tassels of elegant grace and wide expanses of smooth, restful green, lit by jewels and trills and spears of yellow light. I seemed to be striving rather to remember than to see. If I am not deceived, albeit my eyes watched the process with curiosity, yet I clearly foresaw the result. The dimness and distortion fell away like smoke. And now, I was looking at a white caked trampled path, over which a black-green army of trees stood sentinel. I was round-eyed at gorgeous birds on the wing, and flowers waxen, gaudy and gleaming. My boy, there are none such here. There huge monsters wallowed in heat, and unimaginable wee things leapt and scrambled and minced from bough to bough. The whole air shook with their chirrup and purr and drone; the baked earth sweated a dry scent. Monstrous bat-winged insects speckled profusely the black boughs. Honey scent whetted the tongue and the tartness of resinous bark cried out from beneath the honey-scent. Deep in the lazy foetid green of the underwood sparkled quick eyes, and smooth, glossy skins shimmered. There was an atmosphere of ages over the place, and a distressing suggestion that all upon which my eyes looked was of me and in me – my own creatures and creations. But this I know, that myself magnified the scene. The heavy sky, the trees, and all the living things, were a picture painted on a pin's head. God knows more than a German philosopher. So, too, my dear boy, as in a dream of Job, a figure naked and familiar (although his face was turned from me) stalked upon the trampled path. And that figure of a man brought me very near to the terror of my babyhood's dream. I turned to your aunt for comfort, and could not see her. Nor did I awake. Then the awful thought clawed me that I was alive and awake, and with that thought the vision was blinded (so sudden was its going). Then followed a slow easy movement of my eyes, and immediately I was looking upon your aunt's face, bland and young in sleep. I hid my face in her sweet laces, and like any dipsomaniac sobbed loudly. "Why, John," said your aunt sleepily, "you've had a bad dream!" ' Again my uncle paused. 'This wholesome cleanliness of air is admirable,' he added under his breath, sniffing the evening.

I looked at my uncle uneasily. 'More of a nightmare than a dream,' said I.

'It's getting chilly for your aunt,' he replied. Then, after spying through the trunks upon the old lady, he came close to me, and, on tiptoe, whispered this in my ear: 'In eight months that wee creature has walked through centuries. Would dreams be so vile and consistent? Would I, the manager of a bank, cry like any girl at night if every living thing, every tree, rock, and cloud of the world in my skull were not of mine own image? That mote of a man – although he will never turn and show his face to me, try as I may to peer round – that mote of a man is me – me, your uncle. Quick, she's stirring.'

I hastened at his heels to my chair. My aunt woke from her nap, a little peevish. She complained of the dampness. But my uncle, giving her tongue no opportunity to wag nor her mood to fester, taught me how to snare a woman into smiling. Quick to profit, he wrapped a knitted shawl of gaudy wool about my aunt's shoulders, lifted her from the ground with a prodigious puff and a coy scream from the little lady, and trotted away with her into the house. I followed with two basket chairs.

Of course I entitled my uncle's fable *Nerves*. Eccentric would be far too polite a word with which to tell the truth if I were so minded. But as I was brushing my hair I came to the conclusion that it would be undesirable to betray my uncle's confidence to any, least of all to a physician. If his nerves were the progenitors of his visions, a dose or two of valerian might timely teach them their duty. If he was mad, no finical physician could better his condition, and a strait waistcoat would probably kill my aunt. Thus it will be seen that I laughed. Like Sarah, I was afterwards reproved. It surprised me how that in the past odd trifling actions and movements of my uncle must have escaped my attention. For instance, during dinner, as he was poising a wine-glass and testing the colour of his claret in the light of the lamp, he shut his eyes quick, and laid down the glass in confusion. When offering my aunt some tapioca pudding, his smiling pupils suddenly disappeared; he dived under the table, presumably for his napkin. Not only; but also now and again he would mutter a few words, or swear perhaps, or twist his fingers, thereby greatly discomposing a timid, colourless parlour-maid. Such accidents, or their like, must have frequently happened before. To all these drolleries, however, my aunt paid no attention, but nibbled serenely and smiled placidly. When dinner was over, my uncle and I took a turn in the garden. We chatted in a desultory fashion, but it was apparent that only my uncle's tongue was with me; his thoughts were busy with his dreams. At last he began anxiously to question me regarding his behaviour at dinner. I told the truth.

'My dear boy,' he answered bitterly, 'I have tried to look on the tragedy as a farce, but it is useless. I am getting into clammier bog each step I take. My eyes refuse to obey me. I want above all things to spend my life watching. The climax is speeding to a conclusion. I have spied upon the gambols of my hairy ancestry – perhaps Darwin! . . . – and each godless ape was in mine own image. Each transmigration of my eternal – think on't, my boy – eternal self has passed before my eyes, is now. This brood of creatures, of which I am the god and maker, are multiplying like worms in offal; cities teem with ugly and deformed, with lame and vile. Every thought of the past takes human shape. Here one incites to lewdness, here one taints the air with foulness. Here a white-clad, meagre creature struggles and pants for the light. And ever goes that one mite of a man, stalking unheeding and alone under sun and moon. Through sleep and waking, its horrid minuteness, its awful remoteness, troubles my skin; I grow sick. I remember Farquharson, the cashier, took hysteria. (Too much life, my boy.) We twitted him and embroidered him a sunbonnet. A sunbonnet! See this!'

My uncle stopped dead upon the gravel with his face towards the garden. I seemed to *feel* the slow revolution of his eyes.

'I see a huge city of granite,' he grunted; 'I see lean spires of metal and hazardous towers, frowning upon the blackness of their shadows. White lights stare out of narrow window-slits: a black cloud breathes smoke in the streets. There is no wind, yet a wind sits still upon the city. The air smells like copper. Every sound rings as it were upon metal. There is a glow – a glow of outer darkness – a glow imagined by straining eyes. The city is a bubble with clamour and tumult rising thin and yellow in the lean streets like dust in a loampit. The city is walled as with a finger-ring. The sky is dumb with listeners. Far down, as the crow sees ears of wheat, I see that mote of a man in his black clothes, now lit by flaming jets, now hid in thick darkness. Every street breeds creatures. They swarm gabbling, and walk like ants in the sun. Their faces are fierce and wary, with malevolent lips. Each mouths to each, and points and stares. On I walk, imperturbable and stark. But I know, oh, my boy, I know the alphabet of their vile whispering and gapings and gesticulations. The air quivers with the flight of black winged shapes. Each foot-tap of that sure figure upon the granite is ticking his hour away.' My uncle turned and took my hand. 'And this, Edmond, this is the man of business who purchased his game in the city, and vied with all in the excellence of his claret. The man who courted your aunt, begot hale and whole children, who sits in his pew and is respected. That beneath my skull should lurk such monstrous things! You are my godchild, Edmond. Actions are mere sediment, and words – froth, froth. Let the thoughts be clean, my boy; the thoughts must be clean; thoughts make the man. You may never at any time be of ill repute, and yet be a blackguard. Every thought, black or white, lives for ever, and to life there is no end.'

'Look here, Uncle,' said I, 'it's serious, you know, you must come to town and see Jenkinson, the brain man. A change of air, sir.'

'Do you smell sulphur?' said my uncle.

I tittered and was alarmed.

Subsequently I looked up my uncle's man, and had an earnest chat with him, telling him nothing save that my uncle was indisposed and needed attention. Moreover, I did my best to prevail upon my uncle to sleep by himself for a few nights. I thought it safer. But (poor old gentleman!) he seemed to have an unrighteous horror of loneliness. 'Only to be able,' said he, 'only to be able to touch her hand. No sceptic doctors, my boy, let me die wholesomely,' he replied to my earnest entreaties that he should see a physician. I determined to obey him.

The next day he seemed to have recovered his usual

excellent spirits, and although he sometimes fell away into vacancy, his condition in the light of my experience was undoubtledly different from that of many months past. 'I have an idea that I gossiped a good deal of nonsense in the garden yesterday,' said he, buttonholing me after breakfast. 'The sun was hot, very hot. Between ourselves? – that's all right. I had a better night; no nightmares. Eh! E – ay?' In a flash he hid his eyes with his sleeve. 'Er – bless the midges! Come into the garden, my boy,' said he, and forthwith denied his denial.

On Wednesday afternoons when my aunt was upon her parish-visiting, and also at any time that we might snatch, my uncle and I would steal away into the woods or conceal ourselves in a crazy, musty summer-house near the gooseberry bushes. There we would sit for hours together while he narrated to me the doings and adventures of the fantastic creatures which he professed to see. I acted foolishly, perhaps, in consenting to his absurdities, but who would have done otherwise? The charm of his narrations was irresistible. To listen to him as he sat there, with his white eyes, his ragged straw hat upon his head, in the midst of the summer, was fine. Sometimes he would return to the experience of past dreams; sometimes he would look in upon his world, and tell me what he saw there. Whatever he affected to see, moreover, he made me see too. For even, perhaps, gave he not every detail, yet myself by his seeds could raise my own crop of visions of an exact likeness to his. This, too, he was ever at pains to insist upon – that the many beings, the uncouth cities, all that which he had described to me possessed an atmosphere of himself, an intellectual colouring peculiarly his own. He was the unwitting creator, but responsible for his creations. How mad a theory it seems! This, too. 'I see that the end is coming; he treads solitary paths. O that he would flee, and seek for hiding! And the scattered thousands come round about him; they sneak upon his footsteps; they net him in on every side. He passes through villages (which I think I have seen in dreams). The people mock in the streets, and the dogs bark. He journeys through cities that are familiar and yet unknown to me. Danger hides under every leaf. There is a clangour in the air of terror and disaster.' My uncle would carry me away with his enthusiasm, and I would grow with him as eager as a boy, and though it was easy to see that his sickness was serious and that the consequences might be dire, yet with the gentleness of a mother and the intuition of a child he kissed away my aunt's occasional anxieties. He kept to the end the mellow roundness of his cheeks, the vigour of his voice; he neither advertized his pain nor trumpeted his woes. He consistently reviled the doctors. If his perpetual hilarity was sometimes maudlin, he never turned tail nor lacked a pun to the end.

On July fifteenth my aunt came by herself into the breakfast-room, and immediately rustled to me who was sitting in the window-seat, basking in the sun. The sunlight seemed to caress her frailty, to cling to her old laces, her muslins and her trinkets. 'I am afraid, dear Edmond, your uncle is not quite the thing today,' she said affably. 'He seems a little feverish, I think. He tossed in the night, and this morning he was so impatient with his clothes. He alarmed me, dear.'

Just then my uncle walked into the room. He walked in jerks, and collided brutally with the table. When the sunlight fell upon him I noticed a sullen bruise upon his forehead. His arms swung in time to his legs, his left to his left, his right to his right. He lurched directly towards me. I dodged deftly. He sat down upon the corner of the settee, in the place which I had vacated. A fly was buzzing upon the hot windowpane. My aunt stood at my side with her left hand over her mouth. My uncle's head was wagging slowly to and fro. The sun blazed upon his face and scanty hair.

'Like a sunbeam,' said he. 'Like a sunbeam in winter swift and keen. That stone thudded. Another beacon! The city is bloody with flames. No moon tonight. Run, run, run! He'll be met by those mouldy faces. A twist. By the throat!' My uncle's hand clenched upon the blind-cord and relaxed.

'Edmond, Edmond,' chirruped my aunt.

The venetian blind crashed down upon my uncle's skull. He hauled it up without a word, turning fleeting, red, flaming eyes upon us. My aunt knelt down at his feet and set to slapping his hands. I broke the bell-cord, and dashed cold milk into his face, for there was no water.

'The thunder is breaking. The heavens belch their fires; see – like a worm, like a wasp. He'll escape them; he must, he must. Oh God! in their thousands they leap, they skurry, and flee like dead leaves in my garden. Savage and crazy, and implacable as ice. Ah! the granite griffin! He is under, he is under. See the hag, the lewd hag. The air is pitch and be-spattered. The wind shivers. Now growls the thunder, their feet are oats rustling. Oh me! Twist, double, under!'

The maid entered, carrying a dish of kidneys. She stood in the doorway looking at my uncle. My aunt continued to slap his hands and to call plaintively, 'John, John!'

'Lo!' he screamed with gaping mouth. 'He is caught, he is trampled upon and wounded. I am caught. Oh! where the white men with kindly white faces? Are there no white men? None? The granite towers wriggle in their seats. My boy Edmond, my boy, he has turned his face – poor white dead face. He is hand in hand with death . . . he is away, he climbs. They are many as swarming bees. See, hurrah! hurrah!' (His cheer was thin as the song of a wire in the wind.) 'The white men! My boy, very few. Every thought lives for—. We are careless, we are careless. Clutch tight to thy seat, wan mote of a man. Do not heed their savagery. Kiss the cold stone, mote of a man, look to heaven through the lightning-rents. Lucy, your hand, your kind hand. All is ungodly tiny.'

The maid went away.

'Now they fight – in their thousands they gather. Their growl frightens the night. Wan and lurid, mouldy and green and lascivious. He crouches and shakes and sweats on his perch. The smell of blood is sharp to the tongue. The white men fall. They are trampled down. The sky is shaken. The swift tongues of flames are black, for the sky is open – opens wide. It is the light of day. I heard the sound of many—. It is just. Oh, mote of a man!' My uncle's tongue clucked in his throat. He grew silent. His whole body shook spasmodically. The fly buzzed in the sun and danced. Presently my uncle rose to his feet. With neck outstretched (as though led by a halter) he walked across the room. Out by the glass doors into the conservatory he went. The hot heavy scent of his housed flowers rallied behind him and fought with the smell of the kidneys. On my uncle walked between the red pots, and out into the garden where the birds made clamour in the dappled leaves and the earth was alive with insects. He stepped down gingerly upon the gravel and immediately set to running, and as he ran he cried out and flung his arms into the air. The door-frame shut him from me. My aunt and I followed quickly after him. My aunt came first into the garden. When I skipped into the sunlight I saw him again. He was running amuck in the orchard, maddened by blows from the tree trunks and the low-hanging swaying boughs. He frisked hither and thither, to and fro. My aunt hung upon my arm, and with a wee scream greeted every dull blow. I heard the maids sobbing in the kitchen. There was no cloud to hide the sun. Wounded and battered and panting, all sudden in the midst of a blind rush he stopped still and stark. He clasped his hands about his neck. Then with child-steps he laboured patiently toward us. Without doubt or fear he walked over grass and flower-beds until he came to my aunt. He sat down on the low garden seat, saying 'Lucy, Lucy.' Then he was silent.

McGONAGALL
IN THE HEAD

by Ramsey Campbell

RAMSEY CAMPBELL (1946–) has consistently described himself as a horror writer, but has contributed to many anthologies of ghost stories. His novels *The Nameless* and *Obsession* contain ghostly episodes, *The Influence* and *Ancient Images* are ghost novels, while *Midnight Sun* was favourably compared to Blackwood and Machen. His most recent collections, *Waking Nightmares* and *Alone with the Horrors*, contain many ghost stories. Walter de la Mare has suggested that 'the ghostliness of the ghost doesn't much matter' in fiction, and perhaps that excuses the following tale.

HE was on his way to being a reporter. That Monday morning he was early as usual for work, hoping the editor might observe his eagerness. The newspaper office was locked, however, and so Don watched the street through the late October fog of his breath. Buses bearing words and faces scrawled inside their clouded-over windows paraded like a train of elephants through the shopping precinct; girls and young women said 'Brrr' to one another before taking refuge in the hot shops where they worked. Half a dozen schoolchildren whose faces looked bruised by the icy air dodged across the road in front of a lorry laden with washing machines, and the screech of brakes awakened in Don's guts a sensation which felt like hunger and nausea combined. Eyewitness Reporter Don Drake, Our Man At The Scene Of The Tragedy. . . The children skidded on to the pavement, leaving the lorry stalled and fuming, and Tina the receptionist jumped out of her boyfriend's Porsche and waved the rump of her culottes at Don while lingering over a last kiss.

She unlocked the office and switched on the fluorescent lights and ran to press her bottom against the nearest radiator. 'Want to warm me up, Don?'

She'd kicked off her left shoe and was rubbing her right calf with her foot. The cuff of her culotte whispered up and down her stockinged thigh, never quite keeping the promise of a glimpse of bare flesh. 'Just tell me how,' Don said.

'You know where the kettle is, and the coffee's in one of my drawers.'

'I knew that was what you meant,' he said as his discomfort rose from his groin into his stomach.

When a fist rattled the glass of the door he hurried to let in Ted Mull, who dumped his tweed hat on the counter and rubbed his chest vigorously before unbuttoning his overcoat. 'Morning, love's young bloom,' he boomed, tilting his face up and opening his lips as though to catch something in flight. 'Any for me?'

'Coffee, you mean,' Don said.

'What makes you think I was talking to you, squirt?'

'Don't pick on him, Ted. He's doing his best.'

'He's trying all right. Just put it on my desk, son, and give us the milk,' Ted said on the way to comb the remnants of his hair.

The rest of the team arrived before the editor. Stanley Brady responded to greetings by muttering 'Egh' and displaying today's shade and texture of his tongue. Trevor Horrocks, who wasn't much older than Don, blinked anxiously at the editor's door while unwrapping his stringy neck. Bernadette Hain, who wrote the women's page, came last, treating her colleagues to a look of regal disapproval diluted by conscious tolerance. 'It isn't what I'd call a good morning,' she said.

As the clock struck nine the editor strode in, his astrakhan dangling by the sleeve he was about to peel off. 'Morning, Mr Davenport,' the staff said in a ragged chorus.

'Mng.'

That was neutral. 'Mg' was ominous, 'Mrng' expansive. He waved away Don's offer of coffee and turned to the other desks. 'Two minutes.'

Precisely two minutes later the reporters trooped into the inner office. One day, Don promised himself, he would hear what the editor had to say at the morning conferences. All he could distinguish through the door were murmurs, which were enough to distract him from Tina except when her perfume spiced the air. He uncovered his screen and keyboard, then he unclipped his gold-plated ballpoint, which he was saving until he needed to take notes, and laid it on his desk. Then the phone on his desk rang, and he was somebody. '*News*,' he announced. 'Births, marriages and deaths.'

'Deaths?'

'Sorry.'

'Sorry?'

'Deaths.'

'Is there any limit on how long I can be?'

'Over six feet could be a problem,' Don might have said if his professional voice weren't speaking for him. 'Entirely up to you, sir,' he said. 'It's ten pee a word.'

'Poetry included?'

'Whatever you want to give me. You can dictate it to me now if you have a credit card.'

'I'll cough.' The caller did so, sounding as if he was pronouncing the word. 'I'll give you my details at the end of the remembrance. Have you pen and paper?'

'Keyboard and monitor.'

'Dear me. Are you sure those will serve?'

'You have my word.'

'Then here are mine,' the caller said, and adopted a tone that suggested he was reading someone else's. 'Oh Dad we had you all too fast?'

Don had typed the entire line before he grasped what he was being asked. 'That fast is fine. Oh Dad we had you all—'

'—these years,
But every life must end in cough.'

'Tears.'

'When we both stepped through life's door,
After Mum's yours was the first face we saw.
And if we were unhappy at school
You cheered us up, you cough. Cough, cough.'

Don waited for the coughing to subside and said 'You cheered us up, you—'

'Played the fool,' the caller said with a resentment Don thought unreasonable. 'And when we had exams to do,
You gave us help to see us cough.'

'Through,' Don said, typing, resisting the temptation to say 'Are you?'

'You gave us each money to buy cough. Couuggh, cough. To buy cough.'

Don lifted the receiver away from his ear to put a distance between himself and the harsh dry sound. At that remove the coughing sounded even falser. When the caller repeated 'To buy' Don held the receiver at arm's length until he heard the voice continue.

'—a flat,
And lent us more when we needed that.
It took us years to get our degrees,
And it was you who paid most of our fees.
Then you and Mum saw us both wed,
First Sue and then your little cough.'

Don couldn't resist typing 'cough' at the end of the sentence, to be deleted when he went through the text to add punctuation and capital letters and to correct any errors in transcription. There couldn't be much more to come, or he might begin to suspect the call was a joke. 'Your little—'

'Frough. Cough. Fred,' the caller said, and drew a rattling breath. 'Mum sat our babies on her knee,
And cur. Currough. Currough. Currough.'

It *was* a joke. 'And gave you one when they had to pee,' Don heard himself say, and was so nervous of doing so out loud that he typed the line instead. 'And—' he prompted when the coughing trailed off, but there was a breathless silence. 'And gave—'

'What about a grave?'

'Nothing,' Don said, deciding that the call was serious after all. 'On her knee, you were saying, and—'

'And called them each her little flea.'

Don gave the receiver a long slow double-take before he typed the line. 'Carry on,' he said, keeping his face straight, and his voice.

'We've got us all now that you've gone,
And our thoughts of you will still go cough, cough, cough.'

Don typed the last word without speaking it and waited for the coughs to finish. 'Who is the message from and to, please?'

After a silence which seemed longer than was necessary for the caller to catch his breath came the response: 'To Terence Bernard Moore from daughter Sue, son Fred, grandchildren cough, cough.'

'Twins, eh?' Don muttered. 'Flea and flea?'

The silence made him nervous that the caller had heard him, until he – Fred, presumably – said 'Hope and Charity.'

'And called them Hope and Charitee,' Don said under his breath, and more loudly 'So I just need the details of your card.'

'I'll get them now.'

Don waited through a spectacular outburst of coughing and what sounded like the contents of a room being exhaustively overturned, at the end of which he thought the phone had been flung on the floor. Instead the caller said in an aggressively aggrieved voice 'I can't lay my hands on it just now.'

'Then I'm afraid you'll be too late for—'

'I'll send you a cheque. When must you have it?'

'For Thursday's paper, tomorrow morning.'

'I'm writing it now. Goodbye.'

'Of course you are,' Don commented as the phone went dead, and poised his fingers over the keyboard. It would be the work of a few seconds to delete the entire rigmarole, but he should wait for the morning so as to make sure it had indeed been an elaborate joke. The voice had been too old, he reflected, like someone trying to sound older than they were. He was about to call Tina to look at the incredible doggerel when the editor's face loomed beside his own reflection on the screen. 'S,' Don hissed, and managed to say not 'Sorry' but 'Sir?'

'Choking us, is it, Mr Drake, the tie? Finding it hard to talk?'

'No?' Don replied, all he could think of to ask.

'Tidy yourself up, then. We're not at college now, we're in the real world,' Mr Davenport said, and watched while Don pulled the noose tighter.

Don had failed at the interview for the rival newspaper because his hair had been too long, and now his bare nape seemed to bristle with being spied on by his colleagues. Everyone had to please the editor, he told himself. Ted Mull had emerged from the inner office booming 'Of course I will, sir, you can always count on me' as if he didn't care who overheard his slavishness. As the editor headed for the toilet Trevor Horrocks jumped up, gasping 'Oh er Mr Dav' to no effect other than to make Mr Davenport hunch his shoulders, and Don felt better at once. He could rely on his professional voice, and anyone who glimpsed him at his desk would take him for a reporter.

By the end of the day he'd lost count of the births and marriages he'd dealt with, and the rhyming deaths. Why was it death that produced so much doggerel? Perhaps it was a way the living regained control of their lives, even if it meant reducing their experience of death virtually to meaninglessness.

Shops were putting up their shutters as he walked home. The large houses were mostly rest homes, except for those like the one he inhabited, which had been divided into almost as many flats as there were rooms. Otherwise the main difference seemed to be that in houses like his nobody called on anyone else. Cartoon voices climbed from television to television as he raced the time-switched lights up the ragged stairs and let himself into his third of the top floor.

He emptied a can of baked beans and sausages into the pan on the electric ring and fed the toaster its trinity of bread. While he ate dinner he gazed through the windows of the envelopes he'd picked up in the front hall, and having washed up, opened them. The bills weren't quite as greedy as he'd feared, though a reporter's salary would have made them less daunting. He lined up the envelopes on the mantelpiece and tried to read a comic novel, but couldn't lose himself in it, not when he encountered the word 'dead' four times in as many pages: dead letters, beat, good, drunk. He abandoned it and strolled down the hill to the pub opposite the graveyard.

It was the Polytechnic's local, where he had been drinking ever since he'd joined the journalism course. Making his way over the bare floorboards of the snug, which was dimmed by the smoke of a crowd worthy of a rush-hour train, felt like coming home. He was taking his first gulp of Letterman's Bitter when a hand clapped him on the shoulder. 'Dressing for the part?' Paul Prentiss said.

'What part's that?'

'Don't be modest. You've been seen working at your rag. You look quite the hack.'

Don had never cared for the heavy rough humour which went with the chubby scrubbed schoolboyish face, and he liked Prentiss even less for saying 'What story are you after at the moment?'

'At the moment all I'm after is a drink.'

'I can take a hint.' Apparently Don's tone wasn't enough of one, however, because Prentiss bought him another pint and winked over Don's shoulder. 'You're in luck, girls. Two real journalists for the price of one. Meet Don Duck, I mean Drake.'

Don used the lack of space as an excuse merely to wave his free hand without turning. 'So don't keep all the news to yourself, Don,' Prentiss said. 'What's your big story just now?'

As Don drained his first pint, which made him feel as if his head was separating from the rest of him, he deduced why Prentiss was taunting him. 'It was you, wasn't it?'

'You're letting the job get on top of you, Don. I'm not a story, I'm real.'

'It was you pretending to have lost someone. You shouldn't make fun of the dead.'

'Why, can't they keep a straight face? You're never telling us you only deal with dead issues at your rag, when our tutors thought you were so—'

Don took a mouthful of bitter and expelled most of it in Prentiss's face. 'You're so funny, I couldn't help it,' he said as Prentiss spluttered and mopped himself.

He enjoyed the spectacle until the stocky barman grasped his arm. 'I think you've had enough for one night, son. How old are you anyway?'

'Old enough to know when someone's trying to make a fool of me.'

'You can do that all by yourself,' Prentiss shouted as Don struggled to the door, having drained his tankard. He heaved the door open, receiving the night in his face like a dash of ice water, and stalked into his own fog. DISAGREEMENT BETWEEN JOURNALISTS ENDS IN FRACAS, he thought as he was confronted by the smudged stony messages of the graveyard, BECAUSE ONE WAS A JACKASS. He accepted worse rhymes than that every working day. Surely sometime he would be able to draw on his years spent studying in the library, on all those words.

In the morning he waited outside the *News*. By the time Tina straightened up from the Porsche his lips were stiff, his mouth felt clogged with ice. She ran to her usual radiator, and he followed in her perfumed wake.

'Hello, young lovers, whatever you're up to. Make mine black.'

'He isn't in yet, is he, Mr Der—'

'Gagh.'

'You're easily pleased.'

'Mrng.'

Don watched while Tina sorted the mail, delivered by a postman who departed whistling like a blue tit which had almost lost its voice. 'Any for me?' Don eventually asked her.

'A pile.'

None of the letters and cheques related to yesterday's protracted call. He should have emptied the tankard over Prentiss's head. He called up the eighteen lines of verse on the screen and was grinning wickedly at them when his phone rang. He deleted them and immediately wished he'd waited for the noon mail, but it didn't matter: he could remember every word as if they'd leapt off the screen into his skull. 'Births, marriages and deaths,' he said.

Of course the noon mail contained nothing from Fred Moore, and Don felt he should be able to relax. The afternoon brought him mostly births and marriages, which was a relief. That night after his tinned dinner he crouched over the television beside the sink in order to switch channels. An album of black and white faces fluttered past until he settled on a comedy, but he couldn't watch for long when the dialogue seemed to be chanted rather than spoken. 'Crambojingle, crambojingle,' he murmured over and over in bed, and fell asleep wondering where the word came from.

'You'll catch your death one of these days,' Tina said next morning, 'hanging about in the doorway.'

'How's love's young dream today? Time to wake up.'

'Gurgh.'

'Hmmm.'

'Mg.'

'Sorry I'm – Mr Dav—'

'God bless you love we miss you chuck.'

'God bless you love we miss you chuck,' Don confirmed, reminding himself to be professional, not to put words into the caller's mouth, not to listen to rhymes in his head, however tempting they were. Tomorrow was publication day, and then he would have no reason to be uneasy, not that he had now.

That night he went down to the pub, but saw Prentiss through the windows shrouded in breaths. He strolled through the graveyard, where he kept smelling a newly dug grave. Though the stones gleamed darkly over the crystallized turf he was unable to distinguish a single inscription. As he lay in bed his head felt laden with words, but in the morning his mind was blank, thank . . . 'Enough of that stuff,' he muttered as he got himself ready for work.

'Gangway, brrr.'

The rest of the greetings were lost in the bustle as some of the deliverers came to Tina for their batch of newspapers and had to be sent around the back. Don imagined all the words for which he was responsible that week spreading across the town, having begun to fade at the instant they were printed.

It was almost lunchtime when a caller addressed him in a tone he wasn't prepared for. 'Are you answerable for the contents of today's paper?'

'If it's a birth, a marriage or a cough I am.'

'Then where's my father?'

Don was instantly suspicious. 'What name?'

'The name's Fred Moore, and my father was Terence Bernard.'

'I thought you might say that. Not Paul Prentiss, eh?'

'What's that? What are you raving about?'

'Let it rest, Paul, unless you want another in your eye. Haven't you enough news at the *Advertiser* without trying to make a story out of me?'

'Who the devil d'you imagine you're addressing?'

'You've almost got the voice right this time, but you don't fool me. You went on too long last time, that was what gave you away. Nobody living could be that bad for eighteen lines without noticing.'

'I don't think you realize—'

'Sew it up, Paul, before you have a heart attack. There may be real people trying to get through to me.'

Don heard a strangled sound that suggested his warning about the heart attack had come too late, and then there was only the moaning of the dialling tone. He grinned at the receiver before replacing it and waiting for the phone to ring. Just now all the calls were for the switchboard, interrupting Tina's sorting of the lunchtime mail. Eventually she brought him a single envelope addressed to Deaths in a shaky hand. 'Someone must love you,' she said, and hurried back to the switchboard as the editor opened his door. 'Mr Drake?'

'Mr Davenport?'

The editor jerked his permanently frowning slab of face towards his shoulder. 'My office, please.'

Could this be the chance for which Don had been working? He tried to look nonchalant yet enthusiastic as he walked into the inner office, where all the furniture seemed to smell of the pipe Mr Davenport was relighting. Without inviting him to sit the editor leaned back in his chair, thumping the underside of the desk with his knees. 'Enjoying our work, are we, Mr Drake?'

'Certainly are. Am.'

'No ambitions elsewhere?' the editor said through his teeth, making the tobacco in the bowl glow red.

'Elsewhere, well . . .' Don wished he could use his telephone voice; this one wasn't working too well. 'Ambitions, you bet, but when you say elsewhere . . .'

'Take it slow and steady, Mr Drake. Never try to run before you can walk.'

'I'll bet you did. Or didn't, rather.'

The editor stared at him over the fierce red glow. At last he said 'So what's this I hear about your notices?'

'Something good, would—'

Don's voice seemed to stick on the rhyme. 'About a Mr Moore,' the editor said.

'A Mr Moore? Which Mr Moore?'

Don felt as if he was being forced to recite doggerel. He gripped his lips with his fingertips as the editor's voice grew thin. 'A Mr Fred Moore who has just been on to me, wanting to know what became of his father's obituary.'

'If he told you he rang up with it—'

'He didn't, no. His father did.'

'His fough—' Don cleared his aching throat and tried again. 'His father—'

'His father phoned in his own obituary which I'm assured you copied. Don't ask me why he did, it isn't our business to ask. He knew he was dying, his son says, and almost as soon as he'd spoken to you he coughed himself to death.'

The informant could have been Paul Prentiss, Don thought wildly – Prentiss trying to feed the *News* fake news. A single point seemed clear amid the babble of gibberish which the world was threatening to become: whoever the caller had been, he hadn't complained to Mr Davenport about Don's response to his call of a few minutes ago. 'We couldn't publish the obituary,' Don said, inspired just in time. 'We haven't received payment.'

The editor gazed at him as if his mind was on something else entirely. 'You'd better ascertain what happened to it and let the son know.'

'I will,' Don promised, and was fleeing towards the door when Mr Davenport said 'Try taking these.'

'I'm fine, I'm not ill,' Don said, 'I don't need a pill,' and saw too late that the editor was proffering Moore's address and phone number. He clutched them and stumbled out to his desk, where the envelope with the second-class stamp was waiting. As he grabbed it he was afraid he might tear it up, not open, but managed to peel back the flap. The envelope did indeed contain a cheque from T.B. Moore.

Don laid it next to the scrap of paper Mr Davenport had given him, then moved them closer together in an attempt to read them simultaneously without shifting his eyes. As soon as Tina was busy with a call he seized his phone and dialled. 'Mr Moore?'

'Who is it?'

Thank God, Don had succeeded in disguising his voice. 'I'm calling on behalf of Births, Marriages and Deaths. They've had to go out, he has, I mean, but I can tell you your father's cheque has just this moment arrived.'

'Indeed.'

'It was second class,' Don said, thinking that Moore sounded in the mood to take that as some kind of slur on his father. 'I can guarantee your father's piece will be in the *News* next week.'

'You'll understand if I make sure, I'm sure.'

'You rhyme like your dad,' Don managed not to say before breaking the connection. He clipped the cheque and the scrap of paper to the top of his pile of mail, and switched on the monitor. He was hearing the rhythm of T.B. Moore's first line: cough cough, cough cough, cough cough cough cough. He peered at the blank screen and moved his lips, and when the monitor seemed about to flicker in that rhythm he closed his eyes and attempted to mouth. That didn't work either. He couldn't recall a single word of Moore's.

It wasn't urgent, he tried to tell himself. So long as he remembered by next week, nobody would find him out. But his inability to remember felt like a hole in his brain, a vacuum aching to be filled. Moore's rhymes: if Don recalled the rhymes the rest would follow. He was straining to remember just one rhyme when his phone shrilled, and he snatched it up, mumbling a greeting which was all that emerged from the fight of two words to be first past his lips.

'Is that Births, Marriages and Deaths?'

'Yes, this is First and Last Brea—' Don coughed so as to interrupt himself. 'Yes.'

'I didn't quite hear what you said.'

'I deal with the living and—' Don coughed harder. 'No tiss says,' he managed to pronounce.

'Can I have a remembrance next week?'

'All that you need do is speak.'

The woman hesitated, which allowed Don to add 'You can pay by credit card, or send a cheque if that's, cough, preferable.'

The caller dictated her credit card details at once. 'Right, that's done,' Don said. 'Go on.'

'Though it's been years since you said goodbye—
Since you went up into the sky . . . We thought that you would never die . . .'

The choice of rhymes saved Don – their struggle for priority gave him time to choose only to mouth them. He wiped his forehead with the bristling back of one hand and typed her line. 'Go on.'

'The thought of you still makes us cry.'

Don preferred his lines, but he typed hers. 'Go on.'

'Each week in church we light a candle—'

He would be fine so long as he didn't type what he was mouthing. He only needed to say 'Go on' at the end of each line; his professional voice wouldn't let him down. When the caller finished dictating and said 'Is that all right now?' Don managed to confine himself to an affirmative grunt before cutting her off.

His colleagues were returning to their desks with stories from the outside world. Whenever Don had to answer his phone he crouched low over the keyboard so that they wouldn't notice his mouthing outrageous responses to 'She is not dead but gone before' and 'There never was a sweeter mum' and 'We're glad that now you are at rest'. The day was almost spent when Ted Mull stooped to him on the way to the toilet, murmuring 'First sign of madness.'

'At least it's not badness,' Don muttered at his retreating back.

Leaving the office was less of a relief than he'd hoped. He'd anticipated being able to think freely once he was alone, but he was surrounded by words. Everything had a name – street, car, lamp, house – and they seemed to be massing between him and the world. He let himself into his house with The Feeling Of A Key and ran upstairs towards The Taste Of Food. He fed himself a few spoonfuls of baked beans out of the can, and felt as though he was feeding himself the late October cold. He needed to relax in order to think, that was it – he needed a drink. He wouldn't be a journalist unless he had a drink.

The pub felt like a refuge from the cold words standing in the dark. The snug wasn't crowded yet, and the barman who had ordered Don out was off duty. Don sat in a corner with a pint and then with another, turning his back on the room so as to whisper. 'Dead,' he repeated. 'Moore must have said dead. I've got dead in my head.'

He was searching his brain for a rhyme which he was sure was the key when a fingertip tapped sharply on his shoulder. At some point the snug had filled with drinkers and smoke, and Don felt as though the crowd had forced Paul Prentiss on him. 'I want a word,' Prentiss said.

'Because you're a—' Don started to retort, and slapped himself across the mouth. He'd told Fred Moore both Prentiss's name and where he worked, and if he didn't keep his promise to Moore the man might well contact the rival paper. 'Can't you forget I got you wet?' he babbled. 'I'll pay for the damage if you can't cough. You've an empty glass. Let me fill it, you—'

Prentiss was gazing at him with mute amusement. He knew, Don thought: Moore had already been in touch with him. The roar of the crowd – far too many words – engulfed Don. 'You can't make me news,' he shouted at Prentiss, staggering to his feet. 'I'm just here for the booze.'

'I should lay off it for a while if I were you.'

'I've as much right as you have, you—' Don yelled, backing away from the argument which he was afraid he mightn't be able to stop. He mustn't waste time, he had to remember Moore's words before Prentiss could discover he'd mislaid them. He squirmed through the crowd and lunged into the night.

Dark, stark. Gate, fate. Trees, freeze. Willows, pillows. Walk, stalk. Wreath, teeth. Dates, crates. Earth, berth. Stones, bones. Lines, dines . . . None of this revived the verses. When he couldn't think for shivering he went home. If the pit in his brain was sucking in reality and reducing it to words, perhaps lying absolutely still in the dark would clear enough space in his overloaded mind for his memory to work.

At some point he fell asleep. He must have continued to rhyme, however, because when icy sunlight wakened him his brain was laden with pairs of words, while his surroundings seemed more aloof than ever. He was going to be late for work. He dashed cold water on himself, shivered into his freezing clothes and ran stiff-faced out of the house.

Though he was almost on time after all, only Tina was in the outer office. Some big local story must have broken overnight, because Don could hear the buzz of discussion beyond Mr Davenport's door. Ted Mull and Bernadette Hain sounded outraged, and for a panicky few moments Don felt sure they were appalled by something he himself had done. 'Didn't you get much sleep?' Tina said.

'Why, do I look like a creep?'

'That's not what I said.'

'It's what's in your head.'

'Be that way,' Tina said, turning her back on him.

'It's all I can say,' Don protested, almost missing the hook on the wall with his coat in his haste to take refuge at his desk. Once his monitor was switched on he wouldn't need to speak to anyone around him. Just as the screen lit up, Mr Davenport's door opened. 'Ah, Mr Drake. Arrived now, have we?'

'Both of us, you mean, or just me?'

'I didn't quite catch what you said.'

'I'm trying to talk for the dead,' Don muttered even lower as the phone rang on his desk.

He thought it had saved him. He pressed the receiver against his cheekbone, and his jaw dropped as though a bandage had been snatched away. What might he feel compelled to say? 'Is that the births column?' a woman said.

'No need to be solemn,' Don managed only to mouth as he grunted encouragingly.

'Can I put in a happy event?'

'One that you couldn't—' Don coughed so hard it hurt his throat. 'Mm hm,' he said.

'To Dee and Desmond Gray, a son . . .'

Don would be able to cope so long as he mouthed before he typed, he told himself – and then he gaped at the screen. Instead of her line he had typed 'A side effect of a bit of fun'. He could take the call and attempt afterwards to deduce from the screen what the caller had actually said, except that wouldn't work: he wouldn't be able to stop rhyming until he remembered Moore's words. 'Sorry, I'm having a technical hitch. Could you call back a bit later, you—' he gabbled and drowned his last word in the row he made replacing the receiver. As he perched it slightly askew on the rest so that no further calls would be able to reach him, Ted Mull leaned over the monitor at him.

Don thought Mull had noticed his ruse with the phone until the reporter said 'I heard what you said to the boss.'

'That so? Well, I don't give a toss.'

Mull snapped his mouth shut as though he'd caught something in it. 'You'll get nowhere with that attitude, my lad.'

'Then call me a bounder and a rotter and a cad.'

Mull's shiny face was turning several shades of pink and white, putting Don in mind of an iced cake. Bernadette Hain was telling Tina about last night's local outrage – vandalism and, by the sound of it, worse in a graveyard – but Don didn't want to hear; they were more words he would be compelled to rhyme. He closed his eyes and thrust his fingers in his ears, and when he looked again he was alone with Tina.

It was the best he could hope for. He mustn't speak to her. He had to make the most of his chance before she or the editor wondered why Don's phone had ceased to ring. Once Don had reproduced Moore's verses, surely he would no longer need to rhyme – surely he would be able to persuade Mr Davenport to give him a different job. Was it Moore who was filling his head with rhymes in an attempt to recapture his own? The notion felt like inspiration, except that now Don's brain was swarming with the rhymes Moore summoned up: viewer, renewer, lure, cure, immure, boor, endure, spoor . . . Perhaps if Don thought of every single rhyme for Moore that might release him; perhaps if he wrote them all down . . . He was staring with shaky eyes at the screen, convinced that there was something else he had to type so as to clear his head, when a voice said 'Moore.'

Don thought he had spoken aloud until he noticed the newcomer, a man in black with a long mottled face that looked pressed between his bushy sideboards. 'The editor's on the phone, but I'll tell him as soon as he's free,' Tina was saying to him. 'What shall I say it's about?'

'About my father. About his obituary you neglected to publish. I've been trying to speak to someone about it all morning, but it seems that number's out of order. I want to see the obituary before it goes in.'

'You want Mr Drake there. Don, this gentleman wants a word.'

Don felt his lips twitching. They were going to open, he was going to speak, and that would be the end of him. So this was what his nemesis looked like, Moore's grown-up son, no longer little Fred. 'First Sue and then your little Fred,' he thought and mouthed, and gasped. 'Then you and Mum saw us both wed . . .'

All at once the obituary was as present in his mind as it had been while he copied it down, and he was afraid he mightn't be able to type fast enough to record it before it departed from him. He gave Fred Moore a sickly grin and gestured him to wait until Don finished at the screen, and turned away from the counter as his fingers commenced scuttling over the keyboard. Two lines, four, eight, sixteen . . . Though they weren't in order, all eighteen lines were there, thank God. Moore's son was clearing his throat harshly, but Don put the couplets in chronological order before turning back to him.

He didn't trust himself to speak. He went to the counter and lifted the flap and invited Moore in with an ushering gesture, repeating it until Moore stalked frowning through the gap. He gave Moore his chair and stood beside it while the man peered at the screen. 'Oh Dad we had you all these years,' Moore read aloud.

Don heard the late Moore reading the words. Each line

seemed to remove a layer of dead words from his mind. As the son pronounced 'And our thoughts of you will still go on' Mr Davenport came to his office door, demanding 'Is there some problem?'

'Are you the editor?'

'I have that honour. Can I help?'

Moore poked a finger at the monitor, his nail clinking against the screen. 'You can see that this is never published.'

It didn't matter, Don told himself. Since the verses were out of him, the compulsion must be. He sensed that a change was about to take place in his head. The editor marched over and scowled at the screen. 'What exactly is the trouble?'

'We spoke. Fred Moore. You didn't print my father's obituary, and now you're trying to fob me off with this.'

'In what way fob?'

Moore swung one hand at Don. 'Your clerk's made this up. My father was never responsible for this rubbish. As if we haven't been through enough . . .'

Don felt all the rhymes rush back into his head. If nobody believed Moore had composed the obituary he might never be rid of them. His lips shifted, but he mustn't speak. He grabbed his pen from his desk as Fred Moore said unevenly 'Last night someone dug my father up, and – and now this.'

Don clicked the point of the pen out of the barrel and swivelled in search of scrap paper. He mustn't rhyme with Fred Moore's words. This *was* what your father said, he's still stuck inside my head, he's been here inside since the moment he died . . . Before he had time to scribble any of that, Mr Davenport confronted him. 'You're fired.'

No, hired. Give me a chance, don't lead me a dance, don't make me prance . . . Don shoved his hands against the sides of his skull as if he could squeeze out what had lodged in there, and felt the point of the pen scrape his temple. 'Take yourself off to the doctor if you're ill,' Mr Davenport said.

Kill. Don felt his temple begin to twinge as ink mixed with his blood. The rhyme was louder than any of the sounds of the office, the humming of the monitor, the gasps of the men, Tina's scream. It was only doggerel, he didn't have to act it out because he could no longer speak it. Perhaps he had, or else go mad.

THE HOLE OF THE PIT

by Adrian Ross

ADRIAN ROSS was the pseudonym of Arthur Reed Ropes (1859–1933), a Cambridge don. In 1891 he began a new career by writing the libretto of an opera in the Savoy vein, *Joan of Arc*. In the next thirty years he wrote over two thousand lyrics and produced almost sixty musical plays and farces. None of this prepares us for what appears to have been his only work of fiction, 'The Hole of the Pit', published as a novel in 1914 by Edward Arnold and never reprinted until now. While it is dedicated to the author's friend and colleague M.R. James, it owes at least as much to William Hope Hodgson, but it is its own book. Only its extreme rarity has prevented it from being acknowledged as one of the first masterpieces of the novel of supernatural terror.

CHAPTER 1

THIS is the story of a strange and terrible judgment of the
Lord in the deeps; and it has seemed good to me, and to
the one other who knows, to set down in order that which
happened, for the instruction and warning of our
children, to show them the certain end of evil-doing. For
there is need of much exhortation to keep the young from
the taint of that recklessness of unclean living that has of
late years corrupted our people, in spite of the plain
signification of God's wrath by plague and fire, and by
discomfiture before our enemies.

It was, as I remember, the autumn of the year of Our
Lord 1645, and I was but twenty-seven years of age, when
those matters happened which I now set forth. But in
truth I had always been older of look than my years, from
my very schooldays; and seeing this and my strong love of
books, my good parents had bred me for the Church at
Cambridge, and looked for me in time to take a living in
the gift of my cousin, the Earl of Deeping. But my father
and mother both dying in one month of the small-pox, I
was left to my own will; and much misliking the ways of
Archbishop Laud, and inclining towards the doctrines of
those that were called Puritans, I scrupled to enter upon
an office wherein I must do violence either to my own soul
or to the authority placed over me. I returned, therefore, to
my father's estate, where I could make shift to live as
became a gentleman, though little more. Of my wisdom in
holding aloof from the quarrels of religion I was the more
persuaded when our unhappy divisions broke out into
civil war. The Earl of Deeping, though impoverished by
his father's and his own riot and excess, raised a troop of

idle fellows from the countryside, with the help of a few desperate ruffians, the leavings of his service in the German wars, and rode off to join Prince Rupert, sending word to me to follow him with my tenants, which I would in no wise do. Nor could I yield any more to a zealous letter from Mr Oliver Cromwell, afterwards so great (whom I had known at Cambridge), summoning me to play the man on the Lord's side. For in truth I could never see that either party was on the Lord's side, whether the ravaging rakes of the King's army or the slaughtering saints of the Parliament. And had I gone to the wars on either party, I might well have followed the ill example of the good Lord Falkland, ever doubting the right of my own side, groaning 'Peace, peace,' and finding peace at last, after the manner of an ancient Roman, by riding to my death.

Thus doubtful, and being besides of a studious and retired mind, and timid withal, nor loving to look on bloodshed, I kept my house as far as might be, and counselled others to do the same; and the place where I dwelt being far away from any field of fighting, and in especial, three full days' ride from the lands of my warlike cousin, the Earl of Deeping, we were left not merely alive, but unharried by either party. Only once, having occasion to ride a day's journey from my house, I fell into the midst of a score of troopers in armour, who pulled me off my horse and very fiercely demanded of me on which side I was, when as yet I had found no means of knowing on which side they were. But I told them that I was all for peace, and giving them my name, their officer pulled out a list of the gentry of those parts, some marked (as the phrase went) as malignants to be despoiled, and some as quiet men to be spared, among which latter the Lord General Cromwell, as he then was, had written my name. So all passed off well, and at no more cost to me than ale or cider for the troopers and an hour's talk as I rode with the officer, a devout man, and of good parts, but too fond of citing Scripture away from the plain meaning.

In the summer of the year 1645 came the news of Naseby fight, and the utter overthrow, as men thought, and as it proved, of the King's party. Now one of those who fled from that field, after having borne himself bravely but not prudently, was my cousin, the Earl of Deeping, with the wrecks of his troop. He would not follow the rags of the King's army, for he had quarrelled with Prince Rupert on some point, being, I am told, too eager a plunderer even for the no ways squeamish stomach of the Prince. Therefore he made for his own place, Deeping Hold by Marsham, and there that which was to befall, befell him.

On a day in September I sat in my library, and had purposed to read through Dr John Owen's 'Display of Arminianism'. But, to my shame be it said, I soon tired of the divine; and indeed, the discords of our times had spoilt my early relish for controversies of doctrine. In setting Dr Owen again on the shelf, I pushed back a volume of some commentary, and seeking to draw this out, I thrust in two more. So, with the sudden anger that makes children beat the footstools and chairs for tripping them, I flung on the floor first the other volumes of the commentary, and then those that I had thrust to the back. There was much dust on them, and looking into the shadow of the shelf before I set the books in their place again, I saw a little leather book, flat and thin, and stamped on the cover with the arms of our house. Taking it up, I opened on a genealogy of the family of the Earls of Deeping and other their kinsmen, written in a fair hand, with the shields very well blazoned in colours and gold; the whole, as I judged by the last names, some eighty years old, for my great-grandfather ended his branch of the tree. All these names I knew, or nearly all, but as I cast my eye over the pages, it lighted on a string of rhymes in the middle of a leaf:

'When the Lord of Deeping Hold
To the Fiend his soul hath sold,
And hath awaken'd what doth sit
In the darkness of the Pit,
Then what doth sit beneath the Hole
Shall come and take him body and soul.'

I had not beforetime come upon this rhyme of the Earls of Deeping, but it called up remembrances of stories and songs that I had heard and half forgotten on my nurse's knee.

Never had I seen Deeping Hold, in the sea-marshes at the mouth of the river Bere, nor the village of Marsham, on the hill-sides above the creeks. But I had heard legends of a curse hanging over the Lords of Deeping, which had fallen once, if the story might be believed, and was to fall again and no more. And on the one day when I, a mere boy, had seen my cousin the Earl as a tall young man, with fair hair and a small pointed beard, riding with my father, I had wondered at the wildness of his blue eyes, and had thought of the stories my nurse told me. Then I read the rude verse again, and even as I lifted my eyes from the page, my serving-man knocked at the door, and entering, said that Eldad Pentry, from Marsham, desired to see me. I bade the man bring him in, and there came the strangest fellow that I had seen. Of low stature, lean, and with lank hair, and a face of no nobleness, his eyes were yet great and shining, and wide open and staring ever, as if set on something far away behind that which was for him to see. But for these eyes, the man had been merely mean-looking. He was dressed plainly enough in a sad-coloured suit, much stained with dust, and from his belt hung a great old rusty sword of a bigness fitter for Goliath of Gath than for this starveling. I gave him greeting, and asked of his errand.

'I have received of the Lord a message for thee, Hubert Leyton,' he said in a strange and harsh voice, never thinking to doff his hat, whereby I knew him to be a fanatic of some sect, of whom that time had great plenty. 'Arise and come with me, for there is a work for thee to do in the land of Marsham.'

It irked me to have the man mouthing his texts like broken meat, and I bade him, with some sharpness, I fear, to tell me his tale with less Scripture and more sense. He cast his strange eyes upon me, as if he saw somewhat beyond me, where was nothing but the books and the wall.

'I will not be angered by thee, for thou art a chosen instrument,' he said, in the same harsh and drawling tone. 'Listen, and thou shalt hear what hath brought me hither, and wherefore I, a man of peace even as thou art, have girt my sword unto me.'

It seemed to me rather as if he had girt himself unto his sword, a jest made of old time by the learned Tully, and doubtless by many others after him and before. But I was silent, and Master Eldad enlightened me further.

'When the Man of Blood was smitten before Israel,' he said, by which I presently knew that he spake of the battle of Naseby, 'that son of Belial, thy cousin, fled from the battle and came to Marsham. And finding his castle swept and garnished, he entered in with forty other devils worse than himself, and a woman worse than the forty—'

But here I broke in with a question.

'A woman!' said I; 'but what of the Countess?'

His face worked, and he winked with his eyes, and for the first time doffed his hat.

'The Lady of Deeping had been ailing for long,' he answered, and I noted that he spake of her without Scripture. 'A week ago she died, no man of us knows how.'

'God rest her soul!' I said, not weighing my words.

'It is a Popish prayer,' he answered, frowning, 'but I could wellnigh say "Amen" to it. Yea, and much more, God avenge her death on the wicked!'

'What mean you, man?' I cried, for his whole face lowered with sudden wrath and hatred. But at my question his brow was blank again.

'Nay, I know nothing,' he muttered. 'Yet, if two kites be alone with a dove, it needs no seer, Master Leyton, to know that which will be, or that which hath been. And this woman of the son of Belial, this Jezebel, this Delilah—'

'Aye, what of her?' I broke in, for he had called the roll of all the ill women in the Bible.

'She may well be a witch and poisoner,' he said, 'being from the land of all abominations, where the Scarlet Woman sitteth on the seven hills.'

'An Italian,' I guessed, and he bowed his head. ' 'Tis an

ill story, but how can I better it by going thither with you, Master Eldad?'

'Thus canst thou help us, Hubert Leyton. When thy cousin the Earl came to Deeping Hold in the sea-marshes, he strengthened himself there with forty desperate swearing drunken villains of his troop, and mounted cannon on the walls, and gave out that he would hold for the King, though Noll himself were to come. And straightway he sent to us at Marsham, bidding us bring corn and sheep and cattle, ale and cider, butter and cheese and eggs, also bacon and hams great store, to victual the castle for siege. And we, being distressed, besought his good lady to intercede for us, the which she did; but after her dying he was as one beside himself, and vowed he would take by force all that seemed good to him, nor would he listen to us. So I said to the others, "Lo, we are in a strait, and we are but a feeble folk and cannot contend with men of war; let us therefore seek one of his own kindred to plead for us, for he is such a son of Belial that a man cannot speak to him." And all they said that the counsel was good, and bade me go. Now, therefore, arise, and come with me, for we have far to go, and the man hath said that if we bring him not all that his soul desireth by the seventh day, he will burn our houses upon us with fire.'

I knew that the threat was no idle one; the ways of the German wars were well known to us, and my Lord of Deeping had learnt his warfare there, and was like to outstrip his schoolmasters. Yet the business liked me not, for I knew my cousin to be one that feared not God, neither regarded man, and his own life was little to him, and another's less than nought. Yet was he, as I knew, proud of his name and his heritage, to both of which was I now heir as the next in blood, though neither have I taken, for what reason this story will show. Therefore I sat still, communing with myself, and Master Pentry sat also with his great eyes fixed on somewhat beyond me. But after a while, seeing that I was yet in two minds, he rose up and took the great Bible from a desk by the window, and cast it down before me with a clap like a musket-shot.

'Open the Book, Hubert Leyton,' he said; 'and the Lord shall show thee what thou shalt do.'

I have ever thought but little of this divination out of the Scriptures, after the manner of the heathen and their uses with Virgil, though indeed there be many very apt prophecies cited from both, as with the late King Charles. But Master Eldad moved me, I could not say wherefore, and at his speech I opened the Book at a venture and my sight lighted on the ninth verse of the first chapter of the Book of Joshua, so that the man and I read together:

'Have I not commanded thee? Be strong and of a good courage; be not afraid, neither be thou dismayed . . .' etc.

'That is for thee,' said Master Eldad, sharply; 'now read what shall be for me.' With that, he flung over the heavy leaves, and his eyes and mine fell on a verse in the Lamentations of Jeremiah:

'They have cut off my life in the dungeon, and cast a stone upon me. Waters flowed over mine head; then I said, I am cut off.'

I started at that, and looked back over my shoulder at the man; but he was smiling, though grimly, and his eyes were set far away.

'Thus it is ever with me, when I seek an oracle out of the Book,' he said. 'I know what shall happen to me, and yet I go; wilt thou then turn back?'

I put my hand in his, that felt hard and dry like parchment, and said, 'Master Pentry, I will go with thee.'

CHAPTER II

I WOULD have had Master Eldad to stay that night in my house, but he would not, saying that we should return but one day before the week's grace granted by the Earl was ended, and that my cousin would show no mercy, nor would his troopers. So after dinner, I laid up in my mails a suit richer than I was wont to wear, that I might not seem too much the poor scholar in my kinsman's house, of which I was heir, and like to be owner some day; also I took my laced shirts and other matters, Eldad watching me with a sour smile, and muttering I know not what about 'the changeable suits of apparel and the mantles', so that I told him that I cared as little for such vanities as himself, but I would not appear as a sloven to my cousin, or even to the Italian woman. Master Pentry bowed his head, as his way was, and said no more, till presently they led up our horses; but his was sore tired with the journey, being little better than a cart-horse, if the truth were told. Therefore I had out for him the horse my serving-man rode, a strong beast, but slower than mine, and so we departed. I wore an Italian rapier of a new fashion, slender and light in the blade, and apt for tricks of swordmanship; for I had been at some pains to study fence at Cambridge, to clear my wits from over-much reading. Master Pentry had the sword of Goliath of Gath, and a great pistol. But we met with no call to use our weapons, these parts, as I said, being remote from the war; so making what speed we could, not to weary out our horses, we lay at country inns on our way, three nights, and on the morning of the fourth day we were near Marsham.

Now up till then Master Eldad spake little, and that for

the more part Scripture; and when I asked him of the Earl and the Italian woman, he could tell me nought more than I knew already, save that my cousin looked older, and his face fiercer than heretofore, as was like enough. The strange woman Master Pentry had never seen, but those who had met her reported her as of no great bigness or beauty, which made him the more believe her to be a witch. Only concerning my cousin the dead Countess he spake freely, telling me of her good deeds in the village, and how, while her lord was at the wars, she had spent her days in prayer and pious works, with scarce another by her but Mistress Rosamund Fanshawe, her kinswoman. I asked him of this lady, and whether she yet dwelt in the castle. He told me, Aye, and that she was young, and well enough, and kind to most, but, he feared, of a carnal, worldly and unbelieving heart; the which I took to mean that she laughed once or twice and sang snatches of songs to cheer the Countess, and soon wearied of Master Pentry's expounding of doctrine.

Little more than this did I draw from my companion, till we came, about three hours after dawn, to a hill, not steep, but very long, up the which we let our horses pace to breathe them, for our road had lain upward for miles. When we came to the top, Master Eldad touched his beast with the spur. I did the like, and we rode forward swiftly till we passed through a fringe of low trees and bushes that had long stood out as a jagged black edge against the blue sky. Then he drew rein and turned to me, saying, 'Look now!'

And well he might bid me to look, for a fairer prospect had I never seen, nor yet a stranger. Under us the grassy hill fell away steeply, with the white road crossing to and fro like a riband laced across a maid's gown. Then came slopes of cornland golden with harvest, green meadows and fair orchards, with high roofs of thatch peering up among the trees, and deep small dells cut through the hillsides, with little brooks at the bottom, and a church with a square tower, which, Master Eldad told me, was the parish church of Marsham, now without a parson since the death of the last vicar, the Earl of Deeping having other work to do than appointing priests.

So far, the prospect, though fair enough on a morning of sunshine, was such as, thank God, a man could still see on many roads of our England, where even civil war had not roused up Croats or Pandours to burn and plunder foe and friend. But now came in the strangeness of that country-side. Through the plain below us, as we hung on the hillside, was thrust what seemed a grey leafless tree, like an oak smitten with lightning. Then, as I looked again, I saw that the trunk of the tree was a river, flowing at the bottom of a grey cleft, and the branches were winding creeks, now empty, but to be full at high tide. Casting my eyes outward yet further, I beheld a waste of grey sea-marsh, seamed and scarred with darker channels, and patched with green wherever a knoll gave foothold to the coarse grass. Further still, all was grey, the channels grew wider, and a thin mist hung over the salt flats, that seemed to melt away into the distance like a wizard's vision; and I could note nothing clearly, save that on the very edge of the world, as it were, I caught the dazzle of the open sea.

Methought that there was something fearsome in the look of the place, with the grey salt desert lying at the edge of the fair meadows and fields, and reaching up its inlets like the arms of some fabled Hydra or monster of the sea. The strong sun, and the merry wind that sang through the bushes, made that grey waste but seem the more gloomy, even as the sunlight doth when it rests on a thundercloud labouring up across a summer sky. But from these fancies I was called by Master Eldad's voice at my shoulder.

'See'st thou, Hubert Leyton,' he said in his harsh slow tones, 'the house of the son of Belial?' And he pointed a lean forefinger out towards the part where the mist hung thickest over the marsh. For a moment I saw nothing; but presently, as the wind shifted, I caught the sun winking on a weathercock, like a sudden golden flame out of rolling smoke; and with this to guide me, I made out a belfry turret, and then a broad round tower at the end of a blur of shadow in the mist, and lastly a gabled hall and a huddle of buildings along one side of the shadow. All round it were grey steaming wastes of wet marsh, and seams of dull water, and the glare of the mist wearied my eyes.

'This must be Deeping Hold,' I said, turning to Master Pentry. 'How does it keep its place in this shifting sand and shale?'

'Because thy forefathers,' he answered with a grim smile, 'though no great readers of Scripture, were wise enough to build their house on a rock, after the first had been swallowed up. Deeping Hold stands on a rock in the marsh. There is but one other space of sure ground, and that is beyond the castle, where I point my finger.'

At first, following his guidance again, I saw nothing, but as my eyes grew used to the shimmer of the mist, I noted a low sharp point of dark rock, with what seemed the ruins of some rude building hanging to its side, at a mile, as I judged, from Deeping Hold. Wondering what dwelling could have been on so narrow a foothold, I asked Master Eldad of it.

'The old women of these parts say that this was the house of some Popish saint or eremite of ancient time,' he answered, sneering. 'And they will tell you that when an Earl of Deeping, being rebuked by the holy man for ill-living, slew him and brake down his monkish cell, a judgment came on him, and he and his were swallowed of some fabled Leviathan monster. Lo, there was Deeping Hold aforetime, they say.'

He swept his arm around and pointed again to a spot where a corner of wall, as it were the horn of a tower, clung to the edge of a steep above the marsh; and below was a clean sheer fall of rock, as if some immeasurable tooth had bitten a great morsel out of the hill. Then came the heaped boulders of a landslip, half hidden by weeds and bushes, and then a grey slope of shale; and a little way seaward one of the broader creeks at the river mouth ran up near the shore. The channel was well-nigh dry now, but strange of shape; for in the midst of it was a black spot, of some twenty yards across, as far as I could judge of its bigness, and the grey mud around it was like a steep funnel.

'Aye,' said my companion, as he saw that my eyes rested on the ruin and the space below it; 'that black spot they call the Hole, and fable that it hath no bottom, and that down there the Leviathan sleeps with the old Earl and his castle in his belly, till it be time for him to swallow another. But these be old wives' fables. We have wasted over-much time in gazing and babbling. Come!'

I shook my reins, and together we clattered down the steep road, but warily. Yet in spite of his scorn, my mind was full of his story and of the ancient rhyme that jumped so with its purport. And at each turn of the road, when we caught the slowly narrowing view of the shore, and the marsh, I lingered awhile to carry my eyes to the Hole, that lay black and ominous under that shred of the old castle. This I could do easily, for I was much the better mounted, and ever overtook Master Eldad before the next bend of the way. Lastly, a ridge overgrown with brambles took the Hole from my sight, and for that morning I saw it no more, nor, to speak the truth, did I think of it again, for this was to be no holiday time for me. We were got to the foot of the hill now, and rode through a deep lane with brambles bristling up the sides, the blackberries now red, and great foxgloves lingering here and there, and nothing to see but the green banks and the blue sky above, till the earth seemed a peaceful and happy place. Here Master Eldad turned to me as we rode boot to boot for the narrowness of the way, and spake, his harsh voice, so near to my ears, jarring me strangely.

'I must needs gather together the men of the village, Hubert Leyton, that they may meet thee and take counsel what is to be done. If thou wilt rest at mine own house, there is near by a place that we have built for coming together, and there we may meet to-day.'

I had gathered from Master Pentry that he had appointed himself as a minister or preacher to the men of Marsham, and that they had built for themselves what men style a conventicle, not caring to use the parish church, though now left vacant. For himself, he had exercised, so he told me, the calling of a tailor; but thinking it unfit for a messenger of the Gospel to serve man's carnal vanities, he lived, poorly enough, of the gifts his flock made shift to spare him, and the produce of his garden. So I looked for no banquet with him, and could

but hope, frugal scholar as I was, that some farmer might
be moved to mend my host's cheer.

'From yonder corner,' said Master Eldad, as we climbed
out of the hollow lane, 'I will show thee my house and the
tabernacle hard by'; and as he spake, we came to a turn
from which the village showed near at hand, clustered
round the church. I halted and looked thither, and
methought all was strangely still, without crow of cock or
low of cattle, as is the wont of villages. Nor did men seem
to be stirring about the place, nor maids singing, and a
cold fear fell on me that we had come too late. As I
shivered with that dread, Master Pentry, who had been
peering under his hand for the sunlight, called out sharply
and strangely at my elbow.

'It is gone! It is gone!' he cried. 'Hasten! hasten!' and so
put spurs to his horse and pushed on towards the village. I
followed, marvelling what he might have seen so to
distract him, for he rode like a madman, tossing his arms
and raving. But I saw full soon. Skirting the silent village,
he came, and I with him, on a space where I could see
there had been two buildings, of the stone of those parts,
grey or iron-brown in colour. But the foundations alone
were left, or not even these; for in one place a scorched
hollow showed where a wall had been, and the stones and
roof-beams, charred thatch and shards of tiles were
scattered over the earth like scraps of broken meat thrown
for fowls to peck at. Master Eldad threw himself from his
horse and grovelled on the ground within the foundations
of what I judged to have been his conventicle. I lighted
down also, wondering what had wrought this ruin; but on
looking closer at the stones, I smelt a sharp savour that
told me well enough the villainy that had been done. Here
had been gunpowder at work, and none but my
worshipful cousin had laid it. I am no knight-errant
greedy of adventure and thirsting for danger; and I will
own that my first thought was of what welcome I was like
to find from my kinsman when I should go to him as an
ambassador of peace. The careless cruelty that could
waste two barrels of good powder to lay low a couple of
poor hovels, that a truss of straw and a flint and steel had

destroyed as easily, would not grudge a drachm or two to send a ball through my head. But I shook off the thought and went to Master Pentry, who had come partly to himself, and was muttering some of the verses wherein David curses wicked men, the which I have ever relished least of the Psalms.

'Come, Master Eldad,' I said, taking him by the arm and raising him, so that he stood staring before him; ' 'tis a devilish deed, but you shall have your cottage again; aye, and your meetinghouse, if I pledge mine for it. God grant that they have done no worse harm. Let us to the village to see.'

'What worse could they do?' he asked. 'The house of the Lord is broken down and burnt with fire . . .' – and so rambled off into cursing again.

'Why, there be human temples of the Lord also,' I answered, drawing him towards the horses, 'that these villains may have shattered or defiled. Come and save them, if there be yet time.'

My words seemed to mean but little to Master Eldad; and indeed it was a sore blow, and one that might well have dazed him: moreover, I have seen more than once that a man eaten up with the zeal of religion is wont to think but little of the earthly good of others. Still, he roused himself and got on his beast, and I doing the like, we rode together into the hamlet of Marsham. There we drew rein before the little inn, the 'Apple Tree', whose sign hung out bravely, but with black holes through half its apples. The door was barred against us, and we knocked in vain with our hands and the pommels of our swords. Lastly, Master Eldad lifted up his voice, hearing, as I conceive, some sound within.

'John Saunders, John Saunders!' he shouted, 'how long wilt thou leave thy minister outside the door? Come and let us in; there is none here but Eldad Pentry and a friend.'

Methought that if John Saunders were above ground, that summons should bring him; for Master Eldad's voice was not one to be forgotten nor disregarded. And in truth, I heard a stirring within, and after a while, the bars were undone and the bolts withdrawn, and John Saunders, the innkeeper, stood in the doorway. He was a fat man, and had been ruddy of face and jovial as a heathen Bacchus; but some mighty terror had left him pale, with his great cheeks hanging like bags. He started when he saw my horse and clothes, as if afraid that I was some enemy; but Master Eldad lighted down and took him by the shoulder.

'Speak, thou coward!' he said, roughly enough. 'What has happened?'

John Saunders began a rambling story, that I could make but little of; and ever as Master Pentry broke in with some swift question, the innkeeper lost the thread of his tale, and was fain to go back to the beginning again, so that I despaired of learning aught of him. But as he maundered on, I heard a hinge creak across the way, and saw a red head peer out, and then a body follow it. Next, a woman's white face showed in the dark patch of a broken windowpane, and one by one the villagers came out, but timidly, like a cat that has been chased into a hole by a dog, and will hardly venture out for her milk.

Soon Master Eldad and I were in the midst of a ring of pale faces; and on learning from my companion who I was and for what come, they took courage to tell us all that had befallen them, but brokenly, dwelling on small matters, and going over the story again and again, as is the way of country folk and such as have commonly but little to speak of, and much desire to speak. It seemed that the Earl of Deeping, after that he had set the people of Marsham a day to provision his castle, sent some of his men to spy out what was being done to that end; and these fellows, coming to the 'Apple Tree' and paying for liquor, and talking civilly enough (for they were skilful knaves), drew out of the tapster all concerning Master Pentry's journey. Now my cousin the Earl, not hearing that Master Eldad had gone to seek me (nor, had he heard it, would he have believed it), fell into a great and devilish rage (as I learned afterwards, and could even then guess), thinking that the man he hated most of all was gone to fetch the soldiers of the Parliament; and perhaps Master Pentry had done so, were there any such within call. Therefore, without giving any warning to the villagers, or seeking to find out whether they were privy to their minister's plan, the Earl came up the river a little before high tide with thirty men, being his whole garrison but a few, in three flat barges and a skiff, and set his troopers carrying off corn and flour, butter and cheese, eggs and bacon and hams from the houses; Saunders they robbed of his whole provision of ale and cider. Next they fell to catching and chasing the fowls and geese, and driving cattle and sheep and swine down to the barges. The men of the village were afield, save the innkeeper, who dared not say a word, the blacksmith, and an old man or two, who could do naught but curse the robbers, and be laughed at. Of the women, most fled from the place; but the maid at the inn, a wanton jade and fond of talking with soldiers, went with the villains of her own foolish freewill; and the blacksmith's daughter, a well-favoured lass, striving to save her geese from them, two of them took her also to the barges, and her father, making after them, and striking one with a hammer, was beaten down with the butt of a musket and lay speechless for an hour.

So, having taken what they would, and beat in the bottoms of the boats that none might follow, these robbers rowed out with the tide to Deeping Hold; but first the Earl himself went up to Master Eldad's cottage and conventicle, with two of his men that were most with him, each bearing a barrel of powder. In a little while they went back laughing, and as they were at the barges, there came two great thunderclaps, one on the other, and a rocking of the ground, and a great flame and branching pillar of smoke. That sound and sight brought the villagers back in hot haste; and indeed, some of them were already warned by the fleeing women. But as they came on the hills above, they could see the flash of arms on the black barges dropping down with the tide through the grey maze of channel and quicksand that none knew like the men of Deeping Hold.

Since that time, now two days gone, the Marsham men had kept their doors bolted, and their women, and what of their cattle was left, hidden away when the tide rose, lest the Earl's troopers should harry them again; but nought more had been seen of them. So much we learned from the village men and women, with what tears and curses I need not now write.

CHAPTER III

OF MY VOYAGE TO DEEPING HOLD

WHEN the tale of the robbery was told, and an ill tale it was, it behoved us to see what was yet to be done. But first, it being now close on noon, and little fear of the Deeping men till the tide was half risen, Master Eldad and myself must put up our horses, and eat and drink. The villagers had lost much of their stores of victual, but some was overlooked by the plunderers, or hidden hastily by the women when they saw the boats, so that we ate well enough for folk who did but seek to be fed, while our beasts had room and to spare in the cattle sheds. Then we gathered together again in the churchyard, which was higher than the rest of the place, and showed a clear gap through the trees down to the river and the easiest landing-place. Also a watch was set on the church tower, to give us the greater safety, and so we stood and talked together.

Master Pentry, as was his wont, spake first, and with much Scripture, strangely wrested from the true meaning at times. His counsel was to keep no terms of truce with the son of Belial, and to cut him off root and branch with all his house; nor, indeed, did I wonder at his wrath and thirst for vengeance, but I saw not how the thing was to be done. For arms we had none, save his sword and mine, and his pistol; and the rest would be fain to use their pitchforks and scythes without beating them into swords and spears, for the blacksmith was no armourer. Nor (having read something of wars) could I put faith in his prophecy that the Lord would deliver them into our hands. For the Lord has been known to let the worse cause win the field, as was shown by the changing fortunes of our own Civil War, or even more of the war in

Germany, in which either side triumphed in turn, and at last both sank into a baffled peace. Something of this I said to the men, being asked for my counsel next to Master Eldad, who had not waited for the asking; and it was thought good that we should try the course of peaceful treaty before we took up arms. For though our case was well-nigh desperate as against the Earl's ruffians, yet was theirs little better when a Parliament ship of war or troop of horse found time to search them out, nor could they look for aught but hanging as thieves and outlaws, making pretence of the state of war for their private plundering, to whom all generals have with reason shown scant mercy.

So, when I had spoken, and none cared to say further, it was agreed, none disputing save Master Pentry and the blacksmith, that an ambassador should be sent to the Earl under flag of truce, to offer him safe conduct out of the country for himself and his men, and safe keeping for his castle and household stuff, saving only payment for the destruction of Master Pentry's house and conventicle. But, should he reject the terms, we were to declare our purpose of seeking aid from the Lord General Cromwell, whom I knew well, and who had showed me a singular friendship.

Now this last matter was known to my cousin, for he had heard of the letter whereof I spake before, and would therefore know that if I stirred in the quarrel, there was the more likelihood of the Lord General taking it up; also (though I knew it not then) the Earl had in one of his raids plundered some of the General's baggage, and slain a servant of his after a beastly and barbarous manner.

For the choice of our ambassador there was no disputing, seeing that all, without exception, laid the office on me; nor could I well refuse, as having been the first mover of such a course. For indeed I knew that to none other than one of his own quality would my cousin so much as give ear, being of an unmeasured pride and arrogance; nor would any low-born envoy escape a bullet, though he had a hundred white flags. Therefore it behoved me to take the post of honour, none coveting it, and myself least of all.

First, then, I wrote a letter to the Lord General

Cromwell, setting forth the ill deeds of the Earl of Deeping, and beseeching him by the friendship he had for me, and the wrath he bore against murder and oppression, to send a troop swiftly to Marsham, and root out that nest of robbers. This letter I gave to Master Eldad, charging him, if I were kept prisoner or slain, to write on the foot of the letter what had happened to me, and send the whole by a sure messenger on my horse to the nearest post of the Parliament army. So Master Pentry took the writing and duly did with it as I charged him; though (as will appear) I might have spared my pains to secure my life or revenge my death, for all was otherwise ordered.

This being done, there was naught remaining but to repair to Deeping Hold, and there see my cousin. For that I must wait till the high tide was past, and go out with the ebb by boat. Though there was a way across the marshes at low tide to a landing near the castle, yet was the path winding, slippery, and beset with quicksands, where any man not knowing the places as well as the face of his nearest of kin might well be mired and lost; nor could even the skilful be over sure, for it was the nature of those sands to change with a great tide or heavy storm. But in a boat I could scarce come to much harm, being used to handle oars, and strong to swim; for in those parts the sea was like to prove less treacherous than the land.

So we came down to the river together, and found an old boat belonging to one of the men, that the Earl's troopers had overlooked, since it lay in a little creek among the willows. It was small and scarce seaworthy, but we made shift to caulk the seams. Hither they brought my mails, and a staff with a white kerchief tied to it for a flag of truce, and laid them in the boat with the oars, and as all was ready, being now past noon, the tide came in. It was a strange sight to see, for the spot where we were might have been leagues from any coast, as it seemed to me looking down the little creek into the steep trench of grey shale, with the swift river gliding dumbly at the bottom. There was no great wave such as is seen in the Severn river, but a wide hiss and whispering rustle from the marshes, that grew louder and nearer, and then a little wave, grey with mud and crested with thick yellow foam, wrestling up against the current, with others following it, crowding on each other's backs like children at a show, till it passed us; and when I looked round, the river-bed was filling with the dense water, till the grey broken slopes were hidden, and the ripples were leaping at the green rim.

We waited still, till the tide slackened in its flow, and the ridges of yellow foam and lines of slime ceased to strive onwards and caught in the reeds and grasses, and then began to hang on the slopes of the creeks. The time had come, and I stepped into the boat, and the Marsham men pushed it out into the brimming creek. Then, ere I launched out into the ebb, one man after another gave me blessing or warning, the women weeping loudly, and Master Eldad gripped my hand, and standing on the bank, put off his hat and spake earnestly, praying that my journey might be for the glory of God, and the saving of the oppressed. 'And fear not thou, Hubert Leyton,' he added, resting his strange eyes on me, 'for it hath been revealed to me that thy life shall be given to thee for a prey. Launch out into the deep, and follow the main channel till thou come to the place of the beacon; then shalt thou go by the left hand under the shore.'

But here arose a clamour of voices, shrill with fear. 'Not that way!' cried one. 'That channel leads to the Hole.'

'No man goes thither!' cried a woman; 'know you not the story?' Master Eldad shook his hair disdainfully, and looked on them as if he were a very Goliath among the pygmies.

'Heed not old wives' fables!' he said. 'Go in the fear of the Lord, and thou shalt tread on the lion and the adder; the young lion and the dragon shalt thou trample under feet!' – and with that he leant on the pole that he held, and sent the boat out into the river, where the ebb and the current together were swirling down with petty whirlpools of grey thick water and coiling streaks of foam. I set the oars on the tholes and steered the head of the boat down stream; and what with looking over my shoulder to keep in mid-channel, I saw but little of the village folk, and heard only a babble of voices, with here and there some frightened speech of 'the Hole', and again 'the Hole', and Master Eldad harshly rebuking his flock out of the Scriptures.

The stream and the ebb-tide together bore me swiftly down with small labour, save to steer with a stroke or two of either oar when the channel wound. I could see little but the green banks, now edged with a widening riband of wet grey, for the tide had fallen somewhat. It was not long till I glanced over my right shoulder, and saw, standing up from a heap of stones, a stone pillar with a great iron basket half eaten away by the salt winds, and it came into my mind that this must be the beacon whereof Master Pentry spoke. Turning my face to the bow, I saw that the main stream made a sharp elbow on the right hand, but a wide channel went to the left, near the shore, which there ceased, and out beyond was the green and grey tangle of the marsh. This, then, must be the way that my friend had bidden me take, to save a great bend of the main river on my way to Deeping Hold; and somewhere in that channel, too, must be the black deep that the Marsham men feared as 'the Hole'. Something of their fear made a coldness in my blood, for I could not but remember the strange rhyme in the old book; but for all that I turned the boat's head into the broad channel as I passed the basket of the beacon, that looked like the blackened rotting skeleton of some strange beast. The ebb ran but slowly over the shallows, and I pulled at the heavy oars with the sun hot on my face. But the brisk wind that I felt now and again mightily refreshed me.

Little by little the current grew feebler and died away, the wind dropped, and the sun felt warmer than before, so that I was fain to pause and wipe my brow; and at the moment I was aware of a strange smell in the air, as of some dead thing washed up by the sea, cold, foul, salt, and sickening. I looked round me on the water, and saw no such floating carcase such as I thought to see; the channel whereon I floated was dark and strangely still. I cast my eyes up shorewards. There was a band of grey shale, and then a heap of boulders, like the ruin of a cliff, and up against the blue sky a broken horn, as it were, that I knew to be the sole fragment of the old castle; and all at once it came upon me that I must be verily rowing across 'the Hole'. With something of fear, and something of eagerness, I stood up in the boat and looked down over the sides. There was nought to frighten a man, save the evil odour; and this seemed to rise from a certain grey glistering slime, whereof streaks and patches lay on the thick water, or coiled lazily towards the side, and now and then a bubble rose and hung long ere it burst. To one so near the water as I was, the blackness of the Hole did not so much appear as from the height above; but even there I could see that it made a round of some eighteen yards across, as I judged. I was now as near as might be to the middle of this strange place, which I thought, from the slime, to be above the mouth of some pit of bitumen, such as we read of in the story of Sodom and Gomorrah. I looked down, therefore, drawing back my body to trim the boat, and bending my head over the side, till my face was near to the water, which in that spot had no slime, and was clear, and black with depth alone. My sight seemed to travel down into the unfathomable abyss, till light failed; nor did I wonder that the villagers fabled that pit to be bottomless. Yet as I gazed into the darkness, as into a great black agate stone, I seemed to see somewhat moving, and looking more narrowly, it was as if a grey tendril, coloured like the slime, were winding upwards through the blackness and rising swiftly towards me, so that I cried out sharply, as a man will when he wakes from a dream, and at the cry the grey thread wavered and seemed to coil downward out of sight.

I said to myself that this was but a streak of the slime of the pit, and that it behoved me to do my errand to Deeping Hold, where I was like to find more danger than in the Hole. Nevertheless, I could well conceive how the dread of that place came to be fixed in the minds of the men of Marsham; for to speak truth, the smell of the slime and the writhing of that grey riband in the black water made me more afraid than I would own to myself. So, bending to the oars, I rowed on, and in a stroke or two was clear of the dark circle of the Hole, and among the dancing ripples of the channel; and with small labour I won through to the main river, the which, as Master Pentry had told me, made a great elbow and met me further out in the marshes. Now I felt the current again, and was swept swiftly on between wet banks of sand or shale, and growing islands covered with grey grass, or dotted with harsh samphire. In no long time I caught the winking flash of the weathercock on the castle belfry, and then a glimpse of a roof and the hard lines of the walls. Methought that if I could see, I might also be seen, so I took the white flag that had been given me, and set it upright in the bows of the boat.

Nor was I too soon; for as I came round another bend of the stream, I could see a good piece of the wall, and the flash of a steel cap and of a pike; then two or three men came together, and one ran along the wall and vanished, as if gone to tell of my coming. I could see well enough now, for as I had little but guidance to do with my oars, I sat looking to the bow and rowing forward, like a boatman of Venice. So the ebb and the stream swept me on, and the castle loomed larger, till I came out into a wide inlet, and Deeping Hold lay before me on its island, clear of the marshes.

The castle was of no great size, being pent in by the water. The island of rock on which it stood was some fifty yards across, and shaped like a pear, with a mound at the point, on which was reared the keep. The turreted wall was low, and followed the shore of the islet, which rose to four feet or so above spring-tide mark, and the wall added twice as much again. In places the rock had been scarped down to the water; in others a slope of grey shale was heaped against the wall. The whole castle was of one colour with the rock whereon it stood, grey, with stains as of rust; and indeed it was built of the stone hewn out from its cellars and storehouses. At the broader end of the islet stood the mansion, built in the days of Queen Bess, when men feared no more for private enemies; and this house was fair enough, though not great, with oriel windows and a belfry turret with gilded vane. So much I saw well, as the ebb-tide and the river stream bore me down slower in that wide water. The sentinels were watching me curiously, screening their eyes from the dazzle of the sun on the ripples, until I came within short musket-shot; then one of them, levelling his piece, but more in sport than in threat, gave the challenge:

'Who goes there?'

'A friend,' I answered, and came on towards the wall, though I saw no place to land.

'Are you for the King or for the rebels?' he called again.

'For neither!' I answered shortly, somewhat scornful to find such military punctilio in a den of robbers. 'I come for peace, as this sign shows.'

'So you sail under the ensign of the dishclout?' he said, grinning evilly; 'and who and what may your worship be?'

My gorge rose at this insolence from a common sworder, and I spoke, I fear, too sharply for my peaceful mission.

'When thou hast done with playing at soldiers,' I answered him, 'thou canst tell thy master the Earl of Deeping that his cousin Hubert Leyton would speak with him.' The knave on sentry growled somewhat in his red beard, but another by him laughed.

'He touched thee there, man,' he said; 'what need to ask watchwords of one man, and none other within miles of him?' Then he spake to me, who was now close under the wall, fending my boat off from the rock with an oar.

'If you row round the keep, sir, you shall see the gate and the harbour, and I will conduct you to the Earl,' he said, civilly enough, and went down from the wall. The other walked to and fro again, cursing at all canting Roundheads and foreign traitors, and I set to my oars again, for the water was too deep for poling. As I came round the keep, a little window, made of an old loophole cut wider for convenience, was opened, and a head put forth, so that I, looking up unthinking at the sound of the casement, met the eyes of one looking down. It was a maiden, as I deemed, of some twenty years of age, with dark hair curling loosely round the head, as the way then was, and grey eyes (but I minded me not of their colour then) set in dusky circles of weariness and grief. The splash of my oars had startled her, even as the creak of her window caught my ear; so for a brief space we paused, each looking on the other, till I remembered the reverence due to a woman, and put off my hat, waving it, as the fashion of courtesy then was, but, I doubt not, awkwardly enough. She bowed her head, flushing suddenly, and then withdrew it, and I to my oars again, wondering who this might be. But of a truth I had not far to seek, for Master Eldad had spoken of but two women at the Hold, nor could this be one of the stolen village girls; further, he had talked of the Italian as little and not well-favoured. This that I had seen, therefore, must needs be Mistress Rosamund Fanshawe, kinswoman to the dead Lady of Deeping.

So I came round the keep, and saw a little harbour made out of a jutting ridge of the rock, helped with masonry, wherein were moored the barges and boats of the garrison, commanded by two culverins and the loopholes of a barbican tower, through which a way went under a portcullis. Here were more men, some busy caulking the barges, some fishing from the rocks, some idling, in buff jerkins and breeches, and some with boots and hose off. As they gaped on me, methought that I had never seen so many villainous faces in all my life before. For here you had not plain honest English wickedness alone, but the flower of the rascals of all nations. Here was a shock-headed Irish kerne, wrangling over a catch of fish with a burly German, all of his face beard that was not scars, and each flaying the English he strove to speak. A Spaniard, his lip as it were skewered on a stiff moustache, was gambling with a dark Italian, whose hand ever strayed towards his dagger-hilt when the dice ran against him. But each paused in his work or his sport to stare on me and break some jest on my face and garb, nor did any so much as offer to help me tie up my boat. I made shift to do that for myself, and without seeming to mark the knaves, took my mails and went boldly up to the gate, that stood open, and within it was the man who had bidden me row round thither.

He was tall, and had been goodly of face, but for a scar

that seamed his cheek; his hair was yellow, though his skin was tanned with sun and wind; also his dress was rich, though somewhat worn, and not tawdry as that of some of the men. He wore a long sword at his side. He spoke well, yet with a foreign twang, so that I judged him to be some Norlander, belike a Swede, and so it proved; for, indeed, even as many English and Scots served under the great Gustavus, so not a few Swede and German soldiers of fortune came to help the one or the other of our English factions.

'Welcome to Deeping Hold, Mr. Leyton,' he said, with a soldierly courtesy that sat well on him. 'New faces are not so many here that we can be churlish to any friend. May I name my own unworthiness to you as Eric Guldenstierna, once of Upsala, shortened by my men to Gulston of Nowhere, a cornet of my lord's troop, or what Noll Cromwell has left of it.'

I gave the man my hand in greeting before I thought, so frank and manly was his bearing. Then I had nigh plucked it back, for there came on me the remembrance that surely this Swede must have helped my cousin in all his late wickedness, and in how much more and worse before, God knows. Yet I mastered myself, and took my hand back no quicker than need. If mine eyes told aught of the struggle, I know not; Gulston, as I will call him for brevity, laughed shortly, not as one that is merry, and turning, led the way across the castle court, part paven, part living rock. At the door of the house, that stood open, a black Moor in a gay dress was sunning himself, who rolled white eye-balls on us, and loitered within to announce my coming to the Earl.

CHAPTER IV

OF MY EMBASSY, AND HOW I FARED

THE black was long in doing his errand, as is ever the way
of his kind when they see not the whip, and to pass the
time I fell to talk with the Swede. The man was
well-spoken, and had seen much; and his soldierly
bluntness sat well on him. Yet it was a marvel to me that in
all he said there was a scorn of what simple men think
goodness. He had no praise for any of his own side save
for Prince Rupert, and would laugh even at him as a fool,
that cared not to knock his wavering weakling of a master
on the head and take his crown.

'As for your war here,' he said, laughing in his yellow
beard, 'you English know not the meaning of the word.
Noll Cromwell can order his battle indifferent well, and
his saints have swords as long as their sermons; yet where
will you find a real soldier in either host, save one or two
of us from Germany or the Low Countries? Here you shall
march the Ironsides through a village, and not a cottage
burnt or a maiden missing.'

I answered him that such was surely but the proper
Swedish discipline of the wars, as it had been taught by
the great Gustavus himself.

'O aye,' said Gulston, mocking. 'When we began, we
were a sort of Roundheads ourselves, save that we sang
not our psalms through our noses. But the King was a fool,
though a good fighter, and out of the battle old
Wallenstein was my man. Had he not gone star-gazing on
to the pikes of some rascal Irish, he had been our leader.
Wallenstein would never hang a man for a burgher's
purse or a matter of a girl or two. You have no soldiers
here, nor will have.'

I answered him, I fear with some sharpness, that if we

had no such warriors among us, we grew indifferent good hemp to reward them with according to their deeds; but he laughed again.

'I forgot,' said he, 'that men say you are yourself half a Roundhead – and not the half that fights. But I would have you keep your sermons to yourself when you shall meet the Earl and the Signora. To speak the name of hemp might be of ill omen to your worshipful and peaceful self.'

I let his taunt pass, for I was curious to hear more of the Italian woman; so I asked him if he knew aught of her.

The Swede shook his locks and laughed sourly. 'Nay, what I know is soon told,' said he, 'and what I know not, but think, is never told at all. Fiammetta Bardi is her name, and her father was hurt to death by a crowd in Ratisbon. Some called him a wizard, some a scholar. All I know is that my Lord and a few of us took her from the chance of a bath in the Danube, and she has companied with my Lord since then.'

'Know you aught,' I asked him, seeing that it were waste of breath to inquire further of the Signora, 'of the end of my cousin the Countess?'

'I know she is dead, for she is buried by now,' said Gulston; 'and I know she is buried, for that I was by; all else the Earl and the Signora can tell you, if they will. And now will I take my leave, for I see the raven messenger returning.'

With that he put his hand to his hat in a mocking salute, and strode off across the court, and the black, coming forth with somewhat more of alacrity in his manner, took up my mails and asked me to follow him within.

The house, as I have said, was not great, for the builders of it had lacked both space and wealth for that. From the entrance I came into the dining-hall, now empty, where the afternoon sun sent a dusty shaft of light through the western window to the great table. The upper lights of the window were set with painted glass bearing the Earl's shield, argent with a castle gules, that I knew well, though I have not borne it. Two great chairs of carven oak stood on the dais at the head of the table, as was the wont, for the lord and lady of the castle; and as the light fell on the seats I had a strange vision of a shadow in a trailing robe, with a stain of red on the breast, so that I started and cried out sharply, 'What is that?' and with the word I knew myself for a fool, for it was but the play of the light on the wood, and the colour of the red castle in the shield. But when I looked at the black, he was shaking like a man with the ague, and his face went grey with fear.

'Massa see her?' he said, stumbling in his speech; 'Pompey see her many times!' and with that he fell to crossing himself and gabbling of jargon that I judged to be prayers mingled with heathen charms, as is the manner of Africans; nor would he leave his mumbling, though I told him to lead me to his master, but took me to a door at the further side of the hall and pointed to it with a shaking finger; and then, as I signed that he could go, he crept from the place, still muttering his spells.

This vision, though I knew it was but a shadow, joined with the fear of the black, had shaken me strangely, so that I lingered for a while at the door. But the memory of the poor men of Marsham came back to me, and the words of Master Pentry's oracle, and I knocked and was bidden enter.

The room I came into was but small, and somewhat dark, being wainscoted with oak gone black with age. An oaken table stood across the midst, and beyond it a fire was burning bright on the hearth. Two only were in the room, a man and a woman, with their faces turned to the fire; but as I came in, the man rose to his feet, and I knew my cousin the Earl, though changed. He was broader and greater than when I had last seen him, and his hair had touches of grey; but that which chiefly moved me was the wildness of his eyes, which shifted restlessly from my face to the corners of the room, and changed without seeming cause from a flaming wrath to a desperate deadness. Yet he came forward and gave me his hand with a show of friendliness.

'Welcome, cousin!' he said in a voice that would fain sound hearty, 'welcome, whatever brings you here. Let me present to you the Signorina Bardi, a scholar like yourself, and able to discourse of such curious learning as Cambridge men delight in.'

As he spoke, the woman had risen from her seat, and

while my cousin ran on, I had leisure to cast my eyes over her, which I did with the more exactness that I was curious to know the truth of what Master Pentry had told me. As he had said, she was of no great bigness or beauty, under the middle stature, and lean, but supple and well made, as the close robe she wore gave opportunity to judge. Her face had no colour, and her eyes were narrow and near together, and slanted somewhat after the fashion of Easterns. Their hue was greenish, as I came to know afterwards, but she seemed loth to open them to the full. Her hair, which was rolled in a gilded net, was great and red, as in the paintings of Venice, but more dusky, whereby I judged that the colour was of nature, and not of art as travellers say it is with the fair Venetians, who were born dark. She was clad in some dark red stuff, with embroideries about the neck, and wore no ornaments that I could see, save for one great red jewel hanging at her neck, that glowed like a hot coal in the flicker of the fire.

I made shift to bow, and salute her with a word or two in the Italian, at which her lips, that were thin and dusky red, parted in a smile, and her face changed, so that for a flash she seemed beautiful. Her voice also was most musical, with a singing sound in it that made even her English (that she spoke very well) a delight to hear; and in listening to her I almost forgot what she was, and what it was most like she had done or procured to be done. My cousin the Earl looked on us with a snarling smile.

'So she hath bewitched you too, Cousin Hubert?' he said, and I felt my cheek grow hot as he laughed. 'Never blush, man, to follow the head of your house, but sit and empty your budget of news. Stay, it is ill telling a dry story,' and he took up a flagon of Spanish wine that stood at his side, and filled me a Venice goblet to the brim, and another for himself, after the Signora had put it away with a dainty wave of her long fingers. 'Give a health to the King, man, Puritan or none, and drown your conscience!'

'There is no need,' I said; 'to the King, and may he be happily and righteously restored to his due honours!' With that I drank off the wine, which was somewhat too hot for my palate.

'A right Trimmer's toast!' he mocked; 'I will give you a better. To the King, and damn him for a fool that cannot lead and will not follow!'

'Nay,' I said, smiling (for I would not anger him at the start); 'I think I am the better Cavalier of the two, so far as wishing goes, though I own you have fought well for the King.'

'Aye,' he answered, showing his teeth like a dog, 'none has fought better, though I say it; and what is my reward? To sit here in mine own house like a badger in his hole, waiting for the men to smoke me out and the dogs to worry me.' At that the woman sighed with a sort of scornful weariness, and he turned on her. 'And there will be dogs enough to worry the cat that houses in the badger's den, *cara mia!*'

Now I saw my way to speak of my mission, and thrust into the opening.

'There is no need,' I said quickly, 'to think of such a base and wretched ending to the Signora's wisdom and your valour. You are more a lion than a badger, cousin; and I am the mouse in the fable, that may get you out of the snare.'

He gave a great rough laugh. 'A right mousy plan, I doubt not,' he cried; 'some cowardly pettifogging device of feigned submission to save my neck if I will sing psalms through my nose. Here's damnation to all facing-both-ways knaves,' and he filled his goblet and drank it off.

I am by nature and breeding of a quiet temper, and slow to take offence; but at this rudeness my gorge rose.

'My lord,' I said, as calmly as I might, 'if you know what I would say before I speak it, it is plain that I am not needed here, and I have but to accept your own similitude, and leave the badger to the dogs, that may find argument more suited to his comprehension.'

He chafed at that, and felt for his sword that lay sheathed on the table; and I stood warily, cursing his madness and my own folly, yet ready to draw if need were. But as my cousin's eyes roved round the room, they met those of the Italian woman, and I wondered; for it was like the change in a demon that knows the sorceress, or a wild beast that sees the tamer. The fire sank in his eyes, and his hand fell from the sword-hilt; and when he spoke again, he was like a child that has been chidden for rudeness.

'I crave your pardon, cousin,' he said; 'I am a luckless man, and trifles anger me. Drink with me in token that you forgive me, and will be my kinsman and good friend again,' and he filled my goblet and his own with the Spanish wine.

I touched my lips to my glass and set it down, while he emptied his at a draught. 'Come, man, no heeltaps!' he said; 'or I shall think that you bear me malice.'

'No malice,' I answered, 'but your wine is too noble for my poor pate, and I would fain have all my wits to serve you.'

'Well, well,' he said with a wry smile, 'I will drink for you,' and was about to fill again, when the Signora looked at him again with her eyes narrowing. 'No more, *Filippo mio*,' she said in her soft singing voice, and he pushed the flagon away sullenly, and bade me say on.

'Thus is the case,' I began, weighing my words ere I spake; 'here are you with a company of desperate men, cooped up in a corner of the marshes, till it shall please the Parliament men to think of you and root you out. A hard task they will assuredly find it, but the end is certain; also, the more pain you give them, the less mercy will they show. Nor am I sure that your soldiers might not give you up to save their necks, when they saw the game lost; and so should you perish meanly by mere treason. Now, if you will but send away your fellows to their countries, or to the King's forces that yet hold out, you may stay here quiet, no man troubling you; or if you would not seem to submit, you may go forth to the Low Countries, where is no lack of honourable employment for a soldier, and look to find all as you left it here, when the King is restored.'

Thus far my cousin had heard me patiently, only drumming with his fingers on the table; but now he broke in with an oath.

' 'Sblood!' he cried; 'I gave my word to bide quiet, but this is too much! What shall happen to my house and my lands while I starve in the Low Countries? Find all as I left it, forsooth! Nay, I shall find more than I left by half-a-dozen little crop-eared puppies born to the fat Roundhead that will own Deeping Hold!'

'Not so,' I made haste to answer; 'for I will be your bailiff, cousin, and keep your house. Your tenants have sworn to hold what covenant I make with you, and I will send you your rents by a sure messenger. A trimmer I may be, but no man can say that I broke my given word, or wronged any of a farthing. And if the Parliament should take the house away from me, as I see not how they can, I will make shift to send you somewhat from mine own estate.'

He looked at me with narrow eyes. 'And to what end is all this policy?' he asked, sneering. 'Wherefore not stay safe at home and lick Noll Cromwell's jack-boots for my succession?'

'Cousin Philip,' I answered him, though it was hard to speak quietly, 'the poor men of Marsham have trusted their cause to me, and I am bound to them in honour; also, I am of your blood and kin, nor do I greatly care for the Earl of Deeping to be knocked on the head in a paltry scuffle for a common robber. Nay, though I have no cause to love the Signora Bardi, it would irk me to have so much learning and wit sunk in the mire or smothered in the smoke.'

This I said to get the Italian on my side; and assuredly I lied not, for the barbarous superstition of witchcraft had brought many poor women to burning, that were less witchlike than the Signora.

I could see that this moved her, for her eyes widened, though nothing else stirred in her face; and subtle as she was, I could read her mind by my own. The vision of the stake and the faggots, that were then no vain terror, daunted even her high spirit; and on the other side were the fortunes and chances of camp and city, of war and policy and plotting, and the power to be the spider in the web of Machiavel.

So for a space we both abode with our eyes fixed on the Earl, that sat in his great chair, with one leg thrown over the other, drumming with his hand on the table, and his eyes roving round the room. Methought he too could see the wisdom of my counsel, for his brows were frowning with thought rather than anger; and indeed, he was one of good parts, save when his wildness came upon him. At last he leant forward, and his lips parted as if to speak, and I looked for him to assent to the plan I had opened to him; and so it had been, but that in the very beginning of his speech his mood changed. His wandering eyes were fixed in a stare upon the window, and his face was frozen with fear. What he would have said died in his throat, and there came only mutterings that I could not well catch; but I seemed to hear him say – 'Why dost thou come again? I did not slay thee! Hast thou no pity in death?' and other such murmurs, as if he spake to one that we could not see. Thinking that my cousin was smitten with some madness, I turned towards the window, that bore the arms of the house painted on the glass; and for a moment there seemed to me to be the similitude of a white figure with a stain of red on the breast, as the evening sunshine fell on the glass. Yet I knew it to be but the white and red colour of the window, as in the dining-hall before; nor could I think why so common a trick of the eyes should have moved my cousin, that sat bowed in his chair and muttering. Presently he straightened himself, and his eyes were set and staring, yet not now at the window, nor in fear, but rather desperate, as of a fiend more than of a man. I looked for him to fly out on me in a fury, but he did but strike sharply on a silver bell that stood by his chair, and the sound tinkled out through the empty hall beyond. Nor did he say a word more till the black Pompey entered; to whom he spake low in his ear for a minute, and dismissed him, and we sat silent as before.

Lastly, I could endure no longer. 'Cousin Philip,' I said, 'I have told you all my plan; may I not have an answer before I return to those who sent me?'

He made as if he heard nought, and I was about to ask him a second time, when there fell on my ear the heavy sullen strokes of an axe or hammer on wood, at which the Earl stirred in his chair, and an evil smile came on his lips.

'You have your answer, cousin,' he said, sneeringly. 'I have bidden to break up your barge of state for kindling, that we shall lack here in the autumn mists. I am minded to abide here till what ending may be; and seeing that there is no great affluence of company here, I would fain have your learned society to help pass the time. I will not lightly part with mine only kinsman; and though the cheer may be rough, yet a soldier's welcome is yours.'

He had spoken smoothly, yet with a jeering tone; and it angered me that all my policy had but ended in making myself a prisoner to my cousin and his ruffians. I sprang up, facing him, and my hand fell to my rapier hilt; but he never moved.

'Methinks,' I said, 'you have forgotten that I am an ambassador under flag of truce, and that I must give an answer to those that sent me hither.'

'O aye!' he sneered; 'I had forgotten that you were the herald of His Majesty Eldad Pentry, by the grace of Beelzebub, botcher and gospeller to the rats of Marsham. Be content, most punctilious cousin; in not many days I look to deliver them mine answer in person, and you shall be by to hear it. Till then, and perchance afterwards, you must be my guest; and as it grows near to supper-time, I will bid Pompey show you your chamber.' At that he smote the bell again.

Now, I could not leave him thus, but began again entreating him to consider my counsels, and save himself and others from a certain doom; and growing desperate as he answered not, I turned to the Italian woman, and besought her to join her voice to mine, thinking that she had more power over him than I. But at her first words his eyes flamed with anger, and he smote his fist on the table.

'What, you too?' he said, after the manner of Caesar to Brutus in his dying. 'You must needs have me forth to the Low Countries, that you may leave me for a richer gallant or poison me for hire. No, by God! I have you both here, and you shall end with me. Not another word, cousin, or I call Gulston and a file of musketeers to set you up against the wall and shoot you for a Roundhead traitor. If I am a broken man, yet am I still Lord of Deeping Hold, and with men to do my bidding, and store of powder to send all aloft when the end comes. And for you – Fiammetta . . .'

With that he turned and looked on her, and she at him; and her eyes were as those of a snake that bewitches a bird to flutter into its mouth. Yet did not my cousin's eyes droop before hers as beforetime, but shone strangely as a beast's in the night, till I saw her tremble as though with sickness of fear, and turn away her gaze.

Thereupon Pompey came in, and the Earl, smiling at the Signora, bade him take up my mails and lead me to my room.

Nor would I yet yield, but as I strove to speak, the woman beckoned sharply to me to go; and I saw that she was wiser than I, for of a surety my cousin had a devil.

So, with a salutation that he marked not, I followed the black through the empty hall, where the light had now climbed above the chairs, and across the court; and in my head, despite my anger at the treason of my cousin, and my scorn of myself that I had been so easily entrapped, there was ringing the old rhyme of the little book:

'When the Lord of Deeping Hold
To the Fiend his soul hath sold—'

and I fell to thinking of the black deeps of the Hole, and the grey riband winding up from it.

CHAPTER V

OF MISTRESS ROSAMUND FANSHAWE,
AND MY TALK WITH HER

I FOLLOWED the loitering Pompey across the court with steps as slow as his own; for I was sick at heart for the ill-success of mine embassy, and meseemed that through my own folly had ill matters been aroused. Yet, cast about as I would, might I not think how I should have spoken better or done more wisely. Of a surety my plan was such as had commended itself to mine enemy the Italian woman, whose fortune was bound up with my cousin's; nor had he seemed to take it so amiss till he had the vision of somewhat in the window, and thenceforward had he been as one possessed of a devil. Yet could I not feel angered with him as I might with a stranger; for it was borne in on me that there was a doom on the man to be froward and perverse, even as with Pharaoh, whose heart God hardened that he should not let Israel go: and it was given to me as though spoken in mine ear that I should wait and behold the end, nor meddle further with the unsearchable judgments of God.

Wherefore, when I had reached my lodging, which was a little chamber in the thickness of the keep, barred like a dungeon, but furnished well enough for one that cared not for soft living, I changed my apparel without help from the black, and looked from my window over the marshes, whence the sea had now fallen, though it was ever lapping at the foot of the tower. The sun was setting over the hills, big and blood red, and the pools of the marshes seemed red as though a great slaughter had been made there; but overhead there hung one great cloud, shapen like a monster that stretched long trailing arms and claws across the sky. The evening was strangely still,

213

but for the measured pace of the sentinel, and the clank of his pike as he struck it on the stone in turning at the end of his walk. So, wearying of mine own thoughts, I came down the worn stone stairs to the court, thinking that I might speak with some one, though it was not yet supper-time.

I judged that the men of the garrison were at their supper, for the gates were shut fast, and none stirring in sight but a sentry on either wall; also two windows in a room of the castle were litten, and the sound of loud talk and rough laughter came from them, and once a woman's scream, but of no great terror; so I lingered, thinking that perchance I might light upon the Swede or other of the better sort: nor was I mistaken, for presently Gulston strode out from his quarters, that were hard by the guard-room, and greeted me civilly enough. So we stood talking of the wars in Germany, which I judged safer to speak of than our own troubles, and I was able to entertain him with stratagems of war out of Livy and Polybius, and found him apt and eager to hear, though unlearned; and by his voice could I tell (for his face was not read in the shadow) that his contempt for me was shaken, when he heard a mere scholar discourse of the ordering of battles with knowledge; yet I was careful always to defer to him as to one of great experience, and indeed, his speeches were often most pertinent. We were upon the proper mingling of pikemen and musketeers, when I heard steps descending the stairs of the keep, and broke off to see who came; but the Swede only laughed.

' 'Tis but the spectre at the feast,' he said, sneering in his wonted manner; 'the white ghost in the black gown, that sits and never speaks or drinks, and hardly eats – I mean my dead Lady's cousin, Mistress Rosamund. Perchance she may throw you a word, for that you are not one of us. For myself, I grow weary of the sight of her, though full often we see her not for days together. I will present you.'

But it so fell that I needed not his offices, which, I doubt me, would have been of little value with Mistress Fanshawe. For as she lingered in the door of the keep, seeing us in her way, a drunken ruffian of the garrison, who had been sent with supper for the sentinel, came reeling out across the court, and whether taking her for a handmaid or being too far gone in liquor to distinguish, caught her by the arm and strove to kiss her. She broke away from him, crying out with disgust rather than fear; but he followed, and since the drink was rather in his head than his legs, he penned her into a corner of the wall, and was at point to renew his attack, when I ran to help her, and taking the knave by the collar swung him aside. With that he vented an oath or two, and drawing his sword, made for me; so that Mistress Rosamund cried out for help, but the Swede stood still mocking.

I drew also, not knowing the man's skill of fence; but when I saw the roughness of his sword-play, I scorned to do him hurt, but practised a trick that I had often served my unskilled fellows at Cambridge. Keeping him off for a few passes, I made as if to leave my breast open to him, and as he ran at me, I turned his blade under my left arm and locked the hilt to my side, while with my right hand I offered my point at his throat, so that he let go his sword and reeled backwards, and his heel catching on a stone, he fell and so lay gaping. With that, Gulston laughed with somewhat of surprise, and came to me.

'Rarely done, my Puritan!' said he, 'of a truth, for a man of peace, you have some skill of your weapon. But why did you not kill the knave?' And then, kicking the man, that was yet dazed with drink and his fall – 'Giles Warner, get up and give me your sword!' – which when the man did, Gulston smote him on the jaw with the hilt, so that his teeth rattled, and bade him sheathe his sword and never draw it again till he had learned to know hilt from point, and so drove him to the guard-room, leaving me alone with Mistress Fanshawe.

She had stood still in the shadow after that first cry, seeing (as she has told me since) that the man had no skill to hurt me; but now she came to me and laid her hand on my arm, and the first words she spake startled me, for that they were as an echo of the Swede's question. 'Why did you not kill him?' she asked me, sharply, and I could see her eyes shine in the shadow of her hood.

The fierceness of her speech moved me strangely, for her voice was low and sweet, and it seemed not fitting that she should speak with such anger and loathing; insomuch that I stammered, and could find no words to answer her at the first. Nor did I know by what passion and grief she had been so far wrought. Yet I made shift to say somewhat of the man being but a poor drunken sot, nor deserving of death for his rudeness; but she brake in as one distraught – 'Oh!' she said, 'were I but a man, I would kill them all, all! But you are cold like the rest of them, and have no heart to revenge a wrong!'

'Perchance,' I said, for I would not have her think me better than I was, 'I had found it in my heart to hurt him, had it not been all too easy' – and, indeed, I had but needed to oppose my point that he might run on it. 'Yet am I glad that I spared him even out of scorn,' I went on; 'for it is ill shedding of blood for a private quarrel, when there is One that hath said, "Vengeance is Mine, I will repay".'

'Oh!' said she, brokenly, as though a sob came in the midst of her utterance; 'you men are all the same, and when a woman is wronged you can but counsel patience, and fling her a jest or a text as small money to a beggar. I am sick of you all.'

Now this her flying out on me, though assuredly it was but the working of a brain overwrought, did strangely move me, for that I felt that if the one other in the castle – I will not say righteous, but not altogether given over to iniquity – were so to misconceive me, it boded the worse for both of us. Moreover, I knew not wherefore, it cut me to the heart to have her deem me cold and careless of her need, and the more so that I knew myself to be of a timid spirit. But as I was at point to speak to her in mine excuse, the great bell from the turret rang the hour for supper, and gathering her skirts around her, she made haste to the hall, nor could I have speech with her till we were within.

My cousin, the Earl, was already leading the Signora to the high seat at his side, where the Countess was wont to sit, and where the sunshine had made a phantom with blood on the breast but a few hours agone. Mistress

Rosamund looked on her as she sat, and methought there was bitter scorn in the eyes of both. But the Earl greeted me friendly, and presented me to Mistress Fanshawe as an honoured guest, and would have me sit next to the Signora, and made much of me as a kinsman and scholar; nor was the Italian lacking in flatteries and pleasing speeches, whereof she had skill beyond the wont of women, so that it was hard for me to remember that I was kept prisoner in breach of faith; also I could see Mistress Rosamund's eyes dwell on me in scorn as she feigned to listen to the blunt speech of Gulston, that was our only companion at table. Our cheer was but rough, savouring of camp cookery, though served well enough by Pompey and two of the troopers that were the Earl's servants; and only the Swede, that was used to hardness of life, ate and drank heartily, as who might look to go long before he found another meal. There was good Gascony and Canary, though my cousin favoured the Spanish wine, and drank more than he ate; while the Signora took a morsel daintily, and Mistress Rosamund but feigned to eat. The which my cousin marked, and suddenly, with a friendliness that was perchance not all feigned (for his moods ever shifted like the wind), reached over and filled her glass with Gascony, bidding her drink to the health of her cousin and his, and his honoured guest: also he called Pompey to give me wine that I might answer the pledge, and drank to me himself, and bade the Signora drink also. But she excused herself daintily, saying that it was for my kinswoman to pledge first before her, that was but a poor stranger. For the Swede, he had not waited for nice considerations of precedence, but had nodded to me and drained his goblet in one motion so soon as he saw the Earl's lips at his glass.

I could see that Mistress Rosamund was angered by the feigned humility and reverence of the Italian, and her face flushed from its paleness to see the eyes of all fixed on her. Yet she mastered her anger, and raised the brimming glass with a hand that shook not.

'Methinks, Mistress Bardi,' she said, coldly, and dropping her words slowly as a physician might some bitter medicine, 'that forasmuch as you have been so far able to overcome your humbleness as to sit in my dead cousin's seat, you might well venture to drink before my lord's poor kinswoman. Yet will I not cross you in this, but will even pledge my good cousin according to his desert, and wish him many more such merry evenings as this.'

The Earl frowned and muttered somewhat, and the Italian looked at Mistress Fanshawe with narrow eyes; but Gulston brake into one of his great laughs, and called to us to clink glasses after the German custom. At that Mistress Rosamund rose, smiling, and stretched forth her goblet across the table, and I likewise; but whether by mishap or of a purpose, I know not, nor would she ever tell me afterwards, she shocked her glass on mine with such strength that both were broken, and the red wine made a great splash like blood on the cloth.

At this the Earl sprang up, with his face writhen like a madman's, and brake out in a flood of oaths and foul words that I would not chronicle, had I even heard them clearly, and snatched at a knife that lay before him as though to slay Mistress Rosamund, that stood still with the neck of the goblet in her hand, and blenched not; yet before I could speak or go to her help, the Signora caught his wrist and signed to Gulston, that came to his side and took the knife from him; and indeed he was already in part come to himself, and ashamed that he had been so overcome with passion at his own board – perchance more ashamed than for many a worse fault, for he was hospitable after the wont of spendthrifts.

'Cousin Hubert, and you, mistress,' he said, looking on the girl, that answered nothing, 'I am much distempered of late, and a little thing moves me. I crave your pardon if I leave you suddenly' – and at that his eyes fell on the stained cloth again, and a strong shuddering took him, so that the Swede was fain to help him from his seat to the door, and the Signora followed, while Mistress Fanshawe and I looked on each other across the table and stirred not. Pompey, as one that had seen such matters before, took up my lord's flagon of Spanish wine and followed to his apartment, and the two serving-men began to clear the board, for supper had been ended. Nor did Mistress Rosamund move or speak till they had swept off the shreds of glass and taken away the cloth, leaving us alone.

'I am sorry for you, cousin,' she said; 'for though my lord is to-night wrought above his wont, yet may you look for other such passions in days to come. It were better that I should keep my chamber, for I have the unhappiness to anger him. Pity it is that Mistress Bardi was quicker than you, or he had rid the company of my presence for good, and left you to talk of Italian poets to her, that takes great delight in your learning.'

The scorn wherewith she said this cut me to the heart, and I stretched out my hands towards her passionately. 'In the name of God,' I cried, 'why must you so misconceive me? I am as a man thrown into a dark dungeon, where I hear snakes stirring and hissing, and know not which way to step. God knows that I sought not this journey, but came with a single mind to help the poor men of Marsham in their need, and now have I worsened all matters by my meddling; yet I meant well. I am a prisoner here like yourself, cousin, and no flatterer or parasite, nor willing to humour the wicked for hire; yet what am I to do? I must speak them fair, or I shall endanger not mine own life merely, but other and better lives; coward I may be, but I am a true man, and if you shall think basely of me, I must go mad.'

Now while I spake, at the first she looked coldly on me as before, and her scorn made me the more vehement beyond my wont, till I was nigh weeping; but as I despaired of winning her belief, I could see her face change wonderfully, and her eyes grow greater and darker, and her breast heave as though she were stifling for lack of air. I looked for her to break into weeping, and so perchance it had been with any woman less noble to endure. Yet she did but stretch out both hands to me, that I took gladly in mine own.

'Cousin Hubert,' she said – and it pleased me that she had noted my name – 'forgive me that I doubted you. In this house of murder, where men mutter in corners, I know not friend from foe, and scarcely living soul from ghost or devil, and methought you were but another spy like the Swede.'

At that I beckoned to her to be silent, for the door of the Earl's apartment opened stealthily, and Gulston came out; and whether he had heard her latest words I know not, but when he saw he was observed, he came forward carelessly, humming a song, while Pompey drew the curtain behind him.

'What, still quarrelling?' he said, lightly; and indeed, for aught he saw, we might have been as well enemies as friends, for I doubt not that the disorder of my wits showed itself in my face.

Now at his speech it came into my mind that it were well to leave him in his error, if so he thought, for I judged him to be rather cunning than deep in his malice. So on the moment, I answered him according to his bent, deeming that he would not believe that a mere scholar would be subtle enough to feign.

'Indeed,' said I, 'I would not quarrel for a woman's temper, though it cost me a bumper of good Gascony. I was but telling Mistress Fanshawe that my lord had much excuse for his passion, and that it had moved me to anger even at Cambridge to see needless waste of good wine, that we might come to need sorely when the castle lay under siege—' – and other such stuff that I mind not, nor is it worth recounting, but it served my turn. At the first, Mistress Rosamund's face, that I could see dimly in the candle-light, and the Swede saw not, being behind her, grew hard and scornful that I should dare to chide her, and I feared that she might return to her ill opinion of me. But in no brief space her eyes lightened on me, and she smiled a little as though to show that she understood my policy. Then, speaking coldly as before, but with greater scornfulness, that I knew to be feigned, she bade me keep my ratings for college knaves, and mine excuses for those from whom I hoped for favours, and so flung out of the hall as one in a fury, leaving me with Gulston.

'Said I not true?' he asked me, fingering his yellow beard; ' 'Tis a very shrew to-night, though I marvel that she should have been so moved by you. Had we such a maid in camp in Germany, we should soon tame her, but my lord is over kind with women, and the wench has a touch of likeness to his dead lady, though I will vouch for her that she is no saint. You shall do well to shun Mistress Rosamund, if you would bear an unscratched face.' From which I guessed that the Swede had sought to pass the time with dalliance, after the fashion of his kind, and had met with the welcome that I could guess; nor did I love him the more for my thought.

'Nay,' I answered smoothly; 'I am not angered, but grieved to see one so young and goodly in so froward a mind, and I would seek to win her to a temper more submissive and womanly. Nor would I have you hurt her, even if she provoke you; for she is a hostage even as I myself, and hostages in a besieged place have been found to abate the eagerness of attack, and even to save the holders of them in extremity.'

He took my drift as I meant, and played moodily with his sword-hilt as we walked from the hall. 'Think you then,' he said, with something of anxiousness, 'that we shall be besieged here?'

'Unless the King's party recover beyond all likelihood,' I answered him; 'the Parliament generals will assuredly hear of us and send against us.'

'Against us!' he repeated. 'You are not of us, but rather of their faction, and have nought to fear.'

'Your pardon,' I said, laughing, 'I have never heard that a cannon-ball had any niceness in choosing where and whom it should strike, nor that hostages have grown fat when the garrison starved. Rather do I look to be eaten the first when provisions fail. Nor am I of the Roundheads, for that Cromwell himself has asked me to serve with him, and I would not. He would let me perish here, and show his friendship to me by devising new deaths for you and your men.'

'There is something in your words,' said Gulston, as he turned to the door of his quarters. 'I must speak with you again, but not now, for Pompey is yet at the hall door, and he is a spy for my lord on the Signora and the rest, and for the Signora on my lord and the rest, I know not which.

Give you good night!' and with that he was gone, and I to my lodging, well pleased that I had won some ground, and fondly hoping that I might yet save Mistress Rosamund and myself in spite of my cousin, and my cousin in spite of himself.

So I came to the door of the keep, where a cresset burned to light the stair, and was passing in when a voice called me softly from the shadow of the wall, and I knew it was Mistress Rosamund.

'We have but a moment, for the watch will be coming soon,' she whispered quickly. 'Did I not play the shrew well to your pedant, cousin? Have we put the Swede off the scent?'

I told her, Aye, so I thought, and that there were factions in the garrison, as it seemed, and hope of working some good; and then I asked her of how the Earl used her, and whether there were any way of escape from the castle.

So she said, hurriedly, and looking for the guard, that she was not ill-used, and had the girl to wait on her that was the blacksmith's daughter of Marsham, but that she went ever in fear of my lord and of the Signora, but rather of the woman, that dealt in witchcraft and perchance in poison also, and had assuredly wrought the death of the Countess through her own craft and the violence of the Earl. 'They told me,' she said, sobbing through her speech, 'that she died of a flux of blood, and indeed she was ailing long; but how she ended I saw not, yet if she were not murdered, why should my lord be taken with madness at the sight of spilt wine or a blood-red shadow on her chair? Cousin, if you take me not away from this house of evil, I shall go mad.'

'Alas!' I answered her; 'the boat I came in is cleft into kindlings by now, and we should be mired and lost were we to strive to swim to land; but I look to make a party among the garrison, or to find some one that for promise of money or life will help us to a boat. Other hope see I none, save in the hand of the Lord and our patience.'

'The hand of the Lord!' she said, rather in sadness than in mockery. 'Nay then, if we must wait till the heavens open and fire fall on the wicked, we may die first of old age. Preach not patience to me, that have seen the end of my cousin's piety and endurance.'

Now I was grieved to hear such rebellious words from her, and was minded to bring her to a better way of thought; but ere I could think of aught to say, I heard the clash of weapons and the tread of heavy feet across the court.

'The guard comes!' she whispered, 'and they must not see us together. Good night, cousin!' and catching at my hand, she dropped it again and fled up the stair silently, and I followed more slowly, feeling my way to my chamber.

When I had struck a light and looked around, I noted that the key was gone from my door, and there was no means of shutting it from within. Yet I remembered that there was little safety in a lock, when all the household save one might be counted enemies. So without more ado I made ready for bed, and before I had lain down, I heard the tramp of feet on the stair, and saw torches through the crack of the door, and then a key was set in the lock and turned, and I knew that I was a prisoner indeed till the morning. Yet I went to the window and opened it, to see if by chance there was any way out; but the bars were over close for a man to slip between, and though eaten by the sea-wind, they were great and strong and sealed fast into the wall. For a season I lingered, looking out at the night; but the stars were veiled by a mist, and a breeze was blowing cold from the land, till I shut the casement, for meseemed that I could smell the savour of the slime in the water of the Hole, though more like, it was some seaweed or dead fish cast up on the castle wall.

CHAPTER VI

OF THE END OF MASTER ELDAD PENTRY

I HAVE ever been an ill sleeper in beds that were strange to me, and my first night in Deeping Hold was but troubled, though of noise there was little save the wash of the water at the foot of the wall, and now and then the tread of the sentinel on the rampart. Yet could I not compose myself to rest but that a sound would set me thinking, while half asleep, that men came to murder me, and I would start awake and catch at my sword, that hung on the bed-head, before I knew that there was no cause for terror, for that my cousin had no need to deal stealthily if he had a mind to take my life. Also when at last I slept, the horror of a dream would come on me, so that I wakened crying out, yet could I not remember what had affrighted me.

Yet in the end I slept soundly, nor waked till the sun was well above the sea to eastward, and the morning was still and fair, and as I clad myself hastily, the world seemed goodly to dwell in. Also, when I tried the door of my chamber, it opened readily, and I came to the court, no man saying me nay. Men were going to and fro, bearing wood and water, or sallying forth to catch fish or shoot wild-fowl, and methought they seemed less ill-looking than yesterday; also, if they marked me at all, they made no jest on me, wherefore I judged that either the Earl had bidden them show me civility (and they feared him greatly), or the man I had foiled overnight had told a drunkard's tale of my skill at the sword. So I walked to and fro for a space in the court pleasantly enough, till Gulston, spying me there, came out and bade me to breakfast in the hall, where was none but our two selves and Pompey to serve us. We spake but little in earshot of the black, and when we had finished we came to the court again, and I would have sounded the Swede as to my plan for making treaty with the men of Marsham, but at the first word he winked at the hall door, where Pompey was sunning himself; and raising my eyes from the boy, I saw a curtain drawn and the Signora's face against the window, who, noting that she was seen, smiled on us and nodded her head.

I judged, therefore, that I might wait till a fitter season to confer with Gulston, if so be I could trust the man; and we spake of things indifferent, till he turned the talk on matters of fence, asking me of the Italian that was my master, and would have me show him some of the devices of the school with my sheathed rapier; the which I was fain to do, for that no suspicion should fall on us from the Italian. After I had shown a pass or twain, my cousin himself came out to us and greeted me kindly; and when he saw our play, nothing would serve him but that he should have out a pair of foils and try a bout of friendship with me, Gulston standing by for judge. The Earl's sword-play was well enough for a soldier, but showing more of strength than of art, and more reckless than the Swede's, who was ever cool and watchful; while my cousin grew easily heated, and would seek to beat down my foil and waste his strength on the air. But he was apt to learn, and took delight in the exercise, and I taught him a cunning parry and return or two; only the favourite thrust of my Italian master, that I had been at great pains to perfect myself in, I told not to the Earl, deeming it fit that I might have somewhat yet in store to defend myself when the Earl was possessed by his devil.

In no long time he tired of the game, for he was ever restless, and went off to his apartment, and I to mine, being somewhat heated, to rest, and perchance to catch a sight of Mistress Rosamund; but I saw her not till dinner-time, nor could we speak freely, being ever under the eye of my cousin and the Signora, or a servant of theirs. So I was fain to speak of the pictures and poetry of Italy, and then of the secrets of nature and the subtleties of alchemy, though in this I have rather curiosity than knowledge. And so the day wore on, and the Earl's

troopers came back with their fish and wild fowl, and
nought happened, nor was I one hair's breadth nearer my
aim. Only at supper-time we came to talk more freely, and
my Lord speaking of our play with the foils that morning,
and desiring me to do the like on the morrow, Mistress
Rosamund was pleased to make light of my skill when the
Earl praised it, the better to confirm him in his error that
his two cousins were at variance between themselves; and
she saying that it was but folly in me to teach another my
secrets of defence, I laughed, and answered that I had yet
a thrust or two that could save me at the pinch; and at the
word I looked up and caught the Signora's eyes fixed on
me strangely, as though she were revolving in her mind
some subtle device. Yet she said nought, and the evening
passed off with no quarrel, my cousin being merrier than
his wont. Also, when Mistress Fanshawe was gone to her
room, and Gulston was about some business of the
garrison, the Earl would have me in to play chess with the
Signora while he also was busy. Between the moves we
fell to talking, and she asked me of the Lord General
Cromwell and his friendship for me, and other questions
that I answered truly, or perchance with some over-rating
of the general's friendship for me; for indeed, in all his
after greatness, he found never occasion to remember my
name, which hurt my self-conceit, but was to my
advantage when King Charles, now reigning, was
restored to his father's throne. We played not long, for my
cousin, returning, said that he must rest early; so I went to
my room, and this night none locked the door on me, nor
were the garrison making their wonted noise, so that I
slept soon and soundly.

But about the first beginning of the dawn I awaked
suddenly, for my door was open, and half-a-dozen men
armed in breast and backpieces, with swords and
musketoons, were round my bed, who bade me rise and
come with them. Wondering much what this boded, I
arose and clad myself in my travelling suit, making what
speed I might by the light of the torch one of them bore.
When I asked them of the purpose of this haste, none
would say a word; only when I made to gird on my sword,

one of them clapped the mouth of his piece to my breast and bade me leave my rapier, the which I did, for it had been of no use to dispute with them. So I put on my cloak, for the air was chilly, and came down into the court in the midst of the men, and there saw the more part of the garrison gathered, and my cousin the Earl in buff-coat and cuirass ordering them.

The thought passed my mind that perchance he meant to fulfil his threat of shooting me for a traitor, though I knew not what fresh grudge he could bear me; and it was an ugly thought that I should presently be facing a row of ruffians with lighted matches. But my cousin's first words scattered my fears.

'Good morning, Cousin Hubert,' he cried to me. 'I must crave your pardon for breaking your beauty-sleep, but time and tide wait for no man, and we must catch the tide to go and deliver our answer to King Eldad the First of Marsham and his loving subjects; also you, being his ambassador, must be at the conference.'

Now when I knew his purpose, I began earnestly to remonstrate with him, but he cut short by bidding the men set me in the barge, so that I went out at the barbican rather than be roughly handled by his troopers.

In the grey twilight of the hour before the dawn I could mark the two barges swinging at the quay, and a man or two in each; and into one of these I stepped and sat in the stern, wrapping my cloak round me. The oars were ready set on the tholes, and at the fore-part of either barge were a barrel or two and a truss of straw, also a basket of food and bottles of liquor. In no long time out came the men, some two dozen of them, and took place in the barges, with no word spoken; and lastly Gulston and the Earl, whereof the first sat in the stern of the other barge, and my cousin leapt in last by me and bade push off, and presently we were out of the harbour, and the rising tide swept us landward under the wall of the keep.

I sought to speak to my cousin, but he answered not, except to bid me hold my tongue, for he needed his wits for steering; and indeed, it was no easy task to keep a heavy craft from the mud-banks and shallows; and the

Swede, that knew these waters less than his chief, grounded his barge more than once, though he soon got her off again. So with tide and oars we were not long in coming within hail of the shore, and I could see (for the light was growing fast) that we were making for the horn of the ruined castle that overhung the Hole.

Now at this some murmured, for a few of the troopers were of the country, and had heard of the story of that place from their mothers, and had told it to the others; but the Earl held on his way.

'Have you heard the old wives' fable of this place, cousin?' he said to me softly, as he set our course for the round black space of water.

'Surely I have,' I answered him; 'and a strange spot it is, and fit to put fear in men's hearts, as I can well say, for this way came I to the castle.'

'And saw you the monster?' he jeered.

'Nay,' I said; 'somewhat strange I saw, or thought I saw, like a grey snake winding up from the deeps, but I took no harm save an ill odour, like this' – for we were now in the midst of the Hole, and I could snuff the salt foul smell of the slime, but fainter, by reason of the cold.

My cousin answered me not, but cried out to the men in the boats to cease rowing, and set them to muffle their oars that they might not be heard. When this was done, the men were eager to push on, for the smell of the place and the terror of its blackness had daunted them. But before my lord gave the word, he spake in the ear of one of the men by him, who suddenly threw a belt round my arms and buckled them tightly to my side before I knew what he would do.

'Why is this, cousin?' I asked him, being angered at this indignity.

'To save your life, man,' he answered grimly; 'for fear you might be minded, though a man of peace, to strike on one side or the other, and so either meet with your end from a bullet or lose the favour of King Eldad for taking part with your own kin. Now, shall I muffle your mouth, or will you give me your word as a gentleman not to cry out or warn the Marsham men? But if you promise to me and break your word, I swear by my sword that I will fling you into this Hole with mine own hands.'

I bade him rather stop my mouth, for I would be no helper in his enterprise, even under a constrained promise; and he took off his scarf and tied it round my mouth so that I could not cry out. Then he gave the word to row on, but stealthily, and in a stroke or two we were out of the Hole, and making for the basket of the beacon that showed black against a grey cloud. So we came into the river and felt the tide, and were borne up towards the village. Yet was all my cousin's care vain, and Master Pentry was a warier man than he deemed; for as we came near to the village, the prow of the first barge struck on a rope stretched beneath the water, and dragged it some way, and forthwith a bell tolled from a tree by the bank. The Earl swore a great oath, and bade cut the rope, but it was too late.

'Curse on the crop-eared knaves!' he cried; 'they have taken a bell from the church and hung it in yonder tree to give the warning! Row on, men!' and with that he took the scarf from my mouth and bade me bellow my fill if it list.

'Were it not better to go back, seeing we are discovered?' I said.

'No!' he roared. 'A thousand times, no! Give way, men! Catch them before they have their doublets on!'

All thought of stealth was now cast aside, for after the bell we could hear dogs barking and men shouting in the village, and lights showing confusedly in the windows. Therefore the men bent to the oars as rowing a race, and we came speedily to the landing-place under the church. There they made the boats fast, and my cousin leapt out the first and led the one half of his men up to the village, Gulston fetching a compass round the houses to take in the rear any who fought; me they left in the barge, charging the men of the guard to keep me safely, but show me no discourtesy.

Now this command they obeyed, being of that country and holding our house in honour, and one of them proffered me a dram of Hollands, and held the bottle to my mouth; nor was I sorry to be warmed in that chilly dawn. Yet could I not rest, but gazed on the village to see what would hap; for it might be that some of the Parliament soldiers had come to these parts, and then might my cousin find more than he looked for. But it was soon plain to me that little fight, if any, was made, and indeed, as I heard after, Master Pentry's device served only to give the more part of his flock time to flee to the woods. When the Earl and his company ran up among the houses, shouting, the doors stood open, and neither men nor women within; and Gulston and his band, though they made haste to intercept the fliers, could but catch one old crippled woman, that they let go again. The Earl was (so Gulston said after to me) as one beside himself that his devices had failed, and would follow the Marsham men into their refuges; but the Swede withstood him, saying that they would lose the tide and have to stay half a day while the others raised the country on them, and overwhelmed them with numbers. Therefore he gave his word for plundering the place and coming back.

To this counsel the Earl must needs yield, for it was manifestly wise, and the men fell to plunder; but their harvest was small, since some of the cattle and sheep had been kept in the fields, and others had been driven into the woodland. Some bread and bacon they found, and the troops had sport with chasing of fowls; but there was little to reward any. Thereat the Earl fell again into a frenzy, and swore that they should pay for cheating him of his dues, and so took straw from the barns, and wood and pitch that his men had brought up from the barges, and to make an ill story short, fired every house in the place and so left it burning.

Now all this was reported to me, but the rest I saw. First a feather of blue smoke and another sprang out against the clear sky that was now growing of a yellow colour. Then the smoke grew thicker and blacker as the thatch caught, and flames leaped above the trees, and I heard the crackling of the rafters like a fight of musketry. And then came my cousin's men disorderly, by twos and threes, laughing and jesting and carrying their poor plunder.

The sight of their homes burning may well have moved

the Marsham men to madness, for the most of them had ventured back as they saw the troopers leaving the village, and doubtless they came among the houses as the flames broke forth. While the more cautious of them strove to quench the fire, the bolder thought rather of vengeance, and fell on the rear of the Swede's party that came last, with stones and scythes and pitchforks. At that the soldiers faced about, and with a shot or two kept off the villagers, that had but rude weapons; and thinking they had scared the countrymen, they came on carelessly to the boats.

But as they passed a close thicket by a hollow lane hard by the church, there arose a puff of smoke and the sound of a shot, and a man rolled over, clutching at the ground; and ere he lay still, men came running from the thicket and set furiously on the robbers, that were daunted by this sudden onslaught. Foremost of the party was a strange figure that was like an ancient warrior from his tomb, for he was clad all in mail of plate from head to foot, and wielded a great sword, and after him followed others with scythes and sickles; and before any order could be taken, they had slain one more of the Earl's men and wounded three, so that the rest gave back. Only Gulston, crying out on his troopers for cowards, snatched a musketoon from one of them and shot down a great fellow with a scythe as he fetched a blow at him, and made at the leader with his sword; but the blade glanced from the armour, and the other dealt him a blow that had been his end had he not worn an iron plate in his hat, and sent him to his knees half stunned; where he had been thrust through, but that my cousin, who had leapt ashore again at the sound of battle, struck up the sword and engaged the man in armour. For a time they stood striking and thrusting and parrying, unable to hurt each other, for that the Earl was the better swordsman and the other was armoured in proof; but in no long space the armoured man wearied of the weight of his harness and the labour of wielding his great sword, and my Lord, seeing this, put aside the blade and came within his guard and tripped and threw him, and the Marsham men, or such as were left, fled back into the lane.

My cousin bade bring the wounded and dead to the

barges, and bind the prisoner with ropes and carry him thither also; and when the valiant fighter was set in the boat where I was, they lifted the visor of his helmet, and I saw the face of none other than Master Eldad Pentry, flushed with fighting and sore spent, but without shadow of fear.

'Master Pentry,' I said, 'I grieve to see you thus when I have no power to help you.'

'Grieve not, Hubert Leyton,' he made shift to answer between his gasps; 'of a truth it was written before the foundation of the world that thus and no otherwise should I end, and I need not that any should say a word for me. Peril not thy life, for I have taken the sword, and I must perish by the sword.'

As he spoke thus, the Earl leapt into the stern of the barge where we were, and bade push off; then his eyes lightened as they fell on his enemy.

'By God!' he cried, 'we are well met, Master Eldad. I had not thought you could handle so long a needle as yonder sword; and where found you your iron doublet and hose? Stay – I have it – the knave hath stolen the armour of the third Earl, mine ancestor, from the vault of the church. Lo, mine own arms wrought on the breast-plate. Was there no meaner coat that would serve this dog of a ranting tailor?'

Master Pentry did but smile, and his fearlessness was a marvel even to me. 'Aye,' answered he, 'it is easy railing on a bound man, well-nigh as easy as to slay an ailing woman;' and at that word the Earl sprang up with his hand at his dagger, but sat again, as he saw that Master Eldad was nowise moved.

'I will not soil my steel with base blood,' he said, grinning on his prisoner. 'What say you, cousin, what death shall we choose for King Eldad? The axe is for men of gentle birth, like the Earl of Strafford and the Archbishop—'

'Aye,' said Master Pentry, 'and perchance for their master—' whereat a trooper smote him on the lips, but he did but laugh.

'Shall we hang him in the armour he has usurped?' went on the Earl. 'Or shall we roast the hog in armour till he crackles?' whereat Gulston assented with his great laugh, and so did the foreigners of the troop, but the Englishmen of the company murmured.

'Since you ask for my judgment, cousin,' said I, hoping against hope that if I saved not Master Eldad I might yet respite him for awhile, or at the least win him an honourable death, 'I have ever read that in a war of two states, such as this has become, though a civil rebellion in the beginning, it is the custom to spare the life of a prisoner taken in fair and open fight, and hold him for ransom or exchange by cartel, according to the law of nations.'

But at that my cousin cried out on me for a pedant, nor would Master Pentry himself accept my advocacy, for his fanatic doctrine was dearer to him than life.

'Nay, Hubert Leyton,' he said, turning in his bonds, 'between true men and traitors is no quarter given or asked, and thy kinsman is an open rebel to the Parliament of England; nor would I have spared him for thine intercession, if he sat bound as I now.'

The Earl laughed at that speech, and bade the men cease rowing, so that the barges drifted side by side; and looking round I saw that we were come again to the black circle of the Hole.

' 'Fore God, I like thy spirit, man,' he cried; 'tell me what death thou wouldst deal me if I were thy captive.'

Master Pentry looked around him, and marked the spot where we were, and his eyes were great and shining, as though he saw somewhat to us invisible.

'Methinks,' said he, in his harsh and jarring voice, 'the place itself might teach thee, Philip of Deeping. Here, if the story lie not, is the tomb of thine ancestor, to whose name and wickedness art thou heir, and I would but send thee to join him.'

'It is well spoken!' cried out my cousin, pulling at his beard; 'and so shall it be done to thee. Ho, two of you, take him up and fling him into the midst of the pool.'

But the twain that sat on either side of Master Pentry shrank back murmuring, not that they loved him or were unready to slay him, but that being of those parts, they

knew the ancient story of the Hole, and feared to awaken
the monster that dwelt therein; which terror they made
shift to stammer out, being pitiably divided between dread
of the Thing in the pool and of the wrath of their master.
Yet would he not listen, but signed to other two, who,
being ruffians from the German wars, and fearing neither
God nor man, made ready to take up the prisoner. But first
he craved leave to speak, the which was granted him
jeeringly, and he turned to me.

'Hubert Leyton,' said he earnestly, and as though there
were none by but us two, 'fear not for thyself, for it hath
been revealed to me that thy life shall be given thee for a
prey; nor seek to take vengeance for my death, seeing
that, as thou knowest, it was foredoomed from before the
beginning of the world. Surely vengeance shall be upon
the man of Belial, and that by no help of man. And for
thee, son of perdition, get thee back to thine harlot, and
make merry with her, for the time is short.'

But when Master Eldad spake of the Italian woman, the
Earl could endure no longer, and shut down the visor of
the ancient helmet, so that we saw the face of the man no
more; and thrusting me back (for bound as I was, I had
attempted to make in to aid Master Pentry), he gave the
word to the two troopers, that lifted the iron figure by the
shoulders and the feet, and swung it three times, and at
the last hurled it into the midst and darkest of the Hole,
with a great splash of the water, that fell on all in the boat,
and smelt salt and foul of the slime.

When the trouble of the waters was abated, I looked
eagerly over the side of the boat, for it was in my mind that
some strange manifestation might be shown to us. But
there was no sound or sight, nor indeed could we look for
any; for no man, though a strong swimmer and unbound,
could think to rise again in such a weight of armour. A
bubble or twain rose, and no more; so that at the last my
cousin bade loosen my bonds, and gave word to row
homewards, ere we lost the tide.

Now as the men set the oars ready, the pool, that was
still and black with immeasurable depth, grew troubled,
and it was as if a fountain of grey slime were breaking

upwards from the pit, with a great and evil smell, and lastly somewhat black like a man rose from the mid-most of the Hole, and sank again, and rose again higher, like a ball dancing on a fountain; so that Gulston, that was nearest, thrust at it with a boathook that he had caught up, and drew it to him, and we could see that it was of iron.

'As I love,' cried my cousin, 'it is the knave come back to us! Have him in, Eric, and let us see if he be yet alive.' So the Swede, helped by the two men that had cast Master Pentry in (for the others dared not lay a hand to the work) hauled in the thing, that was smeared with the grey slime. But when they raised the visor, the face was gone, and only empty blackness within; and looking into the hollow of the body-armour was there nothing but water and slime. So they cut the straps of the armour with their daggers, and opened the cuishes and greaves, and still was there nothing; till they came to the steel boots (for it was a full suit of plate), and in the right shoe was what had been a man's foot, but the ankle-bones gone, and the flesh shredded out like the claw of a lobster that a man has sucked for the meat. At that sight a great sickness and shuddering fell on us all, and my cousin fell back in his seat like a dead man; but I only, perchance because I had no part in that murder, had strength given me to spring forward and heave that loathsome heap of iron and slime and human flesh over the side into the water, that was now still again, and clear of the slime, and I cried out to the men the while to bend to their oars and escape from that accursed place.

But ere we could win clear of the Hole, for the men were weak with fear at the first, one of our wounded men, methinks Giles Warner, that had beset Mistress Rosamund before, and that had now been sore hurt with a scythe by the man that Gulston slew, sprang up in the barge, screaming out in terror like a beast, and with that the bandage round his thigh slipped, and his blood brake forth in a spout, and so he fell and died, no man marking him save I.

CHAPTER VII

OF OUR RETURNING, AND THE BURIAL
OF OUR DEAD

THE sight of that which had befallen left my cousin's crew,
and even himself, with little thought of what was to be
done, or will to do it; and indeed, it hath been often found
at such times, that men, otherwise bold and apt enough,
are as puppets, ready to work the bidding of any that has
kept his wits. So it was here; for the rough troopers that
were wont to scorn me for a scholar and half a
Roundhead, now bent to their oars as I bade them, and let
me steer them whither I would; till it came into my mind
that if I commanded them to set me ashore, they had no
power to say me nay. Yet would not I make the venture;
for what was there left for me to do on land? Master
Pentry was dead, and the smoke of Marsham village went
up great and black over the hill. The poor men whose
unlucky ambassador I had been had now suffered all the
ill that their tyrant could do to them, and there was none
left to help but Mistress Rosamund; and she to be helped
only by my continuing at Deeping Hold, whereas by my
escape should I advantage none but myself. Therefore I
made no delay, but set the boat's head right for the castle;
nor did I count myself any hero for so determining, for the
strange fulfilment of Master Eldad's prophecy concerning
himself had wrought me to a strong belief that his other
words would not fall to the ground, so that my life should
be given me for a prey.

In no long time, the chance of escape that I had forborne
to take was no longer mine; for the Swede, being
hardened to dangers, nor apt to be moved greatly by
aught that he could not see or handle, recovered his wits
speedily, and began to swear at his crew for a pack of

quaking cowards. At this my cousin stirred in his place, and shook himself like a dog coming out of water, as though to empty his ears of the curse that clung in them. Then, with no word spoken, he snatched the tiller from me, and so steered us homewards; and I, rising, bent over Giles Warner, that lay in a puddle of his own blood, strangely mingled with that slime. Yet was there nought to do, for the man was stone dead; so I made shift to close his eyes, that stared horribly at the sky, and then sat me down in the bows, that I might look back on the land, where the smoke of Marsham village yet went up in a cloud.

But when I cast my eyes shoreward, it seemed as though the smoke had spread abroad over half the heavens, till I knew that this was no smoke, but a storm-cloud drawing up over the land, the blacker for the morning sunshine around us; and as I yet looked, a crooked fork of lightning leapt out in a gap in the hills, and a mutter of thunder came to me.

The suddenness of the storm, and the strangeness of it in time of autumn, moved me to imaginations, and I came nigh to believe that here might be the vengeance of the Lord on murder and robbery. The men also, that could see the growing cloud as well as I, had the same thought, and began to labour at the oars with the strength of fear. So we made good speed to the Hold; and as we rounded the rampart on our way to the haven, the handful of troopers left behind shouted to us and ran to open the gates; also, as we passed under the keep, a casement was opened, and Mistress Rosamund Fanshawe thrust out her pale face, that flushed suddenly as her eyes fell on me, and she drew back her head, leaving me glad at heart, though I knew not why.

So we came to the harbour and made fast; and first, the Earl giving short command, our dead men, being Giles Warner and the two that were slain in the fight, were borne in and laid in an empty store-chamber, till we should take order for their burial. Then the rest of us followed, and my cousin, with no word to me, went up to the door of his hall, where the Signora stood wrapped in a great Eastern cloak, and Pompey by her with a flagon and goblets. The Earl, stumbling for weariness and haste, drained a cup of wine and filled again, nor thought of offering the draught to me that stood apart, or to Gulston, that poured out for himself, asking leave of no man.

The Italian woman spake low and whispering in her own tongue, asking (as I conceive) of the fortune of his enterprise; and he raised his head and answered wearily, 'E morto!' speaking, I doubt not, of Master Pentry. With that a flush came on her face, and her eyes opened and shone green as a cat's. 'How died he?' she asked, smiling as though for pleasure; but the Earl was past the joy of vengeance. 'He is where we shall soon be,' he muttered, yet not so low but that I heard him. 'The curse is loose, Fiammetta, it is loose!' and at his speech her eyelids fell again, and her face was drawn with fear; yet she mastered her dread, and was at point to speak, when the heavens brake open above us in blue flame, and there followed a crash as though the sea and sky were coming together in ruin.

Now the suddenness and greatness of the flash and thunderclap daunted me, though I had marked the black cloud climbing over us; but to the others it seemed as though the day of judgment had come on them. Some of the ruffians fell down for fear, and the foolish maid of the Apple Tree Inn at Marsham, that was chattering with some of the troopers, ran about shrieking that the end of the world was come. Yet was none hurt, nor was this the Lord's vengeance, as we came to know afterwards; for while the most of us stood waiting for some fearful judgment, the next flash shone great and bright but further to seaward, and the thunder was long in breaking, and rather heavy than sharp. With that the rain began to fall in great plashes, growing thicker till it hissed on the stones, and drove all to shelter, myself among the rest; and I had much ado to come to the door of the stairway and climb to my chamber, for I was weak with the weariness and horror of that morning's work, insomuch that I had no thought to shift my clothes, but sat by my window looking into the grey veil of rain that blotted out the hills, till the storm passed suddenly as it had come, and there was sunlight on the land, where a thin feather of steam rose yet from the black scar that had been Marsham. The air that had been sultry with the coming storm was more cool, and a wind blew from the landward, striking chill on me, so that I remembered that I was wet, and changing my garments, came down into the court and walked there, choosing my way between the pools of water, and seeing no man, for no sentries had been set.

I paced the court for some half hour, keeping close beneath the wall, for indeed the air was chilly and damp after the rain, and the wind to my fancy had a savour of the slime of the Hole in it; yet the breezes died away, as I could see by the flag on the turret, that drooped round the pole, and I went up on the rampart to see if Marsham yet smoked. But when I looked over the battlements, I could see no whit of the village, or of the hills behind it, for a mist had risen on the marsh, and was slowly drawing nearer, though wind was none, and the air was dead and damp and chilly, and methought the salt charnel savour was stronger than before; also the sunlight was veiled in white cloud, and the marshes looked more lonely and desolate than was their wont.

Now, as I watched the mist stealthily drawing onward, I heard the sound of feet on the stair of the keep, and presently came Mistress Fanshawe, with a hood drawn over her head, and her maid, the blacksmith's daughter of Marsham. So I made haste to descend to the court, and putting off my hat, greeted her. She hardly answered my greeting, but asked me of the happenings of that morning, the which I told her as I have set them down already, save that I would not speak of that which followed on Master Pentry's end; for when I thought thereon, the dreadfulness choked me, and the savour of the Hole was yet in my nostrils, whether in memory or in the air. Only I took heed to tell her of my will and endeavour to save the man, and how he himself chose his death and the manner of it; for I would not have Mistress Rosamund account me a coward, or slow to help my friends. Yet, need I not have feared, for she herself, as she hath told me afterward, was fain the rather to praise me for my boldness, but forebore, for that

she knew brave men to shrink from hearing overmuch of
their deeds; though belike I had been as greedy to take her
praise as I knew myself unapt to deserve it.

Also I remember that the maid, a well-favoured girl, but
ever glancing this way and that for fear, asked me of the
villagers; so I told her, thinking to comfort her, that none
were slain but Master Pentry and the tall fellow with the
scythe that gave Giles Warner his death wound. Thereat
she asked me earnestly of the man, but I knew nothing
more save that he wore a cap of blue, so far as I might see
him from the barge. But as I said this, the maid gave an
exceeding great and pitiful cry, and called on the name of
a man, and so fell a-sobbing; and when Mistress
Rosamund would have cast an arm around her to comfort
her, she brake from us like a hurt beast and fled to the
door of the keep; nor was it hard to tell that the dead man
had been dear to her, her lover perchance.

Mistress Rosamund gazed after the maid, with her eyes
full of most sweet compassion, and would have followed,
but I stayed her, saying that in such sorrow women were
best alone; also I was loth to lose the chance of seeing
Mistress Fanshawe. So we spake of this and that, that I
remember not, till I saw her of a sudden turn white, and
stagger; and had I not thrown an arm around her, she
would have fallen in a swoon. She recovered herself, and
craved my pardon for what she called her foolish
weakness; but she had felt a sickness and faintness come
over her heart with an ill savour in the air. Of a truth the
smell of the Hole was stronger than aforetime; and as I
looked up, I could see the first wreaths of white mist
coiling through the battlements like the arms of a ghostly
monster, and wrapping the castle in their dank vapour
that grew thicker without breath of wind. Soon the mist
had filled the court, growing thinner or denser in turn,
and the breath of it was a sick loathing and a shapeless
fear.

' 'Tis but the marsh mist,' I said, though mine own voice
sounded hollow and meaningless; and Mistress
Rosamund nodded her head, and spake of the fogs that
would ever beset the castle when the air was suddenly

chill. Yet we both knew that this was no common mist of the river or sea; and when we heard a strange wailing in the air to landward, a great fear fell on me of what might be approaching, for it seemed like the voices of the ghosts that were fabled to flutter over the marshes of Styx. Yet when somewhat white rose above the ramparts and wheeled round our heads, I could see that it was no spectre, but a seagull, and many others following it, till the court was full of birds, circling round the turrets and wheeling above the walls, yet never settling, crying out very mournfully the while, as though in warning and sorrow for somewhat that we knew not and they would fain tell us. For the space of some minutes they continued flying and lamenting, the mist growing thicker the while; then one took sudden flight, and all the rest after him, as though by word of command, and we could see them in a cloud going seaward, for the mist on that side was thinner, till they vanished, still screaming, nor was there a flutter of a wing to be seen in air or on the water or marsh, where commonly were many birds quarrelling and crying over their food.

Now the wailing of the gulls and their flight, as though before some coming peril, moved us strangely; and though we spake it not, one thought was in the minds of both, that these wild creatures, that are nearer to the secrets of the earth and water than we, had come to warn us to flee from somewhat dreadful, or to lament over us if we fled not. But Mistress Rosamund, that was ever brave beyond the wont of women and even of men, shook her shoulders as though to throw off a load of fear, and said lightly that perchance somewhat to landward had frightened the poor gulls, and so went up to the rampart to look, I following. Yet naught was to be seen but the white mist slowly drifting over the marshes, and the dull water lapping at the foot of the wall, with here and there a coiling streak of grey slime.

As we stood gazing, not finding aught to tell us why the birds should have fled, there arose a stir and clashing in the court, and looking down, we saw some of the garrison come forth, talking among themselves, yet soberly and in low voices, with less of swearing than was their wont. After them came Gulston, who hallooed to me and asked me what I did there; and when I told him I had seen a great flight of gulls, and was seeking what had frightened them, 'By Bacchus!' said he, 'as the Signora might say – I have heard tell that these birds are spirits of drowned sailors, and perhaps they were singing a dirge after their fashion for our soldiers. We are a burial party to bear forth the bodies of the men your friends of Marsham slew, and it were but charitable for Your Solemnity to be our chaplain; for we left our parsons to Noll Cromwell at Naseby field, as being too heavy baggage for our haste.'

I had wellnigh told him to take the bodies of his men to the devil that had their souls, so did his fleering jar on me; yet would I not yield to anger before Mistress Rosamund, that had heard all. So I was but turning away without answer, when she laid her hand on my sleeve, and I saw her eyes darken and then glisten with tears.

'Will you not speed these poor dead with a prayer?' she said, 'they did wickedly, but they knew not what they did, and if we forgive them not in death, nor pity them, how shall we look for mercy? Go with them, and I will stay and pray for their souls,' and at that word she caught herself up, and a shadow of a smile was on her lips. 'Oh, cousin!' she said, 'I forgot that you are a Puritan, and will count me a mere Papist. Yet think you that it is wrong to pray for the dead?'

I shook my head, for there was no time to answer; and indeed it has ever been my belief, since I thought deeply on these matters, that the former ill-practices of certain Papists in making a market of the mercies of God have led us Protestants to be over stern in denying a place of repentance after death to such as by youth or ignorance were unable to find the way of salvation. So I turned to go with the men, and when I looked again at Mistress Rosamund, she had bowed her head in her hands over the battlement, and (I doubted not) was praying for the poor wild souls of these three men.

By this time the troopers had brought forth the bodies of the dead, and wrapped them in old sails and cloaks for shrouds; and so, laying them in one of the barges, we pushed off, and rowed through the mist, that was not so thick but that the landmarks were to be known at times. Also the vapours shifted strangely, so that at times we could see down a clear reach of water, like a grey road between white walls, and again we were shrouded in white darkness, and breathing the cold savour of the Hole. So, by lying on our oars when the mist was too dense, and taking our bearings when it lightened, we made towards the land. Yet it was not the purpose of Gulston to bury the bodies on the mainland, which had been perilous, for the countryside was now roused against us, but we shaped our course for a knoll of the marsh, that had been thrown up a few feet above high tides by some old storm, and was now covered with harsh grass and samphire. Here we landed, and some of the men laboured with spades to dig a grave in the close grey shale and sand; and being apt at digging from practice of throwing up forts in the wars, they had soon made a hole, wide enough for the three bodies to lie side by side, but not deep, for in that ground we had soon come to water. Here then the men laid their dead fellows solemnly enough, and stood by while I spake some of the Service for Burial of the Dead, that I knew well, having been bred for the Church; save that, seeing the manner of men they had been, and the business in which they met their end, I could not bring myself to speak confidently of their lot at the Resurrection, but rather commended them to the infinite mercies of the Lord, that are beyond the bounds of our creeds and controversies.

Methought that some of the men were moved by my words, though they understood little; and one man, a Spaniard, with a face tanned like leather and seamed with scars, muttered his prayers in haste with much devotion. When I had done, the men began to fill in the trench above the bodies, and the Spaniard busied himself with binding together two staves he had brought with him, thinking to make a cross.

While they laboured, I stood by the boat watching them, and now and then turning to look at the marsh, when the mist thinned. As I looked, a wind began to blow from the land, lightly at first, but strengthening, and the fog drifted in strange shapes like ghosts, and the smell of the Hole came on the wind, growing stronger, till my heart was sick at the foulness and the chill of it. With the wind, the dull grey water that had been lying still at the edge of the knoll, began to lap at the bank; yet through the sobbing of the water I seemed to hear another sound. At first it was a whisper, far off, but it grew into a noise of sucking, as when water is drawn into a whirlpool or a pipe, and the mist now being in part blown away by the wind, I could see in the channel that led landwards to the Hole, a whirl or funnel of water here and there, that eddied and vanished and then appeared anew, growing slowly nearer, so that I wondered what this might be, and spake to Gulston, that was urging his men to finish and begone from this stinking marsh. But when he turned to look, the whirls in the channel were gone, and naught to be noted save the smell and some streaks of slime that floated past us; whereat he laughed, saying that those waters were full of eddies, and then spat and cursed the stink, and taking a flask from his pocket, proffered it to me; and when I would not drink, he tossed off a dram, to wash his throat clean, as he said. By this time the mound was finished, and the Spaniard, taking the rough wooden cross he had fashioned, and doffing his hat, planted it at the head of the grave, and we were about to go, when the Swede remarked that the end of the grave had crumbled and sunk somewhat, and catching a spade from one of the troopers, heaved a shovelful of the shale and sand on the mound, and slapped the earth with the side of the spade to make all smooth, as children do in building castles in the sand.

Now even as he smote the mound, the end of it crumbled away with a loud sucking sound, and where the hillock had been was a yeasty whirl of grey sand and water and slime. So Gulston gave back with a cry, and leaned on his spade, and we all gazed, while the whirl grew larger, and the mound crumbled away before our eyes, and the cross that was but just planted rocked to and fro and went down with the rest. At that the Spaniard made forward as though to save his handiwork, and I to hold him back, and only in time; for the mound we had reared and the bodies under it were gone, and nothing but a whirling funnel of water and sand. As we looked over the edge, the Spaniard staring as one distraught, and I behind him holding his arm, the whirlpool seemed to open down black to the very deeps, and then filled again with a spurt of slimy water, and in the midst of it one of the corpses, with the shroud gone from it, and the dead hands turning as though in strife to escape. The body was wound, as it seemed, with streaks of grey slime, but the face was bare, and I knew it for Giles Warner, even as I had seen him dead, save that the eyes I had closed were open, and their look was ghastly, so that I could not have borne it, yet might not turn away. Yet, as I gazed, the body was drawn down slowly into the water, the tendrils of slime seeming to tighten around it like cords; and when I looked back, the men were stumbling into the boat, cursing and crying out for fear; and had it not been for Gulston, that kept his wits, they had left the Spaniard and me on the crumbling remnant of the knoll.

In good time we gained the side, and none too soon; for as I heaved the Spaniard over the gunwale, he being palsied with fear, and got my knee on the boat's side, the hold melted from beneath my other foot, and I was fain to cling to the nearest man to clamber in; and where we had made our grave was nought but a grey eddy and the Spaniard's cross tossing in the waters.

No more I saw, for Gulston bade row, and the men bent to their oars, caring not whither they went so it was away from that accursed grave; also, the wind dropping, the mist closed in again, and folded us in a white shadow, so that we went at a venture, grounding in shallows, and feeling for channels with our oars; and mazed with fear as were the men, we might have wandered long in the marshes, had not Gulston bethought himself of his pistols, and firing one of them, in no long time came a musket-shot from the castle, that was nearer than we thought. So we made harbour again, and the troopers crept to their quarters as men broken by fear; but Gulston stayed with me, talking of the strange whirlpool that had swallowed up our dead, and would have it that this was but a sudden sinking of a quicksand, whereof there were many in the marshes. I feigned to assent to his speech, even as he himself feigned to believe it; yet as he went in at the gate and I was following, I looked back on the little port, and as the mist lifted somewhat, I seemed to see a tendril or streak of grey slime coiling round the arm of rock that shielded the harbour, and feeling at the edge of the quay like a finger searching for us blindly. Yet even as I looked, the appearance vanished, nor might I be sure if I had seen aught but a trick of the tide.

CHAPTER VIII

OF MY TALK WITH THE ITALIAN, AND OF CERTAIN MEN THAT WENT A-FISHING

As we came to the court, the Signora was standing on the steps of the hall door, with my cousin at her side, both silent, and, as it seemed, ill at ease, for the Earl's brow lowered as though he were in one of his black moods, and her face had something in it of anger mingled with fear. Yet as the Swede and I came nearer, she lifted her eyes on us, and passing Gulston over as of little account, she smiled on me and greeted me with her foreign courtesy, asking how we had fared. For a space I spake not, finding it hard to choose words to tell what I had seen; and the Swede thrust in, as was ever his wont.

'A fool's errand we have been sent on, to bury men in these cursed marshes of my Lord's,' he said, pulling at his beard. 'We might have spared our trouble, for when the grave was well dug and filled, a damned quicksand must needs open and suck all down, and like to swallow us too, had we not been speedy. God bless the land and the sea, say I, but the devil take this puddle of slime that is neither.'

At that the Earl muttered somewhat in his throat, and smote his hand on the side of the door; but the Signora, letting her green eyes rest on the Swede for but a moment, fixed them on me again as though to draw out my very soul.

'Of a truth,' I said, stumbling in my speech, 'all went much as he saith; the grave, and the knoll whereon it was digged, crumbled away before our eyes, after a strange fashion, and we were fain to flee or be sucked down ourselves. Nay, so sudden was it, that the dread of it yet abides with me.'

'Saw you or heard you anything else, sirs?' asked the woman sharply, though courteously.

'Nay, I saw and heard naught,' muttered the Swede, shaking his head; 'but Master Leyton here spake somewhat of eddies in the water, and I know not what else.'

Thereat the Signora looked at me again, with her eyes wider than their wont, as though eager for what was to hear. So I answered her, telling of the strange sucking noise that I had heard, and of the moving whirls in the water; and when I had ended, she dropped the lids over her eyes and bent her head in thought, speaking not, and we all stood silent, till my cousin lifted his head and pushed back his hair in his wonted way, and laughed loudly, with a desperate and false mirth.

'Why, so it is!' he said, clapping Gulston on the shoulder; 'they are gone, and we have the fewer mouths to feed when Old Noll comes to smoke us out. Of a truth,' he went on, 'we are like to need all our store of victual, for our fishermen have caught not so much as a sprat this day, nor seen a fin. Perchance these shiftings of the sands have frightened the fish.'

At this the Italian lifted her eyes again. 'The fish gone too?' she said. 'You told me not of that, *Filippo mio*.'

'Why, it slipped my mind,' said the Earl, with his mirthless laugh. 'Never fear, Fiammetta, we shall see the fish back again in time for your Friday dinner, or I will send further to seek for some. But it is dry work talking. Come and taste my fresh cask of Spanish, that was broached this morning. If fish fail us, we have store of wine and powder in the cellars, and what more does a soldier need?'

Gulston was never backward in answering a challenge of that sort, and I myself was about to accept my cousin's courtesy, when the Signora looked at me with her narrow eyes, that spake plainly, though without word, that she would have me stay. So I excused myself, answering, as was indeed the truth, that his wine was like to be too noble for my poor brain, and the Earl, waiting not to hear me out in my excuses, took Gulston by the arm and went in, calling for Pompey to bring the flagon. When the sound of their feet had ceased on the flags of the hall, the Signora slipped down and sat on one of the steps, beckoning to me to take place at her side, the which I did. For a space she looked earnestly on me without speaking, then asked me suddenly:

'Signor Uberto,' she said, 'these are strange happenings in land and water. What make you of them?'

I was fain to answer that I knew not of these parts, and of the currents and quicksands of the marshes and channels, but she took me up with a certain scornful impatience. 'O aye,' she said, 'all that is good enough for Signor Erico, or Signorina Rosamunda, but you believe it not yourself, nor does Filippo. Tell me what is in your mind. I am no English girl, to be scared with tales of warlocks, and, scholar as you are, belike I could teach you somewhat of curious arts. Have I not the name of a witch in the countryside?'

I answered something to the purport that peasants were ever prone to think a stranger to be witch or wizard, but she cut me short again.

'Here are we talking follies,' she said, with an angry scorn of herself and of me, 'and the time is flying, and it may be too late. Tell me what you know and what you fear.'

'There is an old tale,' I answered her, 'of a Thing that bides in the deep pit of water they call the Hole; and but the other day, as I was ranging the books in my library, I came on a book of our family, wherein the rhyme was written—'
And so I told her the verse, and she would have me say it over twice or thrice, till she knew it herself. But when I would have gone on to say that this was but an old woman's fable, she stopped me again.

'Do not lie to yourself and to me, signor,' she said. 'There are strange things in this world we see, and in the world unseen, and yet stranger, perchance, in the world of the border. We are in the fall of a heavy peril, and my Lord's great guns and the muskets of his rascal troopers are as straws to ward us, and a straw is your own pretty rapier, though it be good Italian steel, and you have the right trick of using it, signor—'

She had been so scornful of our wasting time in compliments, that when she quitted the business in hand to praise my skill of fence, I could but stare at her in amaze, till she laughed daintily.

'Nay, I am straying from the matter in hand,' she said. 'Pardon me, signor, but I have grown up among swordsmen, and it is a joy to me to see you playing with our good Filippo as a Spaniard fights with a bull. Had you been an Italian, you had entered into your inheritance long ago; an angry word from my Lord, coats off, a pass or twain, a turn of the wrist, and Signor Uberto is the Earl of Deeping.'

I marvelled the more that she should talk thus idly; for I was yet to learn later that the Signora spake no word without a purpose below it and, perchance, a darker purpose or two hidden behind that. So I did but tell her that I was no such master of fence as she would have me, and that I looked on the duello as barbarous, and no more to be accounted civil than Christian, wherefore the Swedish King Gustavus had rightly forbidden it among his officers. As I spake, the Italian woman opened her eyes as though coming back from a dream, and broke in on my homily, waving her hand as if to brush away my reasons.

'Enough, signor,' she said; 'I am partly of your mind. The rapier is a pretty tool, but there is overmuch chance in the duello. A loose shoestring, a mote in the eye, and where is your artist? Nay, a scholar such as you has apter weapons. Signor Uberto, there is upon this house the shadow of a great fear, and the malice of a nameless adversary. What can you do to save yourself and us?'

'I know of no arm but prayer, and no help but the Almighty,' I said, doffing my hat.

'I knew you would say that,' she answered softly, yet with a scornfulness in her voice. 'You Puritani are ever in one story. But the Almighty is far away, and I have seen the good man cry out for help and perish as one of the wicked. There be other spirits, not almighty, yet assuredly potent, that are nearer to help, if one knows their speech.'

I was about to tell her that I had no faith in the invocation of saints, but at that word she caught me up scornfully.

'*Dio mio!* what pedants are you English! Nay, I speak of

others than the saints, though perchance they mask themselves saintly. Think you that I could pray for help to the rotten bones of a stupid friar, that would rub out the wisdom of the ancients to have parchment for the jargon he called Latin? I have better helpers than saints, as you shall yet see – if you be not afeared.'

'I will have no dealings with devils,' I said shortly, rising from the step.

'Who spake of devils?' she answered, looking up at me with narrowed eyes. 'To the wise there is no devil and no saint, but powers and intelligences that are mighty to help or hurt, perilous to compel, and deadly to fools and cowards, but answering to the right word. Much can I do alone, but not enough. Uberto, wilt thou dare to help me?'

As she spake, with more of passion than I had known her to show before, she fixed her eyes on mine, and caught me by the wrist, and it was as if a fetter was laid on my hand and my will. Nor know I how I should have answered her, had not my cousin smitten open the door and come on us, and, at the clash of the lock, the woman dropped my hand, and as it were a veil of grey came over the green light of her eyes. Gulston followed the Earl, and both were flushed with the Spanish wine, and laughing loudly.

'Why, Fiammetta, what hast been babbling so long?' he asked, taking her under the chin and turning her face up, but she writhed away from him like a snake, and looked at him smiling.

'We were but talking of sword play and tricks of fence,' she answered, 'and I was saying to Signor Uberto that were he of mine own country, he might have won himself a goodly name and heritage by his mastery of the sword.'

At that my cousin laughed harshly, and Gulston made an echo. 'Of a truth, cousin,' the Earl cried, 'I had not taken you for so worshipful a sworder, though you are apt at your weapon for a Puritan. And pray, Signora, what name and fortune should my kinsman have won by his rapier? I knew not that titles and estates of nobility came to masters of the sword, even the greatest.'

The Italian's eyes grew narrow like mere slits for malice

as she answered him, 'Nay, my Lord, what say you to the name and estate of the Earl of Deeping?'

My cousin stared, and then laughed again, but not as one well pleased. 'Oh, aye, I take you,' he said; 'a right Italian plan, too. What say you, cousin Hubert? Shall we play a match with the buttons off the foils? You stake a book of sermons, and I this ragged Hold and the rents that none will pay me. Nay, the wager is not fair; shall I throw you in Fiammetta for the prize?'

He spake jestingly, but I could see that in his desperate mood he defied me to take him at his word. But the Signora, having proved her power, was loth to drive him further, even though she was angered at his slighting manner. 'Nay, *Filippo mio!*' she said softly, 'the match were unfair. Signor Uberto is a man of peace, and his tricks of fence would serve him little with the bare weapons. And little as I am worth, I am too good to be the wager of a bout of fence.' So the Earl's mood passed, and he turned to Gulston, that had stared on us blankly the while.

'Eric,' said my cousin, 'the men tell me that they can take no fish with their lines, nor is there any fowl to be seen on the marshes. Send a half-dozen of them forth in a boat with nets and guns, and see that they come not back without a cargo.'

The Swede's face changed, and he shifted from one foot to the other. 'My Lord,' he said, 'I would bid you consider that the men are sore tired with the day's work, and some are feared of the marshes, for the strange quicksands and the evil smell. Also the mist may close in and leave them astray in the channels.'

The Earl's brow darkened, and he swore an oath. ' 'Sdeath!' said he; 'am I captain of a troop of old wives? I know what you would say. Here have some cowardly fools been stuffing the knaves with old fables, till they are afraid of their own shadows. Send forth some of those that were not in this morning's business, and bid them make no more words, or I will flay the hide off them with my dog-whip.'

Gulston shrugged his shoulders, and left us with no more ado; and presently I could hear him routing the troopers from their quarters, till some five of them came forth grumbling, two carrying fowling-pieces and the others fishing-tackle and bait. They were wont rather to take these fishing and fowling cruises as a holiday, yet now they went sullenly, and had they not felt the eye of their master, and known that he would be better than his threatenings, belike they would have let who would go a-fishing. One of them, I remember, turned at the door of the guard-room and went back, as though he had forgotten somewhat, coming out presently with a great sword girt to him, whereat my lord laughed, and would ask the fellow whether he would play at cut and thrust with the cod-fish, but the man answered not. Yet a breeze sprang up and drave the mist away seaward, and a gleam of sun gilded the belfry, till the afternoon looked fair again, so that the men pushed off their boat cheerfully enough, being reckless rascals all, nor apt to mope; and thus they set forth, the Earl crying out to them that if they brought home a full load, fin or feather, they should not lack for ale nor strong waters to wash down the catch.

So we parted, each to his quarters; but, before I sought my chamber, I walked on the rampart for a space, and could see the boat making good speed seaward with oars and a small sail, till presently a shift of wind brought the mist landward again, and I could scarce see the boat, that was dwindled to a black speck on the grey water. Yet I heard no shots, so that it seemed they had found no wild fowl.

Wearying of the grey flats, I sought my room, and cast myself on the bed, for I was sore weary, meaning to rest for a half-hour; yet my head had no sooner touched the pillow than I fell into a deep slumber, that must have endured for hours, and at the first dreamless; but at the last, as I conceive, I had a strange dream, born, as is the way of these visions, of that which I had seen and heard, strangely entangled with other fantasies. Methought that I was at the sword-play with my cousin, and at either elbow of me was a hooded and shrouded form, that I could see, yet I knew, how I cannot tell, that the Earl could not; and as he grew angry and rough in his fence, as was his way when I was too hard for him, the shape on my left hand stretched an arm forth and took the button from my fencing foil, and pointed a long sharp finger at my cousin's breast, saying, in a woman's voice, and that the voice of the Signora, 'Strike! stone dead hath no fellow!' as my Lord of Essex spake in urging the death of the Earl of Strafford. And at that it seemed that the other figure threw back its hood and showed the bare skull of a man with Master Pentry's eyes glowing in the sockets, and spake in his harsh voice, 'Vengeance is mine, saith the Lord!' and would have stayed me, but in my dream I drave my cousin's blade aside with a sweeping parry, and springing forward, thrust him through the breast with the favourite stoccata of my Italian master, and methought the Earl fell with his breast spouting blood, that changed presently to red slimy tendrils creeping over the stones to fasten on me, till I cried out in fear, and then came a great peal of thunder, and I waked with the sweat streaming down my face, and the echoes of the thunder yet trembled in the air.

Now, when I was well awake, I saw that it was dusk, and the dark mist was rolling through my window, bearing the faint foul smell that I knew too well, yet mingled with the reek of powder, whereat I wondered, but not long; for presently the dusky court was lit with a red flash, and there came the great crack of a culverin from the gate, and the smoke mingled with the mist and drifted across the court in strange shapes. So, much marvelling what this might mean, I cast my cloak round me and made haste down the stair, and as fortune would have it, I chanced upon Mistress Rosamund Fanshawe, that was bound on the same errand. She put forth a hand and caught my cloak, asking what this might be, yet could I not tell her, till presently a tall shadow brake through the rolling mist, and I clutched at it, and knew that it was the Swede; and to my question he answered shortly that the fishers had not come back, and the Earl was firing his cannon to guide them through the mist. So I let him go, and went up to the rampart with Mistress Rosamund to listen, and in no long time we heard the sound of a musket-shot, yet far off and muffled as it were by the mist, whereat I rejoiced that the men were returning safe; for in that lonely and fearful place, the worst ruffian seemed a friend, as being at least human. So we stood shivering in the chilly mist, that increased in thickness; and at last came another shot, somewhat nearer, but far off still, and then two or three thick together, and a stillness, and last of all a faint cry of voices, wailing or shouting, that fell suddenly silent, and nothing more.

Presently I could hear my cousin's voice bidding men set a blazing cresset on one of the turrets for a torch to guide the boat homewards; also he bade toll the bell of the hall: but no shout or shot answered for an hour or twain, till the mist lightened somewhat, and the watch on the barbican tower cried out that they saw the boat. So all crowded to the port, and Mistress Rosamund and myself with them; and indeed the tale was true, for we could see a spot of black slowly drifting out of the night towards the quay, till it grew greater, and yet no sign of oar or man. Lastly the boat drave heavily against the quay, and men ran out with torches to see how their comrades had fared, and called to them.

There was none that answered, and the black hulk drifted in till the wavering light shone down into the boat, and we could see that the craft was half full of water, streaked with glistering slime that shone like blood in the red torch-light. Of the men, of their tackle and weapons and the fish or fowl they had taken, was no sign; only in the side of the boat was sticking a broken blade of a broadsword, sunk deep into the wood as though by the frenzied stroke of a madman, and we knew it for the weapon of the man who turned back to fetch his sword, that had profited him little. Other sign to tell the end of these men, there was none.

CHAPTER IX

OF THE SACRIFICE OF THE BLACK FOWL

NOW when my cousin had looked upon the boat, and upon the shard of the sword that was the only sign of his men, he was as one distraught, crying out desperately to launch all the barges and set forth to take vengeance on man or devil. Yet did none stir to do his bidding, and when he would have leapt into a boat, the Signora plucked him back by the cloak and whispered to him, so that he forbore, and she, turning to Gulston, bade all within, and to bar the gates. The which we did, and when we were girt round by the great walls, the fear of the garrison somewhat abated. Yet still they stood huddled and muttering, as if afraid to be alone; till the Italian spake to them smoothly.

'Here is an ill business,' quoth she; 'surely these men were maddened by fear or liquor to set on one another. Doubtless the shots we heard were of the fight, and any that were left alive have cast themselves overboard. Think you not so, Filippo?'

At that the Earl nodded his head, but spake not; but the Swede, falling into her story, sware many and great oaths that he had known such madness to come on men oft-times in the wars, and in wrecks at sea; so the others taking heart somewhat, a double watch was set on the walls, and we went to our quarters. For myself, I cast myself on my bed as I was, with my sword ready to my hand, and so lay uneasily, running to the window at first when the lapping of the water grew louder, and seemed like to the sucking noise that I had heard in the morning, till for very shame I must lie still. Also in the hour before the dawn one of the sentinels loosed off his piece, and brought the more part of us to the walls, with a tale of a black bulk of somewhat that he had seen heaving above the edge of the quay. Yet when we kindled torches and looked, was there nothing; so Gulston put the fellow in ward, with a promise that he should ride the wooden horse on the morrow. Nor were we troubled again, so that toward morning I fell into a doze, nor wakened till the sunlight was bright on my face.

When I looked forth, the day was fair and still, and the mist hung only in the fold of the far hills, also I could hear the men stirring, and one struck up a song. When I came to walk in the court after my wont, all looked to go on as aforetime, nor did the happenings of yesterday seem other than an ugly dream. But presently, as I walked, I heard the sound of groanings from a chamber hard by the guard-room, and it came to me that here was one of those hurt in the fight at Marsham; so when the Swede came forth, wiping the froth of his morning draught from his beard, I asked him how his wounded did.

'One is nigh sound again,' he answered me; 'but the other doth but ill, seeing that his sword-hand was cut through by yonder rascal's scythe, ere I could shoot. We have bound his arm, but I look for him to die, for we have no surgeon among us. Well, it is one fewer for our victuals and a day longer life for our chickens.'

As he spake, I heard a noise of cackling, and a few fowls that were kept at the castle came forth into the court, as the blacksmith's daughter of Marsham, that was maid to Mistress Rosamund, called to them from the door of the keep, and scattered crumbs and broken meats from a basket on her arm. Truly it was a pretty sight and a peaceful to mark the hens pecking between the stones, while their lord and master Chanticleer strutted in the sun like a young gallant in his holiday clothes. So thought Gulston, for he sighed once or twice, and laughed as one ashamed.

'Zounds!' said he, 'I might dream myself at my mother's house by Upsala, fashioning a wooden sword to lead the bonders' boys to war, while the maidens cast the broken barley-bread to the fowls. 'Tis a fair hall, and before the hearth is the skin of the first bear I killed – shall I ever stand thereon again?' and with that he sighed again, and swore, and strode away with his long scabbard swinging against his legs, leaving me to divide the lordship of the court with the fowls.

But when I had walked a turn or two, I marked the Signora put her head forth of the hall door, and seeing me alone, she came stepping daintily to give me greeting, and ask me what I did; and when I answered that I was but watching the chickens fed, she was pleased to ask me in jest whether I were practising divination by fowls after the manner of the ancients.

'Nay,' said I, laughing; 'I have no skill of augury, and fear that I might be counted a scoffer with Claudius the Consul, that cast the sacred chickens into the sea, bidding them drink if they would not eat.'

'Aye, and thereby brought his ships and himself to miserable ruin,' answered she, 'as a warning to all that despise divinations.' At that she broke off suddenly, and gazed earnestly into a corner of the court, where I, for my part, could see naught save a little black hen picking at the stones apart from the rest. Presently the Signora turned to me again, and her eyes were shining as though she had found a treasure.

'Signor Uberto,' said she, 'you remember how yesterday we talked of the unseen powers, and of curious arts that might compel them? Was it not so?'

'Aye,' said I; 'yet have I ever accounted but little of magic.'

'Therein are you right foolish for all your learning,' she answered me scornfully; 'yet if you fear not, you may see somewhat ere long' – and with that she looked again earnestly on the black hen. But while I marvelled what she could see in the pecking of poultry, the wounded man groaned again and called on his Saints, being a Southerner, and she asked me who was sick. I answered as the Swede had told me; and when I spake of the manner of the man's wound, her eyes widened again and grew brighter. '*Ah, povero!*' said she, yet her voice was less pitiful than her words; 'his right hand nigh cut off? I will see the man, and perchance lighten his pain by what of

surgery my father taught me. But first – tell me who cares
for yonder fowls?'

Methought that she would take a fowl to make broth for
the sick man, so I told her that Mistress Rosamund's maid
tended on the poultry, and the girl came forth even then
with another basket of crusts; but when she saw the
Italian's narrow eyes fixed on her, she grew pale and made
her reverence, and so stood.

'Hither to me, wench,' said the Signora, and the girl
came slowly, dragging her feet as one in fetters. 'What is
thy name?' and when she heard that it was Elizabeth – 'It
is well, Elisabetta,' said she; 'See'st yonder black fowl?
Take her up and go to my chamber and wait till I come.'

At this the girl hung back, and began to stammer out
that she was Mistress Rosamund's maid, and had no leave
to go on other errands; but the Italian cut her short.

'Who art thou, and who is the Signorina Rosamunda, to
say what shall or shall not be? Do as I have said, or thou
shalt taste the whip!'

Now it moved me to loathing to hear this stranger speak
so to a free countrywoman of mine own, belike no worse
than her in birth, and surely better in virtue, so I told her
plainly that the wench was no bondslave, nor would I
hear such words to an Englishwoman. Yet the Signora did
but laugh, looking at me with her eyes narrowed to slits.

'Nay,' said she; 'I forgot that here is the land of freedom,
where Jill is as good as her mistress, and Noll Cromwell
better than the King. I will use no violence, neither compel
anyone. Look on me, Elisabetta, and thou shalt see that I
mean thee no hurt.'

Her voice was smooth and sweet as honey, yet hissing
somewhat as a snake's; so the girl took courage to look her
in the face. But when their eyes met, the wench trembled
sore, and writhed her body as though she strove to break
away, but was fast held; and I looked on the Italian, and
her eyes were green and steady, and her lips sucked in as
though she were drawing the life from the other. So they
stood for a space, till the Signora stretched out the
forefinger of her left hand and pointed it at the forehead of
the girl, who shuddered with a great sigh, and without

word walked slowly, dragging her feet, and took up the black fowl, and so went in at the great door, looking back piteously at the Italian as though for mercy that she found not, and then at me, that would have helped her, but knew not how.

'Now must I within, to see if I can help yonder poor man,' said the Signora, yet smiling, as though her meaning were other than her words; but even then Mistress Rosamund called from the stair of the keep, 'Bessie, Bessie!' and when none answered, she ran forth to seek her maid, and so came on us together.

'Your pardon, Signora Bardi and my cousin,' she said, with a scornful reverence to the Italian; 'have you seen my maid Bessie?'

'I have need of Elisabetta for to-day,' answered the Signora; at which Mistress Fanshawe's face flushed, and she beat her foot on the ground.

'Why is this?' she asked. 'Methinks the girl was given to wait me. Surely, if you have need of a woman, there is the maid from the inn, that is as fit to serve you, aye, and fitter perchance, seeing that she loves to company with soldiers.'

Now I feared what the Italian might say or do, as I knew the hatred that was between these two. Yet did she but smile again, and wave a hand after her foreign fashion, as though to put aside somewhat too slight to hold her.

'I cannot stay to bandy words,' she said, 'seeing that yonder poor man needs me. Suffice it that the wench came willingly, nor will she take hurt with me, if she be a true maid. Will you have the other in her place?'

Mistress Rosamund shook her head with no word, and the Signora left us and passed into the chamber where we heard the groaning, and presently came out a trooper to the hall, whence he returned with Pompey the black, that bore a box and some vials, also a chafing-dish of charcoal; and we talked the while of things indifferent, for that the casements of the chamber were open. But when Pompey had entered with his burden, and the windows were shut, I began to tell Mistress Rosamund of the strange talk of the Signora, when there came from the sick man's room a great shrieking cry, and then a babbling in a foreign tongue, and again screams and foul oaths, so that we were fain to stop our ears. Yet in a brief space the cries turned to groans, and fell silent, and presently the Italian came forth smiling, bearing somewhat wrapped in a napkin, that dripped red on the stones, and Pompey followed with her other matters; nor did she waste a look on us, but passed to the hall, as one stedfastly making for a goal. Yet could we well guess what had happened; and also the trooper that had gone in came forth, swearing under his breath as one affrighted, and told me, when I asked, that the Signora had made no ado, but sliced off the man's hand more deftly than any surgeon, and dressed the arm, and so left him asleep with some secret drug from one of her vials. With that he went about his business, and Mistress Rosamund looked on earnestly. 'It is passing strange,' said she; 'a black fowl and a man's hand, and a murderer's, I doubt not! Savours not this of witchcraft, cousin? And what would she do with my poor Bessie?'

I strove to comfort her, saying that I would speak to the Earl that no hurt should come to the girl; and so we went up on the rampart to look abroad. The tide was now full, and the more part of the marshes was a sheet of grey water, darker in the channels, and quiet enough in the pale sunshine; yet was there somewhat amiss in the stillness, where aforetime we had heard fish rising and leaping, or sea-birds crying over their food. Presently Mistress Rosamund grew deathly white, and would leave me, for that an ill savour was in the air; and indeed there was a breath of the smell of the Hole, that I had come to know and to fear. So she went down from the wall, and I continued walking for a space, but marked naught but that a good way from the castle there seemed a whirl of eddies moving swiftly in the water, which passed, and the smell with them; but in some quarter of an hour came the savour again, and the whirls in the water, going the same way as at the first, and so yet other times, till the tide ebbed and I marked the appearance no more, and the day passed wearily.

Now at supper-time we were all gathered together save

Gulston, and as I had promised, I spake to the Earl my cousin of the wench Elizabeth; and he, that knew naught of the matter, asked of the Italian what she would with the girl, thinking it but a women's quarrel, and somewhat angered, methought, that the Signora should take it on herself to command his kinswoman's servant. But the Bardi did but smile after her wicked fashion, and answered him smoothly that she needed the wench for a matter of curious arts that should do her no harm and might be greatly for the advantage of us all; also she bade us come and see for ourselves that very night what she purposed to do, if we had the courage; for that as the business was of great moment, so it was not without danger to herself first, and also to others.

Now when she spake thus, we were all silent for a space, for this matter savoured to us of sorcery and the black arts; also my cousin, whose right it was to speak the first, frowned and sat sullen, as is the wont of violent men that are faced with a danger that they understand not. But Mistress Rosamund, that was ever of a high courage, seeing that no word came from the Earl, leaned toward me over the table and spake earnestly.

'I partly conceive of the nature of to-night's business,' she said; 'nor will it be without peril of our souls as well as of our bodies. Yet is this girl given into my charge, and how can I draw back? Signora, I will come.'

The Italian spake not, but smiled as a man will at the boldness of an enemy; and indeed, though she was an evil woman, she had a man's relish for bravery and learning wheresoever found. Seeing this, I could no longer hold back, and for very shame must make one; and the Earl, awaking from his sullenness, drank off a full goblet and vowed he would be with us. 'We four and the wench,' said he, 'and belike the devil to make the half-dozen – or shall we bid Gulston also?'

The man came in as my cousin named him, and sat down in his place, seeming much distempered. Nor would he answer wherefore he was late, till he had eaten and drunk; when he pushed his platter away, and looking in the Earl's face, 'The man is dead,' says he; 'I have seen him passing and heard his confession, for he took me for a priest in his fever; and an ill story it was, with a dozen murders or so for the best of his deeds.'

'A murderer, and worse?' said the Signora, '*Ah, povero!*' but her eyes shone strangely as though with a secret gladness.

'Well, I'm for sleep now,' said the Swede; 'I go on no more burial parties, day or night. Methinks, signora, your surgery profited him little?'

'I did what I could,' she answered him, with her eyes cast down as in sorrow; 'and sad am I that I could not save him.' The Swede grunted for all answer, and so flung out of the hall; and as he went, my cousin asked of the Italian with his eyes – 'Shall I bring him to-night?' and she shook her head.

' 'Tis a good soldier,' she said scornfully; 'but with wit as leathern as his sword-sheath. Signorina Rosamunda and Signor Uberto, I will send for you.'

So we went to our rooms, and I to watch at my window, for the fear of what was to be kept me from sleep; also once or twice the smell of the slime was strong in my nostrils, and a strange sucking noise, that was more than the wonted lapping of the waters, made me look sharply into the night, that was black and moonless. Yet saw I naught till, a half hour or so before midnight, the black came for me, and I did on my sword and went out; yet looking back to see if I had forgotten aught, mine eyes fell on my little Bible in the Greek tongue, that I ever took to read on journeys; and I thrust it into my pocket with little thought. On the stair was Mistress Rosamund, muffled in cloak and hood, and we followed Pompey to the door of the hall, and up a little stair where I had not before been to a door, whereon he knocked, and so departed in great fear, waiting not till it was opened to us.

The chamber whereunto we came was of a fair bigness, and panelled in oak darkened by age. The floor also was of oak and polished, nor was there a cloth on it, nor any hangings on the wall, nor chair nor other garniture, save one little table curiously wrought of brass after the fashion of a tripod of twining snakes, whereon were two candles lighted, and somewhat covered with a black kerchief. On the floor were four circles drawn with red chalk, or some such thing, of which one was larger, and in each the figure that is called the pentacle or Seal of Solomon; and characters written therein that seemed in the scant light to be of Arabic or other Eastern tongues. Yet though I knew these to be but the customary baggage of sorcerers, I was feared of them as I looked not to be, and more of that which might be under the black veil on the brazen altar, for such it seemed. My cousin was there waiting, but spake not; nor did any word pass before the Signora came to us, strangely habited in a long black robe, and with her hair unbound, and a garland of leaves round her head like an ancient Sibyl.

'You are here,' said she; 'now listen! Stand each of you within one of these figures, nor go out for your lives, whatever you may see or hear, till I bid you.' And when we were set within our pentacles, 'Elisabetta!' she called, 'come hither to me.' At that the girl came forth from the inner chamber, clad in a black robe of strange fashion, and barefooted, with her hair loose, and her eyes staring as though she saw naught, and the Signora set her in the greater circle over against the table. This done, the Italian threw the casement wide open, and the smell of the Hole came in on a little wind, and the candles flickered. 'Ah,' says the Signora; 'it is there, it is there, but we may yet escape—' and she came to the brazen table and twitched off the veil, and there lay, as I half looked to see, the severed hand of the dead trooper, long and lean, and strangely swarthy, with dusky hair on the back, that lay uppermost. By the fingers of the hand she laid a candle that she took from her bosom, and on the floor between the girl and the tripod, a lighted brazier; and so, standing herself in the great circle with the girl, she cast on the coals a double handful of somewhat like incense, that burned with a wavering flame of green and a strong smoke that made mine eyes wink and water, and my head swim as though I were drunken with wine; nor do I know if what I thought I saw after were not in part the work of that devil's incense.

'Now,' says she, 'is it high time for the sacrifice,' and at her bidding the girl laid somewhat black on the brazen table before the hand, and I saw that it was the black fowl that had been chosen in the morning. The bird struggled a little, but made no sound; and the Signora gave to the girl a great knife or short sword bent as a half moon. Even then the clock of the belfry struck the hour of midnight; and on the last beat of the bell, the Italian cried out 'Strike!' and the maid cleft the fowl asunder with one blow, so that the blood of it spirted on her gown and on the dead hand, and hissed on the brazier. So throwing down the knife, she came back into the circle, and standing as one tranced, began to chant a strange song or incantation in some jargon that to my ear savoured now of the Hebrew, now of the Chaldee, now of the Latin, and anon was like the barbarous chatter of black slaves in the plantations. Now when the girl had chanted for a space, there came a puff of air through the window and blew out the candles on the table, so that there was no light save the green flames of the brazier, that the Signora fed ever from a box of her incense. With the wind the fire leapt up, lighting the whole chamber, and I looked toward the brazen altar where the halves of the stricken hen and the hand of the slain man lay.

While I gazed, it seemed to me that the hand was other than I had seen it, being darker of hue, and the nails long and hooked as a bird's claws; also the hair on the wrist was much increased in thickness and blackness, as on the hand of an ape. And whereas the hand had lain flat, it was now bent as though leaning on the table, yet could I see no arm pertaining to it. But presently in the flickering lights and shadows, there seemed to be somewhat moving like a strand of black hair blowing in the wind, that increased in bigness and blackness, yet all disordered and shapeless; and when I looked on the hand again, the fingers of it clutched the strange candle, that came alight without touch of fire, and burned with a green flame; and with that the semblance of the hair writhed about the table and hid the body of the fowl, that we saw no more, only a whirl of wind blew feathers about the chamber, like a flight of black snow, and a savour of burning mingled with the incense. And now the Signora first uplifted her voice in a strange singing manner, and I could tell well what she spake, for she used the Latin tongue, yet rather monkish and barbarous than as the Romans talked. '*Cibum potumque tibi dedi,*' said she; 'I have given thee meat and drink, even flesh and blood of a black victim. What wilt thou give unto me?' Then, whether it were the disorder of mine own senses, or the girl speaking in trance, or verily the voice of a demon, it seemed as though a shrill, chattering voice, as of an ape that could speak, answered her again out of the shadow that had the appearance of hair, saying, '*Quid vis, domina?*' or 'What wilt thou, mistress?' and the green flame of the candle bowed before her.

She stood still for a space before she answered, and the green lights flickered on her face from the brazier and from the candle that was held in the dead man's hand; also it seemed to me, and (as I have heard) to Mistress Rosamund, that in the shade of the Appearance there was a green glowing light as of eyes that turned this way and that. In the stillness that fell I could hear the clapping of the little flames leaping in the brazier, and far out on the marshes, the whisper of the tide, mingled with the strange sucking noise that I had heard before. Lastly, the Signora spake in a tongue that I knew not, pointing to the window, and the Appearance moved somewhat the way she pointed, but, as it were, unwilling; and when she would speak again, and stretched out her arm beyond the ring where she stood, the shadow grew higher, and a long strand of hair lashed back like a whip, so close to me that I felt the wind of it on my cheek, and it was burning; yet did the Signora draw back in time, and the Appearance flickered half way to the window and then back, as I have seen a wild beast that the tamer would have to do some leap or trick. It was of the bigness of a mastiff dog, but I saw not how it was shapen, nor what limbs it had, other than the hand that bore the candle. Only I could note that as it moved to and fro it ever shunned the rings of the pentacles wherein it stood, even as a cat picking her way daintily among pools of water. Also the dread that I had of this Appearance was somewhat lessened, for that it moved sullenly and as in fear.

Yet was this stillness but for a moment's space, for the Signora signed to the wench that stood tranced, and by some art would make her speak the incantation that was (or so it seemed to me) to compel the evil thing to do her bidding. Now when the girl spake certain strange unknown words, the Appearance passed toward the window, and again hung there; till at the last the Italian woman beckoned to the girl, that took up a little rod or wand that I had not noted, and pointed toward the window, and so made after the thing as if to drive it forth. But of that which followed I cannot speak but confusedly, for it seems like the ill dream of a fever, or the vision of a madness. Yet it was to me as though when the maid came from the ring on the floor and approached the Appearance, that it swelled to a huge bigness and blackness, hiding the window, and so flapped and roared like a great sail torn loose in a tempest, and wrapped itself round the wench, that screamed but once and so fell, and all we stood struck still with fear. Only Mistress Rosamund, that till now had turned away from the evil thing, hearing the girl cry, leapt from her place with no fear for herself, and ran to the window, where in the green flicker was a writhing blackness. And I, though I feared greatly, made in to help her, seeking to draw my sword; yet as I felt for the hilt, my hand struck on the Bible in my pocket, and I caught it out as a fitter weapon than steel against the power of Satan. Even as I ran forward, could I see the blackness and the appearance of hair shrink and dwindle, and draw back before Mistress Rosamund, till I could mark the wench lying senseless; but at the window it grew great again and hung over the enemy that did not fear it, being secure in her own purity. But I, that feared for her as she could not for herself, cried out on the name of God, and moved by some spirit that I knew not, flung the book at the blackness and the green glare that had the likeness of eyes; and with a flash of fire and a great noise, whether in mine own eyes and ears only or in very deed, I know not, the brazier was hurled over, so that we were in darkness; and when the Signora found flint and steel and lit the candles, was there nothing but the girl Bessie lying on the floor, and the hand of the dead by itself, and my little Bible. But when we went to take up the wench, she was dead, and her face strangely blackened; also on her throat were marks as though she had been strangled with fine cords. At which Mistress Rosamund fell a-weeping, and the Earl, my cousin, was moved; but the Italian woman broke out into a passion of scorn, with many ill words in the Italian that none noted but I, on the village slut that had lost her own life and the lives of all by her folly. Nor did I know then what she meant; but I have read since in old books of magic, that none can defy the malice of the powers of evil save those that are pure, as is set forth in the stories of the saintly virgins that were beset in vain by dragons and devils; and of a surety there was such a strength of innocence in Mistress Rosamund. Of all this I then thought nothing, but bade the Signora leave her foul speaking of one that she had done to death with her sorcery; and her passion being somewhat abated, she left raving, and stood sullen for a space. Then, as she marked Mistress Rosamund rise from kneeling beside the body of the girl Bessie, she went to her and caught her by the sleeve eagerly.

'Signorina Rosamunda!' she called to her; 'will you not help us in our need, and save yourself from the doom that is upon us? The spirits fear you, and you only, of our company. I will teach you the word of power, and perchance it will avail, for I have seen none that had so high a courage as yourself.'

Mistress Rosamund answered not at the first, but gathered my Bible from the floor, and held it to her bosom ere she spake. 'I have lent myself too much to your evil arts in being here,' she said, gravely; 'and the guilt of this maid's blood lies partly on my soul. If I could save the lives of you all by giving mine own life, without sin, freely would I do it. But I will have no more dealings with the enemy of man. Let me fall into the judgments of God, though they be terrible, and let me not lose my soul to gain a few days of earthly life.' With that she opened the door and left us looking one on another.

The Italian smote her hands together in anger, and turned to my cousin, that had stood the while without word or motion. '*Filippo mio!*' she cried; 'will you suffer us to perish for the pride of this cold girl? You are master here; give command and I will make her say the word of power, if I scourge her to the bones!'

At this I laid my hand on my hilt; and assuredly if the Earl had spoken to do the Signora's bidding, he should have uttered no word more on earth. Yet need I not have feared for him, for in all his desperate wickedness was some spark of honour, and yet more of pride in his house; and now he lifted his hand and spake more nobly than I had yet heard.

'Surely,' he said, with a heavy scorn in his utterance, 'the world is turned upside down indeed when a quacksalver's daughter of the scum of Italy shall talk of scourging a kinswoman of mine own and my dead lady's. Go' – and here he gave her a foul name in the Italian, that I will not set down – 'and take thy carrion with thee, ere I send thee to join thy devils in hell!'

But at this she fell down before him, clasping his knees and crying out for pardon, in that it was but her great love for him and concern for his safety that had made her so desperate; and his mood lasting not, as was his wont, presently they were friends again.

But when we came to lift the body of the wench, it was already blackened and corrupted, so that we cared not to handle it; yet need urging us, the Earl and I made shift to thrust it through the window, the tide being at the full and the current strong. For a while the body floated on the dark water, till there came a breath of the slimy smell that I knew, and a sound of sucking and a whirl in the waters, and no sign more of the dead. So we went forth; but first the Signora cast out from the window the man's hand, that was charred like a coal, and the brazen altar and her other matters of sorcery. 'I have done with curious arts for ever,' says she; 'yet have I mine own self left!'

CHAPTER X

OF MY SWORD-PLAY WITH THE EARL, AND OF THE NIGHT
AFTER

SURELY is there sooth in the old proverb that to-morrow is another day, and wisdom in the way of old men that will forbear to judge of a matter till they have slept on it; for the new dawn often brings new heart to endure, and a few brief hours of sleep avail to carry away the darkness of the soul and mind.

On the morrow of that ugly night of death and devilry was the morning fair again, and clearer than the wont of autumn; and to me, looking from my window at the growing dawn, came the thought that perchance, if the putting off of clothes and lying down to slumber can wipe our hearts clean of so much ill and sorrow, the doffing of our worn and tattered flesh, and the falling asleep that is called death, may lead to an awakening to a new day clearer than the last, yet not unlike, rather than to a glory or a torment too great for our little deeds. Nor have I ceased to comfort myself with this thought, though I have found no divine of any church to hold it other than heresy; so that I have kept my fancy for myself and for one other that will never account me heretic.

When I turned my eyes from the morning to the court of the castle, I could gather that somewhat new was afoot. The troopers were gathered in knots, talking eagerly, some laughing and some sullen, though all cursing; for in the King's army oaths were as many as texts among the Ironsides, yet rather from the fashion of the time than from wickedness in the one host or godliness in the other. One or two of the men were on the rampart, peering eagerly under crooked palms to landward; and as I still looked, came my cousin the Earl with a perspective glass

273

in his hand, and all made way for him to go up and behold what might be toward.

Therefore I clad myself in haste, and went down into the court; and my Lord, turning from the land, saw me and called:

'Hither, cousin, and see where your friends come!'

Now when I was on the platform by his side, I looked landward, as I had marked him spying, but nothing was to be seen save the marshes; so I asked where these friends of mine might be.

'Why, up in the hills, as far as thou canst see,' says he, laughing. 'Hast left thine eyes in thy books, man?'

I strained my sight on the hills, as he bade me, but vainly; and I was about to ask him the answer to his riddle, when I spied a little feather of smoke over the edge of the furthest hill, and told him.

'Aye, that is they,' said the Earl; 'they have lit their fires for breakfast, and a plenteous one, I warrant them. Many is the time I have seen that smoke over the hills in Bohemia, and known that Piccolomini or Gallas was on the road to fight us.'

'Then you think that yonder smoke is made by soldiers?' said I.

'Think? Nay, I know,' he answered. 'I give them for a troop of horse, with Noll Cromwell's orders to knock all on the head that will not take quarter, and hang all that surrender.'

Here one touched him on the shoulder, and he saw the Signora.

'Ah, I forgot La Fiammetta,' he went on; 'for her no steel or hemp will serve, but another puff of yonder smoke.'

She smiled on him with no kindness, and her eyes grew narrow. 'Are the Parliament soldiers come then?' she asked of me.

'We can see the smoke of fires in the hills,' I answered; 'and it is most likely that they are made by soldiers of the Parliament. They should be at Marsham by noon.'

'And at Deeping Hold by Doomsday,' quoth the Earl laughing. 'I am sorry that I beat in the boats, for I would love to fight with somewhat in the likeness of a man. Now

I see not how they are to come at us.'

The Italian woman shook her head in impatience. 'What need for them to do aught?' said she. 'What need for us to care whether they come or go?'

'Why,' says my cousin, 'surely you should not ask that when you have followed our camp over half Germany and all England.' And with that he turned to the troopers, who were looking up at him. 'Men,' he goes on, raising his voice that all might hear, 'these are the Roundheads come to make an end of us, if they can. Here is no flight, nor hope of escape save in fighting. If they promise you life, they will keep their word with a halter. Look to your arms, then, and if we must sleep in hell, let them go first to find us warm quarters.'

He ended, and they gave a great shout and went to furbish their weapons and armour, and the Earl to gaze landward again; but by now was there no smoke to see, the Parliament men being on the march again; so he came down into the court, where were none but the Signora and myself. Now she had not said word again after he put her off, save that while he spake to the troopers methought I heard her mutter '*E matto!*' under her breath. But now she was all smiles, and taking him by the arm, 'Well, *Filippo mio,*' says she, 'if you must needs fight the Roundheads, it behoves you to be apt with your weapon. Will you not have another lesson from Signor Uberto?'

Now these words of hers, perchance so meant, jarred on my cousin's temper, as reminding him that I was the better at sword-play; but he laughed harshly, and bade Pompey bring the foils and other matters, adding that a bout of fence would serve to pass the time, though of little use for battle; 'For,' says he, 'your Roundheads are no nice duellists, cousin, and they will have my head cloven while I am studying in what eyelet-hole to pink them.'

With that Pompey brought us the foils, and I took one and did off my coat; but when the Earl would have done the like, the Signora came before him, and catching up his foil, fell on guard prettily, saying, 'Nay, Filippo, let me have the first bout, for I would fain see if I can handle so long a needle' – and he laughed and bade her go on.

So for a little we were at thrust and parry, and I wondered not a little at her skill thereat; for she seemed to know all the tricks that my Italian master had taught me, and more, and once or twice had well-nigh mastered me, so that I was fain to keep off a thrust rather by strength than art. Yet did she soon tire, or seem to tire; her play grew slower and less artful, till at the last, fetching a lunge at me, her foot slipped and she well-nigh fell forward, and her foil, catching between two stones, snapped short. Thereat she threw down the hilt, laughing at her own discomfiture, and would have the Earl take her place, and he, being nowise loth to show her that he could do better, called for another foil, but Pompey, stammering with fear, told him that none remained unbroken. At that I was fain to give over, but the Italian would not have it so, and would have my cousin take his rapier to my foil; 'For so,' says she, 'Signor Uberto will not hurt you, Filippo, and I am sure you cannot hurt him.'

At that the Earl's brows drew together, and I, fearing lest his rage should take him, made haste to decline so strange a match, for that I was unwilling to set my skin on the hazard of such a bout; and indeed, though I had little fear that the Earl could hurt me by his fence, I feared the chances of the game, wherein I had known men hurt grievously even by the breaking of foils. But the Earl's blood being heated, nothing would content him but a bout with the bare swords; and when the Signora spake against it, he snatched up the unbroken foil (for I had cast it down) and brake it across his knee, and so drew his rapier, and bade me do the same or be called coward. So, as there seemed no way out of it, I drew out my sword and fell on guard, with a great resolution that I would not hurt my cousin, and still less would let him hurt me.

So we fell to at this dangerous play, and at the first the Earl was wary, and I for my part did rather make a show of fighting than fight; for when I thrust, I ever drew back ere I could have hit him, and gave him time to guard; and so did he also at the first. But as he warmed to the work, moved by his temper, and by a mocking word or two of the woman's, his fence grew to be more than play, though still less than cruel earnest, and I had much ado to escape a scratch or worse. So that I cautioned him between thrusts, saying that we should do well to cease, or one or both might take hurt; and perchance he had listened, had not the Signora laughed at my words. At that he came at me the more madly, till I had need of all my skill to keep him off, and of all my patience to refrain from hurting him.

He was swordsman enough to know that I spared him, and grew the more furious, laying himself open as he thrust, and taunting me with my forbearance, till I was angered out of patience, and after my next parry thrust swifter and touched him on the arm, so that a spot of red showed on the sleeve of his shirt. With that the Signora laughed again, and he, either at the smart of the scratch (for it was no more) or at her laughter, was as one possessed of a devil, and made at me so that I was sore put to it not to slay him or be slain, till his breath was spent, and he stood panting and grinding his teeth. This rest I took first to get my own breath, and then to crave his pardon for hurting him, thinking to call him back to the manner of our fight at the beginning. 'For surely, Cousin Philip,' said I; 'I am sorry that I hit you, and you will believe that it was but by chance and not with my will.'

'And wherefore not?' he cried out; 'Why should you not thrust home, if you can, and end all? You have your Roundhead friends to please, and I know not what devils beside, and Mistress Rosamund with her white face, and the canting knave Pentry to avenge. I am one against you all, and I bid you do your worst. Make this a duello to the death, if you will, and be damned for it!'

Now as he spake, panting between his words, and leaning on the wall, and I waited for him, the thought came swiftly on me that here was a man doomed and desperate and desirous of death; a man for whom no mercy would be asked or given from heaven or earth or hell, a man outlawed by God and men and devils. He was past saving; what mattered whether I or another should end him? Whether one of Cromwell's troopers, or a traitor of his own men, or a monster of the great deep, mattered little; his slayer was but an instrument in God's hand, as my sword was in mine, and they that strove to help him would be but partakers in his doom.

So thinking, I made ready to meet him as he took up his weapon and came towards me, his eyes shining with hate and madness; and so sure was I of the secret thrust that I had kept from showing him, that I marked the very fold of his shirt over his breast where I should thrust him through after a pass or twain. And surely (since the best of us have the leaven of Cain in our hearts) I had taken him at his word, had not the Italian woman that watched us, smiling, looked but once into mine eyes, and pointed her forefinger at the Earl, saying, 'Guard yourself, Signor Uberto!' The words were harmless, yet there was that in her voice that said 'Kill him!' and the pointing of her finger called back to me the ill dream wherein I had done in sick fancy the deed that now I would do in truth, and I remembered how in a vision I had thrust my cousin through the heart, and his blood became a nest of red snakes to coil around me. On the instant was my mind fixed, that I would do no evil that good might come; my sword, that was to guard mine own life or quell the public enemy, should be no dagger for the plots of this devil's daughter. Therefore, as my cousin got his breath and came at me again, I dropped my rapier on the stones and so stood, saying, 'Cousin, I am to blame that I hurt thee; and I will not hurt thee further. Thou and I are the last of the house of Deeping; I will not slay thee, and if thou slayest me thou shalt slay a man unarmed.'

For a flash methought that he would thrust me through as I stood, and a horror came over me as he drew back his hand; yet did he but offer his point at my breast, and so stood wavering, for his frenzy was yet strong upon him. Nor do I know what would have befallen us, had not the Swede Gulston come hastily upon us, saying that the Parliament men were to be seen riding over the hills to Marsham. After he had said this the second time, my cousin, as one awaking from an evil dream, ran his hand over his eyes once or twice and fell shuddering; then, with no word to us, he went on up the ramparts, catching up his coat and scabbard as he went, and left the Swede staring at us. To whom I excused myself as best I could, saying that we had been trying tricks of fence with the bare rapier, as our foils were broken, and that having by mischance hurt the Earl, I had ended the bout. With that I also took my scabbard and my coat and went to my chamber, leaving Gulston, that was apt enough at stratagems of war, but in other matters of small quickness of apprehension, yet perplexed. And perchance better had it been for him that I had remained to enlighten him further; but I was weary and spent with labour of body and mind, and thirsted to be alone. Nor did I think aught of it when from the turret stair I glanced in the court and saw the Swede deep in talk with the Signora; I but hastened the more to be out of sight and sound of her, nor rested till I sat on my bed and felt the wind blowing chill at my window, with now and then the sick savour of the Hole.

I stayed thus till the bell rang to call us to dinner, and so to the hall; nor was there aught to mark the rest of the day, save that the Signora was more pleasant and courteous than her wont, and the Swede more sullen and silent. Mistress Rosamund I saw not till supper-time, fain as I was to have speech with her; yet as we rose from table at nightfall, and my cousin gave us brief good-night and passed to his rooms, I made shift to whisper to Mistress Fanshawe that I would walk in the court when the guard had been changed. Nor was there aught else to note, save that with the darkness and the rising of the tide the smell of the Hole increased, till it had been grievous to us, had we not become accustomed to the savour. For the troopers, the coming of their enemies to Marsham had driven their late terrors clean from their minds, that were too narrow to hold more thoughts than one; or if some of them had not forgotten their fear, they made haste to cast it from them, and bend their wits to a new battle with their old enemies, the Roundheads. My cousin, though of a surety he must have known how vain was his care against an adversary that could not well come at him, was eager in setting a watch, and in telling off his best gunners to the culverins on the barbican. Also he was careful, as befitted a captain, to guard well the points of the wall where an escalade might be easiest. Now not far from my turret the wall was somewhat lower than elsewhere, and the shale of the marsh was heaped against the rampart in a mound, that seemed to me, idly looking upon it that day, to be higher than I had seen it aforetime. On this spur of the wall was a little guard-house of stone, with a narrow loop-hole bearing on the marsh, and here were set two sentries to fire on any seeking to climb the wall.

So soon as the watch had gone their rounds, and new sentries were set, I went quietly down the stair of my tower, nor was it long before Mistress Rosamund came from the door of the keep. The night was still and chilly, and the mist had risen from the marshes. No sound was there but the lapping of the tide, and the clanking steps of the sentinels, till presently I seemed to hear the sucking noise that I had noted before, but faint; and the two men in the little guard-house striking up a rough soldier's song, I noted other sounds no more.

While we walked in the mist, then, I told Mistress Rosamund what had been that morning, but doubtfully; for I could not be fixed in my mind whether she would not think I had been weak in sparing my cousin, when one thrust had gone far to save us all from siege and famine, or I knew not what other worse doom. Yet might I have spared my fears; for when I had told her all, but haltingly, she stood and looked on me for a space, and then said earnestly, 'You have done well, cousin, and better than I should have done in your place' – the which when I could in no wise allow, she went on, 'He hath deserved death many times, it may be, yet could you not be his hangman, even to save us all.'

'Had I thought more of your danger,' I said, for I would not have her hold me better than I was, 'I might have slain my cousin. I fear it was but pride and kinship that kept me from revenging the innocent, and I am little less ashamed of forbearing him than I had been of killing him.'

'Well,' says she, with a catch in her throat that was between a laugh and a sob, 'be ashamed of yourself if you will, cousin, but I will be proud of you for both of us.'

At this I was gladder than I had thought to be of aught that I might hear, and caught her hand, that was cold in the wet mist, and had kissed it, but that a puff of wind came in our faces, and she cried out softly and drew back, snatching her hand from me, and yet, as I think, not meaning it; for the wind was filled with the deadly savour of the slime, that made her faint, and I myself was near to stifle with it. Also the men in the little room on the wall must have smelt the like, for I heard one cry out on his fellow, 'Reach me the jack, Tom, else I shall poison with this cursed stink' – and so he drank noisily and cleared his throat with a great hem, and struck up his song again:

'We'll hang up Noll with his crop-eared poll,
　And the hounds of his canting pack;
By one, two, and three, they shall dance on the tree,
　When we bring our good King back—
　　With a hey derry down—'

And the other chimed in with the burden that neither of them was to end in this world; for while they sang, I had marked the sucking noise that I had heard aforetime, growing louder, till it was as the wash of a whirlpool, and looking to the wall, where was a battlement hard by the guard-room, I could see no more the white glimmer of the mist through the break in the coping-stones, but all was black and humped in a mound that grew higher, and with that one of the men brake off his singing and gave a great shout of fear, and the other, as it seemed, sang on for a note or twain, and changed suddenly to a horrid strangling cry, mingled with a grating and cracking as of rock crushed in a miner's mill. A moment I stood tranced with the horror of these noises, and then my manhood came again, and putting aside Mistress Rosamund that would have held me back, I whipped out my sword and made up to the rampart, and as I went, came some of the soldiers running from their quarters, and Gulston doing on his buff coat as he ran, with a dagger between his teeth. But ere I could be at the door of the room, had all cries ended, and only a mumbling voice and the sound of laughter, that daunted me the more; yet I made haste to open the door of the guard-room, where the torch the two men had with them burned yet on the wall.

Well nigh had I fallen as I entered, for the floor was reeking with slime; but naught else was there to see, save one of the men leant against the corner of the wall and laughing softly to himself, as one demented, and then muttering somewhat. Of the other man was no sign save his musket and pike on the stone floor, and the loophole in the wall was scored and jagged at the edges, and dripped with slime. So I stood and stared at the fellow, that gazed on me and laughed and mumbled, twisting his fingers together like a little child; and after me came in the others, yet hanging back, and huddling in the doorway, with wild eyes rolling in the red flicker of the torch. Only the Swede thrust the others aside and took the man by the shoulder, shaking him and bidding him tell where was his fellow.

But he went on twisting his fingers and laughing to himself, and then between his chuckles as it were singing, 'Tom's head's a rotten apple! Tom's head's a rotten apple!' —and naught else, and so laughed again. Nor would he say one word of reason, though Gulston fetched him a great blow on the cheek, that he seemed not to feel, for he left not laughing nor twisting of his hands. So we had him thence to his bed, where he lay laughing and singing of his foolishness till cock-crow, when he shuddered and so died, with no word to tell what he had seen.

CHAPTER XI

As we bare the crazed man to his quarters, came the Earl from his door, with a furred nightgown cast around him, and his naked sword in his hand; and when he heard what I could tell him, he went up to the little guard-room, and thence on the rampart, and I with him; but nought was to see save that which I had seen already, and the slime on the battlements, and the white mist hanging over the black waters, and a silence of death. What my cousin thought I knew not, nor belike did he, for his face was desperate, and he stood by the wall a long time, till he stretched out both arms to the sea, crying out as to some enemy, 'Take me then, if you will!' but there was none that answered, and no sound save the washing of the ebbing tide on the rock. So he turned to me sighing as one wearied beyond endurance, and spake strangely.

'Cousin,' says he, 'why didst not thou thrust home this morning? Thou wast at point to do it, and all had been better for thee and no worse for me.'

I scarce knew how to answer him, for I would not speak of the Italian woman, partly that I was loth to accuse any without strong proof, but rather that I knew her power over him, and feared that she might move him to fasten a worse quarrel on me. So I did but say that I had grown heated with the play, and done foolishly in hurting him; yet had I come to my senses ere worse befell, and craved his forgiveness. 'For,' said I, 'it is written, "Let not the sun go down upon your wrath"; and though it be too late for us to say this, yet let not the sun rise on anger between us twain.'

'Thou art ever a Puritan,' he answered me, laughing

with no mirth, yet not unkindly; 'but thou art better than Noll's saints yonder by Marsham, that will knock a man unarmed on the head to the glory of God. If God take pleasure in such villains, let me serve the devil still.'

I answered him that I for one could not hold that the Lord had delight in the violence of men, though oft-times He might work out His purpose by such tools; and thinking that in this mood I might perchance move him to repentance (his evil genius also being away from his elbow), I said further that it behoved us rather to doubt our own ways than the goodness of God, and that when we had amended ourselves even a little, we should see clearer into His will. 'Even,' said I, 'as we see the stars now, that have been shining all the while, though we marked them not for the mist.' For indeed, while I spake, came a shift of wind from the sea, and the mist rolled away from the marsh, and the night was fair and quiet, with the little sparkles of the stars dancing on the ripples.

Methought I had moved him, but he showed no sign, but turning away from that fair night, 'Well,' says he, 'the tide is ebbing fast, and none can come within a mile of us unseen. So to bed, cousin!' And so he strode off, bidding the sentries in the towers keep good watch; for none would come near the guard-house, that yet reeked of that charnel smell.

So when I had paced the court once or twice, and heard nothing but the call of the watch, and when I came by the troopers' quarters, the babbling of the crazed man (for he died not till dawn, as I have said), I must even betake myself to my chamber with a heavy heart; for I had supped full of horrors, as the play hath it, and but for the thought of Mistress Rosamund (that was with me oft-times now) I had gone near to think the earth a foul and friendless place, and to love life hardly more than did my cousin.

Yet on the morrow, when after a brief and troubled slumber, I awoke to find my window a blank of mist, I remembered rather the fear that hung over us than the hope of converse with another that lay under a like peril with all of us; for though there was at that time no ill savour in the mist, it seemed the cover for I knew not what enemy to come upon us. Yet because there was naught else for me to do, I came down and walked in the court after my wont, and marked naught save the passing shadows of the men; and stopping one of them I asked of the madman, and was told he was dead, and it seemed a little matter to me. So I walked, till the mist lightened somewhat, and I was aware of the Earl coming to me.

'What say you, Cousin Hubert?' says he, 'Shall we have our bout again?' To which I made answer that we had no foils left, else was I willing.

'Why,' says he, smiling, 'let us take our rapiers, but sheathed, cousin; for I would but kill time to-day.'

So, as I had naught against his wish, I bound my sword sheath to the hilt that it should not fall off, and he doing the like, we were at fence for a space, but idly; and thinking to please him, and also to take away the temptation that had gone near to make me a murderer, I asked to show him a new device of sword play, and he being ready, I taught him the trick of the thrust that I had been minded to use on him, and the ward for it; and as he was apt at arms and quick of sight, it was not long ere he learned it nigh as well as myself, and could tell how to prepare for it with a cunning feint that led another, if he knew not its meaning, to bear his hand too low and lay himself open.

Now while I showed him, was the mist still hanging around us, so that none could see what we did; but now the wind freshened, and the vapours thinning, the court was plain in a pale sunlight, and the Signora looking on us from the doorway, and Gulston standing by her. So I ceased, and gave them good morning, and the woman nodded her head, and the Swede came lounging to us, with a swaggering manner that methought sat but ill on him.

'So you will take your lesson with the sheathed swords to-day, my Lord?' he said, grinning in his yellow beard. 'It is right prudent of you.'

Now at this my cousin lifted his brows and pressed his lips together; for the man's words were naught, but there was an insolence in his voice, that made me marvel. Yet I wondered more at the coolness with which the Earl took it.

'Why, surely,' answered he, smiling at the Swede; 'Even I am not a fool two days together,' and with that he unbound the handkerchief from his hilt, and put his sword at his side, and I was about to do the same when Gulston stopped me.

'Will you not spare me a crumb of your learning?' he said, smiling with a show of a soldier's frankness; 'We could not well see you for this cursed mist, but you seemed to be teaching my Lord a pretty trick of fence. Could you not of your bounty show me it again?' As he spake, he looked askance at the Signora, that glanced back at him; and I stood perplexed, thinking that there lay some purpose behind this request, and looking at my cousin for guidance. But he laughed and answered me, 'Aye, show him, Hubert, show him!' and so leaned on the steps and watched us.

Now I could no longer delay, though my mind misgave me that here was some fine plot of the Italian's; so I showed Gulston the thrust I had been taught, and he seemed apter at learning than my cousin, as even the Earl owned. ' 'Swounds, Eric!' he cried; 'you are a better fencer than I thought you. I could not master these Italian tricks in a week of learning. I am but a blunt Englishman, as Madonna here will certify. To it again, Gulston!' And at his word the Swede lunged so aptly with his sheathed rapier that I was over late in my ward, and took a sharp touch on the breast, and the Earl and the Signora clapped their hands. Then I ceased, telling Gulston that I would teach him no more, and feigning a hurt to my vanity; also I was purposed in my mind that I would in no wise show him the parry of the thrust, though I knew not what harm might be therein.

So when my cousin had broken a jest or two on me for my defeat, and the Signora had done the like, but more subtly, and I had answered as best I could (for indeed my wit was never nimble), we stood talking of this and that, till a trooper came from the men's quarters asking what should be done with the man that had been crazed overnight and was now dead.

'Why,' says the Earl, 'Gulston, you will take a burial party in one of the boats, and see that the poor fellow has his rights. Pick me a pair of men, and see it is done ere dinner time.'

At that the Swede's face turned red under the burn of sun and wind, and he pulled at his moustachios, as was his way, and stood a while before he gave answer. So my Lord spake more sharply again. 'You understand?' says he. 'This is no strange thing for soldiers to do in the wars.'

'Aye, but it is a strange thing here,' answers the Swede, getting his speech at last. 'For Mr. Leyton here can bear me out that when we buried the men that were slain at Marsham we were like to be swallowed of a quicksand, or what else I know not, but perchance you may. So I sware, and he heard me, that I would go on no more buryings.'

Now I looked for my cousin to break out into one of his rages; for here was not only flat disobedience, but the manner of the Swede's speech was worse than its matter. Yet if the Earl was possessed of devils, as he seemed full often, this was the cold devil's day, or his pride, which was great, would not let him show that he was moved.

'Well,' says he to the troopers that stood by (for a few more had come forth while he spake); 'if your cornet cares not for catching of a cold, will you bury your comrade, and you, and you—' and he called some of them by name. But they all hung back, divided between their fear of the Earl and their greater fear of the peril on the marshes; nor could I blame them when I remembered what I had seen.

'Nay then,' said my cousin; 'I will never send another on an errand that I fear to go myself. Cousin, will you come?'

Now the Italian had stood silent while Gulston had bearded his officer, and had but glanced up from narrow eyes; but now she brake in, counselling the Earl and myself not to go forth, for that assuredly there was danger to us both. Whereat, as even I could have guessed, my cousin was all the more fixed in his purpose, and I, for very shame, could not leave him to make his venture alone. So he called on the men to make the body ready for burial, and bring it to the harbour, with a pair of spades, the which they did, and laid all in the smallest of the boats, and so stood looking on us as we sat down; and the Signora and Gulston came also unbidden. But when we were at point to push off, first one and then another of the soldiers that were the Earl's own servants came into the boat with us, and took the oars from me as I settled myself to row; and the Swede, seeing this, and bethinking himself (as seemed to me) that he might be counted coward, or belike moved thereto by a look of the Signora, sware an oath and leapt in with us. 'Well, sink or swim,' says he, with a wry laugh, 'I am with you for this bout,' and the Earl, with no word to any, pushed off.

Nor did it seem that any peril would come to us in our errand; for the air was clear, and the sun shone on the marsh, whence the tide had fallen some space, and even the grey flats and stretches were less desolate than their wont. This daunted me the more, for it looked to me as though some ambush lay under the brightness of the day; yet to the men, that were rough and simple of nature, there seemed no cause for fear, and had it not been for the corpse we carried, they had even laughed after their wont.

Not a word did my cousin vouchsafe, but set our course for a wide stretch of shale that lay somewhat to the landward, smooth and grey, with no hollow where an enemy might lurk, and no channel to break the plain; only a space away was a long shadow, marking, as I thought, the course of some ditch or channel like a seam across the marsh. The Swede also sat sullen, playing with his sword hilt, but speaking no word, till we ran the boat up at the edge of the flat, and my Lord giving command, the two troopers carried their dead fellow up to a place where the ground was even and hard, and began to dig a grave; and the three of us sat and watched them labouring, shewing darkly against the sunlit marsh, that was broken only in that place by the shadow of the channel. I looked around sometimes, and listened earnestly, but no swirl in the water was there, nor yet the sucking noise that I had heard; nor did aught strange appear, till the men beckoned to us that they were ready, and my cousin nodding to me, we went up, Gulston following us, and left the boat swinging with a rope to the boathook that we had planted in the ground.

So we came to the grave that was dug for the dead man, and again I made shift to play the chaplain, and with more readiness than the former time, for the soldier that we were burying had perished in no murder or rapine, but in his plain and daily duty; also the extremity of that terror that had reft him of wit and life might be counted by some a fearful retribution for what sins his had been. So I prayed, and my cousin and his men stood with their hats off and waited, and the Swede covered, and aloof from us, till I had done, and the two men filled in the sand and earth above the body; and still the sun was clear and the air calm and still, and no sign of life stirring on the marshes, that were pale in the sunlight, save for the dark streaks of the channels, and chief of these the long shadow that I had noted before to landward, and methought (but I put the fancy aside as idle) that it was somewhat nearer than I remembered.

All being now decently done, I looked for my cousin to bid us go, and the men shouldered their spades ready; but the Earl stopped them. 'Nay, leave them as yet,' he says; 'Maybe you shall need them anon.' And while the men stared on him open-mouthed, and I wondered what this might mean (for he spake quietly, as one that had a purpose), he went up to the Swede, that stood sullen a few paces off, and tapping him on the shoulder – 'A word with you, Eric Guldenstierna,' says he; 'have you forgotten that you dared to disobey the order of your officer but now? What is that but mutiny?' and with that he whipped a pistol from under his cloak. Gulston started, and laid a hand on his hilt; but my Lord saying, 'Draw and you die,' he took his hand away and so stood.

'Had you been Noll Cromwell's man and not mine,' said my cousin; 'you had been pistolled in the castle court, on your first word of mutiny. But we of the King's side, as our cause is the less holy, are less apt at slaying men defenceless. Nor would I risk bespattering a gentle lady like the Signora with your brains, though she has seen worse things perchance. But one of us two goes not back to Deeping Hold.'

'And what will your Lordship do, then?' asked the Swede, sneering. 'Will you have your worshipful cousin and your two men to dispose of me, and save yourself the slaughterer's work?'

'Why, no!' answered the Earl carelessly. 'You shall have your fair chance, little as you merit it; our swords are of a length, and Hubert here shall see fair play, and be priest to the one that dies and ferryman to the other. How sayest thou, cousin?'

But to this I would in no wise consent, for that I held the duello as little better than murder at any time, and most of all when we were in deadly peril, and should hold together for defence rather than turn our hands against one another. Somewhat of this I said; yet could I not move my cousin.

'Thou art no coward for a scholar,' says he; 'but thou hast little knowledge of wars, else thou hadst known that in peril mercy to a mutineer is death to true men. Either I give the dog a chance for his life, or I shoot him down as he stands. Choose thou which it shall be.'

'I will have no part nor lot in the matter,' said I; 'with my will shalt thou neither slay nor be slain.'

'Why then, stand and look on and keep thy conscience warm,' answered my cousin; 'and if he win, let him go free of vengeance. Come, sir, shall we walk?' and as the other nodded without word, the Earl laid down his pistol and did off his cloak and coat, and left them by the boat with his scabbard, and Gulston did the like. Then each with his rapier under his arm, they went back to the place where we had buried the man. 'This place will suit as well as any,' I heard my cousin say, as they came on a bare stretch of the sands beyond the mound that marked the grave. Gulston answered not but by deed. He took his sword in hand, saluted and fell on guard, and the blades clinked together.

Now I had not followed them, nor had the two men, for I would have no share in this quarrel, and the soldiers dared not move without a word from their head. So we stood by the boat, on the shelving bank, and looked at the two that were, it might be, an hundred paces from us, and showed dark against the pale marshland, and beyond them was the dark riband of the channel I had noted, that seemed to have water left there, for the sunlight flickered on a wetness in it here and there. But in a minute or twain I had no eyes for aught but the two that were fighting to the death.

Yet at the first it seemed no more deadly a game than our bouts in the castle court, for that both were wary; and the clinking and grating of the steel as they thrust and parried was like the beat of some strange great clock. The Swede was careful, as I had known him; and my cousin was no whit behind him for coolness. So even a match it seemed that when they ceased and took breath, I had hope that the quarrel might end without blood. When they were breathed, they fell to again, and now grew fiercer, till I heard Gulston vent an oath, and guessed that the Earl had touched him; but he fought on none the less stoutly, and I looked for this duello to last yet a good while, and withdrew mine eyes from the flash of the swords for a moment, resting them on the shadow of the channel, that was grown somewhat wider, so that methought the tide must be flowing. Then, as I looked on the two again, suddenly came the end. I saw Gulston giving back a little, and the other pressing him, and they wheeled so that the Swede turned his back on us; then I marked his blade sweep round swiftly, and he lunged forward in the thrust I had taught him but that morning. I shut mine eyes for a flash, for I deemed my cousin but dead; but when I looked, he stood black against the grey marsh, and Gulston reeled, clutching at his side, and fell, and so lay, and his slayer looked on him for a space, and then came to us slowly, with his sword stained to the hilt.

Truly, if one had to die, I would not that the fight had gone otherwise; yet it sickened me to think that the life of a man could be so ill used, and so lightly lost, and I could say no word to the Earl as he began to do on his coat. Then as he wiped his sword and sheathed it, 'So, cousin,' says he, 'thou art sad that the dog has died a man's death. Yet what does it matter if he has gone first, or I? Hadst thou taught him the answer as well as the thrust, he had been standing here now in my stead. Well, I would I may end no worse than Gulston. Let us go now and do him what honour we may.'

So the men bent down for their spades, and we turned again to the place where the grave had been made, and the Swede had fallen a few paces beyond. But when I looked for the mound and the body, naught could I see but the grey space of the marsh, and no sign that man had been there alive or dead. Then methought that I had turned to another quarter, and I cast my eyes over the plain of grey, but still was there naught save a glistering of the ground, and colours as of a rainbow, as I have seen them on a puddle of slime in the sun. Also the channel beyond, or what I had held to be such, was gone utterly like a smear of chalk wiped from a slate; and a little wind blew to us over the marsh, and the breath of it was salt and foul.

At that a great fear fell on me, and I clutched my cousin by the arm, crying out to make homeward; so he caught up a cloak from the ground, and muffled himself in it, and so came to the boat, and we were with him as soon. The men rowed fiercely, though sight and sound of danger was there none; so in no long time were we at the quay, and all the while my cousin sat with his hat pulled over his eyes and the cloak drawn close round him, and shivered once or twice, as if from cold. And looking at him (for there was naught else to do) I marked that he had taken the Swede's cloak for his own as they lay together.

Now as we drew near the harbour, it seemed to me that I saw a woman on the barbican gazing on us; yet as I looked was she gone, and none but the sentinels to meet us till we came to the court. There stood more of the men, that asked no question of their two fellows, but drew apart from them. At the door of the hall was Mistress Rosamund, and her eyes lightened on me, and her lips moved without sound. Then came the Italian forth, and Pompey bearing a flagon and goblet, and she looked on my Lord that was yet muffled in Gulston's cloak, and his hat pulled over his eyes; and the twain being of a like height and bigness, he seemed the counterpart of the man he had slain. The Signora spake no word, but filled the goblet with wine, and stood waiting and smiling strangely, till the Earl came nearer to her, and threw back the cloak. 'Well, Fiammetta,' says he, 'thou art not rid of me yet.'

Now when he spake thus, her face changed and was convulsed, and she cried out sharply and threw out her arms, marking not the goblet, that flew from her hand and shattered on the stones, and the red wine oozed in the chinks like blood. Also she reeled as though in a swoon, and called on Pompey to hold her; and he stretching out his hands to her, the flagon went to join the goblet. Yet did she recover herself and cast her arms about the Earl, laughing and sobbing as one distraught, and so remained till he shook her off and went in heavily, and the rest of us to our quarters.

Yet must we meet again at dinner presently, and make a show of eating, and speak words that none noted; and the Swede's chair was empty, but Fear sat at the board in his stead.

CHAPTER XII

OF THE POOL THAT CRAWLED

OF that which we spake at dinner-time, as I have said, I have no remembrance, nor did any say much; also, though I held my cousin's cause to be the better in his late quarrel, and would not have had the fight go otherwise, if fight there must be, I had more sorrow for the death of the Swede than I had thought to feel for a mere sworder. We were a little company, beset with many dangers known and unknown, and prisoned on our rock, that was like to prove but a sandy refuge; and sudden or lingering, the end of the leaguer seemed sure. Also from some words that passed between the Earl and one of the men that served us, I gathered that our store of victual was dwindling, nor was I surprised thereat, for it had been as wastefully spent as it had been hastily and wrongfully gathered; and indeed, I remembered that Gulston, in the days when he was yet loyal, had spoken thereof to my cousin, who (being in one of his reckless moods) would take no order, saying that the food would last our time.

Therefore, as soon as we had eaten, I rose from the table, asking leave of the others, and getting a nod from the Italian woman, and went down to the great gate, and finding it open, with a watch set at the side and men in the barbican tower above, I walked on the pier, part of masonry and part of the rock itself, that sheltered the little port, where the barges swayed on their chains with the little waves of the tide, that had risen to the full while we dined, and was now falling, leaving wet stones and shallow pools towards the sea. As I went towards the water's edge, the rocks and stones were slimy, as is the wont after an ebbing tide, so that I had nigh fallen once or twice, and turned back to the drier footing, and went not down to the spot where there lay a larger pool, near to the waves, like a sheet of lead on the grey stone and green weed.

As I came to the gate again (for the mole was but a little one) I was aware of Mistress Rosamund within the gateway, and seeing me, she came out and walked with me, whereof I was glad, for my thoughts were but ill, and it heartened me to see the one face that I knew to cover no memories of bad deeds, nor plots of worse things to come. So as we went to and fro, she asked me of that morning's happenings, and I told her of the fencing bout, and the Swede's disobedience, and the story of the fight; and ever as I told her, she would say, 'And what spake the Signora?' or, 'How looked the Signora at that?'

When I told her of the strange vanishing both of Gulston's body and of the grave of the other dead man, she fell a-shuddering, and gripped my arm, not knowing, as it seemed, and murmuring to herself, 'And it might have been he!' and it gladdened me, though I dared not guess at her meaning.

But when I came to telling of the Earl's catching up the Swede's cloak for his own, and muffling himself in the dead man's apparel, Mistress Rosamund drew in her breath sharply and leaving my arm, smote her hands together, and 'Ah!' says she, 'now I see it all!' At which I was amazed, and asked of her meaning.

'Why, Cousin Hubert!' she said quickly, 'you a scholar and know not what this means? Did you not see, when my Lord did off the Swede's cloak and showed his face, how that woman cried out and dropped the goblet of wine, and called on Pompey to help her, that let fall the flagon, as well she knew he would? Can you not see it now? The wine was for Gulston, if the Earl had been slain, and belike for you also. Me she might have spared for a space to sacrifice to her devil, if he be not sick of a greater wickedness than his own!'

Her words affrighted me, as when I had seen the first grave we digged melt away from under our feet into a whirlpool of slime; and though her meaning was clear to me now, I would not let myself believe in such a black deep of iniquity. 'Nay, nay!' I answered, too roughly, I fear; 'This is surely madness! I love not the woman, nor have cause to; but anyone in her place, good or bad, would have gone nigh to swoon and cast away whatever she held, noting it not. Nay, cousin, give the devil his due!'

Mistress Rosamund turned and smiled on me, but sadly, and somewhat pitifully, as a mother on a child that speaks foolishly.

'Ah, Hubert!' she said, and neither she nor I then marked that she left off calling me 'cousin'; 'thou art no woman, else hadst thou known all this and more long ago. Where are thine eyes? Canst thou not see that behind her cat's eyes there is ever a plot, and behind that another, and behind that again a throng of stratagems, one blacker than another? I tell thee, she eats and drinks and breathes treachery, and plots in her sleep. Nay, see where she stands and murders us with her looks!'

As Mistress Rosamund spake, she waved her hand a little towards the barbican, and there indeed stood the Italian woman, with her hand on one of the culverins, that were ever trained on the mouth of the harbour, that they might be ready against an attack by boats. As I looked up at the Signora, she signed to me, as though in mockery, saying somewhat that I knew not. Then I heard heavy feet on the stone stair, and the Earl's hat and then his head and shoulders rose above the battlements, and he spake to the trooper by the culverin, and looked to his musket; for indeed the sentries were bidden to have their matches ever burning, as is the custom in a leaguered place.

I could see naught clearly of their faces, that were between us and the sky, and showed black against the white blankness; for the sea mist had come up, but thinly, with the tide, and hung in wreaths over the grey shores and leaden ebbing waters. Also I seemed to savour the smell of the Hole, but hardly noted it, for my nostrils had grown used to the odour, when hardly a day went by without some breath of it. Yet, though I marked not her face, nor the Earl's, I saw her lean towards him, and heard her speak in the Italian, what I knew not, save that I caught the word '*drudo*', that signifies a lover; and it came to me that she might be speaking of Mistress Rosamund and myself, for her voice was scornful. Also Mistress Fanshawe seemed to catch that word, and having some knowledge of the Italian, knew the meaning of it; for a redness came into her face, that became her mightily, though I cared not to tell her so for fear of angering her, and she drew hastily away from me, and began walking seaward from the barbican, and I after her, divided between my desire to be near her, and a wish to give no colour to the ill supposings of the Italian; for indeed when a man and a maid walk close together in privy talk, the first fool that sees them can laugh at them for lovers.

Methought that Mistress Rosamund was (as is the way of maidens) more moved by the other's spite than myself; for when I followed her, she did but quicken her pace till she left me some ten paces behind; so, as I would not vex her by a forced companionship, I halted and let her go whither she would. But even as I stood, came a breath of wind from seaward, and with it the cold foul savour of the slime, that was ever a token of danger, and forgetting all else but the peril, I made towards her again, calling on her to turn back. As I spake, she had come nigh to that deeper pool toward the end of the mole; and turning to hear me, she slipped on the stones, that were slimy with weed, and fell with half her body in the water. Yet she seemed not to be hurt, and began to raise herself, and by then had I come to the edge of the pool, and stretched forth my hand, and she doing the like, I looked to help her up. But as I caught at her hand, it was drawn away from me, so that I clutched but the air; and looking again to know wherefore I had missed my hold, I could see a space of wet rock between my feet and the margin of the pool, though I had sworn that I stood in the very water when I reached out my hand. Yet thinking that this was but my lack of skill, I stepped further into the pool and caught at her hand, and again missed it; and looking on her I could see that she clutched on a tangle of the brown seaweed, and pulled it out from the rock; yet was she brought no nearer to me, but the contrary. Also her face, that had been flushed with the fall and the labour to rise, was now pale, and I doubt not (as indeed she told me after), that mine was yet whiter; for in one moment were we ware that this that we took for a slimy pool was slipping towards the sea and drawing her with it to destruction. As I looked, I could see the slimy jelly seething through the shallow water, and winding round her like ropes, and oozing seaward over the rocks, with foul bubbles rising on it. Not a word said Mistress Rosamund, nor could I, for my deadly fear; only I could hear the Italian woman laughing on the barbican.

Perchance her scorn saved Mistress Rosamund and me, for my frozen will awakened, and in a very madness I leapt into that living slime and caught her by the arms and so held her back for a space. More could not I do, nor can I tell how, save by the favour of the Most High, my weak arms were strengthened to hold her against the cords of the abyss. Yet somewhat may I have been helped by the rocks, that were here jagged and beset with sharp barnacles and shells, and broken into narrow winding cracks, so that the thing that we strove against was hampered to come at us; else had we both been sucked down in a twinkling. So I set my feet in a crevice of the rock and held to Mistress Rosamund, that her arms bore the marks for many a days, and I remember that she bade me let go and not die with her; and still could I hear the Signora laughing.

But now, by what sense I know not, that which was drawing us was moved to make an end speedily, and with a strange sucking sound somewhat great and grey and slimy began to rise in the mouth of the harbour, and heave itself toward us like a round wave. And I, seeing the fringe of the thing come oozing and twining up the slope of the mole, cried out in the face of death and closed mine eyes. Even with that came a mighty roar in mine ears, and a rush of wind by me, and a great rain of spray; and when I got my senses again I lay in the empty place of the pool, and Mistress Rosamund beside me, and a great cloud of blue smoke curling above us. So I got to my hands and knees and crawled a little higher; and then I made shift to stand and dash the spray from mine eyes, and could see the barbican, and a culverin smoking yet at the mouth, and my cousin standing thereby gazing under his hand, and two or three of the troopers coming from the gate doubtfully, as men in fear; nor was there sight or sound of that which had lain in ambush for us. So with no small pain we won to the gate, though the way was but little; for the men feared to come half-way to meet us, and cared not to handle us, for the slime clung yet to our garments.

When we came into the court, was my cousin standing above us on the stair to the barbican, and his eyes were shining.

'Well, cousins both,' says he, 'if you will needs play Pyramus and Thisbe, I counsel you to keep on the safe side of the wall. Here be no lions, but worse, mayhap.' With that he gave a great laugh, and the Signora after him, like an echo, and Mistress Rosamund grew red again, and beat her foot on the ground for anger, but anon conquered her pride and went towards him.

'Cousin Philip,' says she earnestly; 'you shall not shame me out of thanking you for my life, that was but lost—' and she had said more, but he brake in on her, as was ever his way.

'O aye,' says he; 'I need no thanks, and least from thee or Hubert here,' – for I was making shift to stammer somewhat of gratitude. 'Nay, man, keep thy sermons till they be dry. Go and shift thyself, or I shall regret that I wasted good powder on thee.'

'And you, Signorina Rosamunda,' says the Signora from the stairs, 'shall I send you the maid with a change of clothes? You have the air – what is the English word? so draggletail!' and she laughed again.

'Aye, Signorina Bardi,' says the other, 'Methinks among the soldiers I might be taken for a camp-follower from the German wars' – and with that she turned to her tower, and I to mine.

But when I had shifted to my other suit, I was fain to cast my hose and boots away, for the smell of the slime clung to them, and made my chamber like a charnel of drowned men. So I flung them from my window and watched them fall on a point of rock some yard or twain from the water's edge, for I had misjudged in my cast. Then I turned to go, but ere I was at the door, I heard a plashing in the water, and went back to the window, but naught was to be seen, only that the bundle of my matters was gone.

CHAPTER XIII

OF THE PATH THAT HAD NO END

NOW when the horror of that escape had somewhat lifted from my mind, and the savour of the Hole was gone from me, was I of a better courage than before, seeing that the thing which beset us might be but mortal, and subject to fear, if not to wound; also my cousin the Earl was merrier at supper than I had seen him, for that he had at last for once baffled the enemy that beleaguered his castle. But in the hearing of the men that served us, he passed off the whole matter as a slip of the foot on the part of Mistress Rosamund, and would have it that seeing us, as he thought, nigh to swooning with the chill of the water, he had shot off the culverin to shake us out of that stupor, wherein we might well have slidden into the sea and been drowned; and we, catching his meaning, fell into his humour, and took his jests easily, though they were rough, and such as savoured of the camp, rather than of the court.

But when supper was over, and the women had bidden us good night and withdrawn to their several apartments, the Earl signed to me to stay; and after the serving men had cleared the platters and gone forth, he locked the door on them, and coming back to the dais where we set, pushed aside his chair, and bade me stand and look on him. So I saw that he stooped to the floor, and taking hold of a ring that I had not before noted, drew up a trap in the boards, that came up easily on its hinges, and without sound. Then he took a candle from the sconce in the wall, and holding it aloft warily, bade me look down. At first mine eyes were dazzled, and I could note naught but darkness; but presently I could see that there was a vault beneath, hewn in the rock, and in it many casks and kegs,

big and little; whereat methought that my Lord would
show me his cellars of wine and liquors, and I marvelled
that he should be so secret, save that perchance he feared
that the garrison might mutiny to get strong drink, as hath
been known in places under leaguer.

'Truly, cousin,' said I, 'thou art bravely provided, nor do
we risk dying by thirst.'

He laughed harshly, and clapped down the door again,
and set the candle back in its sconce. 'Nay, thou simple
scholar,' said he; 'hadst thou been in the wars thou
wouldst know that here is no Rhenish nor cordials. This is
one of Noll Cromwell's powder trains, cousin, that I took
coming from Naseby field, and have kept safe, all save a
pair of kegs that I spent on thy friend Master Eldad to
warm his house for him against his coming. If the thing
that besets us has dread of powder, as by this day's work
would seem, it shall have stuff to stay its stomach. There is
enough here to send the canting knaves of the Parliament
nearer heaven than they will ever go of themselves. I had
thought to baulk Roundheads or monsters of my life, and
go aloft in good company when I could no other; but now
am I fain to see what my powder can do behind good iron
and stone, and feed yonder fiend' (and he jerked his
thumb at the windows) 'with somewhat he likes less than
flesh of men. What sayest, cousin? Will it serve?'

Now while he spake, had I stood in some bewilderment
what to answer, for that assuredly his timely shot had
scared away the monster, if monster it were, that had been
dragging away Mistress Rosamund; yet could I not believe
that the judgment of God could be beaten back by mere
gunpowder, nor that the Earl's artillery would profit him a
second time more than did Satan's engines in the story of
that noble poem 'Paradise Lost', but late given to the
world by Mr. John Milton. So I thanked him, as indeed
was due, for his timely succour, but briefly, for he grew
impatient, as though ashamed of his good deed; and then
I passed to the matter of our provision, that might well (I
said) fail us before the powder. 'For,' said I, 'I have read in
the story of the wars that soldiers have salted their meat
with powder, but not that it would serve instead of meat;

and if we can hold off our enemies, men and worse, from giving us a storm, yet if we starve shall we be none the better.'

'Why, so!' says he, clapping me on the shoulder; 'we shall make a captain of thee yet, Hubert. "O this learning, what a thing it is!" as the play hath it. Surely will I take order for our victual, now that we may have time to eat it,' and with that he gave me good night, and strode off to the men's quarters, and I to my room.

The tide, that had been half-way at ebb when we had adventured on the mole (a thing that we were not like to do again) was now more than half full, and was already lapping on the walls, in those places where they went down sheer; for the island whereon the castle stood being but small, and broken with creeks, the builder of Deeping Hold had been fain to win space by building buttresses down into the holes of the rock, that were never dry save at low tides. Now the great hall of the castle (for though it was of no marvellous bigness in itself, it was yet by far the greatest room there) had been builded out from the rock, to give it what space might be, and the outer wall of it went straight down into the water, with buttresses holding it up; and some way up the wall was an overhanging gallery, where two men might scarcely pass, or one man might walk easily. Now this passage, that led to the rampart at either end, went around the two sides of the hall at a height a little below the foot of the great windows, so that a man standing on the narrow way between the wall and the battlements might see through what panes were of clear glass into the hall itself.

As I think, this pathway was made that the garrison might go round the whole circuit of the walls and see if any foe sought to break in through the wall of the hall, where were no defences, nor could it otherwise be seen from the ramparts save by reaching out beyond the shelter of the battlements. But it was not the custom for the sentries to walk there, there being no turrets for shelter, and also (which perchance weighed more) my cousin had no will for his men to take the excuse of their duty for prying on him as he sat at meat.

As I went through the court to my lodging, musing on my cousin's words, and wondering how so small an advantage as my escape should hearten him so greatly, I was aware of a little sound in the stillness; for of the splash of the waters and the call of the sentries I had ceased to take note, nor did I hear them more than one hears the beat of a clock, so are a man's senses dulled by some few days' use. This new sound was hardly louder than the lapping of the waters, but it was other, being a slow, grating noise, something as of the sea breaking on a beach of pebbles, and rolling stones over stones. So I listened, and judging by the sound that whatsoever might cause it lay beyond the hall, I went up on the wall, and so along the little path whereof I have written, to find if I might see what made that noise, for in our present peril a small thing that was new might grow to a great fear. But as my feet rang on the paving of the pathway (for a footstep sounded hollower and louder there than on the rampart) I could not hear the grating noise for my own walking; nor when I stood still to listen, could I hear it again. Only as I came to the corner of the walk, where it passed to the other side of the hall, could I see that the battlements were somewhat broken and crumbled, as in the way with stone that has stood long in the salt air; nor was there light to see if the breach were new or old. So I turned back, thinking that some pieces of the wall had fallen from decay, and were washing in the water at the foot of the wall; nor did I hear aught but the accustomed sounds of the castle, till I came to my chamber door. Only I remember looking in at the chief window of the hall, where were yet a few embers burning on the hearth, and I saw the shadow of a man going to and fro.

On the morrow I awaked later than my wont, being more weary and shaken than I had thought to be from my yesterday's peril; and the castle was already astir in the mist. So I clad myself hastily, and hearing talk and laughter in the court, I came to the door of my stair and looked to see who might have heart to laugh in our beleaguered place; but seeing only the men of the garrison, I went not out, being unwilling to give them a

handle for mirth; though indeed, since our peril and the
end of the Swede, their roughness and insolence were
somewhat dashed. Yet on this morning, as I judge, the
better spirits of the Earl had given them heart to swagger;
for it is a true saying, Like master, like man. So I kept
myself in the shadow of the doorway, that they marked
me not.

As they jested together, some seven or eight of them,
and as evil-looking ruffians as you should find in all
Alsatia (I mean the part of London so-called), came out the
silly maid of the inn at Marsham, that was now the only
woman in the castle save Mistress Rosamund and the
Signora. So the troopers must needs break a jest or two on
her, that she answered foolishly after her wont, with shrill
laughter, and such rudeness as she knew, though she was
herein far behind the men, that had garnered the foul
words of many lands, and knew the harsh oaths of the
Germans and Hollanders, and the camp talk of Spaniards
and Frenchmen and Italians, that was better for sound but
worse for beastliness. So, feigning to be mad at some one
of these speeches, that she understood no whit (though
had she known the sense of it she had been justly
angered) the wench gave one of the men a clout on the
cheek, laughing foolishly, and he swearing that he would
pay her for it by flaying her face with his beard, that was
like brushwood for stiffness, she fled from him in a mock
terror, and he chasing her, she found no way of escape but
up the stair that led to the rampart. Thither came her
rough wooer after her, and the rest, some half-dozen,
following to see the sport; and one of the sentries, after
she had leapt over his pike that he laid across the way,
joined in the chase, and so they ran, she screaming and
laughing, and they swearing and hallooing as at a hunt, till
they came to the path that led round the hall on the
gallery, and there, one by one, vanished from my sight,
but yet could I hear them yelling, till the girl gave one
dreadful screech, that ended suddenly, whereby I judged
that her pursuer had overtaken her, though her fear
sounded greater than should come from the rough
handling of the soldiers, whereto she was well used. Also I

heard no more of the men, that must by now have come round the corner of the hall; but methought that either the house between kept the sound from me, or that they feared to disturb the Earl, for he was an ill man to trouble in one of his black moods. So I looked for the wench and the others to come out on the rampart beyond the hall. But when I had watched a space and none appeared, I feared that there might be some devilry afoot, and though I liked not to thrust myself into so foul a business, it behoved me to see that the girl took no hurt. So I went upon the wall by the stair, and found naught but the pike that the sentry had dropped to run after the rest, and so on to the corner, and still was none to be seen. But as I was at the turn in the path, and was at point to run round carelessly, came a whiff of the foul smell that I knew well, that I sickened and had nigh fallen; so I laid my hand on the battlement and went warily, and well it profited me; for as I came round the corner of the hall, was the path clear gone, battlements and all, save for a ragged stone or two in the wall, that dripped with slime, and of the wench and the troopers was no sign.

Then a great terror and faintness fell on me, so that I could scarce crawl back to the rampart and down into the court; yet I laboured to reach the ground again, thinking myself but lost till I was off that height, and when I felt the rock under my feet, I fell down and so remained for a space, with nothing left in my thought but fear, and a certain desperate wish that that which beset us would make a sudden end and torture us no longer with dread, so that I went nigh to envy the poor wretches that had gone laughing to their death, and had been spared that death in life of terror.

Nor can I tell but that I had chosen rather to follow them, so great a sickness of my life was on me, had not Mistress Rosamund come forth from her stair, and seeing me yet crawling in the court, ran to me, crying out to know if I had taken a hurt. At the which my senses came to me again, and a shame of mine unmanliness, and I put her hand from me as she would have helped me up, telling her that naught ailed me but cowardice, whereat she was astonished. Then I told her how the gallery was broken, so that those who ran round the wall were miserably drowned; for I would not say more of the manner of the end, nor needed further words, in that she knew without my telling. But when I spoke of my coming to the corner and being like to follow those others, she grew pale, and shivered, and caught me by the sleeve as though to be assured that I still lived, and I was fain to hold her up, till she recovered herself and drew from me, sooner than I would. And therewith, as though ashamed of the weakness that she had so readily pardoned in me, she would have me go and tell the Earl of what had happened. So I found him pacing the hall (for he sat not with the Signora so oft as aforetime) and told him the event as I had said it to Mistress Fanshawe.

He was but moody when I came upon him, for his late show of cheerfulness had been as a blaze of straw; but when I looked for him to fall into a fit of desperation, he did but laugh harshly.

'Well, cousin,' says he, 'a good riddance to the wench, and fair quarters in the warm for my men. A quick death and a merry one is the health we soldiers drink.' Then he asked me more closely of the place where the gallery had broken, and I told him that it lay at the end of the hall where we stood, but that the path above the great window yet stood firm.

'Aye,' says he, after musing awhile, 'I was above, and heard the slut screaming, and came down to bid her be still, and to find if the men were there with her, when I had strictly forbidden them to use the gallery. But when I came was naught to be seen or heard. Well, we are yet enough to handle the guns if need be; but I would that we could turn them hitherward. Duke Bernard of Weimar said to me at the leaguer of Breisach that a corner with no flanking was a door of entrance to the enemy, that could lay his pieces to shoot away the defences sidelong—' and here he took himself and laughed again.

'Look not on me as though I were mad, Hubert man,' says he; for indeed I marvelled that he could remember such matters in our present peril. 'I will lay my life, that is worth less than a little, that in thy last hour will a scrap of Latin or Greek, or a stave of a psalm (thou being a Puritan) beat in thine ears for no reason. Soldiering is my trade,' says he, 'and by the tools of my trade must I end, and the cant of the art military is like to be my last speech. So leave me, cousin, ere I weary thee.'

CHAPTER XIV

OF THE STAIN ON THE WALL,
AND OF THE WAVE FROM THE SEA

MY Lord had followed my counsel, it would seem, and taken order with the victuals; for when we came to supper that day was the fare but scanty and rough, though no lack was there of wine, insomuch that the Italian woman, that was ever dainty in her ways, rallied the Earl on his table, saying that she, for one, was no Puritan, and used to better feeding, even in a camp, and offering as in jest to be our cook. All this she said smoothly, yet her eyes were restless, and answered not to her words, as though the fear that was on the castle had touched her also.

'Why, Madonna,' answered my cousin, 'are we not in a leaguered fortress, with small hope of relief, and must we not be rationed for a siege?'

'No, no,' she broke in, with a feigned petulance, 'it is not for the littleness of the food that I mind, but for your barbarous English cooking and serving. Signor Uberto, would you not wish me to dress you a supper?'

Methought that if I took her at her word I might need no more suppers in this world, but I let my tongue say nought of that, but stammered somewhat of being a plain scholar, and used to English fare and little of it, and how I would not have her spoil her hands by doing service for me, and so forth.

'Why then,' says she, 'and may I not be your camp cook and sutler-woman and cook your meat?'

'Nay, signorina,' says Mistress Rosamund, 'nor belike draw us drink.'

At that word, whereof the Italian knew the meaning, her brows drew together and her eyes grew narrow, and she set her hand to the breast of her gown as though she sought something. Yet did she say naught, for Pompey, the black, that was bringing a dish, and was coming by the wall, cried out in fear and cast the dish from him, and fell down by the table, clinging to the Earl's knees. This moved me strangely, for the boy's black face was grey with terror, and he held to my cousin, that loved him not, nor would be thrust away, but babbled of a noise that affrighted him. And when my Lord kicked him off and bade him stand and speak what noise he heard, could the lad say naught but some jargon about the devil rolling stones in the wall. So the Earl, being angered, caught the blackamoor by the collar of his jerkin, and cuffed him for a cowardly fool; but when he let him go again, Pompey cried out, 'Again! dere he am again!' and so fell as in a fit, moaning and foaming at the mouth.

Now as he fell, were we still for a space, and no sound was there but the gasping of the black; but presently came a muffled noise as of the grating of stone on stone, such as I had heard it the night before. And this grew greater, until it was as if a wave were rolling pebbles on the shingle in the very hall, and yet no appearance of aught; only the sound came from the end of the hall where it gave on the water, and I remembered that outside the wall the gallery had run that was now broken.

All we sat still, and the serving men stood shaking; only my cousin Philip, that was of a high courage, sprang up, and going to the wall whence the noise came, beat on the wainscot, that was old and cracked. And as he smote the wood, he cried out with an oath that he had hurt his hand, for that there was blood on it, and put his fist to his mouth, not thinking, as is the way of all when their skin is broken. But then he spat and swore again, and gulped once or twice as though he were sickened.

' 'Swounds, here is no blood!' he cried, and thrust his hand under a lamp, and it was smeared with gouts of slime, and savoured foully, that he caught up a napkin and rubbed his hand furiously and threw the cloth away; and looking at the place where he had stood, could I see more slime oozing through the cracks of the panels, and crawling down to the floor, and the wood bellying out from the wall.

So I called to him to leave the wall alone, for I guessed full well what was afoot; but he would not. 'Nay,' says he, 'this must be looked into,' and catching hold on the edge of the panelling, that was, as I deem, rotted in places, he tore off a great piece of it, well-nigh to the floor, and showed the stone and plaster of the wall, and catching a lamp, he held it up to show what might be under the wood. Then could we all see how there was a great stain on the wall, and the plaster crumbling away from the stones, as is the way in old and ruinous houses when the damp strikes through the crevices of the building; also the grating of the stones went on, and when it ceased, as it did at whiles, could I hear the waves plashing without, and judged that the tide was high.

Now when we saw that the foulness that beset us had found its way into our innermost citadel, the serving-men stood aghast like men of stone, and the black moaned and muttered to his gods, and for myself I was in a great disorder of mind and could think of naught helpful; but the women sate still and gazed with steadfast eyes on the wall, and I saw their lips move, but heard no word of prayer from Mistress Rosamund or of a spell of sorcery from the Italian. Only my cousin, the Earl, shamed me by his readiness that he ever showed in the face of a present peril, for he cried out loudly that the damp had struck through the wall with the high tide, and drawing his sword, bade the men to bring a brazier, the which they did, sweating with fear of their master and of the appearance on the wall. So I shook off my lethargy and helped, and together we took the burning logs from the hearth and laid them on the brazier, and pushed it close against the wall, that the flame licked the stone, and the slime and water hissed as it dripped from the chinks; and ever as the flame fell the Earl called out for more fuel, for the plaster, and the mortar between the stones, crumbled more and more, and the oozings of slime grew, and seemed to me (though perchance it was but the flicker of flames) to be creeping upward and outward like snakes, and the grating sound grew louder, till it was as though that which was without must needs break in on us.

Yet we nourished the fire, nor noted how the hall was blackened with the smoke; and the men brought wood, and the women sat and watched us, and all seemed like some ill dream. For naught visible was there to fight against but a stain on the wall, and the oozing of slime, and no sound but of the crackle of the fire and the grating of stones, and when these ceased, the plashing of the waves.

Whether this were an hour or twain or yet more, I know not, nor did any know. Only I remember that the men came back at last empty-handed and told my Lord that the wood was done, and he flew out at them for unthrifts and fools, and bade break up the wainscoting and cast it on the brazier, but it was damp and burnt ill, and I looked for the end to come speedily, for that once or twice had I heard a rushing sound, and a splashing as of great stones falling away.

Yet even as I awaited the breaking in of our defences, the grinding of stones ceased, and the oozing of the slime and water, and even the plash of waves was less, so that it seemed that the tide was now fast ebbing. Then Mistress Rosamund arose in her place, and her lips moved with no sound, so that I judged that she thanked God for our deliverance. But the Earl turned and called on Pompey to bring him wine, yet the boy answered not, but lay still under the table, and when his master stooped down and haled him out, the black lay, nor would stir for kicks or curses; and when I felt his breast, was it cold, and his face drawn horribly with fright, and his jaw hung open.

So we judged that he was dead of fear, and hid his body hastily with a cloth, lest Mistress Rosamund should behold it when she came from her seat, for now the table kept the sight from her.

But the Earl went and sat in his great chair, and the Signora by him, and his face was black with the smoke, and he said no word, till he cast his eye upon the eastward window, and marked how the darkness was a little lightened in that quarter. Then turned he to the Italian that sate sullen by him, and spake more softly than his wont. 'Fiammetta mia,' says he, 'we have seen a many dawns together, but here is the last, and let us make merry, for another night shall end our trouble.'

She wheeled to him, and her eyes were scornful of him, 'Why so, Fillippo?' she asked. 'We are not dead yet, nor am I one to give up the game till the last card be played. We shall see other dawns yet, and in better places than this kennel in the marshes.'

'It is my house and the house of my fathers,' says the Earl scowling; 'I will hold it while I can, and then go with it.'

'Oh, thy fathers, thy fathers, with their barbarous names and their ragged pride!' she flung out at him in a rage; 'Who shall know or care when thy castle and thy fathers are sunk in the marsh, mud in mud? Life! life! that have I yet, and that will I hold! Die like a rat in a trap if thou wilt – I will live! I must live!'

I marvelled greatly to see the passion of the woman, now it brake out at the last; nor was it that she feared death, for she had a courage more than womanly: rather was this a fury of disgust in her that her strength and subtlety of spirit and her curious knowledge and arts should be wasted, and the tale of her life cut short ere she had proved her power to the full; and she rejected the imminent doom as a thing unjust to her sovereignty, even as King Charles denied the right of the court that judged him.

But this vehemence of the Signora lasted but a space, and anon she was pleading to the Earl to escape from this prison ere it fell in on us. So he rose wearily, saying, 'Well, Fiammetta, shall we take to the boats and seek to land out of the way of the Roundheads? 'Tis a forlorn hope, yet a hope for thee, and if thou wilt live, why live. Come, Cousin Hubert and Cousin Rosamund, and let us make a plan ere the tide rises again. But first,' says he, 'carry forth yonder carrion.'

So, begrimed as he was, he did on his cloak and went out into the court, that was yet misty and grey in the first morning, and we after him, and the two serving men behind bearing the dead black, that they bestowed in an empty room of the men's quarters; for indeed there was no lack of such, since our numbers had sore dwindled.

So we came to the gate and the barbican tower, where

was yet a cresset burning for the men to watch, and the sentries walking on the walls and crying to one another, and presently were we joined by the two men that had been with us in the hall, but the Earl had strictly charged them that they should say naught of that which had befallen. Some eight or nine of the troopers were at the gate or around the culverins above it, being nigh half of what remained of the garrison, and their faces seemed strange in the red light of the cresset, being wan with fear and weariness, and it seemed to me that we were already like to a company of ghosts among the marshes of the Styx.

Now when the men marked the Earl's face, how begrimed it was, and drawn with care and toil, there went a whisper through them, but none dared speak openly; so he beckoned to them to gather around him under the gate, and the women and I and the two serving men, that were begrimed like my Lord, stood backward from him, and when he saw the troopers nigh him he spake to them.

'Comrades,' says he, 'this is an ill strait that we are in, and needs must we try a desperate remedy. Of fuel and food have we little left, and there is a troop of rascal Roundheads besetting Marsham village, nor are we enough to face them; and this old castle of ours, I doubt, has served its time, and is rotten with age and salt water. But this morning the gallery fell with some few of you, and to-night was the high tide oozing through the very wall of my own hall.'

Here one of the serving men was at the point to say more, but my Lord, hearing him muttering, turned on him with so fierce a look that the fellow shook and was silent. 'What say you, then,' says my cousin, speaking in a manner more friendly that he used to his men, and rather as a soldier to brother soldiers; 'shall we starve here of cold and hunger, or give ourselves to be hanged or knocked on the head by Noll's saints yonder? Surely if one life might ransom the rest, should they have mine, and welcome; but you know their mercy to such as you.'

At that there went a murmur through the men, like the growling of a kennel of dogs; nor could I wonder, for indeed the Parliament men were never tender, even to those that had rendered themselves prisoners.

'Well,' says my Lord, 'we have yet our arms, and no lack of powder, and barges to hold us all. Shall we not take our last chance, and seek to land somewhere out of reach of yonder dogs? Then, if we may not come at them by an ambush, at least may we win through to those that yet hold out for the King, or at worst find a ship to the Low Countries, where is good pay from the Spaniard or the Dutch, which, we care not. Will you venture it with me?'

Some of the men said Aye, with oaths after their manner, but some hung back, muttering that there was a sea-devil besetting the marshes and the water, and we should but sail down his throat.

'Nay then, what talk is this?' asks the Earl, with a great scorn in his voice. 'Are ye my brothers of the sword, or wenches in green-sickness, that ye had rather starve in a rotten hold than take your lives in your hands and sally forth? And what is this fool's talk of a water devil? Here is my cousin Hubert, that will tell you he is a man of peace and no soldier, and he hath ventured forth in a boat with you twice, and no harm come to him, nor to those with him. Shall you be cowards where a Cambridge scholar is bold? Nay, shall you be behind the very women? Wilt thou come with me, Fiammetta?' and the Italian nodded and answered him, '*Si*,' and Mistress Rosamund bowed her head also.

So one and then another of the men, taking courage each from the other, gave their word to try the last venture with him, and my Lord smiled on them, and methought, with his blackened face in the red flicker of the cresset, he seemed like Lucifer among his peers; and he clapped one or two on the shoulder, crying out that they were stout fellows, and worth living or dying with; and all now being at one, he bade open the gate and draw up the boats, that were moored to the mole with chains. So they threw open the gates, and went out, the tide being on the ebb and half way down, as when Mistress Rosamund had nigh perished in the crawling pool; and we stood at the gate and watched them, though the light was but small, for the cresset was burning low, and the dawn was yet faint to seaward, and a mist hung over the water. Yet could I see the men on the mole, as dark shadows against the mist and the low twilight, and the boats black on the oily water, and all seemed peaceful and secure, so that I could scarce believe that we had been fighting for life against that terror of the night.

Now presently came a puff of wind parting the mist, and as I gazed seaward, where a riband of clear grey sky lay on the leaden rim of the water, there seemed to be a rising up as of a heap upon the edge of sight, as when one looks through a twisted glass. Yet as I looked, was it gone; but in a short space I thought to see a rising of the water nearer at hand, as of a wave, and I bethought me of the tales of travellers, how after an earthquake, or by some trick of the tides, a great roller has broken in from the deeps and swept the islands of the South Sea, or cities of the Spanish Main. So I pulled my cousin by the sleeve, and bade him look; yet he saw naught, nor could I, when I turned again.

But in a moment or twain after, as the men still wrought in the boats and on the mole, somewhat heaved up the waters in a heap again, and I was aware of a mound of blackness moving very swiftly toward us, with no crest as is the wont of waves, but round and sleek. So I cried out to the men to beware, and the Earl blew on a whistle, but too late; for as the men heard him, and sought to make for the gate, that smooth hill of water, and what else I know not, rolled full on the mouth of the harbour, and engulfed the jaws of the mole, and while a man might count five was there naught to be seen save a bellying surge, streaked with slime, that rolled up to the very threshold of the gate, yet without foam. Then, as we gazed, was the water sunken again, but of the boats, and the men therein and on the quays was no sign, save the broken chains dangling from their rings, and we stood yet with the hissing and grinding of that strange wave in our ears, and all was still again, and the dawn growing slowly over the dull line of the sea.

CHAPTER XV

OF THE BUSINESS OF THE ITALIAN WOMAN

WHEN that strange and horrid swelling of the waters had ebbed, and left naught of boats or men, but only broken chains and puddles of slime on the stones, Mistress Rosamund was the first of us that spake, imploring the mercy of God on those poor souls so suddenly hurried to judgment. For the rest of us, it shames me to own that I was overmuch busied with my own fear to think of others so soon, for I had looked for the ugly heap of slimy surge rolling in on us to make no stay before it sucked us in also. Nor, seeing that I had been bred a Puritan, was I apt to pray for those that were dead, though I was readier to assent thereto than my teachers had thought a good Protestant might be. And with that, like a very woman, she turned from prayer to the thought of the man that was her friend, and (as I may now confess) sought to be more than a friend; and 'Ah!' says she, 'you saved me from that!' 'Nay,' said I, 'rather my cousin Philip saved us both.'

At the sound of his name the Earl, that had stood in the midst of the gateway staring like a man distraught, heaved a great sigh and turned to us, yet saw us not, for his eyes were inward, and he talked with himself or with one that we saw not.

'All my men gone,' says he, but so low that we could scarce hear it; 'all gone, and yet I cannot go. Truly, Margaret, I was cruel to thee, but thou art more merciless to me. I did but give one blow, nor meant thou shouldest die, but thou hast smitten me daily and nightly. Make an end, woman, nor come to me again with the red stain on thee!'

Then Mistress Rosamund looked at me, and I remembered that the dead Countess of Deeping had been

319

called Margaret. But my Lord went on babbling, and now it seemed that his vision had changed, for he spake to Master Eldad, and called him fool and madman to come in his armour, for that he had been sucked out of it long ago, and suchlike frenzies, till the Italian woman, that had spoken no word, but stood with her head bowed in her hands, raised her face up, and it was ghastly in the dawn, but her eyes were green and shining.

'Fool!' says she to him in the Italian, 'there is none here but the living, and thy saint rests well where we sent her, thou and I. It was more than a chance blow that rid us of her, and more than grapes that made her wine. Yet *I* see her not, nor fear her at all.'

When Mistress Fanshawe and I heard this, we drew from the woman as though she had been leprous; and surely she was of a whiteness like that of Gehazi. Yet the Earl stood stupid, as though her words were naught to him; till presently, with a great cry, he flung his cloak from him, and plucked out his sword, and was for running at her; nor could I find it in my heart to come between them; but she moved not nor spake, but looked on him scornfully, and he made but a pace or two and stood still, and then, with a great curse, he flung his sword on the stones and set foot on it and brake it, and so put his arms about her and pulled her to him, laughing strangely.

'Nay,' says he, 'I will not murder more women, so fear not me. Come, Fiammetta, we will revel to-night, sweet one, and our merry men with us. Shut the gates, knaves, and go to breakfast, and then make ready the hall for feast. Ye shall all sup with me and my new lady, and watch and ward may go hang. What is our muster?' and he ran his eye over the men, that were by now all huddled in the court, gazing on him with amazement. 'Four – six – eight rascals yet left,' says he, 'and four here for the high table, and at supper another guest to make the thirteen. Surely we will give him warm welcome. Come, cousin, shall we to breakfast? There shall be no rations and sparing of our cheer any more, but we will drink the sun up and drink him down again, and so goodnight!'

Now when he ended, with a great laugh, was I sure that

madness had fallen on him, and yet would I not wish him
in his senses again; for had I been in his case (which God
forbid) could I have done no other, being sensible, than
slay the Italian woman first and then myself. But I would
not look on the antics of a madman nor hear his ravings;
for I have ever thought that they who find matter for mirth
in such things are very fiends, whom it were flattery to call
beastly, for that the very beasts do fear or pity madness;
yet have there been men, aye, and women too in these evil
days, not ashamed to make a sport of seeing the wretches
in Bedlam. So without word I turned to my tower, to
spend the little of life yet left to me in meditation and
prayer; for in spite of Master Eldad's prophecy, I looked to
see another dawn on earth as little as did my enemies.
And the like did Mistress Rosamund, and when the Earl
would have had the Signora in with him, she also denied
her company, saying that she had business of her own,
and I marvelled what this might be, but had no will to ask,
for it seemed a little thing to me now what she might be
about, nor could I fear her or aught else. Then understood
I, or had understood had I cared to think at all, how
cowards have been made brave by desperation of their
fear. So I went to the stair that climbed to my room, but
standing in the doorway and looking over the court, that
was empty of men now, and dusky in the twilight of
morning and the shade of the walls, it seemed that a
shadow came from the door of the men's quarters, and
went up to the great door of the hall; and the shape of it
was strange, as of a grey woman bearing a huddled black
thing on her shoulders, and I thought idly on the Italian
and wondered what business hers might be. But the
woman and her burden, that I saw not clearly, were
shortly vanished in the doorway, and no more saw I,
saving that an hour later, looking toward the court, I noted
a red flicker of light in the window of a room that I judged
to be the chamber where the Italian wrought her sorceries,
and a wreath or twain of smoke from the casement.

Now that morning went by like an ill dream, and strive
as I would to set my heart and mind on things of religion,
could I not quiet myself, but was restless. Also when I

sought to read in the Scriptures, were the words empty of meaning as a speech that one hath said over too oft; nor when I prayed was my state the happier. So I fell to thinking of Mistress Rosamund, that was doubtless (or so I held) praying now that we might meet the end with a calm and godly resignation; and she (for so she hath told me since) had the same belief of me, that comforted her in her like restlessness. For be it said to our shame that in that very valley of the shadow of death were our thoughts rather of the creature than of the Creator.

So wore on the day, without sight of the sun, but a grey curtain of misty cloud, and a blackness to seaward; and of our enemies, man or monster, was no sign, and the sea was still and dead. Only about noon I felt anhungered, and sought to see if I might come at any meat; but going to the hall, the door was fast shut, and I could hear a noise of hammering, as though some carpenter were at work, and a voice singing of a camp song, that I knew for the Earl's, though strangely harsh; and the thought of his madness sickened me of my hunger, so that I turned away again and went upon the rampart to walk, for I was weary of sitting still.

Now could I pace my fill, for no sentinels were on the wall any more, and I could nigh make the circuit of the rampart, save in that place where the gallery had been that was broken away. But along the one side of the hall could I still walk, and I looked into the room, that was as a cavern, through a clear pane of the great window; yet was there naught to see but the firelight flickering (for they had found fuel, whence I know not) and no sign or sound more of my cousin and his labours. Little could I see, for that though it was not long after noon, the blackness in the sky to the seaward gathered and rose higher, and though I have small skill of the signs of the weather, yet I augured of a storm at hand, although wind was none, nor foam on the water, but a steady rolling swell that rose and fell against the stones with no sound.

Then as I turned back to the ramparts over the court, came a gust of wind, that moaned through the loopholes, and died suddenly, and the breath of it was faint with a salt foulness; and looking forth to the quarter whence the wind blew, could I see a streak of paler grey on the black waters, and I marvelled foolishly wherefore, if the thing that beset us were indeed there, it had not will or appetite to make an end of us, where were too few now to keep it out. But the patch of grey lay still, wherefore I judged it to be the shadow of some cloud; and indeed the blackness was less above us. Then, hearing steps on the stone, I looked again to the court, and saw the shadow as of a ghostly woman coming through the gloom with a huddled black burden on her shoulders, and as she came near I knew that it was the Signora, and she panted under her load; so, not that I would help her in her business, but for that I could not stand idle and see a woman bear burdens, I came down and made to lend her a hand. Yet when I took hold of that load, I left it again hastily, for I had touched the cold hand of a dead man under the black cloak that was cast over it; but she did but laugh, and casting off the cover, showed me that this was the body of Pompey the black, that I had seen with mine own eyes dead of fright in the hall.

So I was ashamed of my terror, that had been rather of what devilry the Italian might have wrought, than of handling the dead, for this had grown to me a matter of daily use; and judging that she had but been opening the body after the manner of a chirurgeon, to surprise some secret of nature (though I wondered that she should think of her art in that extremity of danger), I asked her what she made with the black.

'You shall hear anon,' says she, yet panting with her toil, 'if you will but aid me to heave this up to the rampart and cast it forth, for I have done with it now.'

So I did as she asked, for I could see no guilt therein, though a labour I liked not; and with no great pain we brought the body up on the wall, and rested it between two battlements. Then the Italian waited and drew breath, and gazed outward a space, till again came a brief gust of wind, and the savour that I had noted before, and I deemed that the greyness of the sea was yet visible, though from the gathering blackness could I not be sure.

But the woman snuffed the air once or twice like a hound, and turning to me, '*Sta bene,*' says she, 'it is well; now fling him out,' and without more words we took up the body, and swung it back and forth once or twice, and lastly cast it out as far as we could into the water, and it went splashing as a boy falling into the sea for sport, and sank, but rose again and wallowed on the waves. So it lay for a space floating idly; but in no long time began the body to drift slowly toward the quarter where I had seen the greyness. Then presently the dead boy went swifter, as though the current carrying him waxed stronger, and lastly rose upright on a swell with the black head and shoulders showing like a swimmer's, and then vanished as though drawn under, nor, if the body rose again, could I see it for the gloom.

So I turned again to the Italian, that had been gazing earnestly after the body, and asked her of her purpose in dealing with the dead black.

'Why,' says she, 'you will be ready to cry out on me and yourself that I thought not of this before, nor you at all. Signor Uberto, when you are beset with rats, do you not lay baits for them with poison? Well, Pompey must serve for our bait to-day, and we have yet hope to win free, if yonder sea-devil have a stomach like other beasts, and be not immortal. And even if our enemy be more than man, may we hope; since my poison, though not blessed by any Holy Father, hath been used by one belike, for it is a right recipe of the Borgia.'

I knew not whether more to admire the courage of the woman or to reprobate her impudence; so I asked her, thinking to shame her, whether this were the poison she had mixed for the Swede, and for aught I knew, for me and others.

'Nay then, Signor Uberto,' she says, 'you know little of me if I would be so ill-mannered as to use that poison on people of quality like you and the Signorina Rosamunda,' and she lengthened out the name as in scorn. 'For you yourself,' went she on, 'never would I seek to poison you, save as a last chance for life, if then. You are a scholar, signor, and a pretty swordsman to boot, and I would be loth to lose two such rarities in one. Truly, Uberto,' and here she leaned towards me a little, and looked in mine eyes, 'there is a brave conspirator wasted in thee. Thou canst see, canst understand what is to do; and then comes in thy cursed religion or duty, or I know not what empty words, and the deed goes by undone. Oh, if thou hadst but taken the chance I gave, and thrust home a day or twain ago, thou hadst then been Earl of Deeping, lord of all in it, men and women, with Mistress Rosamund for the Countess till thou wert tired of her, and then' – and here she drew her lips close together, but her eyes spake for her, and promised I know not what.

Now I could not answer her, being daunted by the naked wickedness of her plotting, and yet mastered by the subtlety and cunning of the woman, and the coolness that could tell all her own devilish deeds as though she had been Machiavel writing of the deeds of Caesar Borgia, and marking how and where each plot had worked or failed. So anon she spake again, but with no passion.

'Then I took the Swede, as a man might use a club when his rapier was denied him,' says she carelessly; 'and you foiled me again, not meaning it, and the club brake in my hand.'

I marked not then how she had thou'd me for a little and then left off, as though she had come near to me and then drawn back, but after, I remembered this and many other things.

'It was by no will of mine, indeed, that they fought,' said I, 'as you know well; yet if fight must be, I would not have had it go otherwise.' But at that she brake out in a passion.

'Oh!' she cried, with an Italian oath of the camp that I set not down, 'that thou shouldst not be a wiser man or a greater fool! A touch more or less wit than thou hast, Uberto, and the Swede had slain Filippo, and come home to my welcome and his cup of wine—'

'And therewith died,' said I, for I remembered what Mistress Rosamund had guessed.

'Nay,' says the Signora frankly, like one in hell that has no need to feign virtue any more, and finds a pleasure in that; 'that were too plain and open. He had died in two days at the least, or I had moved the soldiers to slay him as he lay sick, and charge thee to make their peace with the Parliament. And for the thing out there – who knows if it had not left us, when it had swallowed its dearest morsel? Or we could well have tried my device of to-day—' and here she brake off and clutched me by the sleeve. 'Perchance it has worked by now! Look forth, Uberto, and see if there be any sign on the water!'

So I looked, but the blackness of the sky was now well-nigh like night, and nothing was to be seen save the long smooth waves rolling out of the gloom and lapping up and down without foam.

'If it be dead!' she whispered in mine ear; 'if it be gone away! if it come not to-night, what then? Uberto, what then?' and her breath was hot on my cheek. But I would not see her meaning, or so much as answer her temptation. Nor, truly, was it a temptation to me, though haply in my younger days, when I had gusts of ambition, and thought of myself as having in me the stuff of Plutarch's heroes, I had listened more eagerly. So I but spake to the plain meaning of her words and no more, drawing a little away from her.

'Why,' said I, 'then must we adventure what we were at point to do this morning, and since the boats are gone, must we build a raft and sail under cover of night like shipwrecked mariners, and land in the safest place that may be, leaving Deeping Hold to whoso cares to dwell therein.'

She laughed, mocking me. 'Oh, the wise scholar!' cries she. 'Of a surety that is what we will do, and if the Earl choose to stay here for his life, or longer, shall we pleasure him, thou and I? Nay, say nothing. Even the fool, when he holdeth his peace, is counted wise, which is one of the few sayings of thy Scriptures that I have found worth the remembering. We shall meet at supper, Signor Uberto,' and with that she was gone, leaving me to ponder on what ill meaning her last speech might hold.

So I walked yet on the walls, but nothing was to be seen save the gloom and the swell, nor heard but the fitful gusts and flaws of wind; and I felt a pinching of hunger, for that

I had not broken my fast that day, yet could I not bring myself to go and ask for meat. So I paced up and down the wall awhile, and wearying of the darkness, went down into the court, and presently came out Mistress Rosamund, bearing somewhat between her hands.

'I saw you parleying with her,' says she, and methought with some coldness; 'what had she to say that you were so close with her?'

'More wickedness than I looked to find in man or woman,' I answered in a weariness, for it hurt me that she should think I had friendship with the Italian, 'and more subtlety than I might hear from the Fiend himself. What matters it, Rosamund? Surely we are but dead, thou and I, and if we be no saints, as I know full well of myself, yet shall we be rid of her and her like on the other side.'

But when she saw me weary and faint, she forgot the little thorn of jealousy that will gall the kindest of women at times, and came to me, holding out her burden, and it was a piece of bread wrapped in a napkin. 'Forgive me, Hubert,' says she very sweetly, 'though I may not forgive myself that I spake so to thee. Thou hast not eaten to-day, and art weary, and here is somewhat that I have saved for thee, for I am no such hermit as thou, and could not fast so long.'

I looked on her, and her face was pale and weary in the gloom, and her eyes circled with a shadow, and I knew that she had fasted too, and had saved for me all that she had.

'Nay,' said I, 'thou shalt eat too, else I touch nothing'; and with that I brake the bread in twain, and bade her begin. Yet for a time she would not, saying that she had eaten enough, and felt no hunger, and other sweet lies that the best of women are aptest to tell. Only when I made as though to cast the bread over the battlements, she yielded, and then with pretence that I had given her the greater share; so we sat under the walls in the shadows and ate together, and talked of this and that, and forgot the danger and the darkness that brooded closer, and none came to mount guard, or to trouble us; only now and then could we see lights in the guard-room or the hall, and we judged that the men were drinking, for at whiles came a quavering snatch of song, as though some poor wretch were striving to cheat himself into merriment, and forget his fear. And of what we said to each other remember I no whit, nor assuredly was it worth the treasuring; only I was comforted greatly, and it seemed that the bitterness of death was past, and peril and wickedness but vain and little things, like the foolish flaws of wind that now and again beat against the battlements over our heads.

CHAPTER XVI

Of the End of Deeping Hold

IN this talk, or more often in silence, we sat, for how long I
know not, till a rain began to fall on us, and I bade
Rosamund rise, for I would not that she should be chilled
now, though we both might look to be under the waters
ere the morrow dawned. So we came under the shelter of
a turret, and stood a little. But presently the great door
was cast open, and I heard my cousin's voice calling for
me; so, being unwilling that he should see us together and
perchance break a jest on us in his wildness, I left her in
the shadow and came forward to the door, telling him that
I had been walking in the court, and asking what was his
need of me.

'Why, man Hubert,' says he, with the boisterous mood
still on him, 'I would have thee make thyself brave for
to-night, for it is nigh supper-time, and we have a guest
coming. I will be as gay as I may, and Fiammetta here, and
if thou meet Rosamund, bid the wench wear her best also.'

Now this she heard, standing in the dark, for he spake
loudly, so I but told him that I would see to it, and when
he had shut to the door again, I came back to her and
asked her what she thought, saying that in my mind we
were better spend our last hours in prayer and
repentance.

'Nay,' says she, 'I have said my prayers by now, and I
would fain die without thinking that I denied my cousin
his last desire. Foolish it may be, but no sin; and since I
heard him cry out on his dead wife this morning, have I
forgiven him, as doubtless she hath, and repented of
many ill thoughts of him. He knew not what he did, nor
knows now; and if our folly can help him to end the easier,
why not be fools together?'

It warmed my heart to hear her speak thus, and without thinking that I had spoken no word of love to her, I caught her close to me and kissed her; nor did she struggle, but presently she put me away, saying in a voice between tears and laughter, 'Nay, Hubert, thou shalt see me in bravery for once, if no more, and judge if I cannot ruffle it as well as even Her Highness the Signorina Bardi!'

With that she sped to her room, and I to mine, though since I had come with but two suits, and the commoner was spoilt with the slime of the crawling pool, had I little change of apparel. Yet I clad myself in my best, with what little of price I had, and came down into the court; and the rain had ceased, but the wind was blowing in unsteady gusts, each stronger than the last, and the tide rising fast, as I could judge by the dashing of the waves on the rock and the wall; for all was now dark as the mouth of hell. Yet I found my way to the hall door by the light streaming through it, when the supper bell tolled mournfully like a knell over the desolation of the marshes and the sea; for the door stood open as at a feast, and two men with torches to guide us thither. So coming into the hall, I found my cousin seated in the great chair on the dais at the head of the table, and the seat by him empty, and he was in his best apparel of war, scarlet with gold laces and broideries; and what of plate he had left (for his wars and revels had melted the more part of it), ranged on the high table, and below sat the troopers, all the eight that were left to us, and each with what rags of bravery he had, and their muskets and pikes ranged against the wall. Also a great tapestry was hung over the wall where the stain was, and all the candles that might be put in the sconces were burning, and strange was it to see how all was set for a feast.

So my cousin called me up to my place, but I lingered to see if Mistress Rosamund would come, and presently she entered, wrapped in a cloak, and cast it off ere she went up the hall; and truly it amazed me to see her so royal. For she had on a gown of green silk flowered with gold, the gift (as she told me after) of the Countess when she grew too pious or too sorrowful for bravery; and she glittered in the candlelight like a goddess of gold. Also in her hair and on her neck she wore old jewels of the house of Deeping, that my Lady had left her, and that the Earl let her keep, though the Italian sought to have them; and the likeness which she bore to her dead cousin, or to what the Countess had been in her happier time, made her seem like the glorious body that the apostle hath promised to the righteous at the resurrection.

So the Earl, when he saw her coming, gave a great cry, and greeted her as his sweetheart Margaret, being distraught; yet was he not wholly beside himself, and soon knew her for his kinswoman only. Yet would he have her to sit beside him in his lady's place where the Italian was wont to sit, and bade all the men rise and give her greeting; and she, willing to pleasure him, sat down on his right hand in the place of honour, and I next her.

In this moment came the Italian through the door, and she also was fine, but after another sort, for she wore a robe of red, with broideries of the East, and figures of strange characters, and stones here and there glowing red like eyes, and her great red jewel bound on her forehead. Now when she came to the high table and saw the chief place taken, she stood still, and her eyes narrowed like a snake's, and she felt with one hand in her bosom. But the Earl marked her, and would make excuse; for he could be courtly when he chose.

'Signorina,' says he, 'forgive me that I ask you to sit below me for this one supper. This is the last feast of Deeping Hold, and needs must one of the house sit in the high seat with me. To-morrow shall we dine, aye, and sup together without her, and for many morrows, and belike for longer than we would.'

Not a word spake the Italian, but sat her down at the left hand of the Earl, and played with her rings, that were curious, and some over great for a woman's hand. So we supped, if supper it could be called, when the cheer was but little, and our will to eat less; only the men, that were used to living roughly, and to feeding when they could, fell to heartily, yet stopping at whiles to listen.

Now when we had been at meat about half an hour, the

tempest that had been gathering all the day brake on the castle suddenly with a great clap of wind, that beat upon the windows nigh the place where the gallery had fallen, and whistled through the chinks of the panes, that the candles flickered; and then came other gusts, and then one constant howling and crying of the wind, as though all the devils were loose around us. Also in no long space could we hear the roaring of the waters, as the waves beat on the rock and the buttresses and the foundations of the wall, till the hall shook with their storming; and yet was no sign nor sound of the enemy that we dreaded worse than any tempest, so that the Signora leaned over to me, smiling, and I knew her thought.

My lord marked her smile, and his madness took him again at her scorn. He cried out that the guest was late, and bade lay his place at the foot of the table, for that he was not of gentle birth, and what more folly I know not. But as he ceased, and the men set the place as he bade them (for they feared his frenzy), came a lull in the storm, and it seemed to me that I heard the grinding of stone on stone that had slain Pompey with the fear of it. Then the wind burst again on the castle, and the waves roared higher, but the grating noise grew greater and nearer; and the Signora left playing with her rings and felt in her bosom again, and her face was white as her napkin.

Only my Lord laughed in his mad mood, and cried out that our guest was coming, and filled a great goblet with wine, and bade all do the like and stand up for a welcome; and by now the noise in the wall was like the grinding of a mill that crushes ore in a mine. Also under the tapestry that hid the wall came trickles of water and streaks of slime, and the stuff blew out like a sail, and lastly came a great crashing, and the tapestry was rent away, and the stones tumbled after it, and a ragged hole was burst in the wall. Then the men cried out for deadly fear, and some grovelled on the floor; but the Earl lifted his cup in one hand and drank to the guest, and as he drank came a mighty surge of the sea against the wall, and the crest of it brake through the hole, and somewhat dark was hurled into the very hall; and when I looked on it, it was the body of the black boy.

With that Rosamund, that had endured till then, fell forward with her head between her hands on the table, swooning, so that I, though I looked not to live, was purposed that we two should die forth from that feast of hell. So I caught her from her seat, and with what strength I know not, threw her over my shoulder and fled from the hall, and some two or three of the men perchance may have done the like, but I marked them not. Only I know that I found myself, yet bearing Rosamund, on the rampart, and it seemed to me that the court was all a plash of water from the spray; also the wind buffeted me so that I was fain to cling to the battlements, and drag myself along till I came on the gallery without the hall window, and the lights within made a glow on the darkness, and a buttress of the wall gave shelter from the wind. So I looked within to see when our deaths might come, and prayed that Rosamund might not waken before the end. And I saw how my cousin sat in his chair, and now was the Italian woman in the place beside him, and he held her there with one hand, and of the men some grovelled, and more sat as turned to stone. Then my lord whispered to the woman, as it seemed, and took a candle from the table, and bent to the floor as though to lift somewhat, and I remembered what he had shown me in his cellar, and knew what he was at point to do. But as he bent, he left holding the Italian, and she caught up a knife from her bosom, and stabbed down at him between the shoulders as he rose, so that he fell back into his seat hurt to death, as I judged, and she brake from him, leaving the dagger in him, and came running down the hall. But as she passed by the body of the boy, came a great heap of blackness through the hole in the wall, and washed round her feet that she fell, but rose again, and would have made for the door, when it seemed as though a band of darkness wrapped round her, and drew her down, and twined higher about her, as she fought with it and tore at it, till I saw naught but the red light of the jewel on her head, and then only a writhing in the folds of that blackness, and I sickened, yet could not look away. Then I saw how the slimy blackness grew, and the stones fell away round the hole, and there rolled in what seemed a wave, but it brake not, but spread over the floor, gulfing the men that lay dead or living, struck by fear, till it heaved at the edge of the dais, and lipped over the step like a living tide of slime, and yet with no form that I could tell. But as that foulness drew nigh to his feet, the Earl rose from his chair, though wounded to the death, as I deemed him, and with one hand holding what seemed like a black cord, he set the candle to it, and forthwith a sputter of sparks sprang out under his hand, and ran downward.

Then my strength came back to me, and power to take mine eyes from the loathly sight, and a fortunate madness, rather than any hope of deliverance, drave me to dare the rage of the storm rather than perish by the madness of man. So I gathered Rosamund, that was yet senseless, in my arms, and setting my feet in the battlement, leapt with all my strength outward, and plunged in the waters. And we sank, but I battled to the air again, and was buffeted by the billows, but strove yet to make away from the horror of the castle; and taking the hair of Rosamund in my teeth as she floated, I swam desperately with hands and feet. But ere I had gone far from the wall, even with the swift current of the tide, came a crack like the blast of the Last Judgment, and a blaze of red fire that lit the sea and the marsh, and then darkness and the roar of winds and waters, and great stones and beams raining out of heaven around us, yet none struck us. Then went we down into the depths, and anon were lifted ever upward on a mighty wave, and whirled onwards like straws, and I caught her body in my arms, and remembered naught more.

Now when I awaked, the first thing that I saw was a clear sky yellow with dawn, and a flash of somewhat white above me, and then another, and it came to me that perchance this was Paradise, and wings of angels over me; yet I sighed for somewhat lacking that yet I could not call to mind. But when I sighed, there came a hand on my forehead, and then eyes between me and the sky, and wet hair cold against my cheek, and lips warm on my mouth, and a voice striving to say my name, and sobbing instead. Then I knew that this was Rosamund, and deemed still that we were in heaven, till she drew back to look at me, and I could see a ragged and ruinous wall of stone closing us in, and samphire and rough grass growing up it; and I felt wet grass and rock under me. With that came back the memory of the night till we had been hurled on that great wave, and I raised myself on one arm and looked around.

First saw I Rosamund, that knelt by me, and her goodly gown was sodden and rent, though gold and gems yet glittered from it, and her hair loose and wet like seaweed; and beyond her was a space of troubled water and grey flats, laced with yellow light in the pools, and white seagulls dotted on the grey, and wheeling over the channels. So I knew that I was yet among the marshes, and a living man, and I looked on Rosamund again, and had no sorrow that this was not heaven, as the divines hold it to be, but rather earth grown a heaven; and she took my hand and fondled it, and for a space spake we no word.

But when I came to my full senses at length, being dizzy and sore bruised, but whole in limb, I asked her where we might be, and how we came there; but indeed, had I thought, I knew the place to be none other than the Hermit's island, where, the story ran, an Earl of Deeping had slain the holy man; for no other rock was in the marshes than the castle and this. So as we sat in the ruin of the cell, she told me how she had known naught after that monstrous revel in the hall, till she wakened in the beginning of dawn on the grass of that isle, and felt my arm yet around her, but knew not how we came there; and thinking me dead at first, she had found my heart to beat, and had dragged me with pain to the shelter of the ruin. So I told her what had happened since her swoon, till the time when that great wave took us both; and we kneeled on the grass and gave thanks to God, that had bridled the sea like an horse, that it might carry us to the place that He had appointed.

Then we went forth, holding each other's hands for fear lest we might not be living in very truth, and looked around, and first could I see the hill over Marsham, and the church tower, and a white patch or two by the river that could be no other than the tents of the soldiers.

But when I carried my eyes further along the shore, to where the wreck of the more ancient Hold of Deeping had stood like a horn on the cliff, was there naught to be seen but a ruinous slope of rocks and stones, that stretched out from the foot of a great fresh rent in the hillside, and nearer to us was no black circle of the Hole, but all brown boulders or grey sand; and marvelling greatly how this might be, we dared at last to turn toward the part where we judged the castle to be, for we had not looked thither at first, for fear of what might be to see. But lo! when we cast our eyes seaward over the marshes, was there no golden vane winking at the dawn from the belfry tower, nor roof of the hall, nor keep nor ramparts, only a grey mound of humped sand and shale in the water, and a spike here and there that might be wall or rock, and naught else to mark where Deeping Hold had been, so that I might have thought that all had been an ill dream, were it not for the drenched rags of golden braveries that clad Rosamund.

So we turned from that desolation and looked again to Marsham, and presently we could tell that we not only saw, but were seen; for there came men down the shore, waving kerchiefs and scarves, and we could hear a shouting afar off. Yet we doubted how we might come to them, or they to us, for there were no boats at Marsham, nor more left of the castle barges than of the castle. But when we looked for a path, we could see that the channels of the river, that lay between the rock and the mainland, were changed, and there seemed a way over the sands to nigh the village. So we adventured, painfully indeed, and stumbling, and with fear of quicksands, but found all firm, till we came near to the shore; nor did the soldiers, that I could now see clearly, come to aid us, for the villagers had filled them with fear of the sands, and also they had seen and heard the flame and the crack of the castle through the strange storm of that night. Only when I came within earshot of them, and named myself, did two or three of the troopers ride their horses into the river and hale us across, else had we been too weak to stand against the current.

Now will I make a brief story of the rest. Suffice it to say

that though at first some of the soldiers were distrustful of
us (and, indeed, we were strange to look upon), yet when
they knew us, having heard of us from the country
people, they showed us great kindness, and took us to
their tents, where they brought us food and country
clothes for Rosamund and for me; and when we were clad
and fed, they brought us to their captain. Now when I saw
him, I remembered him for the man that had stopped me
on the highway aforetime, and gone nigh to shoot me for a
Malignant, as the word was; and when I spake of our
discourse, he named me, and was the more kind that he
knew me for a friend of the Lord General Cromwell. So he
would have me tell him all my story, in that he had come
to Marsham on hearing of my need by the messenger that
was sent on my horse, the which he returned me, and glad
was I to have the beast again. But while I rested and ate,
had I purposed in my mind that I would say naught of the
Thing that had dwelt in the Hole, nor of what of strange
and monstrous had happened to our company; for
indeed, when I thought thereof to myself, could I hardly
believe that all was not an ugly dream, and I looked not for
this officer, that was a man pragmatical and set in his own
opinion, to give me credit. So I told him, and Rosamund
confirmed the tale, of the Earl's cruelty and rage to the
men of Marsham, and his murdering of Master Eldad
Pentry, which indeed they already knew or guessed. Also
I said that many men of the garrison had been lost, and
their boats also, by strange accidents, and victual failing
and the very walls rotting, the Earl had fallen in a madness
of desperation, and had held one last feast, to the which
he compelled us to come, and lastly set a train to the
powder under his hall, and so destroyed himself and the
remnant of his company; from which ruin we alone had
escaped, being cast by a great wave on the Hermit's isle.
Now to this, being a plain tale and probable, and fitting
with that which he knew and had heard of the Earl the
captain gave credit, but the people of the village had their
own thoughts, and looked on us with fear as more than
mortal; and if I were to come there now, under a disguise,
and ask of myself, might I find that we had become a

legend, other than the truth, yet hardly stranger.

But I had no will, nor have now, to see Marsham again. Ere we rode forth, Rosamund and I, we called together the people, that were rebuilding of the cottages and farms, and made declaration, in the presence of the officer and his troop, that we, as the only next-of-kin to the Earl of Deeping, now dead, renounced his right and his name, and set free his tenants from all service and rent; also we promised to ratify the same by deed, as soon as the country might be settled. So we travelled with the troop of horse, as naught remained for them to do, till we came to a town where we might suit ourselves with apparel more fitting to our quality. And coming to mine own lands, I bestowed Rosamund with the parson of the parish, a good man and a quiet, nor hot for either party of the Church, till such time as we might be wedded.

From that time there hath nothing befallen us stranger than befalls most men, nor do we love to talk of that which we saw at Deeping Hold. Nay, I was moved to set down this story partly, as I said at the beginning, for a warning of the reward of evil, but partly also, as I must own at the last, that having written all down I might the less think on it again. For I am a man that seek not peril nor pleasure, nor am I at home in camp or court, be the camp Oliver Cromwell's or the court of King Charles the Second. Surely in the common things of life, in birth and growth, in love and wedding and the bearing and rearing of children, in sickness and health, in death and immortality, is enough wonder and pleasure and pain and peril to fill any heart; and each man's, aye, or woman's soul is as a Deeping Hold, with its wayward lord, its ill counsellors, and the Adversary waiting in the Pit.